The Maverick Doc

The Maverick Duo

Emily Forbes · Scarlet Wilson · Joanna Neil

MILLS & BOON

The Maverick Doc

Emily Forbes Scarlet Wilson Joanna Neil

MILLS & BOON

> **DID YOU PURCHASE THIS BOOK WITHOUT A COVER?**
> If you did, you should be aware it is **stolen property** as it was reported 'unsold and destroyed' by a retailer.
> Neither the author nor the publisher has received any payment for this book.

THE MAVERICK DOC © 2022 by Harlequin Books S.A.

The publisher acknowledges the copyright holders of the individual works as follows:

A DOCTOR BY DAY...
© 2014 by Emily Forbes
Philippine Copyright 2014
Australian Copyright 2014
New Zealand Copyright 2014

First Published 2014
Third Australian Paperback Edition 2022
ISBN 978 1 867 24853 8

THE MAVERICK DOCTOR AND MISS PRIM
© 2013 by Scarlet Wilson
Philippine Copyright 2013
Australian Copyright 2013
New Zealand Copyright 2013

First Published 2013
Second Australian Paperback Edition 2022
ISBN 978 1 867 24853 8

TAMED BY HER BROODING BOSS
© 2012 by Joanna Neil
Philippine Copyright 2012
Australian Copyright 2012
New Zealand Copyright 2012

First Published 2012
Second Australian Paperback Edition 2022
ISBN 978 1 867 24853 8

® and ™ (apart from those relating to FSC®) are trademarks of Harlequin Enterprises (Australia) Pty Limited or its corporate affiliates. Trademarks indicated with ® are registered in Australia, New Zealand and in other countries.
Contact admin_legal@Harlequin.ca for details.

Except for use in any review, the reproduction or utilisation of this work in whole or in part in any form by any electronic, mechanical or other means, now known or hereafter invented, including xerography, photocopying and recording, or in any information storage or retrieval system, is forbidden without the permission of the publisher, Harlequin Mills & Boon.

This book is sold subject to the condition that it shall not, by way of trade or otherwise, be lent, resold, hired out or otherwise circulated without the prior consent of the publisher in any form or binding or cover other than that in which it is published and without a similar condition including this condition being imposed on the subsequent purchaser.

All rights reserved including the right of reproduction in whole or in part in any form. This edition is published in arrangement with Harlequin Books S.A..

This is a work of fiction. Names, characters, places, and incidents are either the product of the author's imagination or are used fictitiously, and any resemblance to actual persons, living or dead, business establishments, events, or locales is entirely coincidental.

Published by
Harlequin Mills & Boon
An imprint of Harlequin Enterprises (Australia) Pty Limited (ABN 47 001 180 918), a subsidiary of HarperCollins Publishers Australia Pty Limited (ABN 36 009 913 517)
Level 13, 201 Elizabeth Street
SYDNEY NSW 2000 AUSTRALIA

Printed and bound in Australia by McPherson's Printing Group

CONTENTS

A DOCTOR BY DAY... 7
Emily Forbes

THE MAVERICK DOCTOR AND MISS PRIM 185
Scarlet Wilson

TAMED BY HER BROODING BOSS 365
Joanna Neil

A Doctor By Day...
Emily Forbes

Recent titles by Emily Forbes:

THE HONORABLE ARMY DOC
DARE SHE DATE THE CELEBRITY DOC?
BREAKING THE PLAYBOY'S RULES
SYDNEY HARBOR HOSPITAL: BELLA'S WISHLIST*
GEORGIE'S BIG GREEK WEDDING?
BREAKING HER NO-DATES RULE
NAVY OFFICER TO FAMILY MAN
DR. DROP-DEAD-GORGEOUS
THE PLAYBOY FIREFIGHTER'S PROPOSAL

Sydney Harbor Hospital

These books are also available in ebook format
from www.millsandboon.com.au.

Emily Forbes won a 2013 Australian Romantic Book of
the Year Award for her title

SYDNEY HARBOR HOSPITAL: BELLA'S WISHLIST.

Dear Reader,

I'd like to introduce you to the Anderson sisters—Scarlett, Ruby and Rose—and their search for a happily-ever-after. Scarlett doesn't think she needs one, Ruby doesn't think she deserves one and Rose looks as if she might not get one. But all that is about to change…

In *A Doctor by Day…* Scarlett—the rational, clever eldest sister—is swept off her feet by Jake, a sexy younger man with an unconventional part-time job, who upends her orderly world and steals her heart. And in *Tamed by the Renegade* Ruby, the rebellious middle sister, falls in love for the first time when gorgeous Noah gets under her defenses and teaches her how to love and accept—not only him, but also herself.

These two Anderson sisters might not have a lot in common, but I discovered they both have a thing for good-looking bare-chested men and, as usual, I had fun creating the heroes for my heroines. Jake and Noah are strong and loyal, smart and sexy, with slight nonconformist streaks—perfect for Scarlett and Ruby, even if they take some convincing.

I hope you enjoy these first two stories. I haven't decided if I'll give Rose her own story yet—she's putting up a good case for it in my imagination, but I'm tempted to let you decide. If you'd like to read about Rose I'd love to hear from you. Drop me a line at emilyforbes@internode.on.net.

Until then, happy reading.

Emily

DEDICATION

For romance readers everywhere, this book is written as a thank-you to anyone who has ever read one of my stories.

I started writing this story just after I won the Australian Romantic Book of the Year Award for *Sydney Harbor Hospital: Bella's Wishlist*.

I was thrilled and honoured to win a RuBY, which is a reader-voted award, and I definitely couldn't have done it without your support.

I hope you enjoy this book, too, and in particular Jake. He is my gift to you!

Love, Emily

CHAPTER ONE

'Let me get this straight. Richard proposed and you turned him down?'

Scarlett turned and leant in close to her friend's ear, taking care to avoid the spiky tips of Mel's short pixie haircut. 'Shh,' she whispered. 'I don't want everyone to know and I'm sure Richard doesn't either.'

Mel's voice hadn't been overly loud but this wasn't a conversation Scarlett wanted the rest of the girls in their party to hear. She worked with most of them and she didn't want to be the subject of rampant hospital gossip and she certainly didn't want to be the one to start a tale.

She flicked a glance over their group but most of the girls seemed to be more focused on getting inside the club than listening to her and Mel. Candice, the bride-to-be, was at the front of the line, the long white veil she wore making it obvious she was the hen on the hen's night. The veil was longer than her dress and Scarlett thought she looked ridiculous but what would she know, hen's nights were not really her thing.

Neither was fashion, she thought as she wriggled her toes, trying to encourage some circulation into her extremities. Her feet were killing her. She'd borrowed a pair of platform stilettos to team with her simple black dress. The shoes and her make-up were the only concessions she'd made to dressing up for the night out but the strappy sandals were proving to be a big mistake.

Scarlett's taste in clothing tended towards timeless classics, she wasn't a trend follower. It was a waste of good money, in her opinion, and her feet were now reminding her of her momentary lapse of reason. She couldn't wait to get inside and sit down. The short walk from the restaurant in Leigh Street to the Hindley Street club was about her limit in five-inch heels.

She couldn't believe she was keen to get into the club. Spending an evening at a male revue, especially one called The Coop, wasn't something she had ever done before and she could only imagine what the experience would be like—although if the guy on the door was any example she wasn't going to need to rely on her imagination.

Candice's name was on the door, allowing them to bypass the queue and giving them free entry. Apparently Candice knew someone who worked here and Scarlett wondered where on earth you'd meet someone who worked in a strip club, but as the cute young shirtless guy on the door ushered them inside she decided she didn't care, all she wanted was to sit down.

'I want to hear all about it once we're inside,' Mel said, as another buffed and shirtless male greeted them and led them to their table. The club was dimly lit and it took Scarlett's eyes some time to adjust to the lighting. A T-shaped stage jutted out into the centre of the club, the catwalk stretching into the tables that were clustered around the stage. A mirrored bar lined the far wall and a dance floor hugged the back wall and was already packed with young women dancing and singing. The noise level was high and almost unpleasant, but Scarlett hoped that might work in her favour. Perhaps the noise would make any sort of conversation impossible.

She followed the girls to their table, which was front and centre at the end of the catwalk, and sank into a chair. Jugs of bright green cocktails were delivered, promptly poured into glasses and passed around, and Mel waited only until everyone had a drink before she continued her interrogation.

'So Richard was lying in his hospital bed, recovering from heart surgery, working up the nerve to propose, and then you knocked him back?' she asked, as she sipped her drink. It seemed Scarlett wasn't going to get out of this.

'It wasn't like that,' Scarlett protested. Surely Mel couldn't believe she'd be that heartless.

'Don't tell me he was down on one knee beside his bed?'

'No.' Scarlett shook her head. 'He was out of hospital.'

'Well, that makes all the difference,' Mel teased. 'How did he take it when you said no?'

Scarlett could tell Mel was enjoying her discomfort but she had made her decision for what she knew were perfectly valid reasons and she wasn't going to marry the guy just because he'd had a mid-life revelation.

'He was okay. What other choice did he have really? It was my decision. He can't change my mind. I think marriage is overrated and it's not for me.'

'Don't let Candice hear you.'

'She already knows. Richard showed her the ring he bought me, he wanted her opinion.'

'He bought you a ring!?'

Scarlett nodded.

'What was it like?' Mel's curiosity took another turn.

'Gorgeous,' she admitted. And it had been. A square-cut solitaire, over one carat in size, set in platinum. It was in a traditional setting and was exactly right for her, classic and expensive. 'Almost gorgeous enough that I wanted to accept his proposal.'

'So why did you say no?'

'I was thinking about saying yes but then he started talking about having kids and I freaked out. I don't want kids.'

'Really? How come I never knew that?'

Scarlett and Mel had been friends for years, since meeting on the first day of med school, but Scarlett hadn't realised she'd never shared her feelings about children. She supposed the topic had never come up before now.

'Kids are a huge sacrifice. Believe me, I should know. I've seen what my mother gave up to raise me and my sisters. I've worked really hard to get to this point in my career and I'm not done yet. I'm not going to give it all up to raise a family.'

Scarlett could feel the effects of the cocktails they'd been drinking on top of the wine she'd had at dinner. She could hear her words weren't as crisp as usual, a bit blurred around the edges, a bit of a lisp on the essess. She knew the alcohol had loosened her tongue too. She wasn't normally so forthcoming about her personal life but she and Mel had shared a lot over the years since they'd been paired as lab partners on their first day at uni. They had been the only two who hadn't already known someone—Mel had moved to Adelaide from Tasmania and Scarlett had been a mature entrant.

She'd felt years older than everyone else and hadn't been used to the social nuances of teenagers, even though she'd only just been out of her teens herself. Their isolation had been the only thing they'd had in common initially but they'd both recognised that it hadn't mattered. Over the years their friendship had grown until Mel felt, in a lot of ways, like another one of Scarlett's sisters, only a lot less trouble.

'But you don't have to have kids right now,' Mel countered. 'It could wait until you've finished your final exams.'

'I'd still need to establish myself in anaesthetics before I could take time off and Richard doesn't want to wait. He's forty-three and he's just had a major health scare. It's made him reassess his future.' Richard's recent heart attack and minor surgery had been a big shock to him at a relatively young age and Scarlett knew that coming face to face with his own mortality had been the trigger for his proposal and his reassessment of his priorities.

'You could get a nanny. And a housekeeper. The two of you could afford to pay for whatever help you want.'

'So I get married, have babies and then hire a nanny and a housekeeper.'

'Sounds all right to me.' Mel grinned.

Scarlett shook her head. 'Having or not having kids wasn't my only reason for turning him down. It just didn't feel right. It was more than just his desire to have a family. When he proposed it should have felt like a moment I'd been waiting for my whole life, but I remembered being more excited about getting accepted into my anaesthetics specialty than receiving a marriage proposal, and surely that's wrong. My heart was racing, but not with excitement, I think it was panic. There was no impending sense that this was the next stage of my life and I couldn't wait for it to get started. I could have married him but it would have been for the wrong reasons. At the end of the day, I didn't love him enough.'

She also knew that she'd been scared. Terrified even. She didn't want to have children with someone so much older and who had heart problems. What if he died and left her a single mother? That was exactly what had happened to her own mother and it was not what she wanted in her own future. She didn't love Richard enough to take that chance. It was easier to let him go.

She had thought Richard would be a safe choice, she'd thought he wanted the same things as her. She'd thought his focus was on his career and that because he was already in his forties he wouldn't want children. Wouldn't he have had them by now if that was the case? But when things had turned out differently from what she'd expected, she'd discovered that she didn't love him enough to change her mind. She didn't love him enough to risk everything she'd worked for.

'So that's it. All over?'

'It's the right decision. I know it is. I'm not even sure he loves me either. I think a lot of his plan for the future was driven by timing and circumstances and not so much by his love for me. He had never mentioned wanting children before his heart attack. I think he'd be marrying me for the wrong reasons too.'

Scarlett picked up her cocktail glass. The wait staff was well trained and had obviously been told to make the most of the break in the entertainment to keep the drinks coming. No sooner had one jug been emptied than another was delivered. Scarlett sipped her drink. She didn't really need more but she wanted to let the alcohol numb her a little bit. She didn't want to spend the night thinking about Richard. That chapter of her life was over and she wasn't planning on having any regrets.

She'd been working and studying hard since she was sixteen and she had a few more years to go. She wanted to finish her studies and she wanted time to enjoy the fruits of her labour. She didn't want to be tied down at the moment. Surely that was a sign she wasn't ready for marriage. Surely that was a sign that it was time to have some fun.

'Let's talk about something else. I'm moving forward with my life, starting tonight.'

She looked around at all the women who were getting into the spirit of the evening, not just at Candice's table but throughout the room. She got the feeling she could let her hair down and not be judged. There was a sense of *what happened in the strip club stayed in the strip club* feel to the night. Maybe it was the effect of the green cocktails but Scarlett decided it was time to join the party.

Another round of cocktails had just been brought to their table and this time it was Scarlett who refilled their glasses before she turned her attention to the entertainment. Another set had just begun and the stripper on stage was young and athletic and, in her uneducated opinion, very good at his job. She felt slightly uncomfortable appreciating the 'talent' of the much younger men on stage but considering she was hardly the oldest female in the room, and she was certainly not the loudest in voicing her appreciation, she decided she would be rude not to enjoy the show.

By the time the set came to a close the green hue of the drink was starting to make her feel a bit nauseous. She wasn't used to drinking much, her job didn't really allow for it, and she knew if she didn't make sure to drink some water she'd regret it in the morning.

'I think I need something other than alcohol,' she told Mel. 'I'm going to the bar. Do you want anything?'

Mel shook her head as Scarlett pushed her chair back and stood up, pleased to find she could feel her toes again after resting her feet. She picked her way through the tables, dodging the good-looking, scantily clad waiting staff. She didn't want to make eye contact with them but there didn't seem to be any other polite place to look as she made her way across the room.

The bar staff was all cut from the same cloth as the waiters. They were all men, all shirtless and all cute. Not one of them had any chest hair or any body fat. They were all waxed and tanned and gorgeous and Scarlett gave them each a quick once-over before they had time to notice her.

The barman closest to her was slicing lemons. He was about three feet away and standing in profile to her. He had a sculpted jaw, small ears and brown hair, cut shorter at the sides and longer on top, that he'd obviously run some product through with his fingers to keep it spiked up. The deejay was playing a faster-tempo dance number now and all the barmen were moving to the music. Nothing choreographed, their movements looked natural and Scarlett wondered if they even knew they were dancing. She watched his hips as he kept time to the beat. His abdominal muscles flexed as he twisted to reach another lemon, drawing her attention away from his butt. His skin was smooth and tanned and his triceps tensed as he slid the knife through the flesh.

He finished dissecting the last lemon and scraped the slices into a bowl, using the back of the knife. He slid the cutting board into a sink as he twirled the knife through his fingers. Scarlett held her breath and watched as the light reflected off the blade. She gasped as he lost control of the knife and it left his hand and spun through the air. She watched it fall and waited for it to hit the floor, waited for it to stab into something it shouldn't.

It landed on the floor behind the barman, where it lay innocuously on the rubber matting. No harm, no foul, but he'd heard her gasp and before he retrieved the knife he turned to look at her. He grinned. A cheeky, quick smile that lit up his face and made Scarlett think he made a habit of mucking around and that he didn't mind getting caught.

He held her gaze and winked at her. Scarlett blushed

and quickly broke eye contact but when, out of the corner of her eye, she saw him turn around to pick up the knife she automatically went back for a second look. His jeans had stretched firmly across his butt and Scarlett couldn't help but admire him. His buttocks were round and firm and the denim of his pants moulded perfectly to his backside.

She was still looking as he stood up and turned to face her, catching her by surprise. Her blush deepened and she couldn't pretend she hadn't been checking him out but luckily he didn't seem offended if his broad grin was anything to go by. He didn't seem to mind being stared at but, then, why should he? He was gorgeous and probably very used to it. She didn't imagine she was the first woman to have been caught perving on him.

He ran the knife under hot water and put it to one side. He grabbed a tea towel to dry his hands and then tucked the towel into the waistband of his jeans. Scarlett's eyes followed his movements. His jeans were loose at his hips and as he shoved the tea towel under his waistband the movement pushed his jeans even lower, giving her a glimpse of the diagonal line of his inguinal ligament. When she realised what she was doing she quickly raised her eyes, only to find he was still watching her.

He took three steps and came to a stop in front of her. He was still grinning and Scarlett was flustered, unsettled and unsure where to look.

'What can I get you?' he asked.

His voice was deep but quiet and she found herself leaning towards him as she tried to hear what he was saying. They were separated only by a few inches now and his features came into sharp relief, almost as though he'd been projected onto a glass pane in front of her. His green eyes were deep set and as he looked at her it seemed he could see what she was thinking.

His bottom lip was full even while he was smiling and his nose was perfectly straight, flaring slightly at the bottom into a small triangle. His chin and jaw were shaped like the bottom of a flawlessly proportioned pentagon and the angles of his face gave him an almost perfectly symmetrical appearance. His tanned shoulders were dusted with freckles and his jaw was lightly stubbled, and at close range he looked older than she'd first thought. But he was still young, mid-twenties maybe, definitely younger than her. Not that his age mattered. Sure, he was cute and his body was divine and he certainly looked like he would know how to show a woman a good time, but it was irrelevant to her.

Sexy young strip-club barmen were not her thing, even if they did have the ability to disconnect her brain and make her struggle to speak. He was waiting patiently for her answer and if he could read her thoughts, as she suspected, he was no doubt amused by her lack of reply.

'May I have a glass of water, please?' she managed to ask, just as if it looked like he was about to repeat his question.

Her words sounded strange and she could feel her tongue sticking to the roof of her mouth but she wasn't a hundred per cent sure it was from the alcohol. It could also be because of the half-naked man standing in front of her. She'd seen plenty of naked or semi-naked bodies before but it wasn't every day that one as fine as this appeared before her. Was it any wonder she was struggling to think clearly, let alone speak?

He turned and scooped ice into a glass with his left hand and Scarlett caught a glimpse of a tattoo on the inside of his left biceps, several inky black marks making a dark impression against his skin. He turned to pick up a slice of lemon from the bowl he'd just filled, obscuring his tattoo from view. He dropped the lemon onto the ice and grinned at her as it hit the cubes. His hips kept time with the music as he filled the glass with water and Scarlett's stomach did a peculiar flip as she watched. He looked completely comfortable in his skin and there was something very sensual about his movements.

'Anything else I can do for you?' he asked, as he placed the glass on the bar. His eyes swept over her face, from her eyes to her lips and down to her chest as he spoke to her. Scarlett knew the neck on her dress was high enough that there was no hint of cleavage but she blushed as if she was the one standing there half-naked, not him. His swift gaze was practised, she had no doubt he had plenty of experience at giving women a quick once over, but even she could see the appreciation in his eyes. She could feel her pulse beating between her thighs, and she could feel it getting stronger as the heat in his gaze intensified.

She swallowed and reached for the glass, only to find he hadn't let go of it yet. Her fingers touched his and a surge of electricity shot through her. She snatched her hand back as if the glass was hot instead of filled with ice-cold water.

He was smiling at her again as he pushed the glass closer before removing his hand. His green eyes laughed at her but not unkindly as he asked, 'First time?'

She looked at him in mute surprise. There was no room in her head for conversation as unfamiliar hormones ran rampant through her bloodstream.

'I'd remember if I'd seen you before,' he added, and Scarlett wondered if the bar staff relied on tips. That would explain why he was being so friendly.

But water was free, wasn't it? There was no need to tip and, therefore, no need for him to flirt with her. She'd never had a stranger flirt with her. She wasn't really the type. She knew it was because she never encouraged eye contact, she didn't have the knack of catching or holding someone's attention. She knew the barman had only noticed her because she'd gasped when he'd dropped the knife and she was positive he was only flirting with her out of habit.

She glanced around, partly to confirm that he was actually talking to her and partly to see if anyone was paying them any attention. The bar area wasn't busy; most of the women seemed happy to utilise the club's table service and let the shirtless waiters come to them. The focus of the room was the stage and the tables were set facing that way, which meant most of the women had their backs to the bar. No one was looking at her. No one except the hot barman.

She wasn't sure what she should do in this situation but, since no one was watching her and to ignore him would be rude, she smiled back. 'You have women who come here often enough that you can recognise them?'

'Believe it or not, we get a lot of regulars. Birthday parties and hen's nights are good for repeat business. We've even had repeat customers who hold divorce parties.'

'Divorce parties?'

'The club owner thinks divorcees are an untapped market. Cashed-up women looking for some fun.' He shrugged his smooth, sculpted shoulders. 'He's right and they do seem to enjoy themselves but I take it that's not why you're here?'

She shook her head and replied. 'Hen's night.'

Her eyes flicked across the room to the group she'd come with. No one seemed to have missed her and while she felt as though time was standing still she'd probably only been gone from the table for a few minutes.

As she scanned the room the stage lights came on and started pulsating. The deejay started spinning a eighties disco number and the dance floor cleared as everyone made their way back to their seats and focussed their attention on the front of the room as the next act, an athletic stripper in a sailor's outfit, took to the stage. Scarlett could see the stage from the bar. It was in the club's interest to make sure all patrons had a good view, but she wasn't in any hurry to return to her seat, she was more than happy with the view she had here. She checked again but it seemed as though her absence wasn't being noted. She guessed her company couldn't compete with a semi-naked man gyrating on a stage.

'You're with Candice?' he asked. Apparently he had followed her line of sight.

Scarlett's eyes shot back. 'You know her?' she asked, as she remembered that Candice had known someone who worked here. Was this him?

'We're old family friends,' he explained. He pulled the tea towel from the waistband of his jeans and began wiping the bar. It was already spotless and Scarlett wondered if it was a delaying tactic. Was he delaying so he could talk to her? A warm glow spread through her. She couldn't deny she was enjoying the attention. 'Do the two of you work together?' he asked.

Scarlett nodded.

'Are you a nurse too?'

She shook her head. 'I'm a doctor.'

Her answer surprised him. He'd thought he was a good judge of character and while he didn't think she looked like a nurse she looked even less like a doctor. Her neck was long and slender, her face a perfect oval. Her lips were full and pouty, shiny with a pale pink gloss. In contrast, her eyes were dark and mesmerising. Outlined with kohl, the lids dusted with dark eye shadow and her lashes coated with mascara, her eyes looked as though they could have a thousand secrets hidden in their depths.

Her hair, a brown so deep it was almost black, was thick and she'd pulled it back into a bun at the nape of her neck. His fingers itched to reach across the bar and pull the pins out, to let her hair cascade over her shoulders.

He realised it was the bun that had thrown his judgement off. It was far too severe for her stunning features and gave her the appearance of someone who worked in administration. All she needed to complete the look was a pair of glasses.

On the surface she looked like organised efficiency but his imagination suggested that underneath the surface was a different story. Perhaps he'd been working at the club for too long, he thought as his mind wandered. Maybe he was having difficulty separating fact from fiction, reality from fantasy.

'What's so funny?' she asked.

He shook his head as he realised he was smiling. 'Nothing.' She was a doctor who worked with Candice. It wasn't funny, it was perfect, but the story would keep for another day. 'I'd better get back to work. Tell Candice I'll come over later and say hi.'

He watched as she left the bar and crossed the room to return to her table. He wasn't in a hurry to get back to work—checking her out was far more interesting. Her body was smoking hot. She had poured it into a simple black dress—round neck, sleeveless, zipped down the back. He wondered if she was trying to disguise her assets, but the sway of her hips drew his attention to her narrow waist and round bottom. He was enjoying watching her walk away.

Her dress stopped just above her knees and his eyes travelled lower. Her legs were bare, no stockings, and her calves were pale, her ankles slender. She was wearing heels, ridiculously high heels, which might explain the sexy sway of her hips. He just had time to notice her shoes had a leopardskin pattern before she slid into her seat at the end of the catwalk and the stage hid her legs from view.

He was fascinated. Her swollen lips, mysterious eyes, generous D bust and her unexpected shoes all contrasted sharply with her no-nonsense hairstyle and plain dress. She was a bombshell disguised as a secretary. Which part of her was real? Was she even aware of the bombshell? Was her outfit smoke and mirrors or did she really not know how hot she was? Did she ever let the bombshell out and how could he arrange to be there if she did?

By the time she sat down at her table, Evan, the sailor stripper, had been replaced by Caesar, a muscular man of Fijian descent, who was clad only in a loincloth. The guys were warming the crowd up again with their routines. As Jake mixed a fresh batch of cocktails Caesar backflipped off the catwalk and began dancing through the crowd, looking for a willing participant for his act. Jake watched Candice's friend as he measured and poured. He could see she was trying to avoid eye contact with Caesar, desperate not to be picked and dragged into the spotlight. Just watching her made him grin. She was definitely a club virgin.

He watched as she dipped her head to the side, bringing him into her line of sight. She saw him watching her, a reversal of their earlier roles, but not one to be embarrassed at being caught out, he gave her another wink.

Scarlett felt herself blush again. What was wrong with her? Why couldn't she keep her eyes to herself? Why did she keep seeking him out? She'd just turned down a marriage proposal and yet her head was full of lustful thoughts about a complete stranger.

She tried to focus instead on the dancer, *stripper*—she wasn't sure what they called themselves—only to find that his act was finishing and his spot was being taken by another man, slightly older than the others but just as buff and tanned, who wore tight black leather pants and nothing else. He held a microphone and greeted the audience in a loud, showman's voice, 'Good evening, chicks, and welcome to The Coop.'

'Good evening, Rooster!' A chorus of women's voices split the air as the majority of the audience called out a greeting in return.

'Listen up, ladies, the Himbo Limbo is about to begin. Choose your competitor and send them to me,' he said, as he spread his arms wide in an expansive, all-encompassing gesture that made the muscles on his chest and arms ripple.

'I nominate Scarlett!' Candice shouted, as she bounced in her chair.

Scarlett frowned. She had no idea who this Rooster character was or what he was talking about. 'What on earth is a Himbo Limbo?' she asked.

CHAPTER TWO

'It's just a limbo competition,' Candice told her, 'with a twist.'

Scarlett felt her antennae twitch. She could sense a disaster in the making or at the very least some embarrassment. 'What sort of twist?'

'The "Himbo" part refers to two strippers. Instead of using poles, the Himbos hold the rope,' Candice explained.

That didn't sound nearly as risqué as Scarlett's imagination had led her to envisage but she couldn't understand why Candice was sending her up if it was all so tame. 'Why don't you do it?' she asked, as Rooster called for the nominated hens or chicks to come forward.

'You do yoga, you should be flexible,' Candice replied, 'and, besides, I can't limbo in this skirt, it doesn't leave much to the imagination when I'm standing up straight, let alone if I'm horizontal.'

Scarlett couldn't argue with that, Candice's skirt was incredibly short. She didn't know if she was any more suitably attired, her little black dress was hardly limbo-appropriate, but regular yoga classes meant she was reasonably flexible so maybe it wouldn't be all bad. She hadn't expected games but it was highly likely there would be more embarrassing contests to come and this sounded like it could be one of the lesser evils.

She glanced around the room. Most of the tables seemed to be nominating a participant, although the majority seemed to be brides-to-be, not 'chicks'. She finally clicked why the club was named The Coop—it was full of hens and chicks and one very loud and proud Rooster.

'C'mon, Scarlett, do it for me, it'll be fun,' Candice pleaded.

Scarlett thought it would be about as much fun as getting her legs waxed but she wasn't sure how she could get out of it. It was unlike her to put herself in the spotlight but as the girls continued to egg her on she found herself giving in. Maybe she'd had one too many cocktails, she thought as she said, 'All right, I'll do it.'

Just as she stood up the two 'Himbos' appeared front and centre on the floor beside the catwalk. Scarlett breathed a sigh of relief. At least it seemed as though she wouldn't have to actually get up on the stage. The men were both very toned, no surprises there, and dressed in what could only be described as very tiny, very snug leather shorts. Scarlett thought one of the men was the stripper who had just finished his routine. He had swapped his loincloth for white shorts, which were a sharp contrast to his dark skin but left nothing to the imagination.

The other 'Himbo' was in a pair of slightly more respectable black leather shorts. Scarlett had never thought she'd consider men wearing tiny leather shorts 'respectable' but it seemed as though there was a fair bit about tonight that was going to challenge her traditional and conservative views.

Just when she thought it was safe to join in, the Himbos sprang up onto the stage and Rooster called to the girls, 'Okay, hens and chicks, make your way up to me.'

A spotlight swept the room and came to rest on the gaggle of women gathered by the stage before it moved to illuminate a short flight of stairs leading up onto the catwalk. Scarlett was horrified to realise they were expected on the stage after all but slightly mollified by the sight of the stairs. It was a relief to know they weren't expected to spring onto the stage in the Himbos' footsteps—she certainly wouldn't be springing anywhere in her borrowed platform heels.

The women made a beeline for the steps, eager to get the competition under way, as Scarlett held back. The steps had no railing and she didn't want to get jostled and go sprawling up the stairs in front of everyone. She was going to be embarrassed soon enough just doing the limbo, she didn't need to start by making a complete fool out of herself.

The women clustered around the Himbos as the deejay played dance music. The women and the Himbos were all dancing, with the exception of Scarlett, who tried her best to blend into the background behind the others, although that was hard to do given she was almost five feet eleven inches tall in her five-inch heels. Fortunately Rooster began to introduce the Himbos to the audience, which Scarlett took to mean that the contest would be starting soon and she wouldn't have to be embarrassed for too much longer. The Fijian stripper in the short white shorts, Caesar, was introduced first, followed by Rico, who was introduced as the 'Italian Stallion'. The audience cheered and clapped as the Himbos took their places.

'And now I'd like to introduce our judge for this evening,' Rooster crowed, somehow managing, through sheer force of personality, to keep the attention on himself. 'A favourite among the chicks, our very own Judge Jake.'

The cheers of the audience turned into wolf whistles and the noise in the club reached maximum volume as Candice's friend, the barman Scarlett had been talking to earlier, came up onto the stage. It seemed she wasn't the only one who thought he was delicious.

He had changed his outfit but Scarlett was happy to see he wasn't wearing leather pants—she'd seen enough leather pants tonight to last her a lifetime. He'd changed from regular denim jeans into a black pair, which hugged his thighs. His chest was still bare and he had a length of rope looped over one shoulder and slung across his torso. He jogged across the stage, moving lightly and waving to his adoring audience, and Scarlett's level of embarrassment increased with every step he took towards her. It was too late to back out now but she wished the stage would open up and swallow her. She tried in vain to hide, even though she knew it was futile. He was going to see her standing there sooner or later.

Caesar and Rico had stepped in front of the women, creating some space, and Jake passed them each a black strap, which they fixed around their chests. At the front of the strap, positioned over their sternums, was a hook that looked like a mountaineering karabiner. Jake hoisted the rope from his shoulder and handed it to the Himbos. At each end of the rope was a small metal loop, which Caesar and Rico clipped into the karabiners.

Scarlett's eyes widened in surprise. She hadn't expected the rope to be tied around their chests, she'd expected them to hold it, stretched out between them. That would have given the competitors plenty of space to move but once the rope was tied around their chests and clipped into the karabiners it was quite short and didn't leave a lot of room to manoeuvre. Not, Scarlett thought, that most of the girls would mind, but she had no intention of brushing against half-naked strangers any more than she had to.

Jake waited until the limbo rope was in position before taking the microphone from Rooster and taking over the contest. The girls were asked to line up and after much jostling Scarlett found herself third in line behind two hens, one rather large one and one with an exceptionally long veil. Judge Jake approached each competitor in turn and asked them their name. He showed no surprise when he got to Scarlett and she knew then he'd already seen her on the stage. She just hoped he didn't think she'd volunteered.

Even in her heels she was still an inch or two shorter than him, and she had to look up slightly when she told him her name. Up close she could see that his green eyes were ringed with brown and he winked at her as he repeated her name and Scarlett felt her cheeks redden. She hoped the tell-tale blush wouldn't be noticeable but she suspected the spotlight would only serve to enhance the colour in her face.

With much cheering and clapping from the audience Jake got the contest under way. The plump hen went first and she could almost walk under the rope without ducking, she was so short. The next hen, the one with the long veil, wasn't so lucky. She trod on her veil as she tipped her head backwards to duck under the rope. This pulled her up short and made her fall and she landed hard on her backside. Her faux pas was greeted with laughter from the audience, though not cruel or nasty laughter. Scarlett knew most of them would be laughing with relief that they weren't the ones lying flat on their backs in front of a crowd.

She couldn't work out how the hen had managed to trip herself up but as she was sprawled on the floor and Jake was reaching for her hand to help her to her feet Scarlett just prayed that she wouldn't be as unlucky or as ungainly. She was next in line.

'How confident are you?' Jake asked her, as she moved a step closer.

Scarlett looked at the girls around her, including the

one already disqualified. 'I've done a few limbos in my time,' she fibbed. 'I think I can take this one.' Her knees felt weak and she wondered how she was going to manage to limbo on wobbly legs but her voice sounded surprisingly normal and strong.

She wasn't sure why she'd chosen to announce her lies to the room; she could only assume it had something to do with the challenge in Jake's eyes. She didn't want to look like a complete klutz in front of him but neither did she want to appear timid and pathetic. She didn't normally think of herself as a competitive, win-at-all-costs type of person but she didn't like to fail at anything. She had high expectations of herself and she certainly didn't want to be beaten by these women.

Jake laughed and announced, 'Scarlett Take-No-Prisoners, who is standing in for her hen, Candice, let's see what you've got.'

The girls on her table whooped and cheered as Scarlett easily limboed under the rope and popped up on the other side.

After Scarlett were another six competitors, four hens, one with a rather heavy, awkward-looking tiara holding her veil in place, and two chicks. Two more fell on the first attempt and Scarlett thought the success rate was probably indirectly proportionate to the amount each 'chick' had had to drink.

As the contest continued and the number of competitors dropped, so did the height of the rope. As the rope descended the Himbos shortened it too, bringing them even closer together and giving the chicks less margin for error. Another two stumbled and were eliminated as the rope was lowered to the bottom of the Himbos' rib cages.

The girls were being urged on by their friends but despite the encouragement all but two were out of the competition after attempting to limbo under the rope when it was level with the Himbos' waists. By the time the rope was moved further south to their hips Scarlett's until-now-unknown competitive streak had well and truly emerged and she had no intention of losing tonight. It was now a two-chick race between her and a girl named Tracey and it was Scarlett's turn.

Scarlett sized up the competition. Tracey was several inches shorter than her so Scarlett slid her platform heels from her feet to level the playing field. The rope was very low now and she didn't need to make this any harder than it already was.

'Watch out, Tracey.' Jake laughed. 'The competition is getting serious, clothing is being shed. What else is coming off, Scarlett?'

His green eyes were challenging her again and something in his expression made her want to challenge him back. 'Nothing yet,' she quipped, and was rewarded with a brief spark of something—maybe attraction, maybe anticipation, she wasn't sure—but there was definitely a light in his eyes. She turned her back, wanting to leave him hanging, and shimmied under the rope. She just managed to scrape under without over-balancing.

Jake had stepped around to the other side of the Himbos and was there to take her hand as she straightened. He kept his elbow bent, which kept her close, and his hand warmed her skin where it wrapped around her fingers. He smelt clean, as if he was freshly showered but she knew that couldn't be the case. He smelt good.

She could feel the heat coming off his half-naked body and she knew the skin on his chest would feel as warm and soft as his hand. Scarlett's stomach trembled as Jake continued to hold her hand as they waited for Tracey to take her turn at the limbo. Her body was tingling as Jake's touch awakened her senses and she could feel the pulse low in her belly starting to beat a little bit faster.

Scarlett knew she could pull her hand out of Jake's grasp but she didn't want to. This connection would be severed soon enough and she wanted to enjoy it while it lasted. They watched as Tracey almost made it under the rope before falling at the last hurdle, putting her hand on the ground just before she was ready to stand and thereby disqualifying herself.

Jake let go of Scarlett to help Tracey to her feet. 'I'm sorry, Tracey, you almost did it,' he said as he helped her up, before turning back to Scarlett. 'That makes you our winner tonight.' His smile lit up his green eyes as he added, 'Would you like to see how low you can go?'

Scarlett watched as Caesar and Rico moved the rope down another couple of inches until it was sitting across their groins. She looked back at Jake. He was now grinning mischievously and she knew he was waiting to see if she was up to the next challenge. She shook her head. She'd let him win this round. 'I'm done.'

'All right, here's your prize.' Jake reached his left hand behind him and when he brought it forward again he had a handful of fake money that he must have had stashed in his pocket. Scarlett frowned. What was she supposed to do with fake dollar bills?

He held the notes up in the air and Scarlett got another glimpse of the tattoo on the soft side of his arm. At close range she could see that the inky black marks were stars, five of them in total, their arrangement making a pattern that was familiar to every Australian. He had the Southern Cross constellation tattooed on his skin.

Jake kept his arm held high as he turned through one hundred and eighty degrees, showing the fake money to the crowd, who cheered as he called out, 'Tipping dollars!'

'Tipping dollars?' Scarlett repeated. She had no idea what he was talking about.

Jake lowered the microphone and leant in close as he pressed the fake banknotes into her hand. 'It's to tip the dancers,' he explained. 'Tuck some into the guys' shorts before you leave the stage and share the rest with your group for them to use later.'

The crowd applauded and cheered again as she tipped the Himbos while Jake escorted Tracey from the stage, but before she could follow the crowd began to chant, 'Jake, Jake, Jake!' and she knew she was expected to tip him too. She wasn't certain but she thought Candice might have been leading the call.

Jake was back by her side again. He didn't seem surprised or reticent and she suspected he loved the attention. She'd bet his star sign was Leo. They loved the limelight. She tucked a few notes into his waistband and as her fingers brushed against his hipbone she found herself searching his skin for more tattoos. But the skin of his torso and waist was smooth, tanned and ink-free. Her heart was hammering in her chest and she could feel a blush stealing across her cheeks. Somehow touching Jake felt a lot more personal than when she'd been tipping Caesar and Rico.

With shaky hands she picked up her shoes and fled the stage, retreating to the relative safety of her table.

'That was a side of you I hadn't seen before,' Mel said as she sat down.

'And don't expect to see it again any time soon,' Scarlett replied. Her heart was still racing, making her sound breathless. She hoped everyone would think it was from the exertion of the limbo, although she knew it was a reaction to Jake.

Performing in front of a crowd was completely out of character for her but part of her had enjoyed the chance to pretend to be someone else, someone less worried about behaving appropriately and less concerned about being who people expected her to be. Perhaps it was a case of 'anything goes' tonight or maybe normal inappropriate behaviour was considered appropriate within the four walls of The Coop, but she didn't have time to consider it any further as Mel interrupted her musings.

'I thought it was rather entertaining. But, tell me, who is Judge Jake and how does he know Candice?' Mel asked, as Scarlett handed the remaining tipping dollars to Candice.

'We're old family friends,' Candice interrupted. 'He's coming over now, I'll introduce you.'

Scarlett turned her head. Sure enough, Jake was approaching their table. He was no longer bare-chested, he'd put on a black T-shirt and a black leather jacket but, if anything, he looked even better. No, not better, she thought, but just as good.

Candice made quick introductions before Jake grabbed an empty chair from the table beside theirs. He flipped it around with a practised move and wedged it in between Scarlett and Mel before straddling it backwards. His long legs stuck out sideways and brushed against Scarlett's thigh.

'So you do own a shirt,' Scarlett said, as her eyes raked his torso.

'And a jacket,' he teased.

He was leaning forward over the back of the chair, his arms crossed. The teasing note in his voice and the gleam in his eye made her feel bold. She reached out and ran her hand down his sleeve. 'There's a definite leather theme going on in this place.'

'Hey,' he said, as he sat up straight in the chair, held the jacket on each side of the zip and lifted it slightly, adjusting it on his shoulders, 'this is mine.'

'It's nice.' It was. She could smell the leathery fragrance. She hadn't noticed a leather smell on the Himbos, not that she'd got that close to their shorts.

'Yeah?'

She grinned, feeling more at ease. It was much less stressful now she was out of the spotlight and off the stage. 'Much better than leather pants.'

'Have you ever worn leather pants?'

Scarlett shook her head.

'Well, you should give them a go, you might be surprised at how comfortable they are.'

'You have leather pants too?'

He raised one hand. 'Guilty as charged. Call it part of our uniform. But you might be pleased to know I don't own leather shorts.'

'That's a relief,' she said, but, as much as she thought leather was being worn a little too often around the club, she suspected he would look rather good in leather pants. She suspected he'd look good in anything.

He shifted in his seat and his thigh brushed against hers for the second time. Her nerve endings sparked and it felt as if all the cells in her thigh muscles were straining to get closer to him, as though they were trying to leap out of her skin. She moved her leg away from his before she could be tempted to lean into him instead.

The alcohol she'd drunk tonight had most certainly reduced her inhibitions. Not only had she voluntarily got up on stage, she was now having lustful thoughts about a complete stranger. She was planning on having fun but she wasn't sure if her courage stretched far enough to include Jake. She should go home before she did something even more out of character. Before she could be tempted by a cute young barman who might, or might not, be flirting with her. There was no way she was going to make a move on him, well, not the first move anyway. She needed to get out of here. If he wanted to come with her that was his choice. If he chose to stay behind then she'd assume she'd read the signals wrong. There was a good possibility of that, she thought. She was hardly the most experienced woman at the table.

She'd done her duty to Candice. Surely she could leave now without appearing rude. She leant across the table to speak to Candice, ready to make her excuses. 'I think I might head off, if you don't mind. I had a really busy night on call before working today.'

'How are you getting home?'

'I'll take a cab.'

'Do you want me to come with you?' Mel asked. 'You shouldn't go on your own.' Hindley Street was not the street you wanted to walk down alone.

'I'll wait with you, if you like,' Jake said to her. 'I've finished my shift and was about to go anyway.'

'Perfect! Thanks, Jake.' Candice agreed on Scarlett's behalf without any hesitation. 'That way, Mel can stay and enjoy the rest of the evening. You don't mind, do you?' Candice asked, as she looked at her.

Scarlett didn't want to be accused of breaking up the party so she did what came naturally to her and agreed. 'Sure,' she replied. She'd had a lifetime of experience at being the one to keep the peace, being the one to do what everyone expected of her while her sisters did as they pleased, so of course she agreed, but it didn't hurt that she was more than happy for Jake to keep her company. She knew then that his touch had been deliberate and the thought sent a frisson of excitement through her body.

'Jake is one of the good guys, you can trust him,' Candice added, before she turned to Mel and whispered with a chuckle, 'I'm not denying he could charm a nun out of her habit but that's Scarlett's good fortune.'

As Scarlett ducked her head under the table to put her shoes back on and search for her handbag she heard Candice say something about charm but she couldn't catch the whole sentence. She thought about asking her to repeat her comment but when she found her handbag and looked up she saw that Jake was standing, ready to pull out her chair for her. Not wanting to keep him waiting, she decided that if what Candice had said was important she'd find out some other time.

She followed Jake from the club, aware of several women checking him out as he passed their tables, but their attention was short-lived as another dancer was on the stage and now that Jake was fully clothed there were obviously more interesting things to look at elsewhere. Scarlett didn't mind, she was happy to have him all to herself.

There was a taxi rank opposite the club but the queue was horrendously long, stretching for half a block. Knowing it could take for ever for her turn to come, she released Jake from his obligation. 'It's going to take ages, you don't need to wait,' she said, as they joined the end of the queue.

'I promised Candice I'd look after you.'

'That's okay, I won't tell her.' She smiled. 'Thank you for offering but it's busy enough. I'll be all right,' she said, as she slipped her shoes off. Her feet had had enough and she couldn't stand the thought of another minute standing in uncomfortable high heels. The concrete pavement was rough but cool under her skin and was soothing in an unexpected way. She glanced down the line and saw she wasn't the only one who'd divested herself of her footwear.

'Come on, I'll give you a lift,' he said, looking at her bare feet.

'It's fine, really,' Scarlett insisted. 'I'm just not used to wearing high heels.'

'I'm not going to leave you here and I think we've both got better things to do than stand on the street for an hour.'

His tone wasn't impatient. Maybe she was reading things into his words but the depth of his voice and the low volume made it sound as though the better things he had in mind involved them both and she was tempted to dive in, recklessly, heedlessly, and accept his offer. But her natural inclination not to cause trouble made her ask, 'What if I live miles away?'

'Then that's my problem. I'm not going to retract my offer. I'd look like a jerk.'

She looked up at him. Barefoot, she was now several inches shorter than he was. 'I'd hate to have that hanging over my head.'

'So, can I drop you home?' He grinned and all her objections, few though they were, vanished. She nodded and slipped her sandals back on before following him as he retraced their footsteps.

He led her to an alleyway behind The Coop and Scarlett followed blindly. She knew she would feel unsafe if he wasn't beside her but even though he was virtually a stranger she trusted him. It was an odd situation to be in, she wasn't normally a trusting person, particularly not when it came to men, but she only got good vibes from Jake and he wasn't really a stranger, was he? He knew Candice.

He stopped beside a dark green convertible that had been parked behind a dumpster, which kept it partially shielded from view. The roof was down and there was a cumbersome, heavy steering lock clamped to the wheel.

Jake opened the passenger door and shrugged out of his leather jacket. 'Here,' he said, as he held it out to her. 'It might be a bit cool with the top down but it's a bit temperamental and it'll be quicker and warmer if you wear this.'

Scarlett slipped her arms into the sleeves as Jake held it for her. His fingers brushed her neck as he turned up the collar. The jacket was much too large for her but it was warm and smelt divine, a heady combination of leather and clean male. She didn't bother to zip it, just pulled it close, wrapping it around her like a cocoon.

She sank into the low seat as Jake stowed the steering lock behind them and started the engine. The sound was low and throaty and reminded her of his voice. Scarlett relaxed. She closed her eyes and let the warmth and scent of the leather of the seats and Jake's jacket seduce her. It was nice to have someone else make a decision for her. Not being required to think was a novelty. All her life she had been the one people turned to for advice. She had been the one who everyone relied on to be sensible, responsible, to make the hard decisions, and Scarlett's natural tendency was to carefully consider all angles before making an informed and logical choice.

Letting a stranger give her a lift home was not the sort of thing she did. She wasn't a spontaneous sort of person. Every decision she made was carefully measured, considered and weighed before she acted on it. She was used to being in control. Of her life and of her actions.

Going home with someone she'd just met was the sort of thing her sister Ruby would do. Ruby would have set her sights on a guy the minute she walked into The Coop and wouldn't have thought twice about letting them give her a lift home. Even their younger sister, Rose, was more outgoing than she herself was. She would have walked into The Coop, tossed her blond hair, batted her long eyelashes and her big blue eyes and within minutes she would have had men falling at her feet. She would have flirted expertly and at the end of the night she would have been spoilt for choice if she wanted a lift home.

Scarlett didn't know if she could ever be as confident or as fearless as her sisters but it was kind of nice to step out of her comfort zone for a change. But she knew the only reason she felt safe to do that was because there was a connection with Jake. She wasn't thinking about the physical or chemical connection she felt but rather the safer, more reliable one that was their common friend, Candice. Scarlett knew that no matter how gorgeous and charming a man was, she would never let a complete stranger give her a lift home. She just didn't do things like that.

'Scarlett?'

She jumped as she felt Jake's hand on her knee. She opened her eyes to find they had left Hindley Street behind. The little green car was on the bridge over the River Torrens as Jake headed up Montefiore Hill.

'Are you okay?' he asked, and she realised he must have been speaking to her while she was daydreaming.

'Yes. I'm fine.'

Jake flicked the indicator on to turn at the lookout at the top of the hill. She tried not to notice the cars parked there, certain that the occupants were up to no good as they looked across the city lights. She had never fooled around in the backseat of a car but sitting here with Jake's hand still resting on her knee she could almost imagine what it would be like. But he removed his hand to negotiate the corner, leaving a cold circle the size of his palm on her skin. He drove past the old cathedral and up towards O'Connell Street.

'Are you hungry?' he asked, as the car idled at the next set of traffic lights.

'I am,' she said, as she rubbed at the cold spot on her knee. She was a little surprised to find she was hungry but dinner seemed like hours ago.

'My favourite late-night take-away is just up here. We can grab something to eat there, if you like?'

'Sure.' She thought it was probably a good idea to eat something else and soak up the rest of the alcohol she'd consumed but where they ate was another decision she was happy to let Jake make.

Jake slowed his sports car as they approached the café strip and he searched for a parking space. A car was pulling out from the kerb and he waited, taking the spot in front of a café with distinctive blue-and-white signage. She recognised the café; she'd walked past it plenty of times but had never been inside, but it seemed that Jake knew it well.

'Jake, how's it going?' The guy behind the counter greeted him as they walked in. 'What'll you have, the usual?'

'Sounds good,' he said, before explaining to Scarlett, 'You can't go past George's lamb yiros,' he told her.

There was a huge selection of dishes written on the blackboard above the counter but Scarlett could see the lamb revolving slowly on the enormous spit, cooking as it turned, and the smell carried to her. It smelt fantastic. She'd never tried a yiros before but it was an easy decision. She nodded. 'Make that two,' she told George.

'You want garlic sauce with that?' George asked.

That sounded rather potent and Scarlett wasn't at all familiar with yiros etiquette. Jake was watching her, his head tipped to one side, waiting for her answer. She didn't want to be in close proximity to him if she had garlic sauce and he didn't. Even in a convertible she suspected it could be unpleasant.

'Is that how you usually have it?' she asked Jake.

'Yep.'

'Okay, then.' Scarlett watched as George expertly carved slices of lamb as it rotated on the spit and piled it onto flatbreads and garnished it with garlic sauce and salad before wrapping each yiros in wax paper and handing them over the counter. She followed Jake to a table tucked into the back corner of the café. All around them other patrons were devouring their yiros but from what she could see it was almost impossible to eat daintily. Worried about making a mess of Jake's jacket, she slipped it off and hung it over the back of her chair.

'Do you want to take your shoes off too?' Jake was smiling at her.

She shook her head. 'Not in here.'

'You could take them off on the street, why not in here?' he said, as he tore the wax paper to expose the top half of his yiros.

'We're in a restaurant. Earlier I couldn't face the thought of standing any longer but I'm okay as long as I'm sitting down,' Scarlett said, copying his actions.

'I've never understood why women insist on buying uncomfortable shoes—although they do look great on you.'

'Thank you.' The compliment almost made the pain worthwhile. 'But they're not mine and I didn't realise they were so uncomfortable. I borrowed them,' she admitted. 'Strip clubs aren't really my scene and I don't own anything suitable to wear to one.' She took a bite of the warm flatbread. The lamb was tender and juicy, perfectly complemented by the sauce.

'Going to the club doesn't mean you need to dress like a stripper.' He laughed.

She stuck one foot out from underneath the table, pointing her toes and swinging her foot from side to side. 'You think these look like stripper shoes?'

Jake raised one eyebrow and grinned. 'That wasn't what I meant,' he protested.

'I wonder what my sister would have to say about that!'

Scarlett smiled back before taking another bite of her yiros, only to discover a fraction too late why she should have said no to the garlic sauce as it squirted out of the bread and ran down the side of her hand. She was holding the yiros with two hands, trying to stop it from falling apart, and there was nothing she could do about the sauce that was now running over her wrist and heading for her elbow.

Jake reached across and ran his finger along her forearm, wiping the sauce from her skin. He was watching her as he put his finger in his mouth and sucked the sauce from it and Scarlett felt as though he'd run his tongue along her bare skin. She could see the heat in his eyes and could still feel the heat from his finger as it sent a current shooting through her.

'You've got sauce just here too,' Jake said, and Scarlett held her breath as he stretched his hand out and wiped the side of her cheek. His thumb grazed the corner of her lip and Scarlett couldn't help it—her lips parted under his touch and it was all she could do not to capture his thumb with her mouth. She inhaled deeply as Jake removed his hand and this time wiped his fingers on his serviette.

Despite the fact that they were sitting in a busy café, surrounded by other people, she was aware only of Jake. She ate the rest of her yiros in silence, acutely aware of him sitting opposite her, but somehow she managed to finish eating without any further mishap.

She felt the first wave of fatigue roll over her as she wiped a serviette over her lips and stifled a yawn.

'Are you ready to go?' Jake asked.

She was tired but in no hurry to get home. She was quite happy to sit for a bit longer in his company but she had no reason to delay. She stood as Jake picked his jacket up from her chair and slung it around her shoulders. He left his hand around her back, holding the jacket in place as he walked her to his car. Scarlett had to squeeze in close to him to manoeuvre between the tables and chairs and she could feel the length of his body where he pressed against her. The night air was cool on her skin when he released her to open the car door and she pulled his jacket more tightly around her to make up for the loss of warmth.

Within minutes she had directed Jake to her house. The night was over.

Almost.

Jake was out of the car and was walking her to her door.

'Thanks for the lift,' Scarlett said, as she unlocked her front door.

'It was my pleasure.' He was leaning on the doorjamb, watching her quietly.

'And for supper,' she added, reluctant for the evening to end.

Light spilled from the hallway and fell on Jake, illuminating him where he stood. She was in shadow but she could see Jake's hand reaching towards her shoulder.

'What are you doing?'

'Something I've been wanting to do all night.'

He was leaning forward. Was he going to kiss her? His head was next to hers, his lips beside her ear, and his voice was quiet and deep. She could feel the gentle puff of his breath on her skin as he spoke and then she could feel his fingers in her hair as he pulled the end of her ponytail and untucked her hair from its bun. He pulled her hair forward and loosened it over her shoulders and his hands brushed her skin.

'That's much better.'

Scarlett turned her head and lifted it, just slightly, less than an inch, to look at him. He was still watching her and the way he looked at her made the heat pool low in her belly. She could feel a fluttering of nerves, a tremble in her stomach, but the nerves were anticipatory, not anxious. Jake's green eyes were shining emerald in the light. His lips were millimetres from hers. He dipped his head into the shadow and closed the gap. His lips were warm and hungry, soft yet demanding. His body was lean and hard and his hands on her arms were firm but gentle. Scarlett pressed herself into him as two of them became one.

His hands slid behind her, cupping her bottom, holding her to him.

She wound her hands behind his head as her lips parted in response to the pressure of his tongue.

She was standing on her front porch, kissing a stranger, but he didn't feel like a stranger. Scarlett felt as though she belonged with him, as though she'd known him always. Every cell in her body responded to his touch. Every part of her recognised him, as though they'd met before, and as she kissed him she felt as if she was reuniting with a lover, not making out with a stranger.

She brought her hands to his chest and placed them flat against his pectoral muscles. She grabbed a fistful of his T-shirt, bunching the fabric up in her palms, and dragged him out of the doorway and into her hall.

She should be saying good-night. She should be thanking him for the lift and saying goodbye but the look in his eye and the taste of his mouth had disengaged her brain and she couldn't let him go. Not yet. She knew their first kiss was only a taste of what was to come.

She stepped to her right, towards her bedroom door, and her lips left Jake's mouth. He was watching her closely, his green eyes intense, and she knew he was waiting to see what she would do next. She knew it was her decision now.

She pushed the front door closed and stepped backwards into her bedroom.

Jake didn't wait for an invitation. He stepped towards

her, following her lead. His hands were behind her back and she felt him slide the zip on the back of her dress down and her dress fell at her feet. She stepped out of it, naked except for her underwear and her borrowed heels.

The light from the hallway penetrated the darkness of her room. Scarlett stood still as Jake ran his gaze over her. He dropped his head and kissed her neck. Scarlett arched her back as his fingers trailed after his mouth.

Jake whipped his T-shirt over his head and suddenly there was bare skin on bare skin.

He scooped her up and laid her on her bed.

She bent her knee and slipped a finger under the strap at the back of her sandal.

Jake felt her movement, sensed what she was doing. 'Leave them on.'

Scarlett dropped her hand and let her knee fall as Jake ran his fingers from the inside of her ankle, up her calf to the inside of her knee. His fingers left a line of heat behind and Scarlett felt herself melt at his touch. Her eyes drifted closed.

'Scarlett?'

She opened her eyes. 'Hmm?'

'How much have you had to drink?'

His question startled her. 'Why?'

'I want to be sure I'm not taking advantage of you,' he said, as his hand continued to move higher, to the soft, warm junction at the top of her thigh. He was watching her, waiting for her to stop him, but she couldn't. She was melting in a pool of desire.

'You're not,' she told him. 'I know what I'm doing.'

She actually had no idea what she was doing—this was completely out of character for her—but he didn't know that. He didn't know the real Scarlett. He didn't know that she was normally in control of her actions and emotions.

As far as he knew, she went out every weekend and drank cocktails and danced until dawn. For once, maybe it would be fun to be that girl. She wasn't hurting anybody and she could use some fun.

She wanted to lose herself in his touch. She wanted to lose herself in his embrace. She didn't want to think, she didn't want to make decisions. She wanted Jake to take her away from reality. She would worry about tomorrow another day.

Tonight she intended to take what she wanted and tonight she wanted Jake.

CHAPTER THREE

Scarlett struggled out of bed on Monday morning. She felt unaccustomedly lazy after an indulgent and unusual weekend and it took twenty minutes of yoga and two cups of coffee before she was ready to face the day. Her stint in Emergency was still ongoing and she knew she needed to be focused and sharp while working there, but she was having trouble keeping her attention on what had to be done. Her mind kept wandering off to relive the events of Saturday night.

If she closed her eyes she could picture Jake lying naked and almost exhausted in her bed. They may have only spent a few hours together but she knew she'd always be able to recall the ridges of his abdominal muscles and how they'd felt under his fingers, how his green eyes had lit up when he'd laughed and how it had felt making love to a fit, young and flexible male. It had been quite an experience.

She'd never slept with anyone with a tattoo before; she'd never slept with anyone she'd just met before and never on a first date. They hadn't even had a date—she couldn't count the late-night yiros stop at the café. She still couldn't believe she'd slept with him.

She grabbed a third coffee from the kiosk on her way into the hospital, wondering if she'd have time to drink it and knowing she probably shouldn't. Two cups was probably enough for now. The triage nurse solved her dilemma for her.

'Can you go straight into treatment room three?' she said, as she confiscated Scarlett's coffee and waited for her to sign in for her shift. 'We have a fresh lot of med students and one of them has asked for an anaesthetic consult.'

All day yesterday she'd imagined being someone else, someone more like Ruby, someone who acted spontaneously and did crazy things without regard for others. But one night of rebellion did not make her Ruby. Ruby was the fun sister, Rose was the pretty one, Scarlett was the clever one, and that was the way it had always been. And now she was a doctor and with that hard-earned qualification came certain responsibilities, which included an ability to focus and concentrate. She took a deep breath and shook her head to clear the last of the weekend cobwebs from her mind as she pulled back the curtain and stepped into the treatment room.

There were three people in the cubicle. A blond-haired, angelic-looking toddler, about two years old, was sitting on her mother's lap, cradled in her arms. The mother's face was white, the daughter's face was tear-streaked, and sterile dressings had been draped over her left hand.

The doctor sat opposite the pair and looked up as Scarlett stepped into the space. As their eyes met Scarlett felt as though all the air in her lungs had been knocked out of her. The doctor was the spitting image of Jake. The same green eyes, the same chiselled jaw. The similarity was uncanny.

She knew she was staring but she couldn't seem to stop.

'Hello, Scarlett.' It was the same voice. The same cheeky grin.

'Jake?' There was a stethoscope poking out of his coat pocket, a white doctor's coat. None of this made sense. 'What are you doing here?'

'I'm here on a uni placement.'

'You're a med student?'

'Yep. And this is Margie and her daughter, Skye.' With those few words Jake got Scarlett's attention back on track. She had a job to do, she'd have to deal with the issue of his appearance later.

'Skye managed to grab hold of some exposed live wires on the back of an old electric heater this morning. Luckily she was wearing sheepskin slippers with rubber soles but she sustained third-degree burns to several fingers. She's going to need surgery but I need an opinion as to whether a wrist or arm block would suffice or whether she'll need a GA.'

'How old is Skye?' Scarlett asked Margie, as she took two steps across the room to the basin to wash her hands.

'Twenty-six months.'

'And has she ever had an anaesthetic before?'

'No.' Margie shook her head.

'Let me see the extent of what we're dealing with.' Now that Jake had told her what had happened Scarlett was aware of the odour of burnt flesh but she still wasn't prepared for the state of Skye's fingers.

Jake lifted the dressings and Scarlett noted that he only lifted the side closest to her, keeping the injury shielded from Margie and Skye. The skin on Skye's middle, ring and little fingers was badly burnt. Charred and black, and Scarlett wondered if they'd be able to save them.

'The flesh will need debriding at the very least and most likely she will need plastic surgery. She'll need to be kept very still and that would be an impossibility for a two-year-old, so she'll need a general. I'll book a theatre.'

Scarlett was in a hurry to escape the cubicle. The space was far too small for her and Jake. She couldn't breathe and she knew it wasn't the smell of burnt flesh that was affecting her. It was Jake.

She knew she needed to ignore him. She knew it was better to treat Saturday night exactly as what it had been—a once-in-a-lifetime abjuration of character. It wasn't something she planned to make a habit of and while she couldn't deny she'd enjoyed the experience, a man like Jake didn't fit into her plans. Not even short term. He wasn't her type. He was sexy and fun and she knew she wasn't either of those things.

She gave instructions to the triage nurse and went to change. She was pleased she was going to be busy. She'd worry about Jake later.

She hurried into Theatre, pulling up short when she saw a familiar figure fiddling with the MP3 dock in the corner. Richard was back at work.

Damn. How on earth could she have forgotten his sick leave was finished and that he was returning today?

She knew it was because her head had been filled with thoughts of Jake, so much so that everything else had been wiped from her mind. Added to that, the surprise of seeing Jake again this morning had completely obliterated any chance of her remembering anything else. Guilt burned inside her as she waited for Richard to turn around. She could feel her cheeks flush and her palms were damp with sweat.

Why did it have to be today? She wasn't prepared for this, not now.

She took a few deep breaths as she tried to quell her guilty feelings. She hadn't done anything wrong, and there was no reason to feel guilty. Her business was no longer Richard's business and there was no need for him to know what she'd been up to.

He turned around as their patient was wheeled into Theatre and Scarlett's heart sank as she saw Candice and Mel on either side of the barouche. She prayed they would keep tight-lipped about the events of Saturday night.

The usual flurry of activity—transferring the patient to the operating table and beginning sedation as Mel, who was a plastics registrar, discussed the surgery with Richard—meant there was no time for idle conversation, but as soon as everything was set Candice's first question let Scarlett know she wasn't going to be so lucky.

'Did you get home all right on Saturday?' Candice asked, as she covered their patient with sterile drapes. The tone of her voice made Scarlett suspect she knew more than she was letting on but, judging by the expression on her face, she didn't seem to be hiding anything, although Scarlett was terrified that Candice was going to say more. Candice was an experienced nurse and she was quite capable of continuing a lengthy and detailed conversation while she worked.

'Yes.' She kept her answer short. She didn't want to get into this in front of Richard.

'What did you do on Saturday?' Richard asked, as he prepared to begin putting their patient back together.

'It was my hen's night,' Candice replied.

Scarlett did not want to open a discussion about Saturday night's activities so before Richard could ask any more questions she tried to steer the conversation towards Richard's health instead. He had been off work for several weeks and it would be rude of them not to enquire as to how he was feeling. She glanced at Mel, hoping she would pick up the conversation.

Scarlett felt like a wanton woman. Her behaviour on Saturday night had been completely out of character and even though no one in the room had actually witnessed it, she still felt like everyone could see on her face what she'd been up to. She'd had casual sex with a stranger or, at best, a new acquaintance, only weeks after dumping her boyfriend, who had wanted to become her fiancé and was now standing two feet from her across an operating table. Even though she was entitled to behave as she pleased, the guilt she was experiencing only emphasised the fact she was ill equipped to be acting so out of character. She was far better suited to being responsible and careful and considerate. Being spontaneous might be all right for Ruby but it obviously didn't suit her nature. She needed to remember that.

She let her thoughts drift as she heard Mel take over the conversation. Richard's MP3 was playing in the background. He liked to listen to instrumental versions of bands like Dire Straits and The Police and today it was the Adelaide Symphony's performance of Queen's songs. Scarlett would normally hum along but her mind was elsewhere.

She'd made a mistake. But she'd learn from that. She didn't plan on repeating her error.

She knew she couldn't do casual. She couldn't live in the moment. The moments always seemed to follow her. She didn't know how Ruby did it. How did she go from one man to the next without blinking an eye?

She herself had a tendency to dwell on things, which was why she tried to do the right thing in the first place. She hated feeling guilty or feeling like she'd done wrong, which was exactly how she felt right now, not because she hadn't enjoyed herself but simply because it was so out of character for her. She wasn't like Ruby and she wasn't like her youngest sister Rose either, where she could breeze through life without a care in the world, not minding what other people thought of her. Scarlett didn't want to be judged unless she knew she was going to be judged favourably and she doubted that would be the case if people knew about Jake.

The sounds of Theatre continued to flow around her as she monitored her patient's condition until finally the surgery was finished. Scarlett reversed the anaesthetic and left the patient to be taken through to Recovery.

'Is everything all right?' Candice had followed Scarlett into the scrub room. Scarlett thought about asking her why she hadn't mentioned that Jake would be turning up at work today but she thought better of it. She didn't want to invite questions.

'Of course,' she replied, as she threw her gloves, cap and mask into the rubbish. 'Why?'

'You barely said a word during the whole procedure. Is Richard making things awkward for you?'

'No.' Scarlett shook her head and it was only then that she realised Richard had barely spoken to her. Had he been giving her the cold shoulder or had he been concentrating on the surgery? She had no idea. But she realised she didn't care. Not at all. Working in silence was preferable to making idle conversation at the moment. She had a terrible poker face and she didn't trust herself not to give away her guilty feelings. 'I'd forgotten Richard was coming back to work today. I hadn't prepared myself for that and it threw me off a little.'

It wasn't completely true. Seeing Richard had thrown her but not because he was back at work—it had only bothered her because of her guilt but she wasn't about to air her dirty laundry here. The fewer people who knew about her indiscretion the better. 'I need a coffee,' she told Candice. 'Are you coming?'

Candice shook her head. 'Not yet. I need to go into Recovery first.'

Scarlett was relieved. She didn't want company, she

needed a moment of solitude. She walked through Emergency. The department was busy. Most of the curtains were pulled and people hurried to and fro. Scarlett was grateful to find the tearoom empty. She made another coffee and grabbed a biscuit. She stood by the window with her back to the door. She really needed something more substantial to eat. Her stomach was in turmoil; all the coffee was making her edgy and her nerves were already fraught, but the solitude of the tearoom was more appealing at the moment than braving the cafeteria crowds.

She heard the door open and she half turned her head, more a reflex than anything, to see who was interrupting her peace and quiet. She hoped it wasn't someone who felt like talking. The door opened fully and Jake walked in.

He winked at her. She couldn't believe how confident and cheeky he was, but the combination obviously served him well—it had worked on her. Her knees were shaking and she leant against the window, gripping the ledge with one hand to stop herself from collapsing to the floor. She wanted to touch him, to make sure he was real. She desperately needed to find some self-control. If she wasn't holding on to the window sill she knew she'd probably be halfway across the room by now.

She *never* reacted like this and her reaction irritated her and made her cranky. 'Have you come to tell me why you kept this news to yourself?'

'What news?' he asked, still grinning. 'That I was a med student or that I was coming here?'

'Either. Both.' She couldn't think straight.

'Would it have mattered?'

'Yes.' There was no way she would have jumped into bed with someone who would be turning up at her workplace virtually the next day.

'You never asked what I did.'

'I assumed you worked in a bar.' Scarlett was unsettled.

'You thought that was *all* I did?'

Scarlett shrugged. 'I guess.' He was right. She hadn't asked if he did anything else. She hadn't actually given it much thought. She hadn't wanted to know too much about him. She'd wanted it to be anonymous but she was annoyed with him for saying nothing. Confusion and guilt were making her short-tempered. 'You knew I worked here, you obviously knew on Saturday night that you'd be here today, and you still said nothing.' She felt as though he'd tricked her.

'I didn't think it mattered.'

'It matters to me.'

She felt like a fool. This was why she should never make spur-of-the-moment decisions.

Why hadn't he told her? Why hadn't *Candice* told her?

'Did Candice know you were going to be doing a placement with us?' she asked.

'Yep.'

'Why didn't she tell me?'

'Why would she think you cared?'

He had a point. And Scarlett didn't have an answer.

'What is the problem?'

Where did she start? How did she explain it? Would he understand that Saturday night had been completely out of character for her? Would he understand that her lapse in judgement had risked everything she'd worked so hard for?

It was unlikely. She couldn't expect him to understand.

He crossed the room, coming to stand beside her. She glanced nervously at the door. There was no telling how long their privacy would last. 'This isn't the place for this conversation.'

'No, I suppose it's not. It wasn't my intention to make things awkward, so for that I apologise. Why don't we have a drink together tonight and you can tell me why it matters and I can apologise properly?'

She didn't care about an apology. What she did care about was her reputation. And sleeping with a tattooed med student who worked in a strip club was not the way to get ahead in her career. It was not the way she wanted to catch people's attention. No matter how sexy he was.

Now that she'd recovered from the shock of seeing him, she was able to study him more closely. He was clean-shaven today. His face was all smooth angles and his green eyes had a look of amused interest. He was wearing a crisp white shirt under his white coat and he looked, and smelt, clean and fresh. And young.

He dipped his hand into the pocket of his coat and pulled out a container of breath mints. He offered them to her and when she shook her head he tipped a couple into his hand. Scarlett followed his movements. The mints were tiny against his large palm but it was his long, delicate fingers that caught her attention. She could remember how they had felt on her skin. The pleasure he'd brought her with his touch. It was a shame to think that one night was all she could have but there was no alternative. She had plans that didn't include sexy young male students.

'How about The Botanic at eight?' he suggested. Apparently his plans differed from hers.

'No.' Scarlett gave a slight shake of her head. The Botanic was much too close to the hospital, they would have no privacy there. There were plenty of other pubs in the two kilometres between the hospital and her house and any number of bars in Rundle Street.

Why was she even considering other pubs? Her response simply should have been 'No' and that was that. She could think of half a dozen reasons why she shouldn't meet him but only one why she should. And that reason was enough to have her thinking of alternatives. She needed a chance to make her position clear. He was likely to be on placement in her hospital for the next month and she needed to lay down some ground rules.

The door to the tearoom was opening again and Scarlett had to make a quick decision if she didn't want to risk being overheard. 'How about The Queen's Head?' she proposed, just as Candice appeared.

'Jake! You're here.' Candice bounced over and hugged him and Scarlett took the opportunity to escape from the tearoom while Jake was otherwise occupied. But before she could leave he held up eight fingers—*eight o'clock*—behind Candice's back and nodded at her in silent confirmation of their date.

Only it wasn't a date and Scarlett chose her outfit very carefully to ensure there would be no way Jake could misconstrue the purpose of their meeting. She chose a navy suit jacket and matching pencil skirt. She put a simple white silk camisole under the jacket and pulled out court shoes with a small heel, nothing as ridiculous as the platform sandals she had worn the night she'd met him, and redid her hair, pulling her thick curls into a tight bun. She needed a barrier of power dressing; she hoped it would combat their chemistry.

She spotted him the moment she walked through the front door into the bar. He was in the room to her right, leaning against the bar, keeping an eye on the entrance, waiting for her. God, he was gorgeous.

She was right on time; he'd obviously got there early. She wondered if he'd done it deliberately. And, if so, had it been so she didn't have the upper hand or was he just being chivalrous, not wanting her to wait alone at a bar?

He was wearing jeans and a white T-shirt with a green surf logo on the front that matched his eyes. The stark contrast in the formality of their outfits didn't go unnoticed by Scarlett and she was struck again by their age difference. But it wasn't enough to wipe out the instant surge of attraction she felt when their eyes met. She was aware of other women casting their eye over him as well. He exuded sex appeal and she wasn't the only one to notice, although he seemed completely unaware of the attention.

He straightened up and took two steps across the room, meeting her halfway. He leant towards her and kissed her cheek.

A surge of desire and adrenalin rushed through her and her body threatened to betray her. This was going to be harder than she'd anticipated.

'You came,' he said, as he let go of her hand and straightened up.

Scarlett wondered if he'd really doubted her. She'd bet he'd never been stood up by a woman.

'What would you like to drink?' he asked, as she resisted the urge to put her fingers over the spot on her cheek where she could still feel the imprint of his lips.

'A glass of wine, please.'

'Shall we share a bottle?'

She shook her head and reminded herself to be strong, decisive. *Remember, he must only be about twenty-three*, she told herself. *Just deal with him the same way you deal with Ruby and Rose. Firmly and decisively.* Scarlett was used to dictating the rules. They had to be able to work together.

'I'm not planning on being here very long,' she said. Firm and decisive.

'Ouch.' But he didn't seem to be offended. He was smiling, obviously not taking her seriously despite her outfit and her no-nonsense tone. 'What about something to eat?' he asked. 'Have you had dinner?'

'I'm fine.'

She waited as he ordered their drinks and a serve of beef sliders with fries. He handed her a glass of wine and led her to a table in the corner. It was hot in the pub and Scarlett could feel herself starting to perspire. The back of her neck was damp under her bun. The heat was making breathing difficult, or maybe it was Jake's proximity—he had chosen the chair at right angles to hers, not opposite, and his knee brushed against hers as he sat. She slipped her jacket off, deciding that if he wasn't going to heed her power-dressing message she may as well be comfortable, but she sat, upright, tense and stiff on her chair.

'You can relax,' he told her. 'I can be trusted to keep my hands to myself, much as I would like to do otherwise.' His gaze ran down the length of her arm, from her bare shoulder to her wrist, and Scarlett imagined she could feel a trail of heat on her skin. She shifted in her chair, hoping that another inch of space would break the sensation.

Jake was still smiling. He sipped his beer and said, 'I apologise if my being at the hospital makes you uncomfortable but the fact of the matter is I'm there for the next four weeks so we're going to come into contact with each other. Why is that a problem for you?'

'It's not, as long as we agree to forget about Saturday night. I don't want anyone to know about that.'

'I don't think I can forget about it but I guess I can refrain from mentioning it, but only if you give me a good reason.'

'There're a dozen reasons why. You're a med student. I'm a registrar. I've worked really hard to get to where I am and I don't want to give people a reason to take it away from me.'

'What reason could this give them?'

But Scarlett didn't answer that question as something else occurred to her. 'Is that why you slept with me? Because we were going to be working together? Were you hoping it was going to work in your favour somehow?'

'You asked me in. Remember? Actually, dragged me in might be a better description.' He grinned.

She couldn't remember exactly how he'd ended up inside her house but she did know she hadn't wanted him to leave. But her final choice may have been different if she'd known what the future held. 'I never would have slept with you if I'd known you were going to turn up at my work.'

'So I just have to wait until my placement is finished and then you'll date me.'

'I don't want to date you,' she said.

'I think you do.'

He was smiling again and his smile went deep to her core, stoking the fire that smouldered in her belly just waiting for his touch. She should have ordered a soft drink, not wine, she thought as her resolve weakened with every glance.

'No, I don't,' she said, trying to find that firm, decisive tone she desperately needed. 'I want to pretend that Saturday night never happened and hope that people don't find out. I've worked hard to get where I am. I have a plan and I don't want to jeopardise it by having people look at me differently. I don't have any intention of telling anyone about Saturday night. One-night stands are not my thing.'

Jake took a draught of his beer. She could see him trying to hide a smile.

'Why are you still smiling?'

'Because if one-night hook-ups are out of character for you then maybe I'm in with a chance of getting you to make it two.'

'You could have any woman you wanted. Why me?'

'You have that super-sexy secretary thing going on.'

'You think I look like a secretary?'

'Maybe not so much a secretary, maybe more a high-school principal,' he said. 'When you're dressed all neat and businesslike in your suit and your tidy hair and sitting there bossing me around, I feel like I'm back in the principal's office.'

The picture he painted made her laugh. She'd suspected he had a bit of a rebellious streak. 'Good. That should stop you from wanting to ask me out.'

Jake grinned. 'I dunno, she was pretty hot. And now that I know what happens when you strip back the layers and let your hair down...' He raised an eyebrow and shrugged. 'I had a really good time on Saturday night and, yes, I'd like to do it again,' he said simply, as the waitress placed his meal on the table. 'If I'm prepared to wait until I finish my placement, tell me why I shouldn't ask you out on a proper date.'

'You really want to take me out on a date?'

He nodded.

'But I'm not your type.'

'What is my type?'

'Someone more your own age.'

'How old do you think I am?'

She let her eyes travel over his face. Along the sharp edges of his jaw, across the smooth skin of his cheekbones, blemish-and wrinkle-free, the only lines on his face were smile lines. Her eyes met his. He was watching her just as intently. She reached across the table and pinched a few chips from his plate just to break eye contact as she answered, 'Twenty-three.'

'I'm twenty-six,' he said. 'I had a circuitous path to med school,' he explained, 'but that must put us close enough in age. So now will you date me?'

Scarlett shook her head. 'No. I'm still not your type.'

'And what makes you think you know what my type is?'

'I imagine it would be someone who is used to going clubbing, partying until the early morning.'

'That sounds like you.'

'If I'm out at two in the morning it's because I've been at work. Going clubbing is not my thing.'

'What is your thing?'

The rest of the bar receded into the distance as Jake looked at her. He leant towards her and Scarlett could feel herself being drawn in. He really was far too cute and she was struggling to remember what her thing was. She could feel herself growing warm under his gaze, her skin was burning but she'd already taken her jacket off and she had no more clothing to shed.

'I'm not sure but it's not going home with men who I meet in strip clubs.'

'I beg to differ.'

'I'm not going to date you.' She shook her head again, trying to convince herself as much as him that she meant every word.

'We'll see,' he said.

'You're not listening to me,' she replied, as she reached for her glass of wine. Jake reached for the salt at the same time and his hand brushed her forearm. Scarlett froze, immobilised by the current that raced up her arm. Her gaze dropped to his hand as he lightly curled his fingers around her arm and ran them along the sensitive skin to her wrist. She held her breath, waiting for him to stop touching her but hoping he wouldn't. She was a mess of contradictions. Her body wanted him; it felt as though every cell was straining towards him and clearly ignoring what her mind dictated and Scarlett wasn't sure whether her mind was strong enough to counteract the physical pull.

Jake was watching her watching him, as his fingers came to rest on her skin. 'I am listening,' he said. 'I hear what you're saying and I know you were intent on putting me straight tonight. I've heard what you've said and I see what you're wearing. Don't think I haven't noticed you've ditched your stripper heels in favour of something more demure, but I can also see your reaction to me and your body language is telling me something completely different.'

'That's just chemistry. A physical reaction.'

'And it should be celebrated. We both enjoyed Saturday night—why deny yourself pleasure?'

'But that's my point. Everything about Saturday night was completely out of character for me.'

'You don't like having a good time?'

'I'm not denying I had fun but it was only ever meant to be one night. I didn't think I'd ever see you again.'

'But that's what I don't understand. Why can't we do this again?'

'Because I have a plan.' Scarlett took a deep breath. She had one chance to convince him that getting involved would be a mistake. She had to convince him because by doing so she hoped she would convince herself. She moved her arm, removing herself from his touch as she sorted through her words. 'Usually I make carefully considered decisions. Usually I think about the consequences. Saturday night was just a lapse of control and I'm putting it down to a stressful week and one too many cocktails.'

'It was consensual, wasn't it? You told me you knew what you were doing.'

Scarlett nodded. 'I knew exactly what I was doing,' she admitted, 'but my point is I only intended to do it once.'

'That's a pity. Life should be fun.'

But in Scarlett's opinion life was meant to be taken seriously. That was the way to keep control. She wasn't young and irresponsible like Rose, she had never been like that, and she wasn't carefree and spontaneous like Ruby.

She stood and collected her jacket. She took a ten-dollar note from her purse and left it on the table to pay for her drink. She didn't want to be indebted to Jake.

'I'm sorry,' she told him. 'I have a plan and you don't fit into it.'

Firm and decisive.

And miserable.

But it was for the best.

CHAPTER FOUR

Jake had every intention of respecting Scarlett's wishes. As much as he didn't like, or even agree with, her decision he wasn't going to make her life difficult by making a nuisance of himself. If she didn't want to have anything to do with him he had to respect that. He had been raised to respect women and that included respecting their decisions.

He didn't need to be dating. His final year of studies and his part-time job at The Coop kept him busy enough. University life was almost over and he had to make sure he graduated well if he wanted to be accepted into the hospital of his choice for his intern year. Scarlett was right—scandal was best avoided. He didn't want to jeopardise his career chances any more than she did.

He decided he would respect her conditions for now and he wouldn't ask her out again while they were working together, but once his placement was finished he would see how things lay between them then. Their chemistry had been too good to just let her go without a little bit of a fight.

It would be easy to find things to occupy his time for the remainder of the placement, especially if the last few days were anything to go by. Their paths had barely crossed so his resolve wasn't tested.

Three more weeks, he told himself. He could wait that long, he thought as he glanced at the file in his hand.

A twenty-nine-year-old female had presented to Emergency with abdominal pain. He pulled back the curtain and ducked inside the treatment cubicle. The busier he was the faster time would pass.

The woman lay on the bed, curled on her side, with her anxious-looking partner sitting beside her. He stood as soon as Jake drew the curtain behind him but his movement was restricted by his partner, who kept a tense grip on his hand.

'Doctor, you have to do something, my wife is in terrible pain.' He didn't wait for Jake to introduce himself.

'Is it the baby?' the woman asked. She was the same age as Scarlett and she also had thick, dark hair, but the similarities ended there. Her face was pinched with pain and the knuckles on her right hand were white as she squeezed her partner's fingers.

'You're pregnant?' Jake hadn't noticed that on the file but he hadn't had much chance to look at it.

The woman nodded.

'How many weeks?' She was several kilograms overweight so it was difficult to judge.

'Six.' So her extra weight wasn't all pregnancy-related and there was a chance that she may have been mistaken with dates, one way or the other.

'Have you had the pregnancy confirmed?'

'We did a home test yesterday. It was positive,' the husband replied.

A positive home pregnancy test at this early stage was an indicator but not, in Jake's opinion, full confirmation. He knew he had to treat that news as an unconfirmed pregnancy until he had a chance to do more tests. But an ectopic pregnancy could be the cause of her symptoms and he would need to keep that in mind, although he couldn't afford to rule out appendicitis or other abdominal disorders.

He couldn't be influenced by the couple's suppositions. He needed to confirm a diagnosis, not play guessing games, and to do that he needed more information.

'I'm a final-year medical student—'

'My wife is pregnant and she's bleeding,' the husband interrupted Jake. 'We want to see a *doctor*.'

'The doctors are all busy,' Jake said, concentrating hard to keep his tone even. He addressed his next sentence to the wife. 'You're welcome to wait until one is available but I can't tell you how long that will be.' He suspected she wouldn't want to wait. 'I need to get some details and then I'll call a doctor when we know what is happening,' he explained. 'I can get started with your medical history and the physical exam and a doctor will join us when one becomes available.'

The look of nervousness he had seen earlier in the wife's eyes disappeared. She was in pain and he knew she wouldn't want to wait. A final-year medical student was close enough to the real thing for her. 'Okay,' she replied. Jake could almost see the husband deflate as his wife's agreement took the puff out of him.

Jake called for a nurse. He recorded the details of Angela's symptoms, their onset and severity, her menstrual history and her activities over the past twenty-four hours. He got the nurse to collect a urine sample so he could run a pregnancy test and then he began the physical exam. The medical history he'd taken made him suspect that an ectopic pregnancy was likely to be the cause of her pain but he wanted more confirmation.

'We need a pelvic ultrasound,' he told the nurse.

Sally ducked out of the cubicle to organise the equipment but she couldn't have been more than a few steps away when Angela cried out. She clutched her stomach and bent her knees to her chest. Jake looked at her in alarm.

Her face was completely white and beads of perspiration had broken out across her forehead and upper lip.

A ruptured fallopian tube or burst appendix raced to the top of the list of possible diagnoses. The quickest way to find out the answer now was to open her up.

'Sally!' he called out. The nurse stuck her head back in and Jake tried to disguise the note of panic he suspected was evident in his voice as he told her, 'I need a gynae consult. Right now.'

SCARLETT CHECKED OVER her equipment, ready to anaesthetise her patient as soon as Diana, the gynaecologist, was ready. Their patient, a twenty-nine-year-old woman, was about to undergo surgery for a ruptured Fallopian tube. Apparently she had presented to Emergency with abdominal pain from an ectopic pregnancy and things had gone downhill from there. The general consensus was she was lucky that she'd already been in the hospital and therefore only minutes from help.

She turned her head as she heard the sucking sound of the theatre door as it was opened. Her heart tumbled in her chest as she saw Diana walk in, followed by Jake. He was looking straight at her, his green eyes clear and confident. He was tying his mask and the bottom half of his face was obscured but she didn't need to see all of his features. She'd recognise his green eyes anywhere; the corners crinkled as he smiled at her. She nodded a greeting in return. Her face seemed to have frozen—surprise had taken away her ability to smile.

His mask was green and matched his eyes perfectly. She wondered if he had chosen it deliberately but then she doubted he would have thought of that. While he was gorgeous looking with a body to match she couldn't accuse him of being vain.

He had short-sleeved scrubs on and Scarlett could see the bottom three stars of the tattoo on the inside of his left triceps. It gave her a little thrill to know the reason behind the tattoo. Having that knowledge seemed like such a personal thing and he had shared it with her on the night they had made love. He'd had the Southern Cross constellation tattooed on his arm before he'd taken off overseas for a gap year after finishing school to remind him of where he came from and to remind him that he always planned to come home.

They had lain together in her bed after making love. Jake had wrapped his right arm around her shoulders as she'd lain with her head on his chest and let her fingers trail over the ridges of his stomach muscles. His left hand had been tucked behind his head, in much the same position as it was now, and Scarlett had lifted her hand from his abdominals to run her fingers over each little star. She'd expected the stars to feel bumpy and raised but they had been smooth and flat on his skin. Just the memory of it now made her heartbeat quicken.

He tied the mask easily. He looked perfectly at home in Theatre. He didn't look like a student. He looked comfortable, he looked like he belonged. But Scarlett suspected he wasn't the type of person who would feel uncomfortable anywhere. He'd certainly seemed at home half-naked on a stage in front of a crowd of women so she supposed this setting would be a piece of cake. Two female doctors, two female nurses and Jake—it would be nothing out of the ordinary for him.

Scarlett finally recovered control of her facial muscles and was able to murmur a greeting as Diana introduced Jake and explained that he had been doing the consult when Angela's fallopian tube had ruptured and Diana had invited him to observe Theatre.

'If you stand just to my left you should get a good view of the surgery,' Diana told him.

Scarlett focussed on putting Angela to sleep as she tried to block out the picture of Diana and Jake standing shoulder to shoulder and tried to ignore the tightening of her stomach that she recognised as jealousy. She knew she was being ridiculous. They were only standing together and she had no right to be jealous but Diana was making her a bit crazy. Diana had a reputation as a serial dater around the hospital and Scarlett could imagine her wanting a taste of Jake, but surely not even Diana would sleep with a student?

Diana had made an incision into Angela's abdomen and confirmed what Jake had suspected. Angela had an ectopic pregnancy that had ruptured her fallopian tube.

'This was her first pregnancy, is that right?' she asked Jake.

'Yes. She and her husband said they'd been trying for a while.'

'I think I can repair the tube. I'm going to try,' she said, and explained her reasoning. 'Having one ectopic pregnancy increases her chances of having subsequent ectopic pregnancies. She won't thank me if I don't try to save the tube if it's at all possible. I can't afford to be careless with another woman's fertility.'

Scarlett couldn't fault Diana's skills as a doctor or surgeon but she couldn't help feeling her blood boil as she watched the surgery. As she watched Diana's arm brush against Jake's as she repaired and stitched. But Scarlett knew this was her issue, not Diana's.

Jake was paying close attention to the surgery, asking questions as he looked over Diana's shoulder. Scarlett imagined that Diana could feel Jake's breath on her cheek, just like she had on Saturday night, and she knew she wanted to be the one whose arm was brushing against his.

He hadn't spoken to her. He hadn't looked at her and Scarlett suspected that maybe he was deliberately avoiding her. She didn't want to be ignored. She wasn't sure what she wanted but it wasn't that. Not wanting to show that she was bothered by the lack of attention, she pretended to adjust her equipment but in reality everything was going smoothly with the sedation and there was no need for her to do anything other than monitor the machine.

'Right, that's looking good. I'm really pleased with that outcome.' Diana had managed to repair the tube and was sewing up the incision. There was a noticeable decrease in the tension in Theatre as Diana announced success.

'Scarlett, now the crisis is over there's something I wanted to speak to you about,' Diana said as she snipped a thread. 'I was thinking of asking Richard if he wanted to come with me to Candice's wedding but I wanted to make sure I wasn't stepping on your toes. It is over between the two of you, isn't it?'

Scarlett was mortified. She could feel her cheeks flushing and she was glad her face was half-hidden behind a mask. She would love to have some of Diana's confidence, even ten per cent would be good. She could never imagine announcing her dating plans to a room full of colleagues. But that wasn't the only difference between the two of them.

She had to answer Diana. She couldn't pretend she hadn't spoken directly to her. She looked up and her gaze landed on Jake first. He was watching her from behind Diana's shoulder.

Now he watched her!

Immediately she could feel heat flooding through her. She hated having such primeval reactions to him when he seemed quite unflustered but it reinforced her feeling that she had made the right decision by staying away from him.

Nothing good could come from any involvement. She knew there was a good chance she would lose control.

She quickly averted her gaze, looking at Diana instead. She was a few years older than Scarlett, somewhere in her early thirties. Scarlett wondered if she knew Richard's biological clock was ticking but it wasn't up to her to tell her. Diana might well be hearing the same ticking as Richard. It wasn't Scarlett's business anymore.

'As far as I'm concerned, Richard is a free agent,' she told Diana. 'But I know he's already accepted an invitation to Candice's wedding and I'm pretty sure he'll still be planning to attend. Were you going to ask him as your date?'

'Not yet. I know he's already going but I thought it was a good opportunity to go together without any pressure.'

Scarlett thought inviting someone to a wedding as a first date, even an unofficial one, was buried in pressure. It was a gutsy move but she was actually relieved that Diana had set her sights on Richard as it meant Jake was safe. If Scarlett couldn't have him she didn't want anyone else to either.

'I'm sure he'd be flattered by your attention,' Scarlett said. She could feel Jake watching her still but she avoided his gaze by keeping her eyes glued to her monitors until it was time to reverse the anaesthetic.

But Jake followed her out of Theatre.

'Diana was talking about Richard Thomas, the plastic surgeon, wasn't she?' he asked, as they stripped off their masks and caps.

Scarlett looked down at her hands as she peeled off her gloves. She didn't need to see what she was doing but it allowed her to avoid eye contact. She threw her gloves in the bin as she replied, 'Yes.'

'You could date Richard but not me?' Jake kept the volume of his words low but Scarlett could hear the irritation in his voice. 'Don't you think that's a bit hypocritical?'

'Richard is a senior consultant, no one thinks there's anything wrong with a registrar dating a senior.'

'You don't think people might think you're sleeping your way to the top?'

Scarlett was about to deny his ridiculous accusation but then hesitated. Would people have thought that? Maybe. Not that she would admit he might be right.

Although she had to admit that she'd known dating Richard wouldn't hurt her career prospects so perhaps she was guilty as charged.

She could feel her temper rising. Jake could certainly push her buttons and it annoyed her that he could make her second-guess herself. But she knew it was more than that. All her reactions to him were extreme and she hated losing control but that seemed to be a permanent hazard when she was around him. Extreme irritation. Extreme arousal. Extreme attraction. Extreme awareness. Every reaction, every one of her senses, became heightened in response to him.

'If a registrar can date a senior, why can't a registrar date an intern?' he asked.

'I'm sure they do but you're not an intern. You're still a student.'

'I won't always be. When I'm a registrar and you're a consultant, what will your excuse be then? Is this about me or you?'

She was normally calm, collected and controlled but she seemed to have trouble keeping a lid on her emotions around Jake. She shouldn't be having this conversation with him. She should just walk away but she couldn't make her feet move. She was attracted to him, she wasn't denying that, but once again it was her issue. She had a plan, she was determined to qualify as an anaesthesiologist and she wasn't going to be distracted by an emotion as basic as lust. Not when it could cost her her career.

'This is about both of us. I'm sure we'd be violating all sorts of workplace policies by dating and I for one don't want to be accused of sexual harassment. I am not prepared to jeopardise my career. No matter how tempted I am, nothing is worth that.'

'How about if we keep it low key? Take a leaf out of Diana's book and go to Candice's wedding together. As colleagues. Nothing more.'

'Richard hasn't accepted Diana's invitation yet,' Scarlett was quick to point out.

'Fair enough, but there's no reason to think he won't. She's a good-looking woman, smart, single, he's got no reason not to accept.'

Scarlett felt her stomach clench with another burst of jealousy. Not over the idea of Richard and Diana but because Jake had called her good looking.

'I don't need a lift, thank you, I'm going with my sister Ruby. She used to work with Candice and she's coming to town for the wedding.'

'Is she the one who owns the sexy shoes?'

He was smiling at her, his cheeky grin lighting up his eyes, seemingly unbothered by her rejection of his offer. Did nothing faze him? Was he always so relaxed and easygoing?

She shook her head. 'No, those were Rose's.'

'Another sister? How many do you have?'

'Only two.'

Talking about Ruby made her realise she would provide the perfect distraction. She decided she would focus on Ruby's visit. Ruby always blew into town like a mini-tornado and her sister's presence should be enough to keep her occupied *and* keep her mind off Jake. Ruby would give her enough to worry about and leave no time for sexy med students. Ruby was the perfect solution to her dilemma.

CHAPTER FIVE

Scarlett scanned the crowd as the passengers disembarked from the plane and were disgorged up the ramp and into the terminal. She hadn't seen Ruby for several months and although they kept in regular contact with phone calls and social media it wasn't the same as seeing each other in person. Scarlett paced impatiently. She was dying to give Ruby a big hug and to immerse herself in her sister's latest news. She always had a story to tell.

Ruby was the middle of the three Anderson sisters. Rose was the baby of the family and Scarlett the sensible, oldest sister. Ruby was the wild child, the sister who tried whatever she liked and did whatever she pleased. Scarlett used to wish she was that brave but the fact of the matter was she wasn't brave or rebellious or foolhardy. She was cautious, pragmatic and reliable, and she'd had to decide long ago to let Ruby have the adventures. And Ruby did. There was no denying that Ruby lived her life fully and Scarlett always enjoyed spending time with her, even though it could be exhausting. Ruby was more than a breath of fresh air in Scarlett's world, she was a whirlwind.

The two of them hadn't always been close and there had been plenty of differences of opinion as they'd been growing up. Ruby had caused their mother plenty of headaches and to compensate for Ruby's headstrong behaviour Scarlett had always tried to do the right thing to avoid causing any further stress. She knew that sometimes she'd resented Ruby and her carefree and occasionally selfish attitude but as she'd matured, as they'd both matured, their differences had diminished. When Ruby had left home ten years ago, at the age of sixteen, Scarlett had missed her terribly. And although Ruby had come and gone, she'd never officially returned to South Australia and now Scarlett made sure to make the most of their time together.

A tall, thin woman with shoulder-length platinum-blond curls was walking briskly along the edge of the ramp, dodging fellow passengers and waving. It took Scarlett a moment to realise it was Ruby. Last time she had been home her natural strawberry blond locks had been dyed a dark red but the platinum shade was just as striking and probably better suited to her fair colouring.

Scarlett waved back and took in Ruby's outfit as she waited for her to reach the end of the ramp. Ruby's fashion choices were always interesting and today was no exception. The majority of Ruby's clothes came from markets and second-hand stores and Byron Bay, her current home town, had no shortage of either. Scarlett was constantly amazed that she chose to buy her clothes this way. After wearing second-hand clothes for most of their childhood, Scarlett had vowed she would always have new clothes and the more expensive the better. She chose to save her money and buy a few classic pieces each season, but not Ruby. Ruby was migratory and whenever she moved she'd leave most of her wardrobe behind, donated back to the second-hand clothes stores where it had come from, and pick up thrift-shop clothes that blended into her new environment when she relocated.

Today she was wearing a floaty, ankle-length, tie-dyed skirt with a tight black T-shirt emblazoned with what looked like a movie poster but it wasn't a movie Scarlett recognised. She looked like a stereotypical Byron Bay hippie. A multitude of different-coloured bangles adorned her wrists and ankles and her toenails were painted a bright tangerine. In contrast to her toenails, her fingernails were short, clean and unpainted—nurse's fingernails.

Despite her mismatched outfit she looked clean and fresh. Her hair was newly washed, her face make-up free. Her pale, flawless skin didn't need any help other than a lick of mascara for her eyelashes. Ruby looked like her father's side of the family. There were physical similarities to Rose, particularly now that Ruby's hair was blond, but Scarlett knew that she and Ruby looked nothing alike. And it wasn't just their taste in clothes.

Scarlett hugged her the minute she stepped off the ramp. She was skin and bone.

'You're so thin.'

'I've been too busy to eat.' Ruby grinned as Scarlett released her.

Scarlett recognised that look. 'You know you can stop having sex to eat,' she teased. 'Who is he?'

'Who *was* he, you mean.'

Ruby's relationships never lasted very long and it was almost always Ruby who did the leaving.

'Okay. I'll bite. Who was he?' Scarlett amended as she led the way to her car.

'He was a movie director.'

'You haven't taken up acting now, have you?'

While Ruby chopped and changed hairstyles, addresses and boyfriends almost as often as she changed her underwear, the one thing that had been constant in her life had been her job. Ruby was a nurse, and had nursed with Candice in Melbourne, hence the invitation to the wedding, and it was something that Scarlett thought she loved.

While many other things about Ruby wouldn't surprise her, finding out she'd quit nursing would be unexpected.

'No, no.' Ruby laughed. 'He was directing a small-budget indie flick that was being filmed on the Central Coast, in and around Byron Bay.'

'How on earth did you meet him?' Scarlett asked, as Ruby threw her duffel bag into the car. Scarlett eyed the bag suspiciously. She couldn't imagine what Ruby had packed in there to wear to Candice's wedding. Whatever it was would surely be creased beyond recognition.

'There was an accident on set. Rohan brought the injured actor into the hospital.'

Scarlett was amazed at the different types of men Ruby had dated. In recent memory there had been a pharmacist, a guy who ran a surf school, a teacher and now a movie director, which probably explained Ruby's T-shirt, but Scarlett couldn't work out what they could possibly have in common.

'So what attracted you to him?' Scarlett asked, as she started the car and drove out of the car park.

'He was interesting. They all are. I like a guy who can give me new experiences. Not just in the bedroom,' she said in response to Scarlett's silent smirk, 'although I'm not opposed to that either, but I like seeing the world through different eyes. I guess, most importantly, there's always a connection, some chemistry. And that's hard to resist. When that happens I know I just have to give him a try. If they're good in bed, I'll keep them around for a bit. If they're not...*sayonara*.'

Scarlett thought she understood that feeling now. It was how she felt about Jake and that just served to confirm her idea that he was okay for a fling. Ruby's relationships never lasted long. Obviously chemistry was enough to sustain a short-term fling but did something that burned so brightly fizzle out just as rapidly? It certainly seemed to be the case for Ruby. Jake was sexy and fun but a very unlikely match for herself. She knew someone like Richard, someone meticulous and serious, would be a far better fit for her. If Jake was going to be anything to her it could only be temporary.

'What happened to this one?'

Ruby shrugged. 'They finished filming.'

'Did he break your heart?'

Ruby laughed. 'No. It was fun while it lasted but if he hadn't had to pack up and move on I would have moved on anyway. I was getting bored.'

'At least it means you have time to eat again,' Scarlett told her as she parked the car in front of her house. 'Which is good because we're having lunch with Mum.'

'Really?'

Scarlett could hear the note of trepidation in Ruby's voice. Ruby had a volatile relationship with their mother, which had become strained when Ruby had been a teenager and they had never recovered an easy camaraderie. Scarlett knew Ruby felt as though her mother was constantly disappointed in her. She felt their mother judged her sister and found her lacking. And despite the fact that Ruby had straightened out her life, more or less, she never believed Scarlett when she tried to tell her that their mother loved her and just wanted to feel included in Ruby's life.

Ruby's unpredictable relationship with their mother was one reason she usually crashed at Scarlett's place when she visited. It was always better if Ruby and Lucy had their own space.

'We'll just have a quick lunch and then we'll come back here to get ready for the wedding. Have you got something to wear in there?' Scarlett asked, as Ruby dumped her duffel bag in the spare bedroom.

'Of course. I might even have something to lend to you.'

Scarlett raised her eyebrows. She couldn't imagine that she'd be able to fit into anything of Ruby's. While they were a similar height, Ruby's stick-thin figure was quite the opposite of Scarlett's curves.

'What time is Richard picking us up for the wedding?' Ruby wanted to know.

'He's not. Mel is going to swing past in a cab for us just before four.'

Ruby was frowning. 'Is Richard working?'

'No. We're not together anymore.'

'You're kidding.' Ruby plopped herself on the bed. 'What happened?'

Scarlett hadn't intended to tell Ruby about breaking up with Richard right at this minute, she'd planned to ease into that conversation, but there was no way to avoid the question now.

'Is he still planning on going to the wedding?' Ruby asked when Scarlett had finished giving her the abbreviated version of events. 'Is it going to be awkward?'

'It'll be fine.' Scarlett didn't bother to explain that Richard had accepted Diana's invitation and would be accompanying her to the wedding. That wouldn't matter to Ruby.

'I asked Candice to put me with some hot single guys,' Ruby announced. 'Maybe she's put us together.'

Scarlett immediately wondered if Candice might have put her on the same table as Jake. It had been at least twenty minutes since she'd last thought of him—that had to be counted as progress.

'We can find ourselves a couple of eligible bachelors and organise a double date.' Ruby immediately started thinking about picking up guys at the wedding, which was why Scarlett hadn't intended to say anything about Richard. She'd had some disastrous dating experiences with

Ruby in the past. Their taste in men was about as different as their taste in clothes. Conservative and sensible was Scarlett's motto, which was why Jake was so not her type, and she didn't think she'd ever heard Ruby even *use* the word 'conservative', except maybe to describe Scarlett.

'Or do you already have another beau waiting in the wings?' Ruby asked, when Scarlett didn't reply.

She shook her head. 'I'm not like you. I can't just go from one man to the next.' She wished she could. She wished she didn't have her goals set. She wished she could just be with Jake, even temporarily, without worrying about the consequences. Even though she'd been the one to lay down the rules she had struggled to put him out of her thoughts. He had kept his part of the bargain and had kept his distance around the hospital, but she had been aware of him watching her and she could always tell the exact moment he was anywhere in her vicinity. Her body seemed attuned to his presence; it seemed to pick up his frequency before her brain had registered it. The more she told herself to ignore him the more often she noticed him.

She kept up a constant stream of questions to Ruby as she drove to their mother's house, hoping that listening to Ruby chatter would keep thoughts of Jake at bay. It worked, sort of. And whatever part of her brain wasn't taken up with Ruby's conversation was soon occupied with concern for their mother, who seemed to age noticeably every time Scarlett saw her.

Lucy was only forty-seven but could have been mistaken for someone five, if not ten years older. She was an older, more tired version of Scarlett. They had the same thick chestnut hair but while Scarlett's was still dark, her mother's was streaked with grey. They shared the same dark eyes but Lucy's were underscored with deep shadows and Scarlett knew that her mother's figure had once looked like hers but three pregnancies and years of shift-work and irregular meals as a nurse had combined to sap Lucy's vitality.

This was what Scarlett feared her own future would look like if she succumbed and travelled down the marriage and babies path. In her opinion and experience there wasn't much to recommend it.

The conversation started with the usual discussion about their various careers but Scarlett knew she was on tenterhooks, waiting for something to be said that would set the cat among the pigeons.

It wasn't long before Lucy changed the topic. 'So you haven't settled down yet, Ruby?'

Scarlett held her breath as she wished, not for the first time, that Ruby drank alcohol. She was sure a glass of wine would help to mellow the different personalities and ease the tension but she knew Ruby had perfectly valid reasons for her abstinence and Scarlett couldn't argue with those. She waited for Ruby's response.

'Mum, I'm twenty-six, settling down is the last thing on my mind. I'm in the prime of my life and I intend to have fun while I can. Scarlett is the one you need to talk to. Do you know she's broken up with Richard?'

Scarlett had expected to hear Ruby's usual announcement that she was far too young to even think about settling down but she hadn't expected her to deflect attention from herself by announcing Scarlett's own news.

'Scarlett? When did that happen? Why didn't you tell me?'

Ruby's tactic seemed to have worked. Lucy forgot her usual retort, which went along the lines of the fact that she'd had three children by the time she was twenty-six, which then inevitably led to the argument that only one of those pregnancies had actually been planned and Ruby didn't intend to follow that path. Ruby had a point but although Lucy may not have been terribly successful in either her family planning or in choosing the fathers of her children, she had done her best to raise her daughters. Scarlett knew it had never been Lucy's intention to have three children by three different men but it was the way things had worked out.

Lucy had been a single parent for most of Scarlett's twenty-nine years. She had given birth to Scarlett just after her eighteenth birthday and Scarlett had always felt an obligation to protect her mother as much as possible. Lucy had been unlucky in love and Scarlett also knew that Ruby and Rose, to a lesser degree, had tested Lucy's patience and therefore Scarlett had tried not to add to her mother's burden. She hadn't told her mother about the break-up because she didn't want Lucy worrying about her.

'Are you okay?' Lucy asked, when Scarlett wasn't quick enough with an explanation.

'I'm fine. It was my decision.'

'But why? What went wrong? I thought Richard was what you wanted.'

Richard might have been what she wanted but it had turned out he hadn't been *who* she wanted. If she'd had a checklist she would have put plenty of ticks beside his name, beginning with the fact that he was older than her, settled in his career and didn't want children. She didn't really have an aversion to having a family but she was terrified of being left to raise them alone, like her mother had been. If she was ever going to have kids she'd make damn sure it was with someone who loved her. And there was no guarantee that even that would be enough. Therefore it was safer not to reproduce. In her mind it was safer not to put herself in that situation, although if Richard hadn't changed his mind she may well have stayed with him. She'd even thought she loved him.

Until she'd met Jake.

Whether or not it was simply a matter of timing or circumstances, she hadn't been able to resist Jake. Which meant she couldn't have been in love with Richard, could she? Not when she'd been so quick to fall for Jake's charms and jump into his bed. Ruby bed-hopped but to her credit she had never professed or even pretended to be in love. Scarlett knew now that she had been pretending with Richard.

'I didn't love him.' That was the simplest explanation and the one that would lead to the least amount of questioning.

Scarlett knew her mother had been not so secretly hoping she would marry Richard. Or someone like him. Someone who could take care of her financially and give her the security she had never had. Scarlett had to admit that security was something she craved too but she intended to rely on herself, not another person, for that security. If she was going to get married it would be because she needed something only that other person could give her. It wouldn't be for something she could provide for herself. Her mother had lost one partner to illness, one had simply left and the other had been booted out. Through her mother's misfortunes Scarlett had learnt not to rely on anyone but herself.

Scarlett looked at Lucy. She was so afraid of ending up like her, old and alone. But as much as she didn't want to be alone, she was more afraid of being left. And Richard's heart attack had given her a glimpse of the future and that terrified her.

SOMEHOW BOTH SHE and Ruby managed to get through lunch relatively unscathed but Scarlett was relieved to get home and focus on getting ready for Candice's wedding.

She got out of the shower and stuck her head into the spare bedroom to see what Ruby was wearing. Ruby had dried her hair and had swept it to one side before tucking the end up so it curled and sat just below her jawline. But that was all she'd done. She was still wrapped in her towel.

'Not dressed yet?' Scarlett asked.

In answer, Ruby pulled a slim parcel, wrapped in tissue paper, from her duffel bag. She unwrapped it to reveal a royal blue silk tank-top, heavily embroidered from the shoulders to the waist. Embroidery was another fashion trend that was loved in Byron Bay but at least this garment actually looked new and wasn't tie-dyed, Scarlett thought as Ruby dropped her towel, pulled on some knickers and shimmied into the top.

She didn't bother with a bra; she didn't need one. The top hung loosely from her shoulders and fell just a few inches below her butt. Scarlett waited to see what pants Ruby was going to wear but she just slipped her feet into a pair of strappy silver heels and appeared to be done.

Scarlett raised her eyebrows. 'Is that what you're wearing?'

'What's wrong?' Ruby looked down at her feet. She pulled out another pair of shoes. Neutral peeptoe wedges with an ankle strap. 'These are the only other shoes I have. I think the silver ones go best with the dress.'

So it *was* a dress. 'I wasn't talking about the shoes.'

'What's the matter, then? Don't I look all right?'

Actually, she looked amazing. The 'dress' skimmed perfectly over her long, lean figure and she could get away with the short length as she had fantastic legs. Good legs, courtesy of their mother, were probably the one thing she and Ruby and Rose did have in common, that and the same shoe size. Scarlett couldn't fault Ruby for having the confidence to wear the outfit. Not when she looked so gorgeous. 'You look fabulous.'

'Thanks,' Ruby said, as she twirled in front of the mirror. She was a girl who was used to receiving compliments and she wasn't really looking for approval. 'Now it's your turn. What are you wearing?'

Ruby followed Scarlett into her room and waited as Scarlett pulled her dress from the wardrobe. It was a simple sleeveless shift dress, knee-length and panelled. The centre panel had a floral pattern and the sides were black and cut in at the waist to take the emphasis away from the hips and draw the eye in.

'You can't wear that,' Ruby said.

'Why not?'

'It's okay for an office party or a lunch but it's too casual for an evening wedding and it'll make you look old. I'll find you something else.' Ruby pulled no punches as she began to rummage through the wardrobe. Scarlett had thought the floral fabric gave the dress a fun, celebratory air but Ruby obviously thought otherwise.

'What about this?' Ruby was holding up a silk shirt dress that Scarlett had bought to wear as a top. It had a boat neck, a gathered waist and loose, elbow-length sleeves. In keeping with the sixties style, the fabric was printed with a paisley pattern in pale pink, cream and green.

'I don't know. I haven't got the right pants to wear with it.' Scarlett had intended to wear it with skinny satin pants but all she had were black ones and they had looked wrong against the colour and pattern of the top and she hadn't managed to find the right alternative colour yet.

'Pants! Who said anything about pants?' Ruby cried. 'This is a dress. Put it on, let's have a look.'

Scarlett found her underwear, there was no chance of going braless with DD breasts, and then pulled the dress over her head. It fell to mid-thigh and was much shorter than anything she would normally wear but still several inches longer than the dress Ruby had on.

Ruby was searching the bottom of the wardrobe for shoes. Scarlett would have to remind her not to bend over at the wedding unless she wanted to give all the other guests a glimpse of her undies. She pulled out a pair of neutral pumps and held them out in front of her, her head turned to one side as she looked at them with the dress. She screwed up her nose. The shoes were obviously not to her liking.

'Do you have anything else in this colour?'

Scarlett shook her head.

'That's okay, I'll lend you mine.'

Scarlett smiled to herself; Jake was going to think she didn't own any shoes of her own. *Stop it. Stop thinking about him.*

Ruby disappeared to her room and came back with her nude wedges. 'These will be better.'

Scarlett slipped them on. They were a good choice, the right colour and a better fit stylewise, plus they made her legs look exceptionally long. The floaty sleeves and the neckline preserved enough of her modesty to ensure that overall the outfit wasn't too revealing. It was a win-win.

'Perfect,' Ruby declared. 'Now for hair and make-up. Sit on the bed and I'll fix you up.'

Ruby might not believe in make-up for herself but she had a natural flair for colour and for the dramatic and by the time she'd finished Scarlett felt pretty enough, even if she didn't quite look like herself. But that was okay, she could think of her make-up as war paint. Ruby's ministrations had bolstered her confidence and prepared her for seeing Jake.

CANDICE AND EWAN'S wedding was being held in the garden of the National Wine Centre and as Scarlett made her way through the vines to the chairs placed alongside them she was glad she was wearing wedges. She and Ruby had only just found a seat when Candice's sister, who was the matron of honour, started down the aisle that had been constructed between two rows of vines.

She was accompanied by two angelic-looking children, a flower girl and page boy. Scarlett knew they weren't Candice's niece and nephew and she wondered briefly who they belonged to before her attention was diverted by the bride, who was being walked down the aisle by her father.

The ceremony was lovely, simple and straightforward but heartfelt. Scarlett always loved a good wedding, even if she couldn't quite dismiss the feeling that disaster beckoned. She crossed her fingers, hoping for the best for Candice and Ewan.

As the ceremony ended and she rose from her seat to follow the other guests back to the function centre, she searched the faces for Jake. She lost sight of Ruby as she melted into the crowd that had gathered on the outdoor terrace for pre-dinner drinks, but Scarlett didn't worry. Ruby knew a few of Candice's friends and she'd be fine. She was no shrinking violet. Scarlett had too many nerves of her own in anticipation of seeing Jake to worry about Ruby. Despite their differences, she hadn't been able to stop thinking about him. She hadn't yet found the secret to letting the idea of him go.

She finally found him. He was talking to an attractive couple who appeared to be the parents of the flower girl and page boy. He kissed the woman on the cheek. There was something familiar about her but Scarlett couldn't work out if she knew her. Jake squatted down to talk to the children. He was too far away for Scarlett to hear what he said, but his comments made them both laugh. He ruffled the boy's hair as he stood up and his movements brought Scarlett into his line of sight.

He didn't take his eyes off her and she could read his lips as he excused himself and began to walk towards her. He was wearing a light grey suit and Scarlett had a fleeting thought that this was the most dressed she'd seen him. He had a white shirt under his suit jacket and a green tie that matched his eyes. Even fully dressed, he looked gorgeous.

His walk was fluid and graceful as he crossed the terrace, collecting two glasses of champagne from a waiter as he made his way to her. Scarlett hadn't moved since their eyes had met. She was frozen to the spot, fixed in place by his eye contact, totally under his spell.

CHAPTER SIX

He flashed his cheeky smile at her as he reached her side and that was enough to break the spell and allow her to breathe again.

'You look gorgeous.' He ran his eyes over her and Scarlett felt herself grow warm with his attention. Her makeover, courtesy of Ruby, had bolstered her confidence but not enough to prevent her from dissolving into a mass of nerves under his gaze. The make-up and hairstyle—Ruby had held her hair back with a hairband and teased it behind the band into a sixties style, letting the weight of it fall down Scarlett's back—were not protection enough against the surge of attraction she felt the moment she saw him.

'Champagne?'

Her hand shook as she accepted the glass and a shiver of excitement ran through her as his fingers brushed hers.

'Are you cold?' he asked. 'Shall we move into the sun?'

It was late afternoon and the sun was getting low in the sky, the heat losing its intensity as the day drew to an end. They were standing on the terrace in the shade of the building and Jake moved a few steps into the sunshine. Scarlett followed automatically. Her feet didn't wait for any conscious instruction—it seemed she was programmed to his frequency and she couldn't override her reaction.

'How was your day?' he asked.

Scarlett sipped her champagne as she filled him in on her day's activities and was surprised to find she'd drunk half her glass by the time she'd finished talking.

'So it's been a family affair for both of us today.'

Of course, he'd been talking to his sister—that was why the woman had looked familiar. Their faces were a similar shape, although his sister's was more heart-shaped, less of a pentagon, less angular than Jake's.

'That was your sister you were talking to earlier? Were the flower girl and page boy your niece and nephew?'

Jake nodded. 'That's Mary and her husband, Ted.'

'Are the rest of your family here?'

'Evangeline is. My brothers aren't and my other sister, Ruth, lives in the States. Her first baby is due any day now and my parents have gone over to help her.'

'That's a big family. What number are you?'

'Two older brothers, three older sisters, then me.'

Scarlett smiled as aspects of Jake's personality fell into place. 'That's why you're so relaxed, you're the baby. I bet there was always someone looking out for you and you've never had to worry about anything.'

'And I bet you're the eldest sibling.' Jake grinned. There was no malice in his voice, just laughter. His green eyes sparkled and Scarlett basked in his attention. 'You would always be complaining that the rest never had it as tough as you and that the younger ones all got away with murder.'

In Scarlett's case it was true. She wondered if the lack of responsibility her sisters seemed to feel was due simply to their personalities or also to their birth order. She knew of several studies that indicated that birth order had a lot of influence over personality and she didn't begrudge her sisters, but sometimes she wished she could experience what it felt like to be carefree, instead of constantly thinking about her responsibilities and worrying about doing the right thing. But she knew Jake's comment had been made in jest. As accurate as he was, she was sure he wouldn't really want to know how tough her childhood and her early years in particular had been.

'So you're number one and Ruby is number two?' he asked, and when Scarlett nodded he added, 'Which one is she?' But before she could answer he changed his mind. 'No, don't tell me, I'll see if I can guess.'

'Good luck.' Scarlett laughed.

'I assume by that you mean you don't look alike?'

The champagne had taken the edge off her nerves and she laughed and raised one eyebrow and replied, 'I'll let you be the judge of that.'

'If I guess right, what will you give me?'

She had no idea and when he looked at her as though he wanted to devour her she was too scared to ask what he wanted.

'Can't decide?' Jake grinned, laughing at her with his green eyes and making her stomach flutter. 'Don't worry, I'll think of something.'

His cheeky bravado made her accept his challenge, confident he'd never be able to pick out Ruby. With a tilt of her head and a slight smirk she agreed. 'Okay, go for it.'

He scanned the crowd, commenting on the different women and why they couldn't be Ruby. He had a practised eye but his comments weren't offensive, they were simply entertaining.

'You're supposed to be telling me which one *is* Ruby, not which ones aren't,' Scarlett teased.

'She's the blonde over there, wearing the blue top and no bottoms.' Jake nodded towards Ruby, picking her out without hesitation.

Scarlett laughed at his description, it was exactly what

she would have said, but she was amazed that he'd got it right. 'How did you know?'

'I could tell by her legs.' He looked back at Scarlett before lowering his eyes and running his gaze down her bare legs. The heat in his gaze stirred the pool of desire in her belly and she could feel it spread through her. 'You have the same legs,' he told her.

Self-consciously Scarlett tugged at the hem of her dress, trying desperately to make it longer as she fought the tide of desire.

'Don't,' he remonstrated. 'You have fabulous legs, you should show them off.'

Scarlett blushed, wondering if he could see the effect he had on her or whether the make-up hid her discomfort. His green gaze held hers and his cheeky smile curled the corners of his mouth. She had to look away before she gave in to a crazy notion and leant forward to taste his lips. She looked across the terrace, away from temptation, and her gaze met Ruby's.

Ruby's ears must have been burning. She was looking directly at them and was now coming their way. Scarlett felt a flutter of panic. She didn't want to introduce them. She didn't want Jake to fancy Ruby and in her experience men always did. She didn't want Jake to be like all the others. She knew she was being hypocritical and selfish and she also knew that if Ruby wanted Jake there'd be precious little she could do to stop her, but she wasn't going to stand by and facilitate a meeting. She needed to keep them apart for as long as possible.

As she was deciding on a course of action the flower girl came running up to them, crashing into Jake's knees and distracting Scarlett.

'Papa is coming to pick us up, I have to say goodbye,' she said, as Jake swung her up to sit on his hip.

While he was busy with his niece Scarlett saw the perfect opportunity to make an escape and headed Ruby off at the pass. She touched Jake's shoulder. 'I'll catch up with you later,' she said, knowing he was too busy to stop her.

She intercepted Ruby halfway across the terrace. She tucked her arm into her sister's and guided her over to a drinks waiter.

'Hot guy. Who is he?' Ruby said, as she glanced back to where Jake was still conversing with his niece.

'He's a friend of Candice's.'

'I don't remember her having friends like that when we worked together.'

'He's from Adelaide.'

'That's okay.' She shrugged. 'Is he single?'

'As far as I know.'

'I might have to meet him later.'

Scarlett knew her little interception wouldn't be enough to stop Ruby. Ruby wouldn't wait for an introduction, she'd introduce herself. It was yet another difference between them. She needed to go to the bathroom but she didn't dare leave Ruby alone. She knew the first thing she'd do would be to head for Jake. Scarlett lifted a glass of champagne and a non-alcoholic cider from the waiter's tray before steering Ruby towards Mel. She'd make her keep an eye on Ruby for the time being.

She handed them each a glass, champagne for Mel and cider for Ruby, and said, 'I'm just going to the loo.' She ducked inside the restaurant and almost knocked over the seating plan that was displayed on a board by the main doors. She looked it over quickly. She found her name on table six. Ruby's name was there too. And so was Jake's.

She scanned the room for table six and when she found it she detoured past to check the place settings on her way to the bathroom. She circled the table, looking for her name. She found Ruby's first. To her left was Jake. To Jake's left was her own name.

Candice had put Jake between her and Ruby.

She couldn't think of a worse situation. She couldn't possibly sit next to him all through dinner but she didn't want Ruby next to him either. She picked up her name card before putting it back down. Who should she move? She couldn't move both of them so which one should it be?

Her nerves wouldn't stand being seated next to Jake. She'd have to move herself. She picked up her place card again and switched it with that of another girl at the table, a nurse from the hospital, who she knew was single. Maybe *she* could distract Jake from Ruby.

SCARLETT WAS TRYING to relax and make the best of the situation she'd created when she'd moved her place setting. Her manoeuvring had resulted in her sitting between one of the groom's friends, Simon, and Jake's brother-in-law, Ted. While both men seemed perfectly nice, and Scarlett knew this would be a good opportunity to pump Ted for information about Jake, she was having huge trouble concentrating on their conversation. Her meddling had positioned her opposite Jake and now she had a bird's-eye view of Jake and Ruby. They were deep in discussion, a discussion she was desperate to overhear, but the noise level in the room meant that was impossible.

She realised too late that what she should have done was switch Jake's name card. That way neither she nor Ruby would have been sitting next to him and she still would have only moved one person. But that hadn't occurred to her until now and what's done was done. She would just have to live with the consequences.

From what she could see, Ruby and Jake appeared to be getting on famously. It was what she had been afraid of and it wasn't surprising. Ruby had a lot of her father in her—he was extremely charismatic and was always the life of the party—but she would hate to know that her sister was comparing her to him because he was also a liar and a cheat, two things Ruby definitely wasn't.

Maybe Ruby was more Jake's type, Scarlett thought. She definitely danced to the beat of her own drum and did whatever she pleased, creating her own fun, much like Scarlett suspected Jake did. She sighed and let Ted refill her glass as she resigned herself to the fact that she couldn't control the world and she definitely couldn't control Jake and Ruby. If they were kindred spirits she should be wishing them luck.

She turned her head and tried her best to ignore Jake as she made an effort to engage Simon in conversation while she picked at her dinner. The food looked delicious and she was almost certain it was, but seeing Ruby and Jake together had ruined her appetite.

By the time her main-course plate had been cleared away Candice and Ewan were on the dance floor, dancing their version of the bridal waltz. Slowly the guests began to join the bride and groom. From the corner of her eye Scarlett saw Jake rising from his seat. Involuntarily, she turned her head, expecting to see him ask Ruby to dance, but his eyes were fixed on hers as he made his way around their table to her side.

'Dance with me?' His voice poured over her, softening her resistance with its treacle tones. His green eyes had her fixed in his sights, making her forget where they were and who he was. She couldn't concentrate when he looked at her like that, as if he wanted to consume her, as if she was the only woman in the room. Just a look from him now and she was ready to self-combust. Just a look and she could recall the touch of his fingers on her skin, the warmth of his lips on hers, the weight of his body between her thighs. Her body responded to his gaze and she felt the heat pooling in her groin.

As if he could read her thoughts, the corners of his mouth lifted into a smile that was just for her. He was holding out one hand to help her from her seat. It was hard to resist and automatically she put her hand in his. Her skin came alive as his fingers closed around hers. The heat in her belly raced through her and joined with the fire in her fingertips and her heartbeat quickened as her body came to life.

But as her body woke up, so did her brain. Touching him was enough to make her come to her senses. 'No.' She snatched her hand back, as though she'd been burnt. 'I can't.'

She couldn't imagine being held in his arms while everyone else watched. She couldn't imagine being able to keep her feelings under control while his hands were on her skin, while she could feel his breath on her cheek, while they danced in front of a crowd. It was too dangerous. She'd almost made a big mistake.

'I'll dance with you.'

Scarlett's heart lodged in her throat as she heard Ruby's invitation and Jake's acceptance and it stayed there, making breathing almost impossible as she had to sit and watch and smile while Jake danced with Ruby. While he held Ruby in his arms.

Her hand shook as she poured herself a glass of water and lifted it to her lips. She swallowed hard, forcing the liquid past the lump in her throat. She needed to get a grip on her emotions. She couldn't let him affect her like this. Why did he upset her equilibrium so massively? This reaction was so unlike her. She wanted him but she knew she couldn't have him. She needed to forget about Jake.

He could dance with whoever he pleased, it couldn't matter to her.

But she still wished it didn't have to be Ruby.

RUBY HAD BEEN waiting to get Jake alone and out of earshot of the rest of the table. There were things she needed to ask him. Like what was going on between him and Scarlett. He'd told her he was a med student and that he was doing a placement in Emergency with Scarlett, a rather interesting piece of information that Scarlett had neglected to tell her, and Ruby wanted to know why. She had seen them on the terrace during the pre-dinner drinks and she remembered Scarlett's expression. It had been clear to her that Scarlett only had eyes for Jake—she had been completely unaware of anyone else but him.

She had baited Scarlett earlier, teasing her about meeting Jake, wanting to see if Scarlett let any info slip, but she played her cards close to her chest, just as she'd always done. But it was obvious to Ruby that Scarlett liked Jake and she wanted to know if her sister's feelings were reciprocated.

Jake held her right hand in his left and she could feel his right palm pressing into the small of her back. The pressure was firm enough just to let her know that he knew what he was doing. He had nice strong arms and a good frame and she relaxed and let him lead her around the dance floor.

'Now that we're alone, are you going to tell me what's going on between you and my sister?'

'I don't know what you're talking about.' He avoided her gaze as he spun her out of the way of another couple who looked fairly clueless.

'I'm talking about the fact that neither of you could keep your eyes off each other all through dinner yet you behaved as though you were strangers. Why didn't you move around the table and talk to her? Why were you ignoring her?'

'Because she wants me to.' His gaze was direct this time.

'How do you know?'

'I asked Candice to put Scarlett next to me at the table,' Jake told her, 'and I assume she did, there was no reason not to, yet Scarlett was sitting opposite me. She must have moved place settings to avoid me.'

'Why would she do that? What have you done to her?'

'Nothing. But I think I make her uncomfortable.'

'Because she likes you?'

'Yes,' he admitted. 'But not enough.'

'You should ask her out.' Ruby could never see the point of hanging back. If she wanted something she went and got it, and she figured more people should live by that philosophy.

'I have.'

'Really?'

'Yep.'

'And…?'

'She turned me down. She says she can't date a student. Apparently it's unethical.'

'She's probably right,' Ruby said. 'She's a bit of a stickler for the rules. But surely she's allowed to dance with you tonight?'

'I believe she is.'

'So why isn't she?'

'She doesn't know what to do with me. I don't think I fit into any of her neat little boxes. I suspect she feels I might cause chaos in her orderly world.'

'So what are your plans? You obviously like her too. Are you just going to keep ignoring her or are you going to ask her out again?'

Jake was laughing.

'What?'

'I feel like I'm dancing with one of my sisters. They like to boss me around as well.'

'Well, it sounds as though you need it.'

'Then you'll be pleased to know that I do have a plan. I thought I'd let her have a few more glasses of champagne before I ask her to dance again. She likes me better when she's had a few drinks,' he explained.

'Is that so?'

'Yep. I'll wait for her to relax a bit more and then hopefully she'll be up for some fun.'

'Can I give you some advice?' she asked.

'About Scarlett?'

Ruby nodded.

'Sure.'

'She's not really about having fun. She takes life very seriously.'

'I've learnt that but I'd like to see if I can change her mind. Show her how to have a good time.'

Ruby grinned at him. She suspected that would be something he'd be very good at but she thought it only fair to warn him. 'You'll need to take things slowly. She's not very good at letting people into her world. She's cautious. She expects people to let her down, men in particular. She doesn't like to rely on anyone but herself. For anything.'

'That's okay, I'm not in any hurry. I can do slow.'

SCARLETT FELT AS though she'd been watching Jake dance for hours. He was a good dancer and watching him was certainly no hardship, but watching the succession of partners was becoming tedious.

She wished she hadn't felt so self-conscious, she wished she could trust herself to keep her emotions in check, she wished she could have danced with him. The dance floor was crowded now; she was probably more conspicuous sitting alone at the table than she would be if she was in Jake's arms. He danced confidently. He was light on his feet and had good rhythm. He'd looked like he didn't have a care in the world as he'd danced with Ruby, his sisters, Mel, several of the nurses, Candice—she'd been keeping a mental tally—and now with Diana.

He had removed his suit jacket and she could see the muscles in his butt, back and shoulders flex and relax as he guided Diana around the floor. If he asked her to dance again she'd say yes, she decided. Surely one dance couldn't hurt.

She followed his path around the dance floor, her eyes glued to the crisp brightness of his white shirt, her eyes straining as she tried to see if his tattoo was visible through the thin fabric. He hadn't so much as glanced her way since he'd taken to the dance floor and she felt safe to study him, knowing he was unlikely to catch her out.

She found his tattoo fascinating. She felt as if it was their secret, even though she knew any number of other women had probably seen it but she refused to let her mind dwell on that. She wanted to feel as though they had shared something special. She knew they weren't likely to share anything else, but she could still close her eyes and recall tracing her fingers over the tattooed stars. It would be her memory. One no one could take away.

He lifted his left arm and spun Diana under and away from him and Scarlett's eyes immediately flicked to the inside of his upper arm, to the junction of his biceps and triceps muscles, to see if she could spy the stars. As she searched for the shadow of the Southern Cross she heard someone pull out the chair next to her and guiltily she looked away from Jake to find Richard sitting down beside her.

'Richard! How are you feeling?'

'Surprisingly fit and well. I really feel as though I have a new lease of life.'

She studied him properly for the first time in weeks. He'd aged in that time but it wasn't all that surprising. He'd lost weight but he didn't look too thin, and the fact that he'd lost his tan after stopping his weekly golf game was probably to blame. He was a good-looking man, she acknowledged, but he certainly didn't take her breath away and make her insides go all gooey like Jake did. She realised now she had never had that same intensity of reaction to Richard. Had he ever turned her knees to jelly? She didn't think so. But she'd been happy. Or maybe just not *unhappy*.

'I came over to apologise. Diana told me you knew she was going to invite me to come to the wedding with her but I hope it hasn't put you on the spot. It wasn't my intention to make you feel uncomfortable in any way by accompanying Diana today.'

'It's not a problem,' Scarlett reassured him. 'I was happy for her to ask you.' It was far better than the alternative— that Diana had wanted to ask Jake. 'I want you to have everything you wish for and I'm sorry I couldn't give you what you wanted.' Scarlett didn't bear Richard any ill will. They weren't compatible, and maybe he could be happy with Diana.

Now that he had unburdened himself, his gaze sought out his date. 'Diana doesn't seem to be in any hurry to get off the dance floor.'

Why would she be? Scarlett thought. She was dancing with Jake.

'Shall we join them?' Richard asked.

'Are you up to it?'

'Most definitely.'

She might as well be dancing instead of sitting alone at the table. She took Richard's hand and was curious to discover that she felt nothing. There was no rush of desire, no overreacting nerve endings, no breathlessness. She fought to pay attention to Richard as he guided her around the dance floor but her body had a mind of its own and her eyes kept seeking Jake.

If she had any doubts about her decision not to marry Richard she had her answer now as her eyes found Jake. Even if she could count on Richard to be dependable and committed she knew she could never go back. Their relationship had been convenient and safe, but it had never been exciting. Jake was like a drug and she knew she could easily become addicted to the buzz she got when she was with him, to the surge of attraction and the adrenalin, and that was what she wanted now. She wanted excitement.

She kept her eyes on Jake. While she couldn't imagine being with him long term she knew what she wanted now. Adventure. Excitement. Pleasure. Richard was a good man but she wanted more than that. There was no harm in wanting, was there?

Jake and Diana were getting closer. Scarlett remembered why she didn't like dancing with a partner—men got to call the shots. Richard was guiding her around the dance floor and she had no control over where they went. Jake and Diana were right beside them now and there was nothing she could do about it.

'Shall we swap partners?' Jake asked, directing his question to Diana. Richard and Diana didn't even argue. As if the move had been rehearsed, Jake let go of Diana and she stepped into Richard's arms. Their timing gave Scarlett no option. If she hadn't let Jake take hold of her she would have been stranded in the middle of the dance floor. But as she felt his hand close over hers and the familiar flutter in her belly she thought perhaps she should have escaped while she'd had the chance. But Jake wasn't letting her go.

'I've been waiting all night to dance with you. Just one dance, can you give me that?' he asked, as if he knew she was deliberating over her options.

The band was playing a slower number now and Jake slid his hand further around her back, pulling her in close. His hand was warm against the small of her back and he positioned her so that one of her legs was tucked between his thighs and he was able to control her movements with slight pressure of his hands, his fingers and his thighs. But Scarlett didn't feel trapped or controlled. She felt like part of him. He was light on his feet and she relaxed and let him take over. She'd been wishing she could have just one dance, and this was her chance.

Her breasts were pressed against his chest and she could feel the heat of his body through his shirt. His body was hard and strong against hers. She turned her head to the right and breathed in his scent. He smelt like a summer day, fresh and warm. His left arm was outstretched and she could see the dark shadow of his tattoo through the sleeve of his shirt. She focused on the stars. She didn't need to concentrate on dancing, her body followed Jake's rhythm effortlessly. She wanted to rest her head against him and close her eyes and imagine they were alone but she had to resist and remember where they were. She forced herself to make conversation.

'Where did you learn to dance?'

'I spent years being dragged along to my sisters' ballet classes. When I wouldn't sit still and started complaining, Mum enrolled me in classes too. Not ballet—jazz and contemporary mainly. I loved it and I've never stopped.

When I was in high school it was a good way to get the girls—girls love a boy who can dance. And it comes in handy now for my job.'

Scarlett frowned. 'For medicine?' That made no sense and she wondered if she'd drifted off and had missed part of his answer.

He shook his head and his lips lifted in a smile as he laughed. 'No, The Coop.'

'You need to be able to dance to work behind the bar?' She remembered him moving to the music but his movements had looked completely natural, albeit totally hot, but they certainly hadn't looked choreographed.

'I'm not just a barman,' he said, as he tipped her backwards into a dip and then lifted her upright again before she had a chance to complain that she was too heavy. She knew she wasn't, she knew he had total control, he was ninety per cent sexy, muscled hunk and ten per cent cheek, although she admitted she should allocate some percentage for intelligence as well.

'Sure, there's judging the contests too,' she said, once she'd recovered her equilibrium.

'Everyone at The Coop does a bit of everything.'

He paused and Scarlett wondered what he was waiting for. He had tilted his head to the side as he watched her and once again she had the sense she'd missed something but she had no idea what.

He was smiling at her as he said, 'You do realise I'm a stripper?'

'What?' Scarlett frowned, not sure if she'd heard correctly.

'A stripper,' he repeated. 'Someone who gets paid to take their clothes off in public.'

CHAPTER SEVEN

Scarlett stopped dead in the middle of the dance floor, almost causing a collision.

'I know what a stripper is,' she said, although she still wasn't quite sure that she believed her own ears. But even while she thought her ears were deceiving her, her imagination was taking flight. Her initial reaction was completely visual. She could picture him playing the part. An image of him semi-naked, bare-footed, bare-chested and wearing only jeans was imprinted on her brain from the time they'd first met. If she closed her eyes she could picture the muscle definition of his abdominals, the smoothness of his tanned chest and the perfectly shaped stars of his tattoo. She could imagine him on stage wearing nothing but a cheeky grin and tiny leather shorts, lapping up the attention.

Her heart was racing at the mental picture she had created until she suddenly wondered if he was pulling her leg. She searched his face, looking for a tell-tale grin. She narrowed her eyes and watched him carefully as she asked, 'Is that really what you do?'

'Of course.' She could see no sign of a smirk accompanying his reply. 'What did you think I did there?' he asked as he steered her to the side of the dance floor, making sure they weren't going to get trampled.

'I thought you worked behind the bar.'

'I do but we're jacks of all trades. We're bar staff, waiters, strippers.'

He really wasn't kidding and she had no idea what to do with this new information. She wasn't sure if she should be shocked or intrigued, horrified or excited.

'You really didn't know?' he asked.

Gradually she became aware that they were still standing on the edge of the dance floor. She took his arm and almost dragged him outside to the terrace. She was not going to have this conversation around other people. How would she ever explain sleeping with a student *and* a stripper? She breathed a sigh of relief as he followed her outdoors.

Thank God no one knows we slept together, she thought, and she intended to keep it that way.

'Of course I didn't know,' she told him, as she checked their surroundings to make sure they were alone. 'Do you think I would have slept with you if I'd known?'

'You tell me. You didn't seem to have too many reservations. You didn't seem that interested in the finer details.'

She knew he was right. She'd wanted to do something out of character and she hadn't seen any reason to find out too much about him. She'd simply been looking for a physical connection, not a deep and meaningful conversation. In fact, she'd deliberately avoided any personal discussion. She'd been tempted by a hot stranger and she'd been more than happy to let him scratch an itch for her.

Her anger, which she knew stemmed from surprise and embarrassment, subsided. It was hardly his fault that she was naïve. It was hardly his fault she hadn't asked any questions, let alone the right ones.

'You're right. I'm sorry,' she apologised. 'I didn't stop to think. I didn't want to know anything about you really, other than what I could see. I wanted to pretend I was someone else, someone who was used to having a good time.'

'Well, that's my job. To make sure people have a good time.'

Just how good a time was he talking about? Was that what he'd been doing for her? And how many women had been there before her? She felt a blush steal across her throat and embarrassment made her words stick to the roof of her mouth. 'Do you—? Are you—?'

Jake shook his head. He obviously got the gist of her half-asked question. 'No. My job stops when I leave The Coop. Anything after that is my choice, my time.'

'But you must have picked up other girls in The Coop?'

'Actually, I haven't. I make a point not to. Most of the girls in The Coop are not at their best. Drunk and loud isn't really my type.'

She wondered if she should admit to having been slightly more intoxicated than she was used to but while she'd certainly had more to drink than was usual she knew she'd been in full control. She remembered every blissful minute of that night.

'I noticed you because you were different from the usual clients but I didn't intend to sleep with you.'

'You didn't?' Scarlett blushed. Had she made a complete idiot of herself by kissing him back, inviting him in and then almost begging him to sleep with her?

'Well, not that night anyway.' He grinned and Scarlett relaxed very slightly. 'You were a friend of a friend, I was being nice, offering to walk you to your taxi, but then...' He shrugged.

'So you take your clothes off in front of complete strangers for a living but you don't use your job to pick up women?'

'I do have some morals and it's not all my clothes. It's

no different to being a life model for an art class or a patient for the surface anatomy viva in our exams. I keep more clothes on than they do and I'm paid better and it's fun. There's no harm in it. It's not illegal.'

'I couldn't do it.' Scarlett hadn't had a chance to work out what she thought about Jake being a stripper but she knew it was not something she could ever imagine doing.

He laughed and the sound lifted her spirits. She supposed in the grand scheme of things that finding out he was a stripper was hardly the worst thing that had ever happened.

'No one is asking you to,' he said. 'You were happy to join in at The Coop, though. You have to admit it's good entertainment.'

'I hated it. I was so far out of my comfort zone.'

'What did you hate? The show? The music? The atmosphere? Me?'

'No.' Definitely not him. 'Being on the stage. I had to pretend I was someone else up there. The girl you met at The Coop wasn't me.'

'The girl I met at The Coop came from somewhere.'

'I was pretending I was Ruby,' she admitted. 'I'm the nerdy, shy, clever sister who behaved completely out of character that night. You should be dancing with Ruby, I'm sure the two of you have far more in common.'

Now more than ever, Scarlett wished she was more like Ruby. Surely Jake would rather be with someone who didn't take life so seriously? She was no match for him.

'And I'd rather be out here with you,' he said, as he ran one finger along the bare skin of her forearm, leaving a trail of heat from her elbow to her wrist. Scarlett could feel her nipples tauten in response to his touch and she couldn't think of anywhere else she'd rather be either.

'It's you I want to get to know,' he told her. 'Not Ruby or anyone else.'

'Why?' Scarlett knew exactly why she had slept with Jake but she couldn't understand why he'd want to be with her.

'When I first saw you I thought you were gorgeous and sexy and then I found out you were intelligent and fun as well. I think you're fascinating and I want to see all your different layers. Not just the person you want everyone to see. Do you remember the children's party game Pass the Parcel?'

Scarlett nodded. She knew the game but she didn't have the words to tell Jake that she hadn't gone to parties when she was little. She used to be invited to them but she never told her mother because she knew they didn't have the money for a present and she didn't have a party dress. She didn't want Jake feeling sorry for her. Those days were well and truly behind her, there was no point in bringing up the past.

'You remind me of the parcel.'

She frowned. 'How?'

'You seem to have lots of different layers and I want to unwrap each one and find out what's underneath.'

'I don't have different layers. What you see is what you get. I'm not complicated or interesting. All my life I've been the responsible one, the one who doesn't cause any problems, the one who does the right thing, who worries about what other people think.'

'I disagree. The girl on stage doing the limbo, she's inside you somewhere, underneath that responsible exterior.'

Scarlett shook her head. 'I was pretending. I'm not sure I really know how to be that person and I'm not sure if I want to be. I'm not Ruby and while I admit there are times I envy her I'm not sure that I really want to be her.'

'Are you and Ruby really so different?'

'Ruby is the wild one of our family. She's the fun, outgoing one, the one who has the adventures, the one who doesn't care what people think. If that's what you want, I'm not that person. I've always chosen studying over partying. I'm not a party girl.'

'And I'm not saying you should be. I'm only saying I think there's more to you than you want people to see and I find you fascinating. I want to get to know you. The real you. The complete you. I think we'd have fun together.'

Scarlett couldn't deny that she had fun with Jake but she couldn't imagine it continuing. 'I think you'll be disappointed. I don't think we have anything in common.'

'I disagree.'

Scarlett held up one finger and proceeded to straighten her adjacent fingers as she counted off their differences. 'You work in a strip club. As a stripper. Something I was naively unaware of. You're a student at my hospital. You have a tattoo.'

Jake laughed. 'Well, I happen to think we have plenty in common.'

He gently flexed her index finger, returning it to her palm. 'We're following the same career path. We're at the wedding of a mutual friend,' he said, as the next finger went down, followed by her third finger. 'I have a very small tattoo in a very discreet spot and I seem to remember you rather liked it. And...' he grinned as he closed her fist and finished negating her argument '...you can't hold my part-time profession against me, not when you've only known about it for five minutes, and especially not when you've already slept with me.'

'But I wouldn't have slept with you if I'd known.'

'Liar.' He was leaning in close. His lips brushed her ear and his words were soft puffs of air on the sensitive skin of her neck. 'You might not have slept with me if you'd known I was a med student but you know you wanted me as much that night as I wanted you and, stripper or not, you would have had your way with me.' His hand was on her waist and he slid it around to cup her bottom, pulling her in against him so her belly was pressed into his groin. There was no need to guess what was on his mind. Her nipples hardened in response to his physical reaction, pushing against the soft silk of her underwear, and she knew he'd be able to feel them jutting into his chest. His next words confirmed her thoughts. 'You want me now, too.'

She should have been cross with him. She should have found his arrogance infuriating but she couldn't deny he was right. She did want him. More now than she had on that first night. Now that she knew how her body responded to his touch she thought there would probably always be a part of her that would want him but that didn't make it right. And it had nothing to do with him being a stripper. She just knew they were an incompatible combination. He was too different. But she couldn't deny she was drawn to him. But that just made him different and dangerous.

'Don't be mad, dance with me,' he said.

The music from the band floated through the open doors onto the terrace. They were standing behind a potted tree, partially shielded from view of the guests inside, and Scarlett knew it would be difficult to see them due to the shadows. They were alone but she had no idea how long their solitude would last. She didn't want to have any more missed opportunities tonight. She let the music wash over her as she relaxed against him and let him take control.

He kept his hand on her bottom and held her close against his body. She rested her cheek on his chest. His heart was a steady, soothing beat under her ear. She could have stayed like that for hours but the evening was nearly over. She wished she hadn't been so stubborn, she wished she had danced with him earlier. She could have spent the night in his arms instead of watching all the other women enjoying his company.

She closed her eyes as she dreamed about what might have been.

IT HAD TAKEN him all evening but now he had her right where he wanted her to be—in his arms. He finally had her undivided attention. They were alone, without interruptions. He was convinced he could get her to relax if he had the time. If they had no other distractions and no observers.

He had been aware of her watching him dance for most of the evening. Once again her words had contrasted with her actions. Her dark eyes with their hidden secrets had followed him around the dance floor. He shouldn't find that enticing, he should find it frustrating, but it seemed that every time she contradicted herself it only made him more interested.

He'd meant it when he'd said he found her fascinating. He'd known since the moment he'd laid eyes on her that she was a bundle of contradictions. The serious hairstyle and simple black dress paired with her sexy hip-swivelling walk and the sky-high heels. She was an intriguing mix of sexy and smart.

It had been the contrasts in her that had hooked him from that first glance. Her pouty lips were the type that should be painted red but hers had been slick with a pale pink gloss. Her full lips had promised forbidden delights but had framed a smile that had been hesitant and unsure.

She was an interesting but possibly dangerous package, just waiting for the right spark to set her off. Her performance on stage had hinted at what could be but she had confirmed his expectation later that night when she'd taken him to her bed and he'd been lost in the promise and mystery of her ever since.

He wanted to strip away her layers and discover what was hidden at each level. He had never been so quickly and utterly captivated before. Her contrasts appeared limitless and he was desperate to discover them all. He had never thought that contrariness could be so interesting.

The music stopped, although it took them both a few seconds to notice. It wasn't until they were interrupted by the sound of the emcee announcing it was time to farewell the bride and groom that they realised the band had fallen silent.

Scarlett stayed in his arms. She seemed in no hurry to move and he was more than happy for her to stay right where she was. 'I'm not ready for the night to end.'

'It doesn't have to end yet,' he said. 'Let me take you home.' As he uttered the words he remembered Ruby's cautionary advice to take it slowly.

'And then what? We both know where that would lead.'

'Would that be so terrible?' He'd forgotten his vow to stay away. He'd forgotten he'd agreed to avoid scandal. He was completely under her spell and all he could think of was getting her out of her dress and having her long legs wrapped around him again while he tasted and explored her and learnt her secrets.

'Just think of all the fun we can have.'

'Do you have any idea how much trouble I would be in if anyone found out I was sleeping with a student?'

'It's not the first time.'

'I know. That makes it worse. Last time I could plead ignorance. What's my excuse this time?'

'My irresistible charm,' he whispered in her ear. His lips brushed against her earlobe and he could have sworn he could feel her resistance start to cave. 'I thought you wanted adventure?' he said, as he ducked his head lower and let his lips graze the edge of her jaw. 'You don't need to leave all the adventures for Ruby. I can be your adventure. The first student you seduced. The first stripper you took to your bed.'

'Seducing students and strippers isn't the sort of adventure I had in mind.' She was panting now, her words breathless.

'It's our secret. No one else needs to know.' His fingers brushed her breast, skimming across her nipple as he kissed the hollow at the base of her throat, and Scarlett moaned softly.

She tipped her head back to speak but ended up offering him her throat and he pressed his lips under her jaw over the pulse of her heart, and Scarlett only just managed to get her words out. 'You've only got two more weeks on placement. Can we wait until then?'

'Nine days.'

'What?'

'I've actually only got nine more days, not counting the weekend,' he said, as he ran his hand down her arm and hooked his fingers around hers. 'I guess I can wait that long.'

'Really?'

'Yes, really.' The way he was grinning at her made her think he'd just got what he wanted but she had no idea what that was. 'I was always prepared to wait until the end of my placement. Two more weeks of platonic friendship won't kill me. Especially if you're the prize at the end of it.'

SCARLETT WOKE UP with a start just as she felt Jake's fingers brush over her breast and trail across her stomach. Her eyes flew open and she was surprised to find herself alone in her bed. She would have sworn she wasn't dreaming. Even now her breasts ached with longing and her groin throbbed as her body refused to give up on the idea that Jake was sharing her bed.

Last night when he'd kissed the hollow at the base of her throat it had sent a spear of longing shooting from her belly to her groin and despite her concerns she'd been tempted, oh, so tempted to give in right then and there. But she'd resisted and now she was paying the price—an overactive imagination that refused to accept that Jake wasn't in her bed.

She closed her eyes as she ran her hands over her breasts. Her nipples puckered as she imagined Jake's fingers on her skin and she squeezed her knees together as the nerve centres in her erogenous zones sprang to life. Her fantasy had left her on edge. She needed release but unless she took matters into her own hands she wasn't going to get it. Doing it herself wasn't nearly as much fun. She swung her legs out of bed, deciding to head for the shower instead.

When she emerged from the shower, marginally less frustrated, she was surprised to find Ruby in the kitchen, pouring a glass of orange juice.

'You're up early,' Scarlett said.

'I promised Rose I'd go with her to check out the vintage clothes market. Do you want to come with us?'

Ruby knew of Scarlett's aversion to second-hand clothes. Vintage in her opinion was just another word for second-hand, but she was tempted to go anyway. It wasn't often she got a chance to spend time with both her sisters at once. And going with them didn't mean she had to buy clothes herself.

Before she could answer there was a knock on the front door. 'Is that Rose?' she asked.

Ruby shook her head. 'Too early.'

Scarlett frowned and went to open the front door.

Jake was waiting there, lounging casually against the veranda post as if he popped past every Sunday morning.

'What are you doing here?'

'I came to collect on our bet.'

Scarlett frowned. 'We didn't have a bet.'

'Yes, we did. Yesterday. At Candice's wedding. And I won. I correctly identified Ruby.'

'Oh,' Scarlett said, as she remembered how confident she'd been when she'd agreed to the bet. 'What's your prize?'

He said nothing further. Just smiled his sexy smile and Scarlett had a feeling she knew what he wanted. She held her breath.

'You and I are going to spend the day together.'

She exhaled. She had the perfect excuse. 'I can't. I'm going shopping with Ruby and Rose.'

'Tell them you've had a better offer.' He was still smiling at her.

He had an unfair advantage. Did he know what his smile did to her? She suspected he did. 'I thought we agreed to wait for two weeks?'

'This isn't a date. It's just two friends, hanging out. If it makes it any better we're going out of town. It's highly unlikely we'll bump into anyone who knows us and we're not doing anything wrong.'

When Scarlett still hesitated he added, 'You can trust me. I agreed to wait until I finished my placement before I let you seduce me again. No matter how much you beg I'm not going to let you take advantage of me. Today we are purely platonic. But before you accept my invitation I have a couple of questions for you, in the interests of full disclosure. Do you get motion sickness?'

'No.'

'Do you have a fear of roller-coasters?'

Scarlett frowned. As far as she knew, there were no roller-coasters in South Australia. Where was he planning on taking her? 'No.'

'What about confined spaces?'

She shook her head. She was afraid of being abandoned, of being unwanted, but she didn't have any, or almost any, of the usual phobias. 'Only spiders.'

'Good.'

'Where are we going?'

'Mallala.'

'Mallala?' Scarlett couldn't imagine what a small country town, an hour north of Adelaide, had that could possibly be of interest to her. 'What are we doing there?'

'You'll find out soon enough. We'll have fun, trust me.'

Her curiosity was piqued. 'Can you wait here?' she asked. 'I'll see if Ruby lets me make an excuse.' She didn't want Jake to come in as she suspected he and Ruby would gang up on her and make her go. If she tackled them individually she might at least feel as though she was still in charge of the decision.

'Who was it?' Ruby asked.

'Jake. He's invited me to spend the day with him. He has some secret activity planned.'

'I bet he does.' Ruby's eyes were sparkling as she laughed.

'What's so funny?'

'Nothing, I'm just imagining the activity and I'm amazed either of you have lasted this long. There were enough sparks between you and Jake last night to start a bushfire. The pair of you couldn't keep your eyes off each other. I'm surprised you didn't go home with him after the wedding. You should definitely go.'

Scarlett knew what Ruby was picturing but she also knew she was wrong. Jake had promised a platonic activity and Scarlett believed him. There was no reason not to. For a start, there'd be no reason to drive to Mallala if he wanted to spend the day in bed.

'I'm not sure it's a good idea,' she said.

'Are you kidding me?' Ruby replied. 'It's a terrific idea. He's cute and hot and fun and he likes you.'

'He's also a student.'

'Pah! It's easy enough to sneak around and not get caught if you want something badly enough. If you want *him* badly enough, which I think you do.'

'We've discussed it.'

'Discussed it? What are you wasting your time talking for? Get his gear off.'

'Shh,' Scarlett said. She was very much aware of the fact that Jake was still by the open front door and could probably hear their conversation if he listened hard enough. 'You know me, I like to play by the rules and I like to have a plan.'

'Okay, let's hear this plan of yours.' Ruby was still laughing.

'We're keeping things platonic until he finishes his placement in two weeks' time.'

'Are you sure you can wait that long?'

'We'll have to.'

'And what if his next placement is back in your hospital?'

Scarlett shook her head. 'He wants to do obstetrics and everyone wants to be sent to the city because it's convenient, but it's rare that students get two plum placements in a row.'

'Two weeks is a long time.'

'For you maybe. It will give me time to work out if I really want to do this.'

'Why wouldn't you? He's sexy and cute and smart. Have some fun.'

'I'm not sure I can handle it, handle him,' Scarlett admitted. 'He's so different from my usual type.'

'He's asked you to spend a day with him, not the rest of your life,' Ruby argued. 'Maybe it's time you tried something different.'

'You don't get much more different than a stripper.'

'What?' Ruby inhaled some orange juice and then coughed, sending a spray of juice onto the kitchen bench.

'He has a part-time job at a male revue as a stripper,' Scarlett told her, enjoying the fact that she'd been able to shock Ruby for once. It wasn't often she had that opportunity.

Ruby didn't stay shocked for long. She burst into hysterical laughter. 'I knew I liked him. A naughty streak gets me every time. Have you seen his show?'

Scarlett could feel herself blushing. 'I've seen all I need to see. Thank God no one knows I slept with him.'

'You slept with him? When?'

'The night we met. Before I knew he was a med student.'

'Well, it seems you're already experiencing different as far as he's concerned. That changes everything.'

'I'd forgotten I hadn't told you and it doesn't change anything.'

'What else haven't you told me?'

'Nothing. That's it.'

'Well, that's plenty. Now, stop arguing and go and get ready before he changes his mind. I'm not leaving till tomorrow, we can have dinner with Rose tonight.'

AN HOUR LATER Scarlett slid the hair elastic down her ponytail, letting it sit lower at the base of her neck to accommodate the helmet that she was about to pull on. She wriggled it into place. It was a snug fit but not uncomfortable and the padding muffled the sounds of their surroundings. Jake adjusted the chin strap and Scarlett caught her breath as his fingers brushed the soft skin of her throat.

'You're good to go.' He grinned at her as he pulled his own helmet on.

Jake had brought her to a race circuit in the middle of dry dusty paddocks, and she was about to climb into a V8 racing car for a hot lap. The car was emblazoned with advertising and even though she knew it was the same model as hundreds of family sedans that filled the roads every day it looked fast and dangerous. She wasn't convinced this was a good idea but she didn't want to back out now. She was determined to be brave. Jake had arranged this for her and she was determined to enjoy herself. She had to trust Jake not to hurt her, to keep her safe, but even she could see the irony in that.

He opened the passenger door for her and helped to strap her into the racing harness.

'Sit right back, as flat as you can against the seat,' he said, as he tightened the straps. His hands brushed across her chest as he adjusted the harness and even though she was fully clothed in a fire-retardant racing suit she would swear she could feel the heat of his hands.

Jake slid through a back window into the seat behind her as Sean, their racing driver, double-checked the harness. Scarlett wasn't surprised to find she had no reaction whatsoever to Sean's touch.

Scarlett nervously checked her surroundings. The interior of the car looked familiar, more like the family sedans she was used to, with the exception of the steering-wheel, extra roll bars, the harnesses in place of seat belts and the fire extinguisher that was positioned between her and the driver's seat. On the dashboard in front of her, in place of the glove box, was a horizontal handle. Now that she thought about it, not much was actually that familiar. She took a deep breath and steeled her nerves as Sean climbed into the driver's seat.

The V8 engine growled as he pushed the start button and the car throbbed under her. Sean gave them both a thumbs-up before pulling out of the pits and onto a start line. Scarlett could see the bank of lights at the end of the straight and Sean revved the engine as he waited for the all-clear. He was giving them the full experience. The light changed to green and Sean pushed his foot to the floor and the car shot off down the track. The power of the engine forced Scarlett back into her seat. She didn't think it was possible to sit further back, the harness was so tight to begin with, but she was definitely flattened against the backrest.

She could hear Sean changing gear as they approached the first turn. She was sure he was taking the corner too fast and she grabbed the handle in front of her with both hands, clinging on tightly—at least now she knew what the handle was for—but before she could say anything they had rounded the corner and were flying along the back straight.

Her knuckles were white and she was sure her face was too. It was terrifying. She wasn't sure yet whether it was also fun. She would reserve judgement on that.

As they approached another hairpin turn and the barrier fence loomed large in the windscreen she squeezed her eyes shut.

'It's more fun if you open your eyes.' She could hear Jake's voice and she realised the helmets must have an in-built communications system.

'I'm trying to keep them open but they're refusing,' she replied.

She felt the car change direction and forced her eyes open as Sean put his foot to the floor and they flew past the pits.

'Haven't we finished?' she said, as the pit buildings went by in a blur.

'Not yet. We're doing three laps.'

Another two laps! She wasn't sure she could take it. Her eyes flicked across to the dashboard as Sean came out of the hairpin at the end of the pit straight and hit the gas. She could see the speedometer—did it really read two hundred and sixty kilometres per hour?

She held on tight to the handle in front of her and concentrated on being brave. It would only be a few more minutes. She could manage.

Three minutes later she climbed out of the car on shaky legs. Jake hauled himself out through the rear window, a wide grin on his face.

'Did you enjoy that?' he asked, as he pulled his helmet off before helping her to undo hers.

'I think so.' That had been so far out of her comfort zone she wasn't sure what to think. She was normally so cautious she still wasn't sure what had convinced her to take the challenge and get into a racing car, but looking at Jake, so calm and confident, she knew it was he who had made her feel brave. He made her feel as though she could take on the world and if anything bad happened he'd be there to pick up the pieces. He was teaching her to live in the moment, not worry about the future.

'There's more to come,' he said.

'I'm not sure my heart can take more.' Scarlett wasn't just talking about the racing. Jake had tucked his helmet under his arm and he looked every inch the sexy race-car driver. How was it that he always looked to have everything under control? The wilder things got, the happier he seemed.

'Sean's going to take you out on the skid pan. And this time you get to drive.'

'What?' Scarlett turned to Sean. 'You're going to let *me* drive your racing car?'

'Don't worry, it's insured.' Sean laughed. 'And there's nothing to hit out there. Just flat dirt.'

For the next half an hour Scarlett was let loose on the skid pan. Sean taught her how to deliberately lose control. Deliberating losing control of anything, let alone a moving vehicle, was extremely difficult for her. Her natural impulse was to hit the brakes the moment she felt the rear of the car start to slide out but when she eventually managed to follow Sean's instructions and let the car slide he then taught her to steer into the skid. Eventually she could feel the car straighten and she was able to drive out of trouble. Once she'd mastered the skid pan she felt as if she'd been given the moon.

The minute she pulled the car to a stop in front of Jake she leapt out and ran over to the fence to hug him. 'I did it! I did it! Did you see me?'

'I did. You were brilliant.' He hugged her tight and Scarlett thought this might just be the best day she'd ever had.

'That was so much fun. Thank you.' In the end she'd actually enjoyed losing control. There had been no time to worry about anything, she'd had to use all her energy to control the car and concentrate on doing what Sean told her. There'd been no time to be frightened. 'If that's what adventure is like, I'm a fan.'

'That's adrenalin.' He removed her helmet for her. 'Come on, I think you've earned a drink.' He took her hand as she thanked Sean and walked with her back to the pit buildings, only letting go of her hand to allow her to change out of her racing suit. He was waiting for her when she emerged from the change room and he handed her a soft drink before leading her to a viewing area overlooking the race track. They finished their drinks as they watched other people's laps. It looked just as fast as it had felt.

'I can't believe I actually did that,' Scarlett mused as cars flew past them. 'How on earth did you get into this?'

'My godfather was into car racing. He started in the Car Club and I used to come out here on weekends with him. He was a doctor, a surgeon, but car racing was his passion. He taught me to give everything one hundred per cent.'

'Your car belonged to him, didn't it?' Scarlett remembered Jake telling her that on the night they'd met. The first night he'd driven her home. When Jake nodded, she added, 'Do you ever race your car?'

'No, it's not certified for racing but I still try to make it out here for car club meetings a couple of times a year. MG owners are a rather passionate, eclectic bunch. It's good fun.'

She had to agree—it *was* fun. But the best part had been spending time with Jake. He'd chosen the perfect activity. Away from the pressure of work and people they knew, taking her some place where she couldn't possibly focus on anything other than the matter at hand. There'd been no time to even think about whether spending time with him was the right or wrong thing to do. All she knew was that it felt right. Whenever she was with him she felt as though she was where she was supposed to be.

He was different but Ruby was right. Perhaps different was good. He made her happy and that certainly felt good. She was content just being in the moment when she was with him. It was unusual for her not to be worrying about work or finances or what other people expected of her. It was nice to feel relaxed.

Maybe this was how life was supposed to feel. Maybe she could be relaxed and happy and a little bit adventurous if she was with the right person. Was Jake the right person for her? Could he be?

She glanced over at him as he watched the cars zip by. He was leaning on a railing inside the protective fence and she let her eyes run over the curve of his backside. He was wearing a simple T-shirt and jeans, quite a contrast to the elegance of the suit he'd worn to the wedding and she couldn't decide how she preferred him. In a suit, in scrubs, casually outfitted or naked in her bed? He looked good in anything. And better in nothing.

She was just about to thank him again for the day when her fantasies were interrupted by terrified screams. The screams weren't coming from the racetrack but from behind them. Scarlett whipped around. The screams imparted a sense of urgency, and she saw several car tyres roll from behind one of the pit buildings and go bouncing along the ground.

Jake took off at a run and Scarlett was close behind him.

CHAPTER EIGHT

They rounded the corner of the building. A pile of old car tyres, which Scarlett suspected had once been neatly stacked, had collapsed, sending tyres rolling in all directions. A woman and two children were frantically tugging at what remained of the stack.

'What are you doing?'

'What's happened?' They spoke together.

'My son,' the woman panted. 'He's under here.'

Jake looked at Scarlett but only fleetingly. Before Scarlett could process what had happened Jake was hauling the tyres from the pile and tossing them to one side.

Watching Jake kicked Scarlett into action too.

'Are these also your children?' she asked the woman.

'Yes.'

'Take them around the front, into the building.' Scarlett could only imagine what grisly scene they might be about to uncover. It was better if the children were somewhere else. 'Find someone to keep an eye on them,' she told the mother, as more people arrived on the scene. Jake quickly issued instructions to the newcomers as the woman shepherded her other children out of sight but not without an anxious backward glance and Scarlett knew she'd be back as soon as possible.

Just as the on-site paramedics arrived and the boy's

mother returned, Jake pulled another tyre from the stack to finally reveal the unmoving figure of a young boy. He was unnervingly still, there was not even a slight rise and fall of his chest, and Scarlett feared the worst. She introduced herself to the paramedics and gave them Jake's background as Jake bent his head to check the boy's breathing and simultaneously felt for a pulse.

'Unconscious and in respiratory arrest but he has a pulse,' Jake told the paramedics as he started mouth-to-mouth, breathing for the boy.

Who knew what other injuries he had sustained? Scarlett knew the list could be long. He could have spinal fractures, a head injury, rib fractures, a pneumothorax, just to name a few, but the priority was establishing an airway and getting oxygen into his lungs. They worked frantically for the next few minutes.

Scarlett inserted an endotracheal tube into the boy's trachea to establish an artificial airway and once one of the paramedics was squeezing the ambu bag, forcing air into the boy's lungs, Jake and Scarlett helped to fit a cervical collar around his neck before transferring him onto a spinal board then a stretcher and then into the ambulance. Somehow, in the middle of the frenetic activity, Jake managed to keep chatting to the boy's mother, keeping her informed.

Scarlett breathed a sigh of relief as the ambulance raced away, lights and sirens at full strength. They had done their bit, and had done it well. Now it was up to the paramedics and the trauma team at the receiving hospital. Now that the crisis was over Scarlett found her hands were shaking. By comparison, Jake appeared remarkably unflustered if somewhat filthy from the physical exertion.

'You were unbelievably calm,' Scarlett commented, as she rubbed her hands on her arms to try to disguise her rattled nerves.

'I've been in worse situations,' he replied.

'Really? When?' Despite her recent weeks in the Emergency department Scarlett had never felt under the same sort of pressure that she had been under just then. Working in the middle of nowhere with very limited resources was an entirely new experience for her. When would Jake have experienced worse?

'I spent some time travelling around Asia during my gap year. I was travelling from Vietnam to Thailand when Cyclone Nargis hit Myanmar. The whole area became the true definition of a disaster zone. I volunteered with a charity and what I experienced there was life-changing. I had put med school on hold while I travelled and while I wasn't qualified to give any medical care I volunteered to help in the hospital.

'There were plenty of jobs assisting the medicos for anyone who wasn't squeamish and there were plenty of emergencies and terrible injuries. It was tragic and truly dreadful but any little thing anyone could do could make a difference so it was hugely rewarding at the same time, and it confirmed for me that medicine was what I wanted to do.'

Jake was constantly surprising her. He was far more mature and multi-faceted than she had given him credit for, which made him even more intriguing.

'I had no idea,' she said, but her teeth were chattering and her words weren't very clear. She rubbed her arms again, trying to stop the shaking.

Jake wrapped an arm around her shoulders. 'Come on, let's get you warm and home.' She knew the shivering was an after-effect of the adrenalin but she kept quiet. She didn't want to give Jake a reason to remove his arm. It was comforting. It was perfect. 'There won't be any more racing happening while the ambulance is gone.'

Jake opened the boot of his car, pulled out his leather jacket and helped her into it. He glanced down at his filthy T-shirt. 'This has seen better days,' he said. He whipped it off, treating Scarlett to one of her favourite views—his naked torso, abdominal muscles and tattoo. A familiar surge of longing rushed through her and she wasn't surprised to find that the heat of her reaction counteracted the adrenalin and she stopped shaking.

She was tempted to break her agreement. She was tempted to throw herself at him right then and there, but unfortunately Jake swapped the dirty T-shirt for a clean hoodie that he found in the boot and removed temptation from under her nose.

Disappointed, she climbed into his car. The end of his placement couldn't come soon enough for Scarlett.

One more day.

Less than twelve hours really until she and Jake would be free.

For the past eight days he had been leaving little notes for her, counting down the days. Yesterday he'd managed to tape an envelope to her locker. Inside had been a note that had simply said: *One more day.* The day before that she'd found a sticky note inside a patient's file that had read: *Two days to go.* Today she'd gone into the operating theatre and found an invitation on the whiteboard.

Med students dinner tonight, 7.30, Casa Barcelona. All invited.

Underneath it was a postscript that read: *Only twelve more hours.* She recognised the handwriting and she knew Jake had been in early and left the note for her. She wiped the postscript off before anyone else saw it but she was smiling and his note put her in a good mood that lasted all day.

One more day had become twelve more hours, which had now become a matter of minutes.

Scarlett checked the clock on the theatre wall as she hummed along to Richard's MP3. The final surgery for her shift was almost finished and even the nasty injury sustained by the victim of a dog attack couldn't dampen her enthusiasm and love of life today.

SHE HADN'T WANTED to go to the dinner, she'd had other plans for Jake, but he'd talked her round and she smiled as she walked through the restaurant doors as she remembered what he'd said earlier in the day. 'You need to eat, you'll need your strength.'

They'd ordered shared platters from the tapas menu for the group, and although the food was still coming Scarlett had eaten enough. She was getting edgy. She'd done the right thing, joined in the end-of-placement celebration but now she wanted to get on with the rest of the evening. Jake was sitting beside her on the long wooden bench, his thigh was pressed against hers, and she could feel the heat coming off his body and smell his freshly showered scent. She'd had enough of sitting there politely, pretending to be interested in the conversation and trying to ignore her raging hormones. She wanted to take Jake home, strip him of his clothes and take him to her bed.

She was wondering how she could suggest to him that it was time to leave without being overheard when talk moved onto the students' next placements. They had been informed of their next hospitals just that afternoon and despite her plans she was keen to hear where they were all going.

'You're doing obstetrics, Jake?' someone asked. 'Where are you going?'

'Mount Gambier.'

Scarlett's heart dropped in her chest. He was going to the country.

He must have seen her expression because he stood up from the table without adding anything further. He turned to her and held out his hand as the band started to play. 'Time for dancing,' he said.

She stood too, accepting his invitation. This would give them a chance to talk in private.

'Mount Gambier! That's five hours away,' she said as soon as they were on the dance floor. 'Couldn't you have got somewhere closer?'

'It's a great placement and I'll be the only obstetric student so I should get to do more deliveries than if I was sharing the load with other students,' he said, and she knew she was being selfish. He was right, the placement was important and a good hospital would make all the difference. 'I hear that Annie runs a really good programme,' he added, as he dipped her.

'Annie?'

'Dr Annie Simpson. She's the ob-gyn.' He was grinning at her now. 'There's no need to be jealous, she's way too old for me.'

'How old?'

'Early thirties.'

'Hey, I'm almost thirty.'

'I know,' he said, as he spun her away from him. 'I'm just stirring you. I have everything I want right here,' he said, as he pulled her back into his arms.

Scarlett had no idea what dance they were doing but she didn't care. She didn't need to worry about the steps, she just had to follow Jake's lead.

'I know this isn't what we were hoping for,' he told her, 'but we've got a couple of days before I go so I suggest we make the most of our time and get out of here.'

'You want to leave together?'

'I thought that was the general idea. Tell you what, why don't I leave? Everyone will assume I'm going to work at The Coop. I'll grab a taxi and meet you out the front in ten minutes. You can make an excuse and join me. Okay?'

Scarlett nodded. 'That's a better plan.'

'You're not the only one with a plan,' he said, with a grin that melted her insides.

SCARLETT ROLLED OVER in bed and stretched. She was still half-asleep and she could have quite happily stayed in bed for the day if she didn't have to go to work. The pillow next to her still had an indentation from Jake's head, from where he'd lain beside her for the night. She buried her face in the pillow and breathed in his scent.

She lifted her head when she heard him come into the room. He was freshly showered but only half-dressed. He had his pants on but she was treated to a fine view of his lean, well-defined torso, his ripped abdominals and a glimpse of his tattoo as he put a cup of coffee on her bedside table. He bent a little further and kissed her on the lips before reaching for his shirt and pulling it over his head. He grabbed his car keys and tossed them in the air, then caught them again. It seemed as though his good mood was a match for hers.

'I won't be able to see you tonight, I have a late lecture and then I have to work at The Coop,' he said as he slipped his feet into his shoes.

'You could come past after work,' she suggested.

'It'll be late.'

'That's okay. You can wake me up when you get here.'

'Sounds good,' he said, as he flashed his cheeky grin. His green eyes were alight as he leant over and kissed her a second time before ducking out of the door. She heard the front door open and then close.

In two days he'd be leaving for Blue Lake Hospital in Mt Gambier and she wanted to make the most of the little time they had together before he left. She smiled as she thought about last night. Their time together might be limited for the next month but if last night was anything to go by, they would be able to make the most of any spare moments. She stretched again and sat up, reaching for her coffee cup.

The sudden movement made her feel a little lightheaded and a wave of nausea hit her as she inhaled the strong odour of the coffee. She put the coffee back on the table, deciding to leave it until after her shower. She spent far too long in the shower, leaving herself no time for breakfast, and she left for work with the coffee sitting untouched by her bed. She grabbed a take-away coffee and a cinnamon scroll from the cafeteria but her stomach protested over that combination of flavours too.

She put her breakfast down on a bench in the change room as she prepared to get changed into her scrubs.

She looked up as the door swung open to admit Mel.

'Are you all right?' Mel asked, as she took one look at her.

'Yep, just tired, I think. It's making me feel a little off.'

'You look dreadful. Are you hungover?'

'No.' She wasn't hungover, she'd barely touched any alcohol last night—she hadn't needed to. She'd got by on pure adrenalin. The excitement of being able to go home with Jake without feeling guilty, even if they still didn't tell anyone else what they were doing, had been enough of a buzz. She hadn't needed to drink, not when she'd had Jake.

Scarlett hadn't said anything to Mel about Jake yet. It was early days and she wanted to keep whatever happened under wraps for now, just between the two of them for a little longer. 'I think it must be something I ate last night.'

'Are you going to eat that?' Mel nodded at Scarlett's coffee and scroll, which were on the bench beside her.

Scarlett looked at her breakfast. She'd taken the scroll out of its bag but even the thought of eating or drinking anything was enough to make her feel ill. She shook her head. 'No. It's all yours.'

She bent forward to step into a pair of surgical trousers as Mel picked up the scroll and bit into it. The smell of cinnamon wafted over Scarlett. She wasn't sure if it was the smell or the position she was in but she felt decidedly woozy. She straightened up, hoping that would clear her head. 'I'm not feeling—'

SCARLETT LOOKED AROUND HER. The room looked different but it took her a moment to realise it was because she was lying on the floor. The cinnamon scroll was next to her with a bite out of it. She frowned. She didn't remember eating the scroll. And what was she doing on the floor?

'Scarlett? Can you hear me?'

She turned her head and winced as a stabbing pain shot from the back of her head into her eye socket. Mel was kneeling on the floor beside her. 'What happened?'

'You fainted.'

She frowned. 'But I never faint.'

'Okay, you passed out. Are you hurt?'

'I don't think so.'

She struggled to sit up but Mel put a hand out to stop her.

'Stay there. If you're not hurt I still want to take your BP before you go anywhere.'

Mel ducked out of the change room and came back seconds later with a sphygmomanometer. She wrapped the cuff around Scarlett's arm before inflating it. 'Ninety over sixty. What is it normally?'

'One-ten on eighty,' Scarlett replied. 'I'm fine.'

'You need to eat something.'

They both looked at the cinnamon scroll lying on the floor. 'Not that.' Mel laughed.

'Eating is what got me into this state,' Scarlett told her. 'I think if I eat anything I'll throw up.'

'Shall I run a drip for you instead?'

Scarlett shook her head, wincing again as the movement made her head throb. 'I'm not hungover and I haven't been vomiting. I don't think I'm dehydrated. I just feel off. I'm sure it's just a slight dose of food poisoning or maybe a food allergy of some sort.'

'Could be gastro. Are you having any stomach cramps?' Mel asked, as she took Scarlett's temperature. 'Your temperature's normal. No headaches?'

'I have one now,' Scarlett said as she gingerly touched the bump on the back of her head. 'But I didn't have one before.'

Mel shrugged. 'Okay, you can skip the drip and get up, but only if you agree to go straight home and have plenty of fluids when you get there and something to eat when you can.'

'Just give me a minute, I'll be fine.'

'You need to go home in case it develops into something that could be contagious.'

'I'm sure it's just something I ate,' she protested.

'Maybe. But you did just faint. You shouldn't be at work.'

'Fine.' She felt too drained to argue and the bump on her head was throbbing.

'I'll call past after work and see how you are.'

Scarlett couldn't remember the last time she'd spent the day on the couch. She had an afternoon sleep and woke up feeling like her old self, other than the lump on the back of her head. She put the whole episode down to a lack of sleep, a chilli overload with the tapas menu and no breakfast. Thinking of food made her realise she was actually hungry. She put some bread into the toaster and flicked the kettle on for a cup of tea, thinking it still might be advisable to steer clear of coffee for a little longer.

Mel arrived as she was finishing off the first piece of toast.

'Good, you're eating. Are you feeling better?'

'I'm almost back to normal. I told you it was just something I ate.'

'I know you did but I checked and no one else who was at the restaurant last night is sick,' Mel said, as she dumped her handbag on the kitchen table and rummaged through it. 'I brought you something,' she said, pulling something from her bag.

In her hand she held a pregnancy test kit.

Scarlett stared at the box. 'Why on earth would I be pregnant?'

'You're probably not but you don't have a hangover, you didn't have a temperature or a headache or stomach pain and no one else has been sick. You're just feeling a little off and you haven't been eating.'

'I'm eating now.'

'Have you had a coffee today?'

Scarlett shook her head. 'I've made a couple but I can't stand the smell.'

'When was your last period?'

'Jeez, would you give it a rest?' Scarlett was getting nervous now.

'Well? Do you remember?'

'I'd have to check my diary.'

Mel handed her the test kit. 'Just do me a favour. Take the test and then we can cross that off the list as well.'

Scarlett sighed and snatched the kit from Mel before storming off to the bathroom. There must be a dozen different ailments she could have. Why on earth would she be pregnant? *How* could she be pregnant?

She opened the box and checked the instructions before weeing on the stick. She sat on the toilet and waited, calculating dates in her head while she waited for the time to elapse. She didn't need to check her diary. Her last period had been due on the day of Candice's wedding ten days ago and she realised now that it hadn't come. She'd been too busy at work, too busy thinking about Jake, to notice.

What if Mel was right?

She felt her stomach start to heave and knew she wasn't going to be able to keep the toast down. She stood up from the toilet, flipped open the lid and vomited into the bowl until her stomach was empty.

She rinsed her mouth and spat into the basin. The stick was sitting on the edge of the basin, daring her to pick it up.

Her hand shook as she lifted it from the sink and took it out to Mel.

She nodded at Mel's handbag. 'Do you have another one of these in there?'

'Why? Didn't it work?'

'I hope not. It's positive.'

'Oh, my God. You're pregnant!' Mel jumped out of her chair.

'No. I can't be.' Scarlett shook her head. 'That's why I need to do another test.'

Mel held her hand out. 'Let me see.' She looked at the

window and Scarlett knew what she'd see. Two pink lines. 'You really are pregnant.'

Scarlett collapsed onto the couch. She'd been hoping that Mel would tell her she was seeing things. Seeing pink lines that weren't really there. 'What am I going to do? I don't want a baby.'

If she didn't want children that were planned, what on earth was she supposed to do with an unexpected baby?

'Richard will be over the moon. You don't have to worry about doing this on your own.'

'I doubt that very much.'

'You told me he wants kids. You told me that's why you broke up.'

'It might not be his.'

'What?' Mel's expression would have been funny if the situation wasn't so dire. 'Whose could it be?' she asked.

Scarlett buried her face in her hands. 'God, what a bloody mess.' She took a deep breath. 'I slept with Jake.'

'Oh, my God. When?'

'Candice's hen's night.' She wasn't about to admit to last night's dalliance as well. 'Before I knew who he was. Well, before I knew he was a med student.'

'Oh, my God!' Mel repeated. 'What happened?'

'Remember he offered to walk me to the taxi? When we got to the street there was a huge queue for cabs so he offered to give me a lift home. One thing led to another.'

'Jeez, that was fast work. Candice was right when she said he was a charmer. Didn't you practise safe sex?'

'Of course we did. But something must have gone wrong.'

'So when you said you "can't" be pregnant, you actually could be, you just don't want to be?'

'There's no way I'm having kids, especially not on my

own. And I can't imagine that Jake would want to be a father at this point in time either.'

'It doesn't have to be his, does it?'

'What do you mean?

'Is there a chance it could Richard's?'

Scarlett shook her head. 'No.' She was almost certain it wasn't Richard's.

'Well, there's always more than one option but you don't have to work it all out tonight. It's still very early days and anything could happen. If you really don't want it, maybe that's what you should hope for.'

Scarlett didn't know if she could wish for it all to go away. Not if she really was pregnant. But Mel was right, it was early days and she needed more confirmation than a home pregnancy test. The best she could hope for was that this was a mistake and all she was really suffering from was a bad case of gastro.

'Are you going to be okay? Would you like me to stay the night?' Mel asked.

'No. I'll be fine.'

Scarlett doubted she'd be fine but she'd got herself into this mess and she didn't expect Mel to have to help her sort it out. She'd figure it out one way or another but she needed a bit of time to process what had just happened. She sent Jake a quick message saying she wasn't feeling well and not to come past tonight. She hated to put him off but she needed time and space. She couldn't deal with seeing him just yet.

She was mortified. She had always tried to do the right thing, always tried to behave and avoid trouble. Her sisters constantly did as they pleased while she tried not to cause anyone grief. Most of the time her sisters got away with their behaviour and it was typical of her luck that the one time she did something out of character, the one time she was spontaneous or, dare she say irresponsible, she got into trouble.

She was always the one who helped others. Was she now going to be the one in need of help? And who would she turn to? Her mother? Jake?

If she was pregnant, she was ninety-nine per cent certain it was Jake's. But expecting support from him wasn't fair, he hadn't asked to be a father. Oh, why couldn't the baby be Richard's? At least then she would know the father wanted to be involved, but of course it couldn't be that simple.

She pulled her diary from her bag and double-checked her dates. As she'd suspected, her last period had started four weeks *before* Candice's wedding. Almost six weeks ago. She was ten days late. She was never late.

She hadn't slept with Richard since well before that but she'd slept with Jake almost four weeks ago. It had to be his.

MEL WAS HOVERING outside Emergency the next morning, waiting for Scarlett when she arrived at work. 'How are you feeling?'

'I'm okay.'

'Have you eaten?'

Scarlett nodded. She'd swapped coffee for tea and a piece of buttered toast and so far she'd managed to keep her breakfast down.

'Have you worked out what you're going to do?' Mel asked. 'What you're going to tell Jake?'

'Nothing yet. I want to get the test confirmed first. It still could be a mistake.'

'You mean to tell me you haven't done another home pregnancy test just to see?'

'Of course I have.' She'd gone to the pharmacy last

night after Mel had left and bought three more tests, all different brands, hoping one of them would give her a different answer.

'And?'

'They were all positive.' It was starting to look like she was going to have to deal with it.

'You know as well as I do that any official test is just a variation on weeing on the stick at this stage,' Mel said, effectively negating Scarlett's reasoning for wanting to take a fifth, if somewhat more official, test. 'I think you need to move past denial and work out what you're going to do. You need to talk to Jake. Have you got plans to see him before he goes to the country?'

Scarlett nodded. 'We're having breakfast in the morning.'

'Isn't he leaving tomorrow?'

She nodded again. 'He's driving down with a couple of other med students who are on different rotations. They're leaving at lunchtime.'

'You can't tell him minutes before he gets in the car,' Mel protested. 'Not when he's got a four-and-a-half-hour drive in front of him. That's not fair. Why are you waiting until the last minute?'

'I'm working all day today and he's working at The Coop tonight. Tomorrow is the only chance I've got.'

She was still getting used to the idea that she *might* be pregnant and she and Jake had both been flat out with other commitments over the past two days. She could think of half a dozen reasons why she hadn't said anything, half a dozen excuses for why she'd kept quiet, but she knew in reality she'd been stalling.

'You can't pretend this isn't happening.'

'Why not?' Might be pregnant was a whole different ballgame to definitely pregnant. Definitely pregnant meant having a baby and she wasn't sure she was ready to deal with that. Might be pregnant was working for her at the moment. She was hoping it was all a big mistake and that if she wished hard enough it would go away and she wouldn't have to say anything.

'Because eventually it's going to be obvious,' Mel said.

'If it's true,' Scarlett answered, but even as she uttered the words she knew that all the wishing in the world wasn't going to change the fact that she *was* pregnant. Four different tests had confirmed it, plus her period still hadn't come and the nausea hadn't gone away, neither had her aversion to coffee. Even her boobs were tender and she could swear they were already bigger. People *were* going to notice something, she couldn't keep denying it.

'Don't you think Jake deserves to hear it from you before other people find out?'

Mel was right. Jake would be in the country for the next month. She couldn't delay for much longer. 'Might be pregnant' was rapidly becoming 'time to face reality' and she couldn't risk him finding out some other way. She needed to tell him. She nodded.

'You'll have to go to The Coop tonight, then. I think you might need more than just an hour over breakfast to work this out. I'll come with you.'

'What for?'

'To make sure you don't chicken out.'

SCARLETT HAD SPENT ages choosing an outfit. She knew she should be spending her time working out what she was going to say to Jake but sorting through her wardrobe was marginally less stressful and also managed to distract her from the thought of the dreaded conversation.

She didn't want to look like she was going into a business meeting, neither did she want to look like she was planning on clubbing until the wee hours of the morning, and eventually she settled on a wrap dress made of black jersey. Unfortunately the wrap style highlighted her breasts but she didn't have anything else suitable. She didn't think her boobs could get bigger than their normal DD but it seemed she was wrong and the black fabric wasn't enough to disguise her new dimensions. She'd decided to leave her hair loose, partly to try to soften her look and partly in an attempt to hide her boobs.

She'd also ditched the five-inch heels she'd borrowed last time in favour of pointy-toed black patent leather boots with a two-inch heel. The boots were smart enough but far more comfortable and less stripper-like than the sandals and she thought far more suited to a pregnant woman, even if she did feel knocked up as opposed to pregnant.

But when Mel arrived to collect her Scarlett immediately felt mumsy by comparison, despite her kick-ass, pointy-toed boots. Mel was wearing a very short sequin tank dress with spaghetti straps, and she'd spiked up her short pixie hair and she looked edgy, like someone who belonged in the club. Scarlett's outfit could only be described as conservative next to Mel's.

Scarlett clutched her hands around her small handbag, holding it protectively in front of her as she looked around the club. Looking at the other patrons, she knew she'd be the least likely to be picked as the girl who'd have a one-night stand, let alone get pregnant, but that's was what she was. And even though their 'liaison' had turned into more than a one-night stand she was under no illusion that she and Jake had the sort of relationship that could handle having a baby together. Not yet. And probably not ever.

If ever there was a case of wrong place, wrong time, Scarlett thought this was it. She couldn't begin to imagine telling Jake her news in the club.

She scanned the room, aware that her heart was racing.

She was terrified of telling Jake but Mel was right, he had a right to know. But she was still pinning her hopes on him not wanting the baby either. He was young and still studying. It was hardly good timing for him. He'd probably be scared too. Maybe they had other options.

But then she remembered how he interacted with his niece and that he was contemplating doing paediatrics or obstetrics as his specialty, and she *knew* he would want the baby. Now she had to tell him about the baby *and* tell him *she* didn't want it.

Her eyes flicked over to the bar but she couldn't see Jake. Maybe he wasn't at work, maybe she'd got her wires crossed, maybe she could just go home. She was about to plead her case to Mel when the music started pumping and Mel nudged her in the ribs.

'There he is.'

Scarlett looked to the front of the room where three spotlights illuminated the catwalk. She could see Caesar and Rico and centre stage was Jake. All three of them were dressed alike in white T-shirts that hugged their chests and tight jeans that hugged their thighs, but Scarlett only had eyes for Jake.

The contrast between the three of them—Caesar bulky and dark, Rico lithe and serious and Jake ripped and cheeky—was interesting but Scarlett couldn't tear her eyes away from Jake. Their routine was well choreographed and well-rehearsed. Their movements were in perfect harmony as they played to the appreciative crowd but as Jake strutted down the catwalk she couldn't even pretend to be interested in anything or anyone but him.

As he gyrated his hips and winked at the women she hoped she was blending into the crowd. Jake in performance mode, even while fully clothed, was mesmerising and she wanted to enjoy the show anonymously.

The lyrics were familiar and she found herself moving to the beat of the song.

Jake's hands were at the neck of his T-shirt and she watched in fascination as he ripped his shirt in one smooth movement, tearing it down the middle to expose his chest.

Heat pooled low in her belly as he threw his shirt to one side before running his hands over his chest and along the ridge of his abdominals and down to his groin. She could feel the heat spreading from her stomach to her thighs and she was embarrassed by her lack of self-control.

Jake lifted his hands from his groin and linked his fingers behind his head, and his tattoo pulsed as his muscles flexed. His abdominal muscles rippled as he fell to his knees and women started shoving fistfuls of tipping dollars into his waistband as he winked and bestowed his cheeky grin on them. His star sign was most definitely a Leo.

Scarlett's mouth went dry as she watched the women go wild for Jake and suddenly, seeing him on stage performing for the adoring masses, wasn't so appealing. As he got to his feet he had his hands on his jeans and she knew what was coming next. She didn't need to see this. She didn't need to be reminded that she'd got herself knocked up by a stripper, even one as sexy and as intelligent as Jake. Could tonight get any worse?

CHAPTER NINE

Scarlett was mortified. Her stomach heaved as she watched Jake, Caesar and Rico fall into position for the finale. She couldn't face what was coming next. She turned and fled to the ladies' room before Jake could rip his pants off and stand semi-naked in front of a room full of screaming women.

She was aware of Mel following her as she almost ran to the bathroom. Thank goodness the room was empty—everyone else was enjoying the show.

She got as far as the basins before she lost the contents of her stomach. Mel held her hair out of the way as she waited for her to finish vomiting.

'Wait here,' Mel told her when her stomach was finally empty, and Scarlett rinsed her mouth with tap water. 'I'll bring you a glass of water for a proper drink.'

When Mel came back Scarlett was sitting on a toilet seat with her head in her hands. 'I'm pregnant to a stripper,' she said, as Mel handed her the glass.

'It could be worse,' Mel replied.

'How could it possibly be worse?'

'It's not as if taking his clothes off is all he's good at. He's going to be a doctor, he's also a nice guy, cute, intelligent and, as an added bonus, all his bits appear to be in good working order.'

Scarlett groaned in response before rinsing her mouth again with the last of the water. 'I can't possibly talk to him now. I need to go home.'

'Give me a minute,' Mel said, as she took the glass and ducked out of the bathroom.

'I've left a message with Rooster,' she told Scarlett when she returned a few minutes later. 'I've asked Jake to call past your place when he knocks off. I've said it's urgent so now we can go home.'

IT WAS LATE before Jake arrived but Mel had waited and she let him in before leaving.

He had stopped at the Blue and White Café. Scarlett could smell the yiros and recognised the wrapping.

'Are you hungry?' he asked as he bent to kiss her, before offering her one of the packets.

Scarlett held up one hand, refusing the wrap, and covered her mouth and nose with her other hand. The smell of the roast meat and garlic sauce made the bile rise in her throat.

'What's wrong? Are you sick?'

She shook her head. Her eyes were underlined with dark shadows and she knew she looked pale and tired, especially compared to Jake, who looked fantastically fit and healthy.

'I'm not sick,' she said, as she tugged on his hand, pulling him down to sit beside her. 'I'm pregnant.'

'Pregnant? Are you sure?'

She nodded. She knew she had to accept the facts. She couldn't deny it for ever.

'Shit. Pregnant? How many weeks are you?'

'Six, I think. It could only have happened that first time.'

'But we used protection.'

'Condoms are only ninety-eight per cent effective. Someone has to fall into the two per cent, and apparently it's us.'

'Have you had it confirmed?'

'There's no need. I've missed a period, I'm nauseous, I can't stand the smell of coffee or raw meat or apparently...' she waved her hand at his yiros '...garlic sauce. I've bought every home pregnancy test the pharmacy sells and they all came back positive. And my boobs are bigger.'

Jake smiled.

She stared at him as tears welled in her eyes. She felt like crying and he was smiling? What was the matter with him? She swallowed, fighting not to lose control. 'You think this is funny?'

'No, I know it's not,' he said, as he took one of her hands in his. Her hand felt cold against his warm palm. 'But I must say this isn't one of the first conversations I imagined us having when we moved on from our platonic status. I thought we might start with dinner and a movie. I was looking forward to getting to know you better, not choosing colours for a nursery.'

'Stop it.' Her voice caught as she fought back the tears. She couldn't believe he could see humour in their situation.

She shook her hand free from his hold but he wasn't going to let her go easily. He wrapped one arm around her shoulders and pulled her into him, resting her head against his chest as he kissed her forehead.

'Sorry. In our family we use humour when we're out of our depth. Somehow it helps make a crazy situation seem not so bad. In a family our size there's always someone with a bigger problem.'

'I'm not sure that it gets bigger than this.' Her voice was muffled against his body.

'Sure it does. People have been having children for thousands of years and plenty of them weren't planned. Other people cope. We'll manage too.'

'But I don't want children.'

He sat back, putting some distance between them so he could see her face. 'What do you mean, you don't want children?'

His tone suggested he'd never heard anything so ridiculous. Did he expect, just because she had a womb, that she had a desperate desire to reproduce? That one of her life's ambitions was to be a mother? He was about to learn a lot more about her than he'd bargained for.

'I didn't think you would want them either,' she said.

'Someday, in the future, definitely.'

'This isn't the future. This is happening now.'

He took hold of both her hands and fixed her in place with his green eyes. 'And so we will deal with it now. We can handle this.' His gaze was unwavering and she wanted to believe him. She almost did. Almost.

But she was scared.

'I'm not sure that I can.'

'Why not?'

'Because I don't want to. It's typical of my luck that the one time I do something out of character, something unplanned, I get into trouble. This wasn't ever something I wanted. This is why Richard and I broke up. He wanted children and I didn't. I wasn't prepared to give up my life to marry him and become a mother and I definitely don't want to be a single mother.'

'You don't have to go through this on your own, you know. It's my responsibility too.'

Scarlett shook her head. 'You can't promise that.'

'I can promise whatever I like.'

'There's nothing stopping you from walking away.'

'Nothing except my sense of duty and responsibility and family.'

'But you didn't ask for this any more than I did, and when it all gets too much? What then?'

He didn't answer immediately and Scarlett began to worry about what he was going to say. His answer surprised her.

'What is this really about?' he asked. 'I haven't said or done anything to make you think that when I give you my word I can't be trusted. What is bugging you?'

'Apart from the fact that I'm pregnant?' She managed a half smile, although she suspected it looked more like a grimace.

'Apart from that,' he agreed.

'I've seen how hard it is to raise a family, especially as a single mother. My mum had me when she was eighteen and I have never met my father. Mum struggled constantly to provide for my sisters and me and I have seen the sacrifices she had to make, and while I appreciate what she has done for me, for all of us, I don't want to be like her.'

'You've never met your father? But what about Ruby and Rose?'

She knew what he was asking. 'We're half-sisters. We all have different fathers. Our mother had three children by three different men. My father left before I was born. Ruby's father was a liar and adulterer. He had a whole other family in Melbourne that Mum didn't know about until she fell pregnant with Ruby. He was quite happy cheating on his wife but when Mum fell pregnant he got scared and went running back to Melbourne.'

'And what about Rose's dad?'

'He was lovely.'

'Was?'

Scarlett nodded. 'He married Mum when I was eight. That was the happiest time for all of us. We still didn't have much money but we were a family. But he died when I was sixteen.'

'What happened?'

'He was much older than Mum and he died suddenly of a heart attack. Mum has been on her own ever since.'

'Does your father know about you?'

Scarlett nodded. 'He knew Mum was pregnant. Mum told him. That's only right, isn't it? The father should know?' she asked, seeking confirmation from him.

'Most definitely. Do you know where your father is?'

She shook her head. 'No.'

'Have you tried to track him down?'

'I figure he doesn't want to see me. He could have looked for me. He could have looked for my mother. He knew where to start at least. But this isn't about my father. This is about me. I've watched my mother struggle as a single mum. I've seen what she gave up to raise me and my sisters. I've lived it and I don't want to battle for the rest of my life. I know what it's like to be poor, to wear second-hand clothes, to share a bed with my siblings, to say no to birthday parties because we couldn't afford to buy a present, and I can't consider putting my career on hold to raise a child. I've worked hard to make something of my life and I'm not done yet. I don't want to give it up now.'

'Why would you have to give it up?' he asked. 'You don't need to worry. You didn't get into this situation on your own. It's my responsibility too and I won't let you down. I know you're scared but I'm not going to abandon you. We are in this together.'

He was handling the news far better than she'd expected, far better than she was, but she wasn't sure if she could believe him.

'How can you be so sure? This has come completely out of the blue. We might end up hating each other,' she said, but she was thinking, *You'll end up leaving me.*

'Whatever happens, it will still be my child.'

'Are you saying you really *want* to be a father now?' She had assumed he wouldn't want a baby either at this point in his life.

'I'm saying I don't like the alternatives and you can trust me to do the right thing.'

Trusting men to keep their word wasn't something she was very good at, particularly when they were promising to stay. She appreciated the sentiment but she wasn't convinced she believed it and she was too tired to give it the consideration she needed to. She couldn't think about it any more tonight. The sun would be up in a few hours and she needed some sleep and so did he.

'I need some time to think about this.'

He didn't push her. He just nodded. 'Do you want me to delay the drive tomorrow? I can leave later.'

'No. We need more than a couple of hours to think this over.'

'All right. But don't make any big decisions without talking to me first, okay?'

'Okay.'

Jake kissed her gently on the lips, his touch light and soft and warm. Scarlett closed her eyes, savouring his taste. He rested his hand on her stomach, deliberately or not, she wasn't sure, but her belly fluttered under his fingers. She knew it was just her normal reaction to his touch but part of her imagined it was the fluttering of a tiny baby. 'Look after yourself. I'll talk to you soon,' he said. And then he was gone and she was alone.

She knew it wasn't his fault, she knew he had to go, but she couldn't help but feel he was already leaving her.

HE WAS ALMOST HOME. It had been a long first week on his country placement. The hours in Obstetrics were always erratic and often long but it was the additional stress of

Scarlett's unexpected pregnancy that had pushed the limits of his endurance. He knew Scarlett was worried about him managing the long drive at the end of a working week and even though he'd told her he was fine, that he was used to long hours, he felt tired and he knew apprehension was contributing to his fatigue.

When he had spoken to Scarlett during the week he'd heard the consternation in her voice and he knew she was still undecided about the pregnancy. He couldn't admit to himself that she was undecided about the baby. Their baby, his baby. His child.

Even though the timing wasn't perfect he was excited about the news, but Scarlett's hesitancy was certainly spoiling the moment. He could understand how their very different upbringings were causing conflicting emotions for them both but he hadn't expected her to be so set against the pregnancy. He'd meant it when he'd said he'd be there for her. He would support her in any way she wanted, but his child came first and he knew he would fight for his unborn child with every cell in his body until he took his last breath.

He had spent almost every spare minute of the past week looking at his options and getting the finer details from his brother-in-law, Ted, who was a family lawyer. But what Ted had told him hadn't eased his mind or solved his dilemma.

According to Ted, and in Australian law, a father had no rights over an unborn child. If Scarlett didn't want this baby apparently there wasn't much he could do about it, but he refused to accept that as final.

He drummed his fingers on the steering-wheel as he waited for the traffic lights at the bottom of the freeway to turn green. Fifteen more minutes and he hoped he'd start to get some answers.

It didn't go quite as he planned. With Scarlett, nothing ever went as planned.

He had imagined presenting a reasonable, logical and rational argument to convince Scarlett to have their baby, but all sensible thought evaporated as soon as he saw her.

She greeted him at the door wearing a silk robe, which was loosely tied at her waist, and he knew that with one tug the robe would fall away and that underneath she'd be naked.

He managed to resist until she had closed the front door and then he reached for her. His mouth covered hers as his fingers undid her robe. Scarlett moaned as his fingers brushed her bare skin as he pushed the robe from her shoulders. It fell to the floor with a soft rustle as he scooped her up and carried her into her bedroom, and all arguments were forgotten as they made up for the week apart.

THE GOOD MOOD lasted until they were both spent and satisfied. Until he had showered and they were sitting in the kitchen, sharing a midnight supper of scrambled eggs.

'I've been thinking about our situation. I think we should get married,' he said.

'What on earth for?'

'I know you're scared. I thought if we were married it would give you security. I want to raise our baby together, as a family.' Jake had thought he had worked out where her reluctance was coming from. She wanted financial security but he suspected she also wanted emotional security, and he was prepared to offer her that.

'We both know that being married is no guarantee that a relationship will last,' she argued. 'It's no guarantee of anything and it's not the 1960s. I don't want to get married because I'm pregnant. I don't even want to be pregnant.'

Had he misread her story so badly? He had tried to see things from her perspective but had he still got it completely wrong?'

'This could be the adventure you're supposed to have.'

'This is not my idea of an adventure.'

She obviously hadn't changed her mind over the past week. He was prepared to do the right thing, he was prepared to support her in any way she wanted, but his child had to be his priority. He moved to Plan B.

'Scarlett, I want this baby. I want our baby. I know you're worried about doing this on your own but I want to be part of this. If I have to I will raise our baby alone but I need one thing from you, I need you to stay pregnant. I'm begging you, please, don't do anything rash.'

'You work in a strip club. How on earth are you going to have time to raise a baby?'

'You and I both know I won't be working there for ever. At the end of the year I'll be a doctor. I'll be an intern. I won't be working in the bar and I will have a decent income.'

'And then you want to specialise. You'll be studying for years to come. You can't take time off to care for a baby and neither can I. The future doesn't take care of itself.'

'I have money saved, I own my apartment, I can provide for my child.'

'I appreciate you want to do this but in my experience men don't stick around. What happens when you're working eighty-hour weeks as an intern? What happens when you want to travel back to Asia? What happens when you start to feel trapped? I'll end up alone with the baby, a single mother.'

'Have I told you about the programme at Blue Lake Hospital?' he asked. 'Annie Simpson, the obstetrician who is supervising me, runs a programme for teenage mothers in conjunction with the high school to help the girls to finish school and keep their babies. If teenagers can do it, you can too.'

'This isn't part of my plan.'

'We can make a new plan. We can work this out. Together. You're strong and smart and you're not going to have to do this alone.'

'I'm not strong enough. I'm not like my mother.'

'You don't have to be. I will be there for you.' But it was obvious to him now that Scarlett didn't think he would be enough. 'What has your mum said?' he asked. Maybe someone else's opinion would help her to see sense.

Scarlett didn't reply, she just shook her head.

'Have you told your mum about the baby? Have you told Ruby?'

'No. I don't want to tell anyone. I don't want it to be real.'

'Why haven't you said anything?'

'I'm worried that Mum will be disappointed in me.'

'Your mother raised three daughters on her own. If anyone will understand, she will.'

'I don't want to repeat her mistakes.'

'Has she ever told you that you were a mistake?'

'I know I was.'

'You were unplanned but she chose to have you. Do you think she'd want you to make a different choice? You have a career, you have my support. You're in a much better position than she was. Has she ever complained about the sacrifices she made? Has she ever told you she didn't want you?'

'No.'

'I think you should talk to her. You can't make decisions based on your mother's experiences. Especially if you don't really know what her experience was. You are in a very different position. Can I ask you, please, before you make a decision, will you do me a favour and talk to your mum?'

It took all weekend but Jake finally thought he'd managed to convince Scarlett to at least talk to her mother. He knew that conversation could go one of two ways but he hoped it would persuade her to keep the baby. He was prepared to raise a child, his child, alone if he had to. He had no doubt he could but he'd prefer to do it with Scarlett. He knew they could do it together, he just had to convince her to trust him and that was the difficult part. He wasn't sure how he was going to achieve that but he wasn't going to give up yet.

CHAPTER TEN

Scarlett sat on the couch opposite her mother. Her heart was racing and her hands were shaking so badly she had to lace her fingers together and hold her hands in her lap to disguise the tremor. She was more nervous now than she'd been when she'd told Jake the news. She was only here because Jake had asked her to let her mother know. He had been so supportive she felt she owed him this at least.

Jake made her feel good about herself but she wasn't feeling so good at the moment. She felt like she was letting him down. She wasn't being the person she knew he wanted her to be. She wasn't sure if she *could* be that person. Was he asking too much or was she being unfair?

She sat quietly, waiting while her mother poured their tea. Her mother always insisted on making tea properly, in a warmed teapot and using fine bone-china cups. Scarlett normally found the routine soothing and had asked for tea specifically for that purpose, but today nothing was comforting.

'What's the matter, darling?' Lucy asked, as she passed Scarlett her cup and saucer. 'Nothing's so terrible that you can't tell me about it.'

'How do you know something's wrong?'

'I'm your mother, I can tell when something is troubling you.'

She took a deep breath. 'I'm pregnant.'

'Oh, thank God.' Lucy moved seats, coming to sit beside Scarlett as she hugged her. 'I'm so pleased.'

'You are?'

'Yes. You look exhausted and you look like you've lost weight. I thought you were going to tell me you were sick. But pregnant! That's exciting.'

Scarlett hadn't expected that. 'Is it? I thought you'd think I was crazy.'

'Why?'

Scarlett shrugged. 'Another Anderson female getting knocked up while single.'

'It's hardly the worst thing that can happen,' Lucy replied matter-of-factly, 'but you don't sound thrilled with your news. Are you having doubts?'

Scarlett nodded. 'I don't want to be pregnant. It's really not part of my plan, short term or long term. I broke up with Richard because he wanted kids. His heart attack was the catalyst for his change of mind but it scared me. I was terrified I'd end up alone, raising his family, and that was not what I wanted for my future.'

'Is Richard the father?'

Scarlett shook her head. 'No. It's more complicated than that.'

'What are you going to do?'

'I don't know yet. Do you ever think of how different your life would have been if you hadn't fallen pregnant with me? Did you ever think of not having me?'

'No.' Lucy shook her head. 'Not once. My life would certainly have been different but it couldn't have been any better. I wouldn't want to change a thing.'

'But I saw how hard your life was. I've lived through the struggle.'

'I'm not pretending that being a single mother is easy

but you're in a much better position than I was. You're twelve years older than I was when I fell pregnant, that puts a completely different spin on things, and you have a career. A very good career.'

'I always thought Ruby would be the one to make a mistake. I would have placed money on Ruby being in this situation before me.'

Lucy smiled but refrained from commenting. She never compared her girls. 'Don't think of your pregnancy as a mistake,' she said. 'A baby is a gift. I know you want a different life to the one I've had. I want that for you too. But if I had to choose between having you girls or having an easy life I would do it all again, exactly the same. I love you more than anything in the world.

'I know it hasn't always been easy but the best things in life are often the things worth fighting for. Not everything in life works out exactly how you'd like it to or planned for. But some of life's surprises can be the best things that ever happen to you. Sometimes they can take you on an adventure you never expected.'

Scarlett wondered why everyone kept talking about adventure. What were they seeing that she wasn't?

'I don't know if I have the courage to be a single mother.'

'You'll find the strength if you need to. Trust me, once this baby is born there is nothing you won't do for him or her. I know you've worked hard at your studies but that just means that you will be financially secure. You can raise a baby. You'll be surprised at how your priorities will change. I know you—once you hold that baby in your arms you will do anything to protect him or her. A mother's love is like no other. You'll wonder how you ever doubted yourself.'

Lucy sipped her tea before asking, 'But why are you assuming you'll be a single mother? What about the baby's father? Does he know? How does he feel?'

'He wants the baby. He wants to be involved.' Scarlett didn't tell her mother that Jake had offered to raise the baby on his own if need be. She wasn't sure how she felt about that yet.

'Is it serious between you?'

'I don't know. I thought it could be but it's only early days. I was looking forward to seeing how things developed between us but being pregnant is a complicating factor I wasn't expecting and I'm not sure now if we've missed our opportunity. If I have the baby nothing will be the same again but if I choose *not* to have the baby that will change everything anyway.'

'Are you considering a termination?'

'I don't think I'm brave enough to go through with it. And Jake wants the baby. Knowing that, I don't think I could do it. It doesn't seem right. None of this seems right.'

'I've always been a big believer in the saying that things happen for a reason. Do you love Jake?'

'I don't know that either. When I'm with him everything feels right, as if my world is in balance. I'm not aware of anything else when he's beside me. He calms me and excites me at the same time. I feel alive. I feel happy. I feel like I'm the person I'm supposed to be.'

'That's how I felt about your father.'

'Really?'

Lucy nodded. 'I loved your father. We might have been young but nothing was as important to me as he was until you came along.'

'What happened to you both? Why wasn't he around?'

'I thought he would be. I thought we were going to raise you together but his family had other plans. They didn't want him throwing his future away by becoming a teenage father. His family moved interstate, they deliberately took him away and they paid for me to terminate the pregnancy.'

'You were going to have a termination?' Scarlett's stomach dropped. She'd had no idea her mother had considered not having her. She was horrified to think she might not have existed and she knew then that as much as she wished not to be pregnant, there had never really been any question that she wouldn't keep the baby.

'Obviously I couldn't do it. I had to keep you.'

Scarlett had always believed her father knew about her. What if that wasn't the case? What if he thought the pregnancy had been terminated? 'Does my father know you kept me? Did you tell him?'

'Yes, of course. Your grandparents made sure of it. But I never heard anything from him.'

'And you never tried to find him?'

'No.' Lucy shook her head. 'I always hoped he'd come looking for us but he never did. He broke my heart and I was angry and afraid, but I recovered once I had you. I had to. I poured all that love into you and tried not to think about your father.'

'Are you sorry about how things worked out?'

'I have no regrets. I've been lucky in so many ways. I got something wonderful from our relationship. I got you. Love is a gamble. A risk. You can't make someone love you but you have to be prepared to take the chance that they will. But the one thing you don't have to gamble on is the love you will feel for a child of your own.'

Her mother's words resonated with her. It was time to stop wishing for a father she'd never known, for a father who had never wanted to know her. She couldn't change the past and she'd wasted many years wishing for something she wasn't going to get. He didn't deserve her time. She didn't owe him anything. She owed her mother and now she owed it to her unborn child to look after him or her. She had other priorities. She put her hand over her stomach. She could feel a mother's love already.

She saw her mother notice her gesture. 'Sometimes you have to trust in yourself and sometimes you have to learn to trust other people,' Lucy told her. 'You have one life to live and this is it. Nothing matters except this baby. You'll realise that soon enough. You'll work out what the right thing is to do.'

Scarlett had the opportunity to give her own child the very thing she herself had wanted. Her own child had a father who wanted her and she couldn't deny her child that right. She had to do her best for her own baby and that included giving it a chance to know Jake.

SCARLETT SLOWED HER car as she approached the outskirts of Penola. She was almost there. Another forty minutes and she would be with Jake.

The countryside was getting prettier. This was wine country, the famous Coonawarra district, and rows of grapevines ran in perfectly straight lines out into the distance on both sides of the road, their symmetry only broken by the occasional enormous old gum tree or small creek or picturesque stone building. Many of the numerous wineries had modern cellar door and visitor facilities but the town itself looked as though it hadn't changed for a hundred years. She stopped to buy a cold drink and stretch her legs but didn't want to waste precious minutes dawdling here when she could be on her way to Jake.

She got back on the road and her mind wandered as she drove out of town. She wondered if they'd have a chance over the weekend to come back here for a meal as most of the wineries appeared to have a restaurant, or maybe they could just browse in some of the shops.

The road veered to the right around a blind corner and Scarlett eased her foot off the accelerator, her unfamiliarity with the highway making her cautious.

She rounded the corner and was shocked to find herself face to face with a wine tanker that was halfway across the road and taking up most of her lane. Desperate to get out of its way, she yanked on the steering-wheel and was relieved when the truck missed the side of her car by inches. But her relief was short-lived.

Her evasive action had forced her partially off the road and before she could correct her drift her car was hit by the airstream from the moving truck and forced further sideways. She felt herself losing control of the car as her outside tyres lost traction on the loose stones at the roadside. Her speed and momentum took over and carried her car completely off the road.

The car was skidding across the dirt but somehow she managed to resist the temptation to hit the brakes and instead remembered what Sean had taught her on the skid pan. *Steer into the skid.*

It had seemed strange then and it seemed even stranger now, but she tried to do what she'd been taught. She turned the car into the skid.

But she was still sliding. She hoped the car wasn't going to roll.

She waited, fighting to get the wheels aligned. Her knuckles were white as she gripped the steering-wheel and waited for the car to straighten. She knew she was supposed to wait until the moment the wheels were aligned again before she accelerated out of the skid. Were they aligned yet? She didn't know.

She was aware of a scraping sound and an occasional thwack of branches as the car careered through the scrubby bush. This was a totally different experience to the skid pan. On the skid pan there'd been no outside interference, nothing to interrupt her concentration and nothing that had really been a threat to her safety. Looming in the passenger window was a tree, more than one, actually. There certainly hadn't been any trees in the middle of the skid pan.

She had no clue what to do now. If she did nothing, she was going to hit a tree.

Were her wheels aligned yet? She had no idea.

Her survival instinct took over. She took a chance and touched her foot to the accelerator pedal, hoping her wheels were aligned, hoping and praying she could now drive out of the skid. The car surged forward as she depressed the pedal but she didn't have full control and she felt the back of the car slide sideways again.

The car was fighting her. There was nothing she could do.

She heard the crunch of metal, a thud and her world went dark.

'Jake, we've got a consult in Emergency. MVA with a pregnant woman.'

Jake's eyes flicked to the clock on the wall. He hadn't heard from Scarlett yet, he'd expected her in the last half hour. His gut contracted so violently he thought he was going to throw up. He felt the blood rush from his head and he gripped the counter at the nurses' station as he tried to steady himself.

'Jake?' He felt Annie's hand on his shoulder. 'Are you okay?' Her words were jumbled, the sound of the blood rushing from his head loud enough to partially drown out her voice.

'Scarlett.' His voice caught in his throat and sounded husky and hoarse. 'Did they give you a name?'

'No.' Annie shook her head. 'But whoever it is, she's alive. Let's get down there and we'll find out.'

There was an ambulance in the bay. The doors were open and the paramedics were unloading a stretcher. Jake caught a glimpse of raven hair and he took off, sprinting past Thang, the doctor on duty.

'Jake! What are you doing?'

'That's my—' What was she? Girlfriend, partner, mother of my child? How did he describe her?

She was his everything.

He loved every contrary and complex thing about her and he wasn't going to let anything bad happen to her. He'd promised to take care of her and that started now.

Seeing her lying pale and still on the stretcher with her dark hair spread around her she looked like Sleeping Beauty, except for the bloody gash at her temple. His heart beat a loud and angry tattoo in his chest. She was injured. But how badly?

He was by her side and his hand sought hers. 'Scarlett?'

Her eyelids flickered open and he could see her searching for him. Her eyes darted from side to side. Her neck was immobilised in a cervical collar and she couldn't turn her head. He hoped the collar was only a precaution. 'Jake?' He leant over the stretcher as the paramedics wheeled her inside.

'I'm here.' He squeezed her fingers gently and relief flooded through him as he felt her squeeze his fingers in return.

'The baby?'

'Let's get you into an exam room. Everything will be okay.' He hoped he was right.

He ran his eyes over her as they rushed her inside the hospital. She was covered with a dusting of fine white powder from the airbag but apart from the gash at her temple he couldn't see any other external signs of injury.

She was taken straight into a treatment room. Jake followed but Thang stopped him just inside. 'We need to do a general exam,' he told him, and Jake knew Thang meant him to wait outside.

'I'm fine. I want you to check the baby first.' Scarlett lifted one hand from the stretcher, holding it up to stop Thang. Jake saw her wince with the movement but she didn't back down. 'I'm a doctor too, I know I don't have any life-threatening injuries.' She looked at Jake, her dark eyes pleading with him. 'Don't you think I'd tell you if there was anything serious, anything that could harm the baby?'

A week ago he wasn't sure if he could have given her the answer she wanted but looking at her now he knew her concern for their child was genuine. Something had happened in the last week that had made her certain about this baby. Something had made her become the mother he knew she could be.

His heart swelled with love. For Scarlett and their baby. He smiled and nodded. 'Scarlett's right,' he told Thang. 'Let's check the baby first.'

'Are you really okay?' he asked once Thang had agreed with the order of examination and Scarlett had been transferred from the stretcher to a bed.

Scarlett nodded. 'I'm fine, thanks to you.'

'Me?'

'I think if you hadn't taken me on that skid-pan exercise, things might have been a lot worse. That might have saved my life but I'm still worried the baby—'

'All right, that's my cue,' Annie interrupted. 'I'm Annie Simpson, the ob-gyn. Let's have a look at this baby, shall we? How many weeks are you?'

'I think maybe eight.'

'Have you had any prenatal appointments?' Annie asked as she took control of the situation.

'No.'

'Any unusual symptoms—spotting, cramping, pain?'

'Now or before?'

'Before today.'

'Just morning sickness but I've got pain here now.' She lifted her shirt and ran her hand lightly across her lower abdomen.

The nurse wrapped a blood-pressure cuff around Scarlett's arm and slipped an oxygen monitor onto her finger, while Annie flicked the ultrasound monitor on and squeezed gel onto the transducer head of the ultrasound. 'If you're eight-weeks gestation, an abdominal ultrasound will tell us what we need to know. This gel will be a little cold, I haven't had time to warm it up,' Annie said, as she squeezed a little onto Scarlett's stomach.

Jake pulled a chair beside the bed and held Scarlett's hand. Annie adjusted the angle of the monitor so everyone could see and then began to sweep the ultrasound head across Scarlett's belly. A black-and-white image appeared on the screen. They all knew what they were looking for.

A black pocket appeared on the screen. Scarlett's uterus. Inside the pocket was a tiny figure, shaped like a jelly baby.

'Oh.' Scarlett lifted her hand and reached for the screen, almost as though she wanted to hold the baby.

Annie moved the ultrasound head slowly. 'There's a good strong heartbeat.' They could see a tiny flicker of a pulse on the screen. 'That's a good sign.'

A tear rolled down Scarlett's cheek. Jake leant over and gently kissed it away. 'It's all fine,' he told her. 'We're all going to be fine.'

Annie pushed a few buttons and took some measurements. 'Your baby seems perfectly okay and I'd say you're pretty spot on with your dates. It all looks about right for eight weeks. You can see the limb buds, the arms and legs just here.' She pushed another button and printed a picture. She handed it to Scarlett. 'Congratulations, the first picture for your album.'

'Can you believe it?' Scarlett said, as they stared at the picture. 'It's really happening.'

'I wish I could give you some time together but Thang will want to come in and examine Scarlett now,' Annie told them.

Jake nodded. He intended to stay with Scarlett but Thang banned him from the exam room.

'I should be in there with her,' he said to Annie, as he paced nervously outside.

'Let Thang do his job,' Annie told him. 'He doesn't need you hovering over his shoulder. The baby is fine and Scarlett seems okay too. You can relax.'

But he couldn't relax. Not until he knew the state of affairs.

Thang reappeared from the exam room. He pulled off his gloves as he delivered a reassuring summary. 'Soft-tissue injuries in the main. Whiplash, mild concussion, some bruising from the seat belt and possibly a cracked rib, but overall it seems as though she was very lucky. No apparent liver, kidney or spleen injuries. She's refusing any pain relief so she really just needs rest. You can go back in now.'

'Can I take her home?' Jake looked at both Annie and Thang.

Thang nodded while Annie replied, 'Ordinarily I'd keep her in for observation—'

'I promise not to let her out of my sight.'

'All right. I'll arrange for someone to collect her things from her car. It'll be towed into town, but she'll need a few things in the meantime, some clothes and toiletries and the like. Why don't you organise that and then you can come back and pick her up?'

Jake hadn't considered the practicalities. All he wanted was to get Scarlett out of here and into the five-star accommodation he'd booked for them for the weekend. It had been a far better option than taking her to the hospital accommodation he was sharing with two other med students but Annie's suggestion made sense and the sooner he followed her instructions the sooner he'd have Scarlett to himself.

'Are you in pain?' Jake asked her.

'No. Well, yes, but I'm okay.' Talking was painful. *Breathing* was painful but Scarlett wasn't going to complain. She was lucky to still be doing those things.

She lay in the warm bath that Jake had drawn for her and she felt good, battered and bruised but good. The accommodation was gorgeous. The marble bathroom was huge and luxurious and their room had a soft king-sized bed, a log fire and French doors that opened onto a private patio area overlooking the expansive grounds of the rural resort. It was a room made for champagne and romance but she'd have to make do with the romance. Surrounded by bubbles of a different kind, cocooned in the warm water and drinking a hot chocolate while candles flickered on the basin edge, she felt quite decadent. 'I can put up with some discomfort now that I know the baby is okay.'

'You sound far more positive than you did a week ago. I was worried you weren't going to have the baby. What's changed?'

Jake was sitting at the end of the bath. He was wearing jeans but his chest and feet were bare. This was one of her favourite Jakes. She ran her eyes over his naked torso. 'Why don't you join me in here and I'll tell you.'

'I don't think there's room for me.'

'I'll make room.' She smiled and slid forward in the bath. She watched as Jake stood and unbuttoned his jeans, dropping them to the floor along with his underwear. Just a glimpse of him naked was enough to elevate her pulse.

He slipped into the bath behind her, pulling her back to nestle between his thighs. Scarlett could feel his arousal and she was tempted to take advantage of it but she knew she needed to tell him what she was thinking, and if she didn't take the opportunity now who knew when she'd have another one?

'You were right,' she said, as he wrapped his arms around her. 'I had a few things to sort out but Mum and I had a big talk, like you asked, and she made me realise some things about myself and my life.

'Growing up, I always wished I had a father. I wanted to be like the other girls at school. I used to make up stories about why my dad wasn't around. I think my favourite was when I told everyone he was a spy, and when I was older and Mum married Rose's dad I claimed him as my own and said he'd just returned from a secret mission. Rose's dad was lovely and he treated me like I was his own daughter. I don't think I would have been any happier with my own father, but part of me always felt as though something was missing.

'Mum has only just told me that my father's family wanted her to terminate the pregnancy, terminate me, which was something I never knew. When Mum told me I realised I could never do that and was never thinking that way. I was just wishing I wasn't pregnant, which isn't the same thing as not wanting the baby. Accepting I was pregnant was my major hurdle.

'I spent years wishing I had a father when I should have been grateful that I had a mother who loved me and chose to keep me. Knowing how much easier things would have been for her if she had terminated the pregnancy made me realise that I am in the same situation and I am choosing to make the same decision she did. All I wanted was a father of my own and I want to be able to give my own child the chance I never had. It wouldn't be fair of me to take that away from the baby or from you.

'But I should warn you. Trust is difficult for me. Because Mum's relationships didn't last I expected the same from mine, and I know I often don't give anyone a chance. I expect them to leave. My mother and my sisters have been my roots. They keep me anchored to the ground and I've always worried that if I give myself to someone else they might rip me from the roots and then discard me. I felt I might disintegrate and disappear like the seeds of a dandelion blown by the wind. But the past is just that, and it's Mum's past, not mine. I need to take a chance.'

Jake kissed the side of her neck, just at the point where it joined her shoulder. 'I will be your shelter,' he said. 'I will protect you and any little seeds that fall from you. Those seeds are the beginnings of a new family, our family, and I will protect you all and be there always. I promise you. Will you do this with me?'

Scarlett nodded. 'I want to see whether we can build a relationship. I was worried that this pregnancy had ruined any chance we had but then I realised it was me who was jeopardising that. If you're prepared to trust in us then so am I.'

'Do you want to look for your father?'

'No. I've thought about this a lot this week. Why I've never gone looking for him myself when I've had years when I could have searched for him. But I know it was because I was scared to. I didn't want him to reject me. I don't know if I never want to find him but that is a question for another day.

'What I do know is that I want my own child to know you. That's what's important now. I need to build my own future, our future, and to do that I need to trust in you and believe that we can make this work or at least be prepared to give it our best shot. I can't continue to make assumptions about my life based on the past. I need to look to the future and I want you to be a part of that. Starting now.

'I am going to focus on you, me and our baby. On seeing if we have a relationship that can work. You were right. Things haven't worked out exactly as I planned but they may turn out to be better. This will be the biggest adventure of my life and if you are prepared to go on it with me I think I might just survive.'

THEY HAD MADE love in the enormous bed. Scarlett had insisted she was fine and he'd been unable to resist, although they had taken it slowly, carefully and tenderly. She was propped up in bed, her dark eyes enormous in her pale face, but despite her pallor he thought she'd never looked more beautiful.

He had drawn the curtains and lit the gas log fire and the room was illuminated only by the soft light of the flames. Now was the perfect time to give Scarlett his present.

He reached into the drawer of the bedside table where he had hidden the package earlier. 'I have something for you,' he said, as he handed her a gift bag.

Scarlett peeked inside and pulled out a wooden matryoshka doll.

'She's beautiful. What is she for?'

'For you. She reminds me of you.'

Scarlett frowned. 'She does?'

'Yes. Remember when I described you as the parcel in the pass-the-parcel game?'

Scarlett laughed. 'Yes. Not the most flattering description.'

'I agree, and I've decided that you're still layered but perhaps you're more like one of these dolls. Complex but within every layer is something else equally as interesting and equally as valuable.'

'Where on earth did you find her?' Scarlett asked. 'She even looks a bit like me,' she said, as she studied her closely. The first doll was a woman with her dark hair pulled into a bun and with an intricately detailed face, dark eyes and full lips, dressed in a white doctor's coat with a stethoscope around her neck.

'I had her made for you. There's a local artist who makes these to order. This is you in all your different complexities. The doctor,' he said as Scarlett separated the first doll to reveal one wearing a replica of the paisley dress she'd worn to Candice's wedding. 'The party you.' Next was Scarlett the sister. The artist had painted tiny images of Ruby and Rose on either side of her, and then there was Scarlett dressed in white, a lace veil covering her dark hair.

'Is this a wedding dress?'

Jake nodded as Scarlett shook the doll. Something rattled inside.

She looked at him, her dark eyes wide. 'I'm not ready for marriage. It's not a ring, is it?'

'It's okay, open it.' He smiled.

Inside was another doll. Still Scarlett but this time dressed in a simple pale pink shirt. It still rattled.

'There's one more,' Jake said.

Nestled inside was a tiny doll.

Scarlett lifted it out. It was a dark-eyed baby wrapped in a swaddling cloth.

Jake picked up the final empty doll and pushed the two halves back together before cupping it in his hand. 'This doll is you, the mother, and this...' he rolled his finger over the baby '...is our baby. There's no ring. Not yet. I am going to marry you but only when you are ready. I believe we were meant to meet at this point in our lives. This baby is meant to be ours and we are meant to be together. Married or not, we're ready for this.' He kissed her gently before asking. 'Do you remember why I got my tattoo?'

Scarlett nodded. 'To remind you to always come home.'

'You and our baby are my home now. I will always be there for you. For both of you. I want to marry you because I love you.' He rested his hand over her belly. 'I love you both. Just tell me when you are ready.'

Scarlett closed her palm around the baby doll, cradling it in her hand. She slid her hand under Jake's and wrapped his fingers around hers, holding them together. 'I'm not ready yet but I know this is where I'm supposed to be. With you. I love you too.'

EPILOGUE

'Can you believe it? In one week you'll be Mrs Chamberlain.'

Scarlett was in the kitchen, chopping vegetables for a salad, when Jake came up behind her and wrapped his arms around her swollen belly as he kissed her neck. It was ten days until Christmas and the temperature had been climbing steadily for weeks. Scarlett was feeling huge and uncomfortably pregnant but the touch of Jake's hand was enough to make her forget her discomfort.

'I can't wait to see you walk down the aisle.'

'Don't you mean waddle?' she said, as she turned her head and smiled at her fiancé.

'No. You look beautiful. This last trimester suits you,' he said, as he slipped his hand inside her loose camisole and cupped her breast.

Scarlett moaned as his fingers teased her nipple, sending shivers of longing through her. She didn't know about this last trimester suiting her but it had certainly fired up her libido. It seemed all Jake had to do was look at her and she felt like ripping all his clothes off. Hers too.

'I have something to show you,' Jake said. 'An early wedding present.'

'Ooh, what is it? You know I love presents.'

In reply Jake pulled his T-shirt over his head and the

sight of his naked torso almost made Scarlett forget about the present. He was too gorgeous for words. He had finished his undergraduate medical degree and left his job at The Coop in order to spend more time with her before he started his internship, but he had kept up his exercise routine and still looked fabulous.

Scarlett ran her eyes over his body in appreciation and it was then she noticed a sterile dressing on his left upper arm.

Concern flooded through her. 'What happened to you?' she asked, reaching out one hand towards his arm.

Jake's fingers teased the edge of the dressing, pulling it from his skin where it had covered his tattoo.

'I got a new tattoo,' he told her.

He lifted his arm and Scarlett could see two new stars inked on his arm at a forty-five-degree angle to the Southern Cross.

'What are they?'

'Alpha and Beta Centauri, the Pointer Stars.' He pointed to the first star, furthest from the Southern Cross. 'This one is you and this one,' he said, pointing to the second new star, 'is our baby. The two of you will always guide me home. Every time you see these stars I want you to remember that you can depend on me. I love you and I can't wait to spend the rest of my life taking care of you.'

Scarlett linked her arms around his neck. 'I do know that. It's one of the reasons I agreed to marry you.'

'What were the others?'

'You make me feel safe, adored and happy. I love you and if we didn't have to wait for all our siblings to get home I'd marry you tomorrow.'

'Haven't you learnt by now that I'm a patient man?'

'I have learnt that. It's another reason why I agreed to

marry you. You waited so long for me to give you an answer I thought you deserved it to be yes.

'Five months was about my limit,' he teased. 'Any other reasons spring to mind?'

'Yes. I can't resist your tattoos.'

'You like these.' Jake grinned at her and flexed his biceps.

'I do.' She ran her fingers lightly up his arm and reached behind his head. She pulled his forward and kissed him hard on the mouth. 'Shall I show you just how much?' she whispered. She dropped her hands to the waistband of his shorts and discovered his reaction was as intense as hers. 'It looks like you're not that patient after all.' She laughed.

'There is only so much waiting I can do in one lifetime,' he said, as Scarlett divested him of the rest of his clothes. 'And it seems I've just run out of patience,' he added, as he scooped her into his arms and carried her off to bed.

* * * * *

The Maverick Doctor And Miss Prim
Scarlet Wilson

**Also by Scarlet Wilson
in Harlequin® Medical Romance™:**

AN INESCAPABLE TEMPTATION
HER CHRISTMAS EVE DIAMOND
WEST WING TO MATERNITY WING!

**These books are also available in ebook format
from www.millsandboon.com.au.**

**Praise for
Scarlet Wilson**

"Stirring, emotional and wonderfully absorbing, *It Started with a Pregnancy* is an impressive debut novel from a fabulous new voice in category romance: Scarlet Wilson!"
—*www.Cataromance.com* on *It Started with a Pregnancy*

"Scarlet Wilson continues to get better with every book she writes! West Wing to Maternity Wing is a tender, poignant and highly affecting romance that is sure to bring a tear to your eye. With her gift for creating wonderful characters, her ability to handle delicately and compassionately sensitive issues and her talent for writing believable, emotional and spellbinding romance, the talented Scarlet Wilson continues to prove to be a force to be reckoned with in the world of contemporary romantic fiction!"
—*www.Cataromance.com* on *West Wing to Maternity Wing*

Dear Reader,

When I was asked by my editor if I would be interested in writing a duet, I was delighted and jumped at the chance. The Center for Disease Control in the U.S. has always fascinated me. I work in public health, and love all the work around infectious diseases and immunisation campaigns. The CDC always features heavily in any plague/outbreak/epidemic films that are made, and I was excited at the prospect of having a story along those lines and set about creating my own fictional organisation, the Disease Prevention Agency, for my *Rebels with a Cause* duet.

But all stories need to have fabulous characters, and I instantly fell in love with my hero in *The Maverick Doctor and Miss Prim*—Matt Sawyer, wounded bad boy and very much like his namesake, Sawyer in *Lost*. He's the kind of guy you know deep-down has real good in him. It's just going to take a special woman to unearth it.

My sassy heroine, Callie, is a girl out of her depth. She takes the initial call at the DPA and assembles the team, but her mentor is taken unwell on a plane and she's left in charge of a situation that is clearly bigger than any she's coped with before.

Her only option is to turn to Sawyer for help. After all, he worked in the DPA previously and has the expertise she needs. So why doesn't he want to help? It makes quarantine very interesting….

Both my characters in this story are grieving. And both deal with their grief in their own way. Needless to say, I let them get their happy-ever-after. It just takes a while to get there!

Please feel free to contact me via my website, www.scarlet-wilson.com. I love to hear from readers!

Scarlet

The second story in Scarlet Wilson's *Rebels with a Cause* duet

ABOUT THAT NIGHT…

is also available from Harlequin® Medical Romance™

DEDICATION

This book is dedicated to my two fabulous and entrepreneurial brothers-in-law, who have put up with me for more years than I care to remember. For Sandy Dickson and Robert Glencross, thank you for everything that you've done for me and my family and for taking such good care of my sisters!

CHAPTER ONE

Chicago

"Okay, beautiful, what you got for me?" Sawyer leaned across the reception desk as the clerk glared at him.

Miriam cracked her chewing gum. "You've been here too long—you're getting smart-mouthed."

"I've always been smart-mouthed."

"And get a haircut."

He pushed his shaggy light brown hair from his eyes then tossed his head. "The long-haired look is in. Besides—I'm worth it."

The clerk rolled her eyes and picked up three charts. "You can have two sick kids with chicken pox in room six or a forty-three-year-old female with D&V behind curtain two." They lifted their heads in unison as the noise of someone retching behind curtain two filled the air.

He shuddered. "Give me the kids." He grabbed the charts and walked down the corridor. His eyes skimmed the information on the charts. Ben and Jack Keating, aged six and seven, just returned from abroad with chicken pox.

He pushed open the door. Unusually, the lights were dimmed in the room. The two kids—brothers—lay on the beds with a parent at each bedside. Alison, one of the nurses, was taking a temperature. She walked over to him, her pregnancy bump just starting to emerge from her scrub trousers. "Sickest kids I've seen in a while," she murmured.

He gave her a smile, his natural instinct kicking in. "You safe to be in here?"

She sighed. "After three kids of my own it's safe to say I'm immune."

Sawyer crossed the room quickly, leaving the charts at the bottom of the beds. Alison was right. These kids didn't look good. Chicken pox could be a lot more serious than a few itchy spots.

"Hi, I'm Matt Sawyer, one of the docs. I'm going to take a look at Ben and Jack." He extended his hand towards the mother then the father, taking in their exhausted expressions before turning to the sink, washing his hands and donning some gloves.

He walked over to Ben. In the dim light it was difficult to see his face, but it looked as if it was covered in red, bumpy spots. "Hi, Ben, I'm just going to have a little look at you."

The six-year-old barely acknowledged that he'd spoken. He glanced at the cardiac and BP monitor, noting the increased heart rate and low blood pressure. At first touch he could feel the temperature through his gloves. He pressed gently at the sides of Ben's neck. Unsurprisingly his glands were swollen. There were a number of spots visible on Ben's face so he peeled back the cover to reveal only a few angry spots across his chest but a whole host across his forearms.

The first thing that struck him was that all of the spots were at the same stage of development. Not like chicken pox at all—where spots emerged and erupted at different times.

Alarm bells started ringing in his head. *Be methodical.* He heard the old mantra of his mentor echoing around him.

He moved to the bottom of the bed and lifted Ben's foot.

There. The same uniform spots on the soles of his feet. He stretched over, reaching Ben's hand and turning his palm over. Red vesicular spots.

He tasted bile in the back of his throat and glanced across the room to where Alison had switched on her telepathic abilities and had already hung some bags of saline and was running through the IV lines.

"Where were you on vacation?"

The boys' father shook his head. "We weren't on vacation. I was working. We've just come back from three months in Somalia. I work for a commercial water-piping company."

Somalia. The last known place for a natural outbreak of this disease.

"Were any of the locals you came into contact with sick?" There were a million different questions flying around his head but he didn't want to bombard the parents.

Mrs Keating nodded. "We were in the highlands. A lot of them were sick. But we didn't think it was anything too serious. We actually wondered if we'd taken a bug to them—we were the first people they'd come into contact with in years."

His reaction was instinctive. "Step outside, please, Alison."

"What?" The nurse wrinkled her brow.

He raised his voice, lifting his eyes and fixing them on her, praying she would understand. "Wait outside for me, please, Alison."

The atmosphere was electric. She was an experienced nurse and could read the expression on his face. She dropped the IV lines and headed for the door.

"Is something wrong?" Mr. Keating started to stand.

Sawyer crossed to the other bed. Jack was lying with

his back to him. He wasted no time by pulling the white sheet from across Jack's chest and tugging gently on his shoulder to pull him round.

Identical. His face was covered. Red, deep-seated round vesicles. All at the same stage of development, a few covering his chest but mainly on his forearms. He opened Jack's mouth. Inside, his oral mucosa and palate were covered. He checked the soles of his feet and the palms of his hands. More identically formed red spots.

He could feel chills sweeping his body. It couldn't be. *It couldn't be*. This disease had been eradicated in the seventies. No one had seen this disease since then.

Then a little light bulb went off in his head. Hadn't there been a suspected outbreak a few years ago that had turned out to be chicken pox? The very thing that this was presumed to be? He ran the list of other possibilities in his head. He knew them off by heart. Anyone who'd ever worked in the DPA did.

But the more he stared at the spots the more convinced he became that it was none of the alternatives.

"How long since the spots appeared?"

The mother and father exchanged glances. "A few days? They had a rash at first then the spots developed. They've got much worse in the last day. But the boys had been feeling unwell before that—headaches, backaches, vomiting. We just thought they'd picked up a bug."

Sawyer felt as if he was in a bad movie. Why him? Why did this have to happen while he was on duty?

Would someone else recognize this? Realize the potential risks? Or would they just chalk it up to a bad dose of chicken pox and discover the consequences later? He'd put all this behind him. He'd walked away and vowed never to be involved in any of this again. He was in the middle of Chicago—not in some far-off country. Things like this didn't happen here. Or they *shouldn't* happen here.

And right now that was he wanted to do again. To walk out that front door and forget he'd ever seen any of this.

He looked at the long inviting corridor outside. He wasn't a coward. But he didn't want this. He didn't want *any* of this. The kind of thing that sucked you in until it squeezed all the breath from you.

A shadow moved outside the door.

But there was the killer. A pregnant nurse standing outside that door. A nurse who had been working with him and had contact with these children. Could he walk away from her?

He glanced upwards. It was almost as if someone had put her here so he *couldn't* walk away. His conscience would never allow him to do that.

If only he didn't know she was pregnant. If only that little bump hadn't just started to emerge above her scrub trousers. That would make this a whole lot easier.

Then he could walk away.

He took a deep breath and steeled himself. He was a doctor. He had a duty of care. Not just to his colleagues but to these kids.

These very sick kids.

He looked back at the parents. "I need you to think very carefully—this is very important. Did you fly home?"

They both nodded.

"When, *exactly*, did you first notice the rash on the boys? Before or after you were on the plane?"

The parents looked at each other, screwing up their foreheads and trying to work it out.

A detailed history could wait. He knew enough already. He wasn't part of the DPA any more. This was their job, not his. The notification part he could handle—setting the wheels in motion so the processes could take over.

Isolation. Containment. Diagnosis. Lab tests. Media furore.

In the meantime he had two sick kids to take care of and staff members to worry about. Let the DPA do their job and he could do his.

He pulled his smart phone from his pocket and took a picture of Jack's spots and then Ben's. "Wait here."

Alison jumped as he flung the door open. "What on earth's going on?" She matched his steps as he strode down the corridor to Reception. "Don't you think you can get away with speaking to me like that. I want to know what you think is wrong." He watched her as subconsciously her hands went to her stomach. This day was just about to get a whole lot worse.

"Did you touch them?"

"What?" She wrinkled her nose.

"The spots. Did you touch the children's spots?"

She must have read the fear he was trying to hide behind his eyes. "I think I did." She looked as if she might burst into tears. Then realization dawned. "I think I had gloves on." Her voice grew more determined. "No, I'm *sure* I had gloves on."

"And when you took them off, did you touch any other part of your skin?"

Her face crumpled. "I don't think so. But I can't be sure."

His hands landed on her shoulders and he steered her into the nearest free room. He knocked the water on with his elbows and pulled the hand scrub over, opening up a scrub brush for her. "Scrub as if you were going to Theatre and don't stop until I tell you."

She looked pale, as if she might keel over. But her reactions were automatic, pumping the scrub, covering her hands, wrists and forehands and moving them methodically under the running water.

He watched the clock. One minute. Two minutes. Three minutes. Four.

"Sawyer?"

He nodded. "You can stop now."

"Do you know what it is?" She was drying her hands now.

"I think I do. I'm just praying that I'm wrong. Come with me."

They reached the desk. Miriam had her back to them and was chatting loudly on the phone.

Sawyer leaned across the desk and cut the call.

She spun around. "What are you doing?"

"We're closed."

"What?" Several heads in the surrounding area turned.

"You don't have any authority—"

"I do. Get me Dr. Simpson, the chief of staff, on the phone." He turned to face the rest of the staff. "Listen up, folks. As of now, we have a public health emergency. The department needs to close—right now." He pointed at Miriam. "Let Dispatch know not to send us any more patients."

He turned to one of the security staff. "Lock the front doors."

The noise level around him rose.

He put his hand on Alison's arm, pulling her to one side. "I'm sorry, honey, but that isn't chicken pox. I think it's smallpox. And we need to contact the DPA."

Atlanta

CALLIE TURNER STOWED her bag in her locker and nodded at a few of her colleagues getting changed. She glanced in the mirror and straightened her skirt, taking a deep breath as she gave herself a nervous smile and pulled at her new haircut—an asymmetric blonde bob.

It was meant to signify a new start—a new beginning for her. It had looked fabulous in the salon yesterday, expertly teased and styled. Today it just looked as if she was halfway through a haircut. This would take a bit of getting used to.

First day at the DPA.

Well, not really. An internship and then a three-year specialist residency training program completed within the DPA. All to be part of the Disease Prevention Agency. Eleven years in total of blood, sweat and lots of tears.

All to fulfil someone else's dreams. All to pay homage to someone else's destiny.

Today was the first day of the rest of her life.

She pushed open the door to the telephone hub. "Hi, Maisey."

The short curly-haired woman looked up. "Woo-hoo! Well, look who picked the lucky bag on her first day on the job." She rolled her eyes at Callie. "Go on, then. Who did you upset?"

Callie laughed and pulled out the chair next to Maisey. "No one that I know of. This was just my first shift on the rota." She looked around. "It's kind of empty in here. Where is everyone?"

Maisey gave her a sympathetic glance. "You should have been here two hours ago. They're assembling a team next door. We've got a suspected outbreak of ebola."

Callie's eyes widened. First day on the job and she was assigned to the phones. The crazy calls. While next door the disease detectives were preparing to investigate an outbreak. She bit her lip. "Who took the call?"

Maisey smiled again. "Donovan."

Callie sighed. Typical. The person who took the call usually got to assemble and lead the team. Donovan had a knack of being in the right place at the right time.

Unlike her.

She stared at the wall ahead of her. Someone had stuck a sign up: "Normal People Don't Phone the DPA."

Never a truer word was said. The phone next to her started ringing. She bent forward and automatically picked it up. It would be a long day.

Four hours later she'd spoken to three health officials, crazy bat lady—who phoned every day—two over-anxious school teachers, five members of the public, and two teenagers who'd obviously been dared by their friends to ring up. Right now all she could think about was a large cappuccino and a banana and toffee muffin.

Her stomach grumbled loudly as she lifted the phone when it rang again. "DPA, Callie Turner, can I help you?"

"This is Matt Sawyer at Chicago General. I've got two kids with suspected smallpox."

She sat up instantly as her brain scrambled to make sense of the words. All thoughts of the muffin vanishing instantly. This had to be a joke. But the voice didn't sound like that of a teenager, it sounded like an adult.

"Well, aren't you going to say anything?" He sounded angry. Patience obviously wasn't his strong point.

She took a deep breath. "Smallpox has been eradicated. It's no longer a naturally occurring disease, Mr. Sawyer."

"Listen, honey, you can call me Doctor. Dr. Matt Sawyer. Ringing any bells yet?"

She frowned. Matt Sawyer? The name seemed familiar. Who was he? And why was he speaking to her like that? She put her hand over the receiver and hissed at Maisey. "Hey, who's Matt Sawyer?"

Maisey's eyes widened instantly, the disbelief on her

face obvious. She skidded her wheeled chair across the room next to Callie. "You're joking, right?"

Callie shook her head and pointed to the phone.

Maisey bent forward and pulled the phone away from her ear, replacing it with her mouth. "Outbreak, dead pregnant wife, disappeared off the map."

The pieces of the puzzle started to fall into place and become vaguely familiar. Of course. She *had* heard of this guy. In fact, everyone in the DPA had heard of this guy. He was like a dark, looming legend. But it had been way before her time.

Her training and natural instincts kicked in. There was a protocol for this. She pushed her chair under the desk and pulled up a screen on her computer. "Hi, Dr. Sawyer. Let's go through this."

The algorithm had appeared in front of her, telling her exactly what questions to ask, why and when. She started to take some notes.

"You said you're at Chicago General. Whereabouts in the hospital are you?"

She could almost hear him sigh. "The ER."

"What are the symptoms?"

"Two kids, returned from Somalia a few days ago. Ages six and seven. Very sick. Febrile, uniform red spots mainly on their faces, forearms, palms and soles. A few on their trunks. Low blood pressure, tachycardic, swollen glands."

She was typing furiously. Somalia. The last known place to have a natural outbreak of smallpox. It did seem coincidental.

But there were a whole host of other diseases this could be. She started to speak. "Dr. Sawyer, have you considered chicken pox, herpes, scabies, impetigo—"

"Stop it."

"What?"

"I know you're reading from the list. I've considered all those things. It's none of them. Check your emails." He sounded exasperated with her.

"What do you mean?"

"Lady, do I have to tell you everything twice? Check your emails. I just sent you some photos. Have you ever seen spots like that?"

She clicked out of the algorithm and into her emails. Sure enough, there it was. Everyone in the DPA had a generic email address starting with their full name. He was obviously familiar enough with the system to know that. There was no message. She opened the attached photos.

Wow.

The phone was still at her ear and she moved her face closer to the screen to examine the red spots. No. She hadn't seen anything like that before—except in a textbook.

"Show the photo to Callum Ferguson," the low voice growled in her ear.

Callum Ferguson. The only person in their team who'd actually been through the last smallpox outbreak. The only person who'd seen the spots for real. Only someone who'd worked here would know something like that. This phone call was definitely no hoax.

"Give me two minutes." She crossed the room in big strides, throwing open the door to the briefing room where the ebola team was assembling.

"Callum, I need you to take a look at something urgently."

"Kind of busy in here, Callie." The large Scotsman looked up from the floor, where he was packing things into a backpack. Callum was well past retirement age but nothing seemed to slow him down, and his age and experience made him invaluable on the outbreak team.

She lowered her voice, trying to avoid the glare coming across the room from Donovan.

"It's Matt Sawyer on the phone. He needs you to look at something."

Callum looked as though he'd just seen a ghost. His hands froze above his pack. He started to stutter, "Wh-what?"

She nodded and he stood up wordlessly and followed her out of the room.

In the few seconds she had been away from her seat, everything had changed. Her boss, Evan Hunter, was standing in front of her computer, staring at her screen, his two deputies and Maisey at his side. The phone receiver was still lying on the desk.

No one spoke. They just moved out of Callum's way as he reached the screen. His heavy frame dropped into Callie's chair and he glided under her desk.

"Well?"

Evan Hunter wasn't renowned for wasting time. The scowl on his face was fierce and made Callie raise her eyebrows. Hadn't someone told her there had been no love lost between him and Matt Sawyer in the past?

Callum, normally red faced, looked pale. He turned to Evan Hunter and nodded. "I'm sure. I never thought I'd see this again," he whispered.

Everything around them erupted.

Evan pressed his hand on Callum's shoulder. "You're off the ebola team. This is yours—it couldn't possibly be anyone else's, seeing as Matt Sawyer is involved. You're the only one who's ever managed to assert any control over that loose cannon. I want you all over him. Pick your team." He looked at his watch. "It'll take ninety minutes to fly to Chicago. I want you packed and ready to go inside four hours."

He turned and swept out the room, his deputies scurrying after him. Callie was shaken. Had this really just happened?

Callum's voice continued in low tones on the phone. He wasn't even looking at the algorithm she'd pulled up on the screen. His eyes were still fixed on the photo.

"You're sure there's no possibility that this could be intentional—a biological terrorist attack?" He was scribbling notes as he listened. There were a few more mumbled questions before he replaced the receiver.

"Was it him? Was it definitely Sawyer?" Maisey looked fit to burst.

Callum nodded. "It was him." He stood up slowly, obviously still in thought. "I guess that means he's all right, then." He touched Callie's arm. "Get ready, Dr. Turner. This could be the experience of a lifetime."

"I'm on the team?" She could barely contain her excitement. It was only made slightly better by the look of disgust on Donovan's face over the other side of the room.

Callum smiled at her. "You know the rules, Callie. You took the call—of course you're on the team."

"I'll be ready in half an hour. Let me get the updated plans." She rushed off, her heart thumping in her chest.

First official day on the job and she was on the outbreak team investigating an apparently eradicated disease. Isabel would have loved this.

CALLIE SHOVED HER bag in the overhead locker and sat down next to Callum. Everything was happening so fast. She hadn't even had time to think.

The doors of the plane were already closed and they were starting to taxi down the runway. The cabin crew was already in their seats—the safety announcement forgotten. The normal rules of aviation didn't seem to apply today.

This was the biggest team she'd ever been part of. There had to be around thirty people on this plane. Other doctors, epidemiologists, case interviewers, contact tracers, admin personnel and, most worrying, security.

Callum had the biggest pile of paperwork she'd ever seen. He was checking things off the list. "Vaccines—check. Protocols—check. N95 filtered masks—check. Symptom list—check. Algorithm—check. Three-hundred-page outbreak plan..." his thumb flicked the edges of the thick document "...check."

He leaned back in his seat. "And that's just the beginning." A few minutes later they felt the plane lift off. Ninety minutes until they reached their destination.

"What have you done about containment plans?"

He nodded at her question. "I've identified a suitable building for a Type-C containment. Arrangements are currently being made to prepare it. In the meantime we've instructed Chicago General to switch their air-conditioning off. We don't want to risk the spread of the droplets. They don't even have suitable masks right now—only the paper ones, which are practically useless."

He shook his head. "Those spots were starting to erupt. These kids are at the most infectious stage of this disease."

Callie shuddered. A potentially deadly disease in an E.R. department. Her mind boggled.

It didn't matter that she was a completely rational person. It didn't matter that she specialized in infectious diseases. There was still that tiny human part in her that wanted to panic.

That wanted to run in the other direction.

The strange thing was that there were colleagues at the DPA who would kill to be in her shoes right now. Her very tight, uncomfortable shoes. Why hadn't she changed them before they'd left? Who knew how long she would be on her feet?

She hesitated. "Who are you relaying the instructions to right now?"

His eyes fixed on the papers in front of him. He didn't look so good. "The chief of staff at Chicago General is Max Simpson. He's following our instructions to the letter. Or rather Matt Sawyer is following our instructions to the letter. He's the only one with any experience down there."

There were small beads of sweat on his brow. He reached into his top pocket and pulled out some antacids.

"You okay?"

He nodded as he opened the packet and popped three in his mouth.

Callum was the calmest, most knowledgeable doctor she'd ever worked with. She'd worked side by side with him through lots of outbreaks. She couldn't ask for a better mentor. But even he looked a little scared. Maybe it wasn't just her after all?

Or maybe it was something else entirely.

She lowered her voice. "He was your protégé, wasn't he?"

"My what?"

"Matt Sawyer. I heard he was your protégé."

Callum grimaced and shook his head. "Do me a favor. Don't let Sawyer hear you call him that. That would tip him over the edge that I presume he's currently dangling on."

"What do you mean?" During all the frantic preparations Callie hadn't had any time to find out more about Matt Sawyer. Only a few whispers and hurried conversations here and there.

This was her first real mission. She'd been out as a danger detective before—when she'd been completing her specialist residency training. But this was her first real chance to prove herself. To prove that she was a worthy member of the team. To prove to them—and herself—that she deserved to be there.

It didn't sound promising if the doctor who'd made the initial call was unstable.

She looked at the pile of papers on Callum's lap. The outbreak plans, the containment plans, the paperwork to use for contact tracing, the algorithms. A plan for everything. A piece of paper for every eventuality. Just the way she liked it. Just the way she'd learned to function best.

Rules and regulations were her backbone. The thing that kept her focused. The thing that kept everyone safe.

Callum followed her gaze. "This could get messy."

"What do you mean? With the disease? The casualties?" She hadn't even stopped to think about that yet. She still had her public health head on, the one that looked at the big picture. She hadn't even started to consider the individuals.

Callum looked kind of sad. "No." He gave a little grimace again. "With Sawyer."

"Sawyer? Aren't you happy to see him again?" She was confused. Hadn't they been friends?

"Under any other set of circumstances I would be. But not here. Not like this. This will be his worst nightmare. Sawyer walked away from all this. The last thing he wants to do is be involved in another outbreak. I can't imagine how he's feeling."

"He's a doctor. He has responsibilities. He has a job to do." She made it all sound so straightforward. Because in her head that was the way it should be.

He sighed. "Things change, Callie. Life gets in the way. Sawyer doesn't live by anybody's rules but his own. He didn't even follow protocol today. He should have notified the state department first but he didn't. He just called the

DPA. He called *you*." He emphasized the word as he placed a hand on his chest.

She'd missed that. Miss Rules and Regulations had missed that. In her shock at the nature of the call it hadn't even occurred to her that Sawyer should have contacted the state department first and *they* should have contacted the DPA.

How could she have missed that?

She didn't need anyone to remind her that things could change—that life, or lack of it—could get in the way. She was living proof of that.

Seeds of doubt started to creep into her mind. She'd missed the first rule of notification. And if she'd missed that, what else would she miss? Should she even be on this team?

Rules were there for a reason. Rules were there to be followed. Rules were there for everyone's safety.

Then it really hit her. What was happening before her very eyes.

The last thing she needed to do right now was look at the wider picture. She needed to concentrate on the picture right before her.

Callum was turning gray, with the slightest blue tinge around his lips. His skin was waxy and he was still sweating. His hand remained firmly on his chest.

"Callum? Are you okay?" She unfastened her seat belt and stood up, signaling to some of the other members of the team. "That's not heartburn, is it?"

He shook his head as she started barking out orders to the rest of the team. "Get me some oxygen. Find out how soon till we get there. Can we get an earlier landing slot? Speak to the pilot—it's a medical emergency."

They literally had every piece of equipment known to

man on this plane. Unfortunately, most of it was in the hold. And none of it was to treat a myocardial infarction.

She cracked open their first-aid kit, monitoring his blood pressure and giving him some aspirin. She pasted a smile on her face. "Things will be fine, Callum. We'll get you picked up at the airport and taken to the nearest cardiac unit."

His hand gripped her wrist. "I'm sorry, Callie. I shouldn't be leaving you to deal with this. Not with Sawyer. You two are like oil and water. You won't mix. Not at all." His head was shaking.

Callie's stomach was churning. The thought of facing the legendary Sawyer herself was not filling her with confidence. But right now she would do or say anything that would relieve the pressure on Callum. Anything at all.

"Everything will be fine. You'll see. Don't worry about a thing, Callum. I can handle Sawyer."

Famous last words.

CHAPTER TWO

"Who are you and where is Callum Ferguson?" Not waiting for an answer, the man with the shaggy hair pushed past her and looked behind her. With his broad frame and pale green eyes, on another occasion she might have looked twice. But she didn't have time for this.

Great. The welcoming party. And he was obviously delighted to see her.

She struggled to set the box down on the reception desk. There was only one person this could be. And she intended to start the way she meant to continue. This was business.

"Here are the N95 masks. Make sure anyone that goes into the room with those kids wears one. And make sure it's fitted properly, otherwise it will be useless."

He hadn't moved. He was still standing directly in her path. "I asked you a question."

She almost hesitated but that would do her no good. She needed to establish who was in charge here. And it was her.

"Matt Sawyer? I'm Callie Turner and I'm leading the team." She turned towards the door as the rest of the team fanned in behind her, carrying their equipment.

It was like an invasion. And the irony of that wasn't lost on her.

She tilted her head. "I'd shake your hand but you're already an infection control hazard, so forgive me."

Did she look confident? She certainly hoped so, because her stomach was churning so much that any minute now she might just throw up all over his Converses.

She walked around behind the desk and started pulling things out of the boxes being deposited next to her. "Lewis, Cheryl, set up here and here." She pointed to some nearby desks.

"I'm only going to ask you one more time. Where is Callum Ferguson?"

He was practically growling at her now. And that hair of his was going to annoy her. Why didn't he get a decent haircut? Wouldn't long hair be an infection control hazard? Maybe she should suggest he find an elastic band and tie it back, though on second thoughts it wasn't quite long enough for that.

She drew herself up before him. This man was starting to annoy her. *Did he think she was hiding Callum Ferguson in her back pocket?* "I'm sorry to tell you, Dr. Sawyer, that Dr. Ferguson became unwell on the plane en route."

He actually twitched. As if she'd just said something to shock him. Maybe he was a human being after all.

"What happened?"

"We think he had an MI. He's been taken to the cardiac unit at St John's. I heard it's the best in town."

She waited for a second while he digested the news. Would he realize she'd checked up on the best place to send her colleague, rather than just send him off to the nearest hospital available? She hoped so. From the expression on Sawyer's face she might need to win some points with him.

Why did the thought of being quarantined with this man fill her with impending doom?

SAWYER WAS ABOUT to explode. And Miss Hoity-Toity with her navy-blue suit, pointy shoes and squinty hairdo was first in line to bear the brunt of the impact.

It was bad enough that he was here—but now to find out that the one person in the DPA he absolutely trusted *wasn't* going to be here?

The thought of Callum Ferguson having an MI was sickening. Sawyer had almost fallen into the trap of thinking the man was invincible. He'd spent the last forty years investigating outbreaks and coming home unscathed.

Please let him be okay.

He scowled at Callie Turner as she issued orders to those all around him. Did she realize her hand was trembling ever so slightly? Because he did. And it wasn't instilling him with confidence.

He planted his hand on his hip. "How old are you *exactly*?"

He could see her bristling. Her brain was whirring, obviously trying to think up a smart answer. She walked straight over to him and put both of her hands on her hips, mirroring his stance.

"Exactly how old do you want me to be, Sawyer?"

He couldn't wipe the smile from his face. Smart and sassy—if a little young. The girl showed promise.

"So what happened to the hair?"

He'd already caught her tugging self-consciously at one side of her hair. As if she wasn't quite used to it yet. "Were you halfway through when you took my call?" He took a piece of gum offered by nearby Miriam and started chewing as he watched her. He could tell she was irritated by him. Perfect. Maybe if he annoyed Miss DPA enough, he could get out of here.

Except it didn't work like that and he knew it. Still, he could live in hope.

She dumped a final pile of papers on the desk from her box, which she picked up and kicked under the desk. Yip. She was definitely mad.

She grabbed the heavily clipped document on the top of the pile, strode over and thrust it directly against his chest. It hit him square in the solar plexus, causing him to catch his breath.

"My haircut cost more than you probably make in a month. Now, here—read this. And it isn't from me. It's from Callum. He said to make sure it was the first thing I gave you—along with the instructions to follow it to the letter."

He pulled the document off his chest. The DPA plan for a smallpox outbreak. All three hundred pages of it. He let it go and it skidded across the desk towards her.

"I don't need to read this."

She stepped back in front of him. "Yes. You do. You've already broken protocol once today, Dr. Sawyer. You should have contacted the state department *before* you contacted us. But, then, you know that, don't you? You don't work for the DPA anymore, Dr. Sawyer."

He cracked his chewing gum. "Well, that's at least one thing we agree on."

She glanced at her watch. "So, that means, that as of right now—five thirty-six p.m.—you work for me. You, and everyone else in here. This is my hospital now, Dr. Sawyer, my jurisdiction, and you will do exactly what I tell you." She jerked her thumb over her shoulder. "And it's all in that plan. So memorize it because there'll be a pop quiz later."

She kicked her navy-blue platforms beneath the desk

and started to undo her shirt. "Where are the scrubs and protective clothing?" she shouted along the corridor.

"In here," came a reply from one of the nearby rooms.

"Let's go see these kids," she barked at Sawyer over her shoulder as she headed to the room.

Organized chaos was continuing around him. Piles upon piles of paper were being pulled from boxes, new phones were appearing and being plugged in all around him. He recognized a couple of the faces—a few of the epidemiologists and contact tracers—standing with their clipboards at the ready.

He could hear the voices of the admin staff around him. "No, put it here. Callie's very particular about paperwork. Put the algorithms up on the walls, in the treatments rooms and outside the patient rooms. Everyone has to follow them to the letter."

So, she was a rules-and-regulations girl? This was about to get interesting.

He wandered over to the room. Callie was standing in her bra and pants, opening a clean set of regulation pale pink scrubs. Last time he'd worn them they'd been green. Obviously a new addition to the DPA repertoire.

The sight made him catch his breath. It was amazing what could lurk beneath those stuffy blue suits and pointy shoes. The suit was lying in a crumpled heap on the ground, discarded as if it were worthless when it easily clocked in at over a thousand dollars. He could see the label from here. Maybe Miss Hoity-Toity did have some redeeming features after all.

Her skin was lightly tanned, with some white strap marks on her shoulders barely covered by her bra. She was a matching-set girl. Pale lilac satin. But she didn't have her back to him so from this angle he couldn't tell if she favored briefs or a thong...

Her stomach wasn't washboard flat like some women he'd known. It was gently rounded, proving to him that she wasn't a woman who lived on salad alone. But the most intriguing thing about her was the pale white scar trailing down the outside of her leg. Where had that come from? It might be interesting to find out. His eyes lifted a little higher. And as for her breasts...

"Quit staring at me." She pulled on her scrub trousers. "You're a doctor. Apparently you've seen it all before." She tossed him a hat. "And get that mop of yours hidden."

She pulled her scrub top over her head and knelt in the corner next to her bag. She seemed completely unaffected by his gawping. Just as well really.

Sawyer reluctantly pulled on the hat and a disposable pale yellow isolation gown over his scrubs. She appeared at his side a few seconds later as he struggled to tuck his hair inside the slightly too big cap.

"Want one of these?" She waved a bobby pin under his nose with a twinkle in her eye. She was laughing at him.

"Won't you need all of them to pull back that one side of your bad haircut?"

She flung a regulation mask at him. "Ha. Ha. Now, let's go."

They walked down the corridor where the lights were still dimmed. She paused outside the door, her hand resting lightly on his arm.

"Let's clarify before we go in. How many staff have been in contact with these kids?"

He nodded. He would probably answer these questions a dozen times today. "Main contact has been myself and Alison, one of our nurses. We're estimating they were only in the waiting room around ten minutes. One of the triage nurses moved them through to a room quickly as the kids were pretty sick."

Her eyebrows rose above her mask. "I take it that you've continued to limit the contact to yourselves?"

"Ah, about that."

"What?" Her expression had changed in an instant. Her eyes had narrowed and her glare hardened.

"There's a problem."

"What kind of problem?"

"Alison's pregnant. Eighteen weeks."

She let out an expression that wasn't at all ladylike. He hadn't known she had it in her.

"Exactly. I haven't let her go back in. She's adamant. Says there's no point exposing anyone else to something she's already breathed in anyway. But I wasn't having any of it."

He could see her brain racing. There was the tiniest flicker of panic under that mask. "But the vaccine…"

He touched her shoulder. "I know. We don't know the effects it could have on a fetus." He shrugged. "I don't know if you've come up with any new research in the last six years, but I wouldn't want to be the doctor to give it to her."

She nodded. "Leave it with me. I'll take it up with the team." She turned back to the room. "We need to get some samples."

"It's already done."

"What?" She whipped around. "Why didn't you say so?"

He sighed. "What do you think I've been doing these last few hours? I'm not that far out of the loop that I don't know how to take samples. Besides, the kids were used to me. It was better that I did it."

She nodded, albeit reluctantly. "And the parents?"

"I've taken samples from them too. They're all packaged and ready to go. Let's find out what we're dealing with."

"I want to see the kids first."

Now she was annoying him. "You think I made their spots up? Drew them on their faces and arms?"

"Of course I don't. But, like or not, I'm the doctor in charge here. I need to see the spots for myself. Get some better pictures than the ones snapped on your phone. I need to be clear that you've ruled out everything."

She was only saying what he would have said himself a few years ago. She was doing things by the book. But in his eyes, doing things by the book was wasting time. That was why he hadn't bothered with the call to the state department. Best to go right to the source.

And this family might not have that time to waste. Just like his hadn't.

It made him mad. Irrationally mad. And it didn't matter that the voices in his head were telling him that. Because he wasn't listening.

"For goodness' sake. Don't you have any confidence in my abilities? I've been doing this job since you were in kindergarten. I could run rings around you!"

She pushed her face up next to his. If it weren't for the masks, their noses would be practically touching. "You're not quite that old, Matt Sawyer. And it doesn't matter what I think about your doctoring abilities. I'm in charge here. Not you. We've already established you don't work for the DPA any more and I do. You know how things work. You know the procedures and protocols. You might not have followed them but I do. To the letter." She put her hand on the door. "Now, do your job, Dr. Sawyer. Take me in there and introduce me to the parents."

CALLIE LEANED BACK against the wall in the sluice room. She'd just pulled off her disposable clothing and mask and dispensed with them in line with all the infection control protocols.

She let the temperature of the cool concrete seep through her thin scrub top. Thank goodness. With the air-conditioning turned off this place was getting warm. Too warm. Why couldn't this outbreak have happened in the middle of the winter, when Chicago was knee deep in snow, instead of when it was the height of summer? It could have made things a whole lot simpler for them. It could also have made the E.R. a whole lot quieter.

Those kids were sick. Sawyer hadn't been kidding. They were *really* sick. She'd really prefer it if they could be in a pediatric intensive care unit, but right now that was out of the question.

And even though it seemed like madness, in a few minutes' time she was going to have to inoculate them and their parents with the smallpox vaccine.

Then she was going to have to deal with the staff, herself included.

There wasn't time to waste. The laboratory samples were just away. It could be anything up to forty-eight hours before they had even a partial diagnosis and seven days before a definitive diagnosis. She didn't want to wait that long.

She knew that would cause problems with Sawyer. He would want to wait—to be sure before they inflicted a vaccine with known side-effects on people who might not be at risk. But she'd already had that conversation with her boss, Evan Hunter. He'd told her to make the decision on the best information available. And she had.

She wrinkled her nose, trying to picture the relationship between the man she'd just met and Callum Ferguson, a doctor for whom she had the utmost respect. How on earth had these two ever gotten along? It just didn't seem feasible.

She knew that Sawyer had lost his pregnant wife on a mission. That must have been devastating. But to walk away from his life and his career? Why would anyone do that? Had he been grief stricken? Had he been depressed?

And more to the point, how was he now? Was he reliable enough to trust his judgment on how best to proceed? Because right now what she really needed was partner in crime, not an outright enemy.

If only Callum were here. He knew how to handle Sawyer. She wouldn't have needed to have dealt with any of this.

Her fingers fell to her leg—to her scar. It had started to itch. Just as it always did when she was under stress. She took a deep breath.

She'd made a decision. Now it was time to face the fallout.

"Are you crazy?"

"No. I'm not crazy. I've already spoke to my boss at the DPA. Funnily enough, he didn't want you sitting in on that conference call. It seems your reputation has preceded you."

"I don't care about my reputation—"

"Obviously."

"I care about these staff."

He spun around as the crates were wheeled into the treatment room and the vaccine started to be unloaded. One of the contact tracers came up and mumbled in her ear, "We're going to start with a limited number of people affected. The kids, their parents, Dr. Sawyer, yourself and these other four members of staff who've had limited contact."

"What about Alison?"

The contact tracer hesitated, looking from one to the other. "That's not my decision," he said as he spun away.

Callie swallowed. She could do with something cool to drink, her throat was dry and scratchy. "Alison will have to make her own decision on the vaccine. There isn't enough data for us to give her reliable information."

She saw the look on his face. He looked haunted. As if he'd just seen a ghost from the past. Was this what had happened to his wife? Had she been exposed to something that couldn't be treated because of her pregnancy? This might all be too close to home for Matt Sawyer.

"Okay." He ran his fingers through his hair. It hadn't got any better now it had been released from the cap. In fact, it seemed to have grown even longer. "Do me a favor?"

She lifted her head from the clipboard she was scribbling on. "What?"

"Let me be the one to talk to Alison about it. If there hasn't been any more research in the last six years, then I'm as up to date as you are."

She took a deep breath. She didn't know this guy well enough to know how he would handle this. He was obviously worried about his colleague. But was that all? And would his past experience affect his professional judgment?

"You can't recommend it one way or the other, you understand that, don't you?"

She could tell he wanted to snap at her. To tell her where to go. But something made him bite his tongue. "I can be impartial. I'll give her all the facts and let her make her own decision. It will come better from someone she knows."

Callie nodded. He was right. The smallpox vaccine came with a whole host of issues. She was already questioning some of the decisions that she'd made.

Alison was at the end of the corridor in a room on her own, partly for her own protection and partly for the protection of others. She'd been in direct contact with the disease—without any mask to limit the spread of the infection. In theory, because she hadn't had prolonged exposure in a confined space, she should be at low risk. But she'd also been exposed to—and had touched—the erupting spots. The most infectious element of the disease. Pregnant or not, she had to be assessed as being at risk. "You know I have to do this, right?"

He was glaring at her, his head shaking almost imperceptibly—as if it was an involuntary act.

"We have the three major diagnostic criteria for smallpox. This is a high-risk category. Those parents look sick already. They're probably in the prodromal stage of the disease."

The implication in the air was there, hanging between them. If they waited, it could result in more casualties and the DPA being slaughtered by the media for wasting time. That was the last thing anyone wanted.

"Callie? We have a problem."

Both heads turned to the DPA contact tracer standing at the door. "What is it, Hugo?"

She stepped forward and took the clipboard from his hand.

"It's the parents. They can't say for sure if the rash came out during or after the plane trip home."

"You're joking, right?" Callie felt the hackles rise on the back of her neck. This was one of the most crucial pieces of information they needed. Once the rash was out, the person was infectious. This was the difference between three hundred passengers on a plane being at risk or not.

Hugo looked pale. "Mrs. Keating is sure they didn't have a rash before they got on the plane. And she's almost sure they didn't have it on the plane, because the kids slept most of the journey. They went straight home and put the kids to bed—she didn't even get them changed. It wasn't until the next day she noticed the rash, but it could have been there on the plane."

Callie cringed, as Sawyer read her mind. "Prodromal stage. Did they sleep because they were developing the disease or did they sleep because it was a long flight?" He put a hand on Hugo's shoulder. "You have to establish if she noticed either of the kids having a fever during the journey." He paused, then added, "And make sure they didn't change planes anywhere." Sawyer rolled his eyes to the ceiling, "Or our contact tracing will become a nightmare."

Hugo nodded and disappeared back through the door.

Sawyer watched her as she fiddled with the clips in her hair. She was consulting the plan again. There seemed to be one in every room he entered. A list of procedures. A multitude of flow charts.

She didn't like it when things weren't exactly to plan. Then again, she'd never been in charge of an epidemic before.

He could be doing so much more for her. He could be talking her through all this, helping her out. Liaising more with the team back at the DPA—even if that did mean dealing with Evan Hunter.

He knew all this stuff inside out and back to front.

But he just couldn't.

It didn't matter that he was stuck in the middle of all this. There was a line he didn't want to cross. He had to take a step back. He had to focus on the sick children.

He picked up another disposable gown and mask. "The IV fluids on the kids probably need changing. I'm going to go and check on them." He paused and turned his head just as he left. "You need to go and make an announcement to all the staff. You need to bring them up to date on the information that you have." He hesitated, then added something else.

"It's not only the natives that will be getting restless. We've got patients here who've been quarantined. They won't understand what's going on. They won't know what to tell their relatives."

She gave the slightest nod, as if the thought of what she was going to say was pressing down on her shoulders. He almost withered. "There's a public address system at the front desk—use that."

His phone beeped and he headed out of the room and down the corridor, pulling the phone from his pocket.

Violet.

He should have known.

No, he should have texted her first. She must be frantic.

He flicked the switch to silent and pushed it back into his pocket. She would just have to wait. He would deal with her later.

CALLIE COULD HEAR the raised voices as she strode down the corridor. "Why can't I leave? I'm fine. If I stay here, I'll get sick. You can't make me stay!"

It was inevitable. People always reacted like this when there was an outbreak. It was human nature.

The hard part was that Callie didn't want to be here any more than they did. But she couldn't exactly say that, could she?

The reality check was starting to sink in. She was in a strange city, in the middle of a possible outbreak of a disease that had supposedly been eradicated. She wasn't ready for this. If she closed her eyes for just a second, she could see Isabel in the middle of all this. This had been her dream from childhood—to work at the DPA at the cutting edge of infectious disease. She wouldn't be feeling like this. She wouldn't be feeling sick to her stomach and wanting to go and hide in a corner. Isabel would be center stage, running everything with a precise touch.

But Isabel wasn't here.

And that was Callie's fault. Her beautiful older sister had died six years earlier. Callie had been behind the wheel of their old car, taking a corner too fast—straight into the path of someone on the wrong side of the road. If only she hadn't been distracted—been fighting with her sister. Over something and nothing.

That was the thing that twisted the most. It was the same argument they'd had for years. Pizza or burgers. Something ridiculous. Something meaningless. How pathetic.

She fixed her gaze on the scene ahead. Isabel would know exactly how to handle a man like Sawyer. She would have had him eating out of her hand in five minutes flat.

Okay, maybe not five minutes.

Sawyer probably wasn't the type.

But, then, Isabel had been a people person. She'd known how to respond to people, she'd known how to work a crowd. All the things that Callie didn't have a clue about.

The voices were rising. Things were reaching a crescendo.

It was time to step up. Whether she liked it or not, it was time to take charge.

She pushed her way through the crowd around the desk and jumped up onto the reception area desk. "Is this the PA system?"

The clerk gave her a nod as she picked up the microphone and held it to her mouth. Adrenaline was starting to course through her system. All eyes were on her. She could do this. She pressed the button on the microphone and it let out a squeal from automatic feedback. Anyone who hadn't been listening before was certainly listening now.

"Hi, everyone. I'm sure you know I'm Callie Turner from the DPA. Let me bring you up to speed."

The anxiety in the room was palpable. The eyes staring at her were full of fear.

"You all know that we're dealing with two suspected cases of smallpox. That's the reason why the E.R. has been closed and we've enforced a quarantine. The samples have been collected and sent to the DPA lab for identification. The laboratory tests for smallpox are complicated and time-consuming. We should hear back in around forty-eight hours what type of virus it is—whether it's a type of pox or not—but it takes longer to identify what strain of virus it is. That can take anything up to seven days. So, until we know if it's a pox or not, we need to stay here. We need to try and contain this virus."

"I don't want to be in isolation," one of the men shouted.

"You're not," Callie said quickly. "You're quarantined—there's a difference. Isolation means separating people who are ill with a contagious disease from healthy people. The children who are affected have been isolated. Quarantine restricts the movement of people who have been exposed to someone or something, to see if they will become ill. That's what we're doing with all of you." Her hand stretched out across the room.

She could still feel the tension. Anxious glances being exchanged between staff and patients. She could see the questions forming on their lips. Best to keep going.

She tried to keep her voice calm. "The incubation period for smallpox is around twelve days but it can range from seven to seventeen days. Smallpox is spread person to person by droplet transmission. It can also be spread by contact with pustules or rash lesions or contaminated clothing or bedding.

"A person with smallpox is considered infectious when the rash appears, but at the moment we're going to consider any affected person infectious from the onset of fever. This should help us control any outbreak. It's important to remember that only close contacts—those who were within six or seven feet of the infectious person should be at risk."

She was talking too quickly, trying to put out too much information at once. She was hoping and praying that someone wouldn't pick up on the fact that they could be quarantined together for seventeen days.

"Should? What do you mean, 'should'? Don't you know?"

Callie took a deep breath. She didn't blame people for being angry. She would be angry too. But as she opened her mouth to speak, Sawyer got in there first. He'd appeared out of nowhere, stepping up alongside her, his hand closing over hers as he took the PA microphone from her.

"This isn't like some disaster movie, folks. A person with smallpox doesn't walk, coughing and spluttering, through a crowd and infect everyone around them. For a start, most people infected with smallpox don't cough anyway. And the last data available from the DPA shows that the average person affected can infect around five to seven people. And those would only be the close contacts around them. Let's not panic. Let's keep this in perspective."

She was watching him, her breath caught her in throat. He was doing what *she* should be doing. He was keeping calm and giving them clear and easy-to-understand information.

Part of her felt angry. And part of her felt relief.

She was out of her depth and she knew it.

The DPA was a big place. And she was a good doctor—when she was part of a team. But as a leader? Not so much.

Put her in a room with a pile of paperwork and she was the best. Methodical, good at interpreting the practical applications of a plan.

She could do the patient stuff—she could, obviously, or she wouldn't have made it through medical school or her residency. Actually, some of it she had loved. But she'd enjoyed the one-to-one patient contacts, patients a physician could take time with, understand their condition and give them long-term advice. Not the hurried, rushed, wide perspective of the DPA.

But, then, the DPA had been Isabel's dream, not hers. She'd never wanted this for herself.

And now? She was stuck with it.

"So, that's it folks. We'll let you know as soon as we hear back from the labs. In the meantime, we'll have arrangements in place to make everyone more comfortable with the facilities we have here." He raised his eyebrows at her. "It could be that in a few hours we move to somewhere more suitable?"

She nodded wordlessly. He must have known that Callum would already have put the wheels in motion to set up a category C facility for containment.

"In the meantime, follow the infection control procedures on the walls around you. Take a deep breath and show a little patience. We're all scared." He pointed at the figures lining the walls with their clipboards, "It's important we help these guys out. Tell them everything you know." He looked back at Callie. She was sure that right now she must resemble a deer caught in a set of headlights. "And if you have any questions, Dr. Turner is in charge. That's it for now."

He jumped off the table and headed back down the corridor.

The room was quieter now, the shouting had stopped.

Her legs were trembling and she grabbed hold of a hand offered to her as she climbed down off the table. Heads were down, people working away, going about their business. One of the security guards was helping one of the nursing aides carry linen through to another room to help set up some beds.

Callie knew she couldn't leave this. She knew she had to talk to him. Even though he was trying to put some space between them.

"Sawyer." She was breathless, running down the corridor after him. "I just wanted to say thank you. For back there."

His green eyes fixed on hers, just for a second, before they flitted away and he ran his fingers through that hair again. Her heart clenched, even though she couldn't understand why. He was exasperated with her. "That was a one-off, Callie. Don't count on me to help you again." He turned and strode back down the corridor, leaving her standing there.

Alone.

CHAPTER THREE

"You need to manage things better." He couldn't help it. There were probably a million other ways to put this more delicately, but Sawyer didn't have time to think about nicer words.

Her head shot upwards. There it was—that rabbit-in-the-headlights look again from her.

He hated it. Because it made his stomach churn. He didn't know whether to be irritated by it or whether he really wanted to go over and give her a quick hug.

"What on earth do you mean, *'manage things better'*?" She made quote marks in the air with her fingers as she repeated his words back to him. He could see the lines across her brow. She was tired and she was stressed. And he understood that. It was part and parcel of the job at the DPA.

He could feel his lips turn upwards. She looked even prettier when she was cross.

"What are you smirking at?" She stood up from behind the desk. A desk lost under a multitude of piles of papers—no doubt more copies of plans and protocols. A few sheets scattered as she stood.

His smile broadened. He could tell she really wanted to stop and pick them up.

She was in front of him now, her hands on her hips. "What?"

He liked that. Sometimes she just got straight to the point. No skirting around the edge of things.

He gestured to the door behind him. "You need to clarify some things about the vaccination. There are still a lot of questions out there."

She sighed and ran her fingers through the short side of her hair. "I know. I'll get to it. I've got a million and one things to deal with." Her eyes flickered in the direction of the hidden desk.

"Then delegate."

She started, as if the thought of actually delegating horrified her.

"But I'm responsible—"

"And you need to be visible. You need to be seen. You have to be on the floor—not stuck in some office. You can make your decisions out there, not from behind a desk."

He could see her brain ticking, thinking over his suggestions. Truth be told, she'd been delegating from the minute she'd walked in the door—just not the important stuff.

"And you need to do something about Alison."

Her eyes narrowed. "I thought you wanted to deal with Alison."

"And I have—we've had the discussion about the vaccine. She hasn't decided what to do yet, but I think she'll opt on the side of caution and say no."

"So what's the problem?" She'd started to walk back over to the desk.

"The problem is she's a nurse. She's stuck in a room at the bottom of the corridor. Isolated. Quarantined—"

"You know that's not the case."

He touched her shoulder. "But she doesn't. You need to tell people, explain to them what the difference is. You explained that to the masses—but you need didn't explain it to her. She's in there frightened and alone. You need to communicate better." He could feel her bristle under his touch. "Alison needs to do something. I understand you think she might have been exposed but you can't leave her sitting there for hours on end." He picked up a pile of papers from the desk. "Give her a list of phone calls to make for you. Let her do some of the specialized phone contact tracing."

"She can't do that. That's a special skill. You need of hours of training to do that properly," she snapped.

He could feel the frustration rising in his chest. "It's only a list of questions! She's an intelligent human being. Give her something to do. Something to take her mind off things."

He grabbed the first random thought that entered his head. "Let her organize the food, then! Something—anything—to stop her thinking that if she hadn't come to work this morning she wouldn't have risked the life of her baby."

He could see the realization fall on her face. And suddenly he understood.

She was a big-picture girl. The perfect person for public health. She didn't individualize, or personalize, the other side of the job. The things that affected normal people.

He took a deep breath. He wasn't trying to make this harder for her. He knew she'd been thrown in at the deep end.

Part of him wanted to offer to take over, even though he knew that would never be allowed to. And part of him still wanted to run for the hills.

He hated this. Everything about this situation grated on him. He'd thought he'd be safe.

He'd thought he'd distanced himself enough to never to be in a situation like this again. How often did an E.R. notify an outbreak on this scale? Rarely.

And this type of disease? Well, let's face it, not in the last thirty or forty years.

No matter what his brain told him, he would not allow himself to be dragged in. Even though he was right in the middle of everything he needed to keep some distance. He needed *not* to have responsibility for this outbreak.

She was hesitating. He could see it written all over her face. Then the decision was made. It was almost as if he could see a little light go on behind her eyes.

She looked him square in the eye. "You're right. I can give her something to do. Something that means she's not at risk to herself or anyone else around her." She picked up a list from her desk. "She can order the food supplies, linen supplies and any extra medical supplies that we might need. The food's turned into a bit of a nightmare in the last few hours." She picked up a hefty manual from her desk, ripped out a few sheets and attached them to a red clipboard. "This will tell her everything she needs to know about how to arrange the delivery of supplies that keeps all parties safe."

Her eyes swept around the room.

It was almost as if once she'd made a decision, that was it. She was ready. She was organized. The courage of her convictions took her forward. She could be great at this job, if only she had confidence in her abilities. And she would get that. It would just take a few years.

A few years that she would normally have had in the DPA, working with their most experienced doctors.

His thoughts went back to Callum and he glanced at his watch. "I need to make a phone call."

Her hand rested on his arm. The warmth of her fingers stopped him dead.

"I need you to do one more thing for me before you go."

She was looking at him with those big eyes. The ones

he preferred not to have contact with. This was where his gut twisted and he wanted to say no. Say no to anything that would drag him further into this mess.

There was a new edge to her voice, a new determination. She handed him a file from the desk. "I need you to look over this with an independent eye. You've been out of the DPA long enough to make an assessment."

He was confused now. What was she talking about? Instinctively, his hand reached out for the file.

"You told me to delegate. Everyone thought the next smallpox outbreak would be deliberate—a terrorist act. Nothing we've seen here supports that. All the information from the parents and contacts would lead me to suggest this was a natural outbreak—however impossible or improbable that may be."

He was nodding slowly. It was one of the first things that Callum had asked him. It was one of the most immediate priorities for the DPA: to try and determine the source.

"I need you to look over the rest of the evidence the contact tracers have collected. I have to phone Evan Hunter in the next half-hour. It's my professional opinion that this isn't a terrorist act." Her voice was wavering slightly. This was one of the most crucial decisions she would make in her lead role for the DPA.

Everything she was saying made sense and he knew that she would have read and analyzed the evidence to the best of her abilities. But time was pressing. If there was any threat to the general population, they had to know now.

He understood what this meant to her. And he understood why she was asking him.

It wasn't just that he'd told her to delegate. It was that this could impact on everything. The actions and reactions the world would have to this outbreak.

She had to be right.

She had to be sure.

If Callum had been here, this would have been on his head. But even then, he would have had Callie to bat things back and forth with. To agree with his decision-making.

She didn't have that.

She didn't have anyone.

So she was asking the one person here who might have those skills.

He laid his hand over hers. "I'll make the phone call. It will take two minutes and then I'll close this office door and look over all this information. If I have even a shadow of a doubt, I'll let you know."

Her shoulders sagged just a little. As if she'd just managed to disperse a little of their weight. "Thank you," she said as she walked out the door.

Sawyer watched her leave, trying not to look at her rear view in the pink scrubs. He couldn't work out what was going on. One minute she was driving him crazy. The next?

He slumped back in the chair a little, the mound of paper in front of him looking less than enticing. His phone slipped from his pocket and clattered to the floor.

It was like an alarm clock going off in his head.

Violet. He really needed to contact Violet.

His sister worked at the DPA and must be going crazy. She would have heard his name bandied about by now and know that he must be in the middle of all this.

His phone had been switched to silent for the last few hours and he glanced at the screen and cringed. He'd known as soon as he'd called the DPA that his number would have been logged in their system.

It made sense that she'd tried to get in touch with him— after all, he'd changed his number numerous times in the last few years—only getting in touch when he could face it.

He really didn't want to know how many missed calls and text messages he'd had from her. It just made him feel even guiltier.

When his wife had died and he'd walked away from the DPA, he'd also more or less walked away from his family.

It had been the only way he could cope.

He couldn't bear to have any reminders of Helen, his wife. It had been just too much. He'd needed time. He'd needed space.

On occasion—when he'd felt guilty enough—he'd send Violet a text just to let her know that he was safe. Nothing more. Nothing less.

She deserved better and he knew that. He just hadn't been in a position to give it.

The one saving grace was that no one in the DPA knew they were related. She'd started just after he'd left. And the last thing any new doctor needed was to live in the shadow of the family black sheep.

He turned the phone over in his hands and looked at his watch. The mountain of paper on the desk seemed to have mysteriously multiplied in the last few minutes.

He would phone Violet. He would.

But right now time was critical. He had to do this first.

CALLIE WAS MAD.

But she was trying not to show it.

Everything he'd said was right.

The doctor who was apparently bad-tempered and temperamental was making her feel as if she was the problem and not him.

The worst thing was he'd sounded clear-headed and rational. He was right, she did need to delegate. No matter how alien the concept seemed to her.

So she'd delegated the most obvious duty to him. Evan Hunter would have a fit.

But she was in charge here. Not him. And since Callum wasn't here, she had to rely on the one member of staff who had some experience in this area—whether Evan Hunter liked it or not.

"Callie?"

She'd reached the treatment room. One of the second-year residents was emptying the refrigerated container of vaccines.

"What is it?"

"How many of these do you want me to draw up?"

She shook her head. "None—yet." She glanced at the face of the resident, who was obviously worried about doing anything wrong. A few years ago that would have been her.

"Have you used the ring vaccination concept before?"

The resident shook her head.

In the midst of all this madness Callie had to remember she had a responsibility to teach. To help the staff around her learn their roles. To lead by example.

The words started repeating to a rhythm in her head.

"Ring vaccination controls an outbreak by vaccinating and monitoring a ring of people around each infected individual. The idea is to form a buffer of immune individuals to prevent the spread of the disease. It's a way of containment."

"And it works effectively?"

Callie gave a small smile. "We thought it did. Ring vaccination was held as essential in the eradication of smallpox. For the vast majority of people, getting the smallpox vaccine within three days of exposure will significantly lesson the severity of the symptoms."

"What about people who were vaccinated before against smallpox? Aren't they already protected?"

Callie shook her head. "It's a common misconception. Why do you ask?"

"One of the men in the waiting room said he'd had the vaccination as a child and he wouldn't need anything."

Callie smiled. "Last time ring vaccination was used for smallpox was in the late seventies. But if he was vaccinated then, he would only have had protection for between three and five years. There might still be some antibodies in his blood but we can't assume anything."

"Would we vaccinate him again?"

"It depends where he falls at risk. In the first instance, we vaccinate anyone who has been, or may have been, exposed to someone who has the infection."

"He was sitting next to the family in the waiting room."

Callie nodded. There was so much about this that wasn't written entirely in stone and open to interpretation. "Then we need to assess how much contact he had with the family—and for how long."

"And that's where all the guessing games start."

The deep voice at the door made her head jerk up. Sawyer was standing with her file in his hand. He walked over and held it out towards her. "You're right, Callie. It didn't take long to review the information." He shook his head. "There's absolutely nothing there to hint at anything other than a natural outbreak—the very thing the DPA declared could never happen."

The sense of relief that rushed over her body was instant. She'd been scared. Scared that she'd missed something—that she'd overlooked something important. Something her sister would never have done.

It was the first time today she actually felt as if she might be doing a good job.

She took the file from his hand. "I guess we don't know everything, then," she murmured.

He gave her a lazy smile and raised one eyebrow at her. "Really? You mean the DPA hasn't managed to find its way into every corner of the universe to see if there are any deadly diseases left?"

Her eyes were scanning the sheets in front of her. She shrugged. "It makes sense. The Keatings said that it was the first time the locals had come into contact with outsiders."

"First contact. Sounds much sexier than it should."

She raised her eyebrows at him. "Sounds like a whole can of worms."

The resident lowered her head and busied herself in the corner of the room. In some ways Callie wanted to do that too.

She wanted to take herself out of the range of Sawyer's impenetrable stare. It was making her hair stand on end and sending weird tingles down her spine.

She felt like a high-school teenager on prom night, not an experienced doctor in the midst of an emergency situation.

She picked up one of the vials on the countertop. "I guess I should lead by example."

He was at her side in an instant. "What do you mean?"

"If I'm going to recommend first-line vaccination, I guess I should go first."

"Are you sure about this?"

Callie almost laughed out loud. Was he joking? "Of course I'm not sure. But I've got to base this on the evidence that I've got, no matter how imperfect it is. If this is smallpox, I've a duty of care to protect others and contain the virus. You, me, the parents—anyone else assessed as 'at risk' should be vaccinated."

She picked up the diluent and delivered it swiftly into the container holding the dried vaccine. Her hands rolled the vial between her palms, watching the liquid oscillate back and forth.

"I think you should wait. I think we should have a definite diagnosis before we start vaccinating."

She nodded. In an ideal world that made sense. But this wasn't an ideal world. It was a completely imperfect situation. If she hesitated, she put people at risk.

This was her decision. The buck stopped with her.

"There are risks attached to any vaccine but this vaccine was widely used and we've got a lot of data on the issues raised. I've reviewed our medical notes. There's nothing in my history, your history or the parents' that would prevent vaccination. The only issue is Alison—and she's already told me she's decided against it."

There was an expression on his face she couldn't fathom. Something flickering behind his eyes, as if the thoughts in his head were about to combust.

This man was almost unreadable.

Was he relieved or mad? Did he want Alison to have the vaccine and put her baby at risk? Or did he want her to take her chances without?

Obviously, she knew the outcome—but that didn't help here.

Had Sawyer's wife been in similar circumstances and avoided a vaccine because she had been pregnant? Or had she taken a vaccine—that was untried and untested on pregnant women—with devastating consequences?

It was almost as if he'd gone on autopilot. He washed his hands, lifted a syringe and needle and tipped up the vial, plunging the needle inside and extracting the vaccine. "If this is what you want, let's do it."

She was stunned. She'd thought he was going to refuse—going to argue with her some more and storm off. This was the last thing she'd expected.

"Are you going to get vaccinated?"

He nodded almost imperceptibly. "Of course."

She tilted her head and raised her eyebrows at him, the question obvious.

"I'm working on the assumption you're going to say that only vaccinated personnel can work with the kids. These kids are mine. They're *my* patients. I won't let you keep me out. And if a vaccine is what it takes…" he shrugged "…so be it."

The words were stuck in her throat now.

The thing that seemed to pass her by. The people thing.

The thing she really wanted to concentrate on, but her public health role wouldn't let her. She'd learned over the years just to lock it away in a corner of her mind.

But it was the thing that was on the forefront of *his* mind. And it was affecting his reactions. If only she could have the same freedom.

He was prepared to take a vaccine with known side-effects in order to keep looking after these children.

And no matter how hard she tried not to, she had to admire him for it.

There was only one thing she could do.

She turned her arm towards him. "Let's do it." Her voice sounded confident, the way she wanted to appear to the outside world. Her insides were currently mush.

His finger ran down the outside of her upper arm. Totally unexpected. The lightest of touches. She heard his intake of breath before he went back to standard technique and pinched her skin.

It was over in the blink of an eye. She never even felt the bifurcated needle penetrate her skin. It wasn't like a traditional shot and she felt the needle prick her skin a number of times in a few seconds before it was quickly removed and disposed of.

"You know this won't be pretty, don't you?"

She nodded, automatically reaching up and rubbing her arm. "I know what to expect. A red and itchy bump in a few days…" she rolled her eyes "…a delightful pus-filled blister in another week and then a scab."

She washed her hands at the sink as he drew up another dose of vaccine and handed it to her, pulling his scrub sleeve up above his shoulder. She could feel herself hesitate, taking in his defined deltoid and biceps muscles. Did Sawyer work out? He didn't seem the type.

"Something wrong?"

"What? No." She could feel the color flooding into her cheeks. How embarrassing. He hadn't given her arm a second glance.

Concentrate. Focus. He was smirking at her again, almost as if he could see exactly what she was thinking.

She scowled, pinched his arm and injected him, delivering the vaccine in an instant. It was as quick as she could get this over and done with, so she could turn her back to dispose of the syringe.

"Ouch." He was rubbing his arm in mock horror. "It's all in the technique, you know."

"Yeah, yeah." She started washing her hands again. "You're not supposed to rub your arm, you know."

He shrugged. "Everyone does. It's an automatic response. Being a doctor doesn't make me any different." His arm was still exposed, and this time, instead of focusing on the muscle, her eyes focused on the skin.

It was full of little pock marks and lumps and bumps. The obvious flat scar from a BCG vaccination. He followed her eyes and gave her a grin. "A lifetime's work. Chicken pox as a child, then a whole career's worth of DPA vaccinations."

She pulled up her other sleeve. "Snap."

His finger touched her skin again and she felt herself suck in her breath as it ran over her BCG scar. He was standing just a little too close for comfort but seemed completely unaffected.

He turned and smiled at her. "At least you don't have chicken pox scars." Maybe it was the lazy way he said it or the way his smile seemed kind of sexy.

"Oh, I do. Just can't show them in public." She couldn't help it. The words were out before she had time to think about them. She was flirting. She was *flirting* with him. What was wrong with her?

That was the kind of response that her sister might have given. The kind of response that had men eating out of the palm of her hand and following Isabel's butt with their eyes as she walked down the hallway.

But this was so *not* a Callie response.

What was she thinking of?

It wasn't that she was some shy, retiring virgin. She'd been on plenty of dates and had a number of relationships over the years. But she wasn't the type of girl who walked into a bar and flirted with a man. She was the kind of girl who met a man in a class or in a library, and went for a few quiet drinks before there was any touching, any kissing.

She wasn't used to being unnerved by a man. To find herself flustered and blushing around him. It made her cringe.

But Sawyer seemed immune. Maybe women flirted with him all the time? He just gave her a little wink and crossed the room. Now he was in midconversation with the second-year resident, explaining where some of the supplies were kept and how to access them.

He obviously didn't feel heat rising up the back of his neck to make him feel uncomfortable.

She took a deep breath and moved. Out to the madness

of the corridor, where the incessant sound of phones ringing must be driving everyone mad.

She picked up the nearest one as she passed. The voice made her stop in her tracks.

"Callie? Is that you?"

Evan Hunter. It must be killing him to be stuck at Headquarters instead of being in the thick of things.

"Well?" His abrupt tone was hardly welcoming.

It was beginning to annoy her. Every phone call she'd had from this man had started with him snapping at her and shouting orders. Wasn't he supposed to be supporting her?

He knew she'd been flung in at the deep end.

"Hold on." She set down the phone, ignoring the expletives she could hear him yelling as she walked over to the whiteboard on the wall. The DPA team was well trained. Every piece of relevant information and the most up-to-date data was right in front of her. She didn't need to run around the department asking a barrage of questions.

She watched as a member of staff rubbed one number off the board and replaced it with another. The potential 'at risk' group was now at five. Not bad at all.

A list of queries had appeared around the containment facility. She would need to get onto them straight away.

The only glaring piece of information that was missing was around the plane. There was the number of passengers, with the number of contact details obtained. Three hundred passengers—with contact details for only seventy-six.

This was taking up too much of her team's time. They needed to deal with the issues around the containment facility. It was time to delegate.

She could feel her arm tremble slightly as she picked up the phone again. Isabel would have been fit for Evan

Hunter. She would have chewed him up and spat him out. It was time to embrace some of her sister's personality traits.

"Evan?"

"What on earth were you doing? When I call I expect—"

She cut him off straight away. "What have I been doing? What have *I* been doing? I've just been getting my smallpox vaccination and I've just inoculated another member of staff. I've been assessing our most up-to-date information to determine whether or not this is a terrorist attack." She glanced at the clock. "Information I wasn't due to present to you for another eight minutes. And, incidentally, my professional opinion is that it's not.

"I've also been trying to keep the staff and patients here calm and informed about what's going on. I'm trying to find out how Callum is but no one will tell me anything. I'm having problems with the containment facility. We can't make all the contacts for the plane passengers." She was starting to count things off on her fingers.

"We're just about to vaccinate those exposed—but we have a pregnant nurse to consider. Oh, and Sawyer is driving me crazy." She took a deep breath. "So, how's your day going, Evan?" She couldn't help it. The more she spoke, the more she felt swamped, the more she felt angry that Callum wasn't at her side. The more she realized that Evan Hunter, boss or not, should be doing more to help her, not adding to the problems.

The silence at the end of the phone was deafening. Her heart rate quickened. Had she just got herself sacked?

No. How could he? Not when she was in the middle of all this.

She heard him clear his throat. "Point made."

She was shocked. "What?"

"Point made, Callie. What do you need?"

For a second she couldn't speak. *What did she need?* Apart from getting out of here?

"I need you to take over the plane contacts. We've got three hundred passengers and only contact details for seventy-six. I also need you to take over the viable threat assessment for these people as our details are sketchy. I'll get one of the contact tracers and epidemiologists to conference-call you." Isabel used to quote the English expression *"In for a penny, in for a pound"* before she took a risk. Somehow, it seemed apt.

"Fine. I can do that. Anything else?"

She felt like a girl in a fancy department store on a fifty percent sale day. But nothing else screamed out at her. "Can you magic me up some pediatric ICU facilities?"

"That might be a little tricky."

"Didn't think so. Never mind. I'll let you know if I need anything else. When can I expect to hear from the lab?"

"That's what I wanted to tell you."

Oops. She almost felt bad for being snarky with him.

"The samples have been received and are being processed. It's only been a couple of hours. In another ten we should be able to tell you which virus type it is. That will give us something to work with."

She nodded as she scribbled notes. "That's great."

"And, Callie?"

"Yes?" This was it. This was where he blasted her for the way she'd just spoken to him.

"Leave Sawyer to me. I'm going to try and find out where he's been and what he's been doing these last few years. Let him know who's in charge. Only use him if you have to. He's not part of the DPA anymore."

She could feel the steel in his words and instantly regretted her outburst that Sawyer was driving her crazy. "He's actually been quite helpful. He's just a little…" she struggled to think of the word "...inconsistent. One minute he's helping, the next he looks as if he could jump out the nearest window." She looked over at the window next to her. The sun was splitting the sky outside. She almost felt like jumping out the window herself and heading for the nearest beach. Chicago had good beaches, didn't it?

Her stomach rumbled loudly. What she wouldn't give for pizza right now.

Evan was still talking.

"Sorry, what?"

"I asked if you wanted another doctor sent in."

"No. Not right now. If things progress, then probably yes. But let's wait until we have the lab results. You're dealing with plane passengers and hopefully things are contained at our end."

Her brain started to whirr. She couldn't really understand why, in the midst of all this, part of his focus was on Sawyer. Surely Evan should just be grateful that she had any help at all? No matter how reluctant.

She rang off and stared at the phone. Her stomach rumbled again loudly. She didn't have time to figure that out right now.

Along with many other things, it would have to wait.

CHAPTER FOUR

"Sawyer? Are you in here?" Callie stuck her head around the door into the darkened room. It was three a.m. and she could make out a heap bundled against the far wall, lying on a gurney.

The heap moved and groaned at her. "What?" He sat up and rubbed his eyes.

"Oh, I'm sorry," she whispered, searching the room for any other sleeping bodies. "Have you just got your head down?"

He swung his legs off the gurney and stood up, swaying a little. She walked across the room and put her arm on his. "I'm sorry, Sawyer. I didn't realize you were sleeping."

"I wasn't," he snapped.

She smiled at him. "Yes, you obviously were."

"What's wrong? Did something happen to the kids?" It was almost as if his brain had just engaged.

She tightened her grip on his arm. "No. I'm sorry. Nothing's changed. The kids are still pretty sick. Laura, one of the DPA nurses, is in with them now. I've kept Alison away, just like you said. She's still down at the other end of the corridor in a room on her own." She held up a paper bag and waved it under his nose. "She's doing a great job, by the way. She got me banana and toffee muffins."

"Oh, okay." The words took a few seconds to sink in then he scowled at her. "What is it, then?"

"It's Max Simpson, the chief of staff. It's three a.m. and I've just realized I haven't seen him yet. I've been so busy with things down here."

She could see the realization appear in his eyes. He grimaced.

"What is it?"

"Yeah. I meant to speak to you about Max too. I sort of made an executive decision there."

"You did what?" She was on edge again. What had he done now? He'd already broken protocol once. Had he done it again?

He shook his head. "I'm sorry, Callie, I meant to talk to you earlier. Max is the reason I'm here."

"What are you talking about? I don't understand."

"Max has prostate cancer. He's undergoing chemotherapy—midway through a course. He's immuno-compromised. So I told him he can't be anywhere the possible threat of infection and he can't be near anyone we immunize—including us."

The words struck home. For a second she'd thought he was going to say something unreasonable—something to get her back up. Instead, Callie felt the tenseness ease out of her muscles. Another piece of the jigsaw.

"So, what? You're covering for him right now?"

She could see the hesitation on his face. "Yes, I guess I am. Max was a real hands-on sort of guy. He dropped out of his clinical commitments a couple of months ago and has just been doing a few days' office work a week. He wants to keep his hand in during his treatment but couldn't manage any more. I was only supposed to be here for two weeks, covering someone's vacation leave. But I met Max, he liked me and asked me to stay and cover his clinical work in the E.R. for a few months."

She was trying to read behind the lines. Trying to understand the things that he wasn't telling her. She couldn't work this guy out at all.

Matt Sawyer's reputation had preceded him. Apparently when his wife had died, he'd had the mother of all temper tantrums, telling everyone around him what he really thought of them. She could only imagine that Evan Hunter had been one of them.

But here he was describing how he was helping out a sick colleague. Someone he'd only met a few months ago.

Was it just everyone at the DPA he hated? Did he blame them for his wife's death?

She could see him searching her face. Was he worried that she would be unhappy for him not putting her in the picture before now? Or was he worried she would actually see his human side? The side he'd tried to hide from her when he'd said his help had been a one-off event.

She wrinkled her nose at him. It was late and she was getting tired. Her defenses were weakening as she approached that hideous hour in the middle of the night when her body was screaming for her bed.

"I don't get you, Matt Sawyer," she whispered.

"What don't you get?" He took a step closer. The lights in the room were still out and the only light was from the corridor outside, sending a warm, comfortable glow over them both. He'd changed into the regulation DPA pale pink scrubs. Pink on a man. Whose idea had that been? He made them look good, though. Kind of inviting.

He reached up and gave one of her wayward locks at little tug, a sexy smile crossing his face, "This hair of yours, it's driving me crazy. I keep wanting to grab a pair of scissors and lop this off."

Her hand reached up too, brushing the side of his face and touching his brown hair that was mussed up around his ears. "Likewise," she whispered.

For a few seconds neither of them spoke. Callie had no idea what she was doing. She was in the middle of the biggest potential outbreak of her career, in a strange city, with no real idea of what could happen next. There was nothing in the plan about this. There was nothing that told you what to do when your colleague was sick and you had to take over the management of a situation like this. She needed a friend. She needed someone to reach out to.

"I saw your hand shaking earlier. Are you scared, Dr. Turner?" His voice was low, barely above a whisper. No one else could possibly hear them.

"Scared?" she repeated. "Matt, I'm terrified." She felt a whoosh of air come out of her lungs. It was the first time she'd said the words out loud. She'd spent the last twelve hours thinking them but she couldn't have imagined actually saying them to someone. It was like laying herself bare. To a man she hardly knew. It had to be a recipe for disaster.

He raised one eyebrow. "Like I said earlier, we're all scared. There's not a person in this E.R. right now who wants to be here—except, of course, for a few DPA geeks. Most people would sell their right arm to get out of here." He touched the side of her arm, running the palm of his hand up and down it. "Fear of the unknown is one of the most terrifying fears that there is."

She nodded, knowing what he was saying was true. There was something soothing about his voice. Something reassuring.

Her hand touched the side of his cheek. He almost flinched. She could see it. But he stood firm, his pale green eyes fixed on hers. "I can't work you out, Matt Sawyer. You're supposed to be a bad boy—a rule-breaker. Mr. Nasty. But right now I'm seeing a whole other side to you."

He wrinkled his nose. "What's that smell?"

"What smell?" She sniffed the air around her. "I can't smell anything."

"It's weird. Like strawberries or fruit or something."

She smiled. It was proof that they were standing too close to one another. "It's raspberries. It's my shampoo."

He moved even closer, his nose brushing against the top of her head as he inhaled again. "Almost good enough to eat," he murmured.

She couldn't wrap her head around all this. Maybe it was the time of night and her befuddled brain. She'd heard that Sawyer had lost it after his wife had died, had finished treating the patients he'd had to, had roared at everyone and walked off the job. He'd refused to make contact with anyone after that.

But here he was. Obviously struggling. But here.

His hand reached up and tightened around hers. There was an edge to his gaze. A shield going up right before her eyes. "What do you want to know?"

"I don't *know* that I want to know anything. I guess I just want to find out for myself. If I'd listened to Evan Hunter, I wouldn't have spoken to you at all when I got here, but I like to go on instincts."

"And what are your instincts telling you, Callie Turner?"

Wow. What a question. Because right now her instincts were telling her she was acting like a seventeen-year-old girl rather than a twenty-nine-year-old woman.

He moved their hands from the side of his cheek to resting both of them on her breastbone. Could he feel her heart beating against the skin on his hand? A man who had seen her virtually naked a few hours before?

What was she thinking about? Outside, down at the

desk, there were a million things that she should be doing. Being in here, with Matt Sawyer, wasn't on the list that she'd prepared earlier.

But the words came too easily, "My instincts are telling me that Callum Ferguson is one of the wisest men I've ever known. And if he had hope for you, then maybe I should too."

He was even closer now. She could feel his breath on her cheeks, warming her skin. He bent forward, his lips brushing the side of her ear. It felt like the most erotic touch she'd ever experienced. "What if I told you I'm still a bad boy? What if I told you I left my last two jobs in Alaska and Connecticut before they could fire me?"

And then it happened. Callie just let go. Just like she'd done on the phone earlier with Evan. She didn't think, she just acted. She spoke the words that came instantly into her brain. *What was happening to her?* "I'd say you found problems in the places you were working. I'd say you told them what was wrong and how to fix it. I'd say they probably didn't like it."

He tilted his head to one side, the lazy smile still fixed on his face. "I knew you were young. I thought you didn't know anything. I thought you only followed rules."

His words were supposed to be teasing but something else happened.

Something flooded through her veins. Adrenaline, laced with fear.

She shouldn't be doing this. She shouldn't be in here with him. It was compromising her ability to think straight.

He was right. Following rules was what she knew. Following rules was *safe*.

Last time she hadn't followed the rules it had ruined her life.

No. It had ruined her *sister's* life.

So, getting involved with a rule-breaker?

Not an option.

His phone buzzed, in that gentle, quiet way it did when it was switched to vibrate instead of ring. She sprang backwards. "I need to go, Matt." She pushed the door open, flooding the room with light.

"Wait!" He grabbed her arm as he glanced at his phone. "I'm guessing here as I'm not sure of the number but I think it's my sister. She's the only person I know who would be so persistent."

"Your sister?" The words cut through her like a knife. Her back-to-reality jolt was instant. "You have a sister?"

Something had just happened. And Sawyer didn't understand it. One minute they'd been almost nose to nose in the darkened room—as if something was about to happen. The next minute he had almost seen her building the wall around herself.

He had no idea what had made her just snap like that.

Miss Hoity-Toity had looked almost inviting a minute ago. For a second he'd almost thought about…

No. Not possible. He didn't think like that any more. Well, not unless he was in a bar and halfway through a bottle.

But for a few seconds she'd looked vulnerable. She'd looked like someone who could do with a hug. And he wasn't the hugging type.

And that smell from her. The raspberry shampoo. More enticing than any perfume he'd ever smelt.

It was weird what confined spaces could do to a person.

She was still looking at him with those too-wide eyes. What was with her? What was the big deal?

"Yes, I've got a sister."

"I meant to ask you if there was anybody you wanted

to notify that you had been quarantined. Haven't you told her what's happened?"

His eyes fixed on the floor. This wasn't going to be pretty. "My sister's called Violet. Violet Connelly." He waited for the penny to drop.

And it did.

"Violet Connelly's your sister?" Her voice rose, filling the quiet room.

He leaned against the doorjamb and folded his arms. He was well aware he was trying to look laid back, but he was feeling anything but. All of a sudden he was hit by a wave of emotions that he didn't want to deal with. He tried to focus on the face in front of him. "Yes. Why so surprised?"

"Violet Connelly is your sister?"

"You've already said that and I've already answered."

She wrinkled her nose. It made her look kind of cute. "Why hasn't she said anything? I've never heard her mention you and I've been at the DPA for the last three years."

"I'm the family black sheep." Explanations weren't really his thing. It seemed the easiest solution.

"Bull. Violet's not like that at all."

Okay. Maybe not.

"And why don't you have your sister's number in your phone?"

He shifted uncomfortably. "I've been out of touch for a little while."

"With your sister?" Her voice rose in pitch. "How can you be out of touch with your sister?" Little pink spots had appeared on her cheeks.

"She has a different name. How come?"

"So now you're getting personal?"

"Don't get smart, Sawyer. You've just told me a woman I've worked alongside for the last three years is your sister. Violet's a sweetheart and she's never mentioned you once. Why?"

He shrugged. He really didn't want to have this conversation. It was way too uncomfortable. And it was bringing up a whole load of guilt that he really didn't want to consider. "It's complicated."

Now she looked angry. That middle-of-the-night woman angry. Never a good sign. "Don't give me the *'it's complicated'* crap." She raised her fingers in the air again. "Tell me why on earth she would keep something like that secret? Maybe Evan Hunter was right—maybe we should be looking a little closer at you."

He could feel the pent-up anger build in his chest. His temper was about to flare. Here. In the middle of the hospital. In the middle of a crisis situation.

He turned and flipped on the light, walking over to the nearby sink and running the cold tap. He bent over and started splashing water on his face. How dared she? That was almost an implication that he was involved in this crisis situation.

This woman didn't know him at all. Didn't know anything but hearsay and gossip. If she knew even the tiniest part of him she'd know he'd do anything to get out of here.

He could feel the pressure building in his chest. Wasn't it bad enough that she'd just reminded him how guilty he felt about pushing his family—and his sister—away? He felt as if a truckload of concrete had just been dumped on his head.

As if this situation wasn't already bad enough.

Now she was making him think about things he'd spent the last six years pushing away.

He grabbed some paper towels and dried his face. Breathed in through his nose and out through his mouth. The flare was reducing. He didn't feel the urge to hit a wall any more. He was trying to think reasonable, rational thoughts.

But Callie Turner was still there. Wondering what she'd just witnessed.

He turned to face her. "Try walking in Violet's shoes for a while, Callie. Her brother's reputation is in the doghouse and she's just about to start her residency at the DPA. You know how important that is so why would you do anything to spoil it?"

She took a deep breath. He'd looked so angry a second ago.

But no wonder. She'd said something completely unforgiveable. She'd more or less accused him of being responsible for the smallpox outbreak. And he obviously wasn't.

Callum had already told her how difficult this would be for Sawyer. He was the one person here with more experience than her. Whether she liked it or not, she needed him. The last thing she should be doing was insulting him.

And more to the point, he was right. She hadn't told anyone about Isabel. She couldn't have dealt with the reaction that she'd been in a car crash that had killed her sister—a sister who would have given anything to work at the DPA. She hadn't let anyone in on her secret. Why should Violet?

She was telling herself to be reasonable and rational.

But something was skewing her thought processes. He had a sister. And it had caught her unawares.

It seemed ridiculous. Half the world had a sister. But most of the time she was prepared. She was ready. This time she hadn't been.

It didn't help that Violet Connelly was one of the sweetest people she knew. Not unlike Isabel. The fist squeezed around her heart even tighter.

She met his gaze. His face was flushed; he was still holding back his anger.

She'd kept her family secret too. She hadn't done anything to spoil her job at the DPA. She hadn't gone to her interview and said, *Well, actually, this was my sister Isabel's dream and since I was driving the car that killed her I feel I owe it to her.*

She took a deep breath, "I guess I wouldn't do anything to spoil it," she murmured.

He moved closer to her, the edges of his hair now wet around his face. "Our mum got remarried when I was a teenager. Violet was still quite young—she changed her name to our stepfather's. I didn't."

She raised her eyebrows at him. "What? You mean you were a rebellious teenager, Sawyer?" Anything to lighten the mood, anything to ease the tension in the room that was still bubbling away in her stomach. Anything to release the squeezing around her heart.

He nodded slowly. Then something else jarred into her mind.

"Does Evan Hunter know Violet's your sister?" She'd spoken to him numerous times on the phone today. "It was Evan that wanted you checked out."

He rolled his eyes. "I know that. Evan and I go way back. I haven't had a chance to phone Violet yet. I meant to, I just got caught up in everything. She's texted me and called me. She must have heard my name mentioned at the DPA. I need to fill her in on the details."

"You mean she didn't know you were here?" She couldn't keep the shock out of her voice. Why on earth would his sister not know where was?

He hesitated and for a second looked kind of sheepish. For a man with a reputation as a bad boy it almost didn't fit.

"I kind of dropped off the radar."

No. She didn't get this. She didn't get this at all.

"What do you mean? I know you didn't tell anyone at

the DPA where you were—in a way, I almost kind of get that. But your sister? Your own sister, Matt?"

Her voice was raised. She couldn't help it. He had a sister. He had options. Options she didn't have.

How on earth could he do that? How long had he been off the radar? Six years?

Six years of no contact? It was unthinkable.

Her voice was shaking. "How could you do that, Matt? You have a sister who clearly loves you. She must have been frantic with worry. She's still frantic with worry. Why would you do that to her? Why would you put her through that?"

There it was again. That action. The one he always did when he was thinking of an answer. He ran his fingers through his hair. "It's not as bad as it sounds."

She stepped right up to him. "Really? How? How is it not as bad as it sounds? Explain to me, Matt."

She was mad. She could never have done that. Never have cut Isabel out of her life for six years. It was unthinkable.

Nearly as unthinkable as being responsible for her own sister's death.

"I texted her. Not often. Just every now and then to let her know I was safe."

"And that was supposed to be good enough?"

He flung his hands up in frustration and shouted, "You don't know, Callie. You don't know anything. That was as much as I could manage. I needed time. I needed space. I didn't want anything familiar around me. I wanted to get my head straight."

"For six years?" She was shouting back.

His lips tightened. She knew there were tears threatening to spill down her cheeks. She couldn't help it. What a waste. He'd dared to risk his relationship with his sister.

A relationship she'd give anything to have again. It made her hate him.

"Not everything in life is part of a plan, Callie. Maybe if you get some life experience, you'll find that out."

She felt as if he'd just punched her in the ribs.

He couldn't be more wrong if he'd tried.

But, right now, in the middle of the night, she was hardly going to fill in the blanks to a man she hardly knew.

It was time to get some perspective. He had no idea how much those words had hurt. And she'd no intention of telling him.

Distance. That's what she needed.

Being in an enclosed space with Matt Sawyer was doing weird things to her. Being in an enforced quarantine for up to eighteen days would plain drive her crazy.

"Sawyer!"

The shout came from down the corridor, followed by the sound of thudding feet. They both sprang to the door at once, yanking it open and spilling out into the hallway.

"What is it?"

The nurse was red faced, gasping for breath. "There you are. I need help. Jack's struggling to breathe—he needs to be intubated. The spots must be causing his airway to swell." She glanced from one to the other. "Tell me we've got a pediatrician who can do this?"

Their eyes met.

They didn't have pediatric intensive care facilities. They were an ER—not a PICU. Their options were limited.

Sawyer grabbed a gown and a mask. "I'll do it." He started to run down the corridor before she could ask any questions. "Get me a portable ventilator," he shouted over his shoulder.

Her head flooded with thoughts. What did the plan say? Were there algorithms for intubating smallpox patients?

Were there risks attached to ventilating this child and possibly allowing the spread of disease?

There was no time to think. There was only time to act.

Sawyer had already sprung into action.

And for once she agreed.

CHAPTER FIVE

Everything happened in a blur. A portable ventilator seemed to appear out of thin air.

The fear that had been hanging around everyone, crystallizing in the air, was pushed to one side.

Jack's stats were poor, his lips tinged with blue, but his face was red with the strain of struggling for breath.

Intubating a child was never easy. Particularly a child who was panicking. Sawyer was at the bedside in a flash. "Give me some sedation."

The nurse next to him nodded, pulled up the agreed dose and handed him the syringe.

Sawyer leant over Jack. The panic flaring behind the little boy's eyes was obvious. Sawyer tapped his arm at the point where Jack's cannula was sited. "I know you're having trouble, little man. But I'm going to help you sort that out. I'm going to give you something to make you a little sleepy then put a tube down your throat to help you breathe. It will make things much better."

On a normal day he would have given a child some time to ask questions. Then again, on a normal day he wouldn't be doing this. He administered the drug quickly, waiting for Jack's muscles to relax.

A few seconds later his little body sagged and the whole team moved seamlessly. Sawyer positioned himself at the head of the bed. "Give me a straight-blade laryngoscope and the smallest ET tube you've got."

Callie pulled the light closer, trying to aid him as he slid the tube into place. It didn't help that it was the middle of the night and there was no natural light. It would be tricky to intubate a partially blocked airway, not something that she would ever wish to attempt. It had been a long time since she'd been in an emergency situation like this. DPA callouts usually involved febrile kids and adults and lots of sick bowls and emergency commodes.

On occasion, people got really sick and died. But Callie didn't usually get involved in that side of things. She was usually left to consider the big picture—the spread of disease.

Watching a little kid struggle for breath was something else entirely.

She gave a sigh of relief as Sawyer slid the tube into place and attached the ventilator. There was a murmur between him and nurse standing at the bedside as they set the machine. Callie frowned. Who was she? She didn't recognize her.

In fact, she didn't recognize half the people in this room. Was this what happened in the case of a medical emergency? Isolation procedures were ignored?

She squeezed her eyes shut as she tried to rationalize her thoughts. Isolation procedures weren't being ignored. Everyone in here had the regulation disposable gowns, masks and gloves in place. But there was a whole host of new people in this room—not just the restricted one or two.

One of the residents was talking in a low voice to the parents, trying to calm them. Another nurse was standing next to the half-pulled curtain next to Ben. She was leaning over him, obviously trying to distract him from the events surrounding him, telling him a long-winded version of the latest kids' movie.

Another guy came through the door. "You wanted a pediatrician? You've got one."

Callie's head shot up. "Where on earth did you come from?"

She couldn't see his face properly behind his fitted mask but his eyes flitted over to her and then instantly away. His priority was obviously the child, not the surrounding bureaucracy. "Upstairs," he said, as he walked over to the bed and started to fire questions at Sawyer, who turned to face him.

"Wish you'd got here five minutes ago," he said.

Callie was incredulous. "*Upstairs?* What do you mean, upstairs? This unit is closed. There's no one going out and no one coming in." Her hands were on her hips.

She was watching her whole world disintegrate around her. The first rule of quarantine: no one in, no one out. "Which door did you come through? Who let you through? Didn't you realize there was a quarantine in force down here? Do you know you've put yourself at risk by walking into this room?"

She was shouting. She couldn't help it. Next she would have infected people running down the streets and the media crucifying the DPA for not handling the outbreak appropriately. Evan Hunter would be on the phone telling her she was a failure.

"Callie." It was Sawyer. He was right in front of her, his pale green eyes visible above the mask. "Calm down. We put out a call for a pediatrician. We can't handle these kids ourselves."

"You did what?" She couldn't believe it. This was the problem with delegating. Mistakes got made. People did things they shouldn't. People did things that put others at risk. "Who gave you the right to do that?"

"I did." Sawyer's voice was calm but firm. "Decisions like this get made all the time. I'm in charge of the clinical care of these patients. And, as much as I don't like to admit it, this is getting beyond my level of expertise." He nodded towards the pediatrician. "Dan's great. We discussed the risks a little earlier. He knows he'll need to be vaccinated."

"It's much more than that!" She exploded. She couldn't help it. "Once he's vaccinated he may be able to look after these children but it'll put him out of commission for the general hospital for nearly a month. There's no way a doctor exposed to the smallpox virus through vaccination can be near anyone who is immuno-compromised. "Did you even think about that, Sawyer? Did you even consider it? And it's not just him. Who are all these people?" Her hand swept around the room. "They'll all need to be vaccinated too!"

"Stop it." She could sense his gritted teeth beneath the mask. He leaned closer, "You're making a scene and, quite frankly, it's not helping. Do you really think you're telling me anything I don't know or haven't already discussed with Dan? Do you really think these people don't already know the risks attached to coming into this room?"

She could feel the tiny hairs stand up at the back of her neck—and not in a good way. But he wasn't finished. "The difference between you and me, Callie, is that I know when I'm beaten. I know when to look for other options—options not in the plan. It's time you learned some new skills. Not everything in life is down in black and white."

He turned and walked away from her, leaving her stunned. She watched the second hand tick around on the clock on the wall in front of her. Less than twenty minutes ago she'd almost been in a compromising position with him.

Then, in the blink of an eye, everything had changed.

He made her want to cry. He made her want to scream. He was truly and utterly driving her crazy. The tears had automatically pooled at the corners of her eyes.

And it wasn't just the fact he behaved like an insubordinate teenager. It wasn't just that standing near to him made her hair stand on end or that sometimes there was wisdom in his words, even though they weren't in the plan.

It was the fact that in the midst of all that she just didn't know what she thought of him. She didn't know how to *feel* around him.

She was focused. She was precise. She followed the plan. Most of the time she'd helped develop the plan. And back in Atlanta these had seemed smart, comprehensive plans. Back in Atlanta they had seemed to cover every eventuality.

But they didn't cover the Sawyer element.

Not at all. They didn't cover the get-under-your-skin clause.

A smell drifted past her nostrils. What was that? She glanced at her watch—it was nearly five in the morning. Where had the time gone?

"Pizza," came the shout from down the corridor. She walked quickly along the hallway. She had to get out of there. She didn't have any pediatric skills and Dan clearly had things under control.

She also needed a chance to regroup.

Twenty pizza boxes were being descended on from every angle. It was like a plague of locusts. Someone was reading the tops of the boxes, shouting out what was in each one. "Hawaiian. Ham and cheese. Vegetarian." Arms appeared from everywhere, grabbing at the outstretched boxes. "Tuna and pineapple? Who on earth ordered that?"

A smile broke over her face. Alison had taken her responsibilities very seriously earlier when Callie had asked her to organize food for the patients and staff.

She'd asked what Callie's favorites were and so far she'd magicked up banana and toffee muffins and her favorite pizza. She pushed her way to the front. "That's mine." She held out her hand for the box.

The guy behind the desk wrinkled his nose in disgust. "Take it," he said as he moved on to the one underneath.

She smiled and drifted off with her pizza box. She'd learned early on as a junior doctor that ordering takeout was a whole new skill. Order something simple that everyone liked and you would never see it. Sweet and sour chicken, pepperoni pizza, chicken tikka masala, all would disappear in a blink of an eye. Order something a little out the ordinary and no one would touch it with a bargepole.

Tuna and pineapple pizza was an acquired taste. Isabel had sworn by spinach and anchovies. Even the thought sent a horrible tremor down her spine and made a smile dance across her face.

Sometimes the memories were good. Sometimes the memories were fun.

The typical teenage fights over clothes and boys had almost been blotted from her mind. The competition between them in medical school continued to hover around her. Isabel always had to be first to see their exam results. To see if she'd beaten Callie. But it had been a pretty even split. Both of them had excelled in different areas. Callie in planning, anatomy and biochemistry and Isabel in epidemiology, diagnostics and patient care. If things had gone to plan, they could have been a dynamite team.

Callie leaned back in her chair, her appetite leaving her abruptly. It always happened like this.

She was fine, she was focused. Then it would hit her again—what she'd lost. Just tumbling out of nowhere, like a granite rock permanently pressing on her chest.

The grief counselor had told her she'd get over it. It would just take time. But every year—particularly if there was an event that Isabel had especially enjoyed—it just seemed to shadow her all the more.

She turned her head to the right. The pile of paperwork about the type C containment building. The place that was currently having power issues. Would Isabel really have handled all this better? Would Isabel have been better organized than she was?

Would she handle Sawyer better than she was?

Her leg started to itch again and her hand automatically went to her scrub trousers and started scratching. She didn't have time for this. She didn't have time to be morose. She had a containment facility to sort out and there was no time like the present. Why should city hall officials get to sleep when she couldn't? She took a bite of her pizza and lifted the phone.

THE CHILDREN WERE as settled as they could be. The parents had been calmed, and in the end Dan had decided to give Ben some sedation too. Nothing about this situation was ideal and the little guy had become hysterical when he'd realized there was a machine breathing for his brother.

Sawyer breathed a sigh of relief. His too-big scrub trousers seemed to have given up trying to stay in place, partly due to the missing elastic at the waist and partly due to being weighed down by the phone in his pocket.

What time was it in Atlanta? He looked at his watch and tried to count it out. But what did it matter? Violet had been trying to phone him for hours. Whether he liked it or not, it was time to call her back.

He lifted his hand. Then pressed it down again on the desk.

He couldn't remember the last time his hand had shaken like that.

Come on. This was easy. It was one phone call.

So, how come the voices in his head had to will him on?

He took another breath and lifted his hand again, trying to ignore the shake. His fingers slipped and he missed the buttons.

Darn it. What kind of a fool was he?

Three-year-old kids could dial a phone—why couldn't he?

Concentrate. Get this over with. It would only be a few minutes out of his life.

The first time would be the worst. Once he'd done it, the heavy weight pressing on his chest might finally lift and let him breathe again.

Stop thinking about it, you moron—just dial!

He pressed the buttons on the phone, praying it might automatically jump to voicemail.

He didn't even hear the first ring. "DPA. Can I help you?"

"Violet Connelly, please."

There was a few moments' silence as the call was connected. He resisted the huge temptation to hang up and hide.

Hang up and go and find a beer.

"Violet Connelly."

He could almost picture her in his mind, doing ten things at once with the phone perched between her shoulder and her ear. Even at this time in the morning she'd be multi-tasking.

"Hello?"

Patience had never been her strong suit.

"Hey, Violet." His voice cracked.

There was a loud crash. All he could imagine was that her chair had just landed on the floor. "Sawyer? Sawyer?"

He cringed, guilt flooding through him. The concern and anxiety in her voice was crystal clear. He should have texted her hours ago. Why hadn't he? Ten seconds. That's all it would have taken.

Scrub that. He should have phoned her six years ago. Not just send the odd random text from an occasional phone.

"Yeah, it's Sawyer."

Some not very ladylike words spilled down the phone. The concern had quickly been replaced by anger. "'Hey, Violet'? Is that the best you can do? Six years, Matt. *Six years!*"

"I know. I'm sorry but—"

"You're sorry? *You're sorry?* You've got to be joking. I've been trying to phone you for hours. *Hours.* You logged that call here hours ago, Matt. You must have known I would hear about it straight away. I've been trying to contact you ever since. I've been frantic."

"Violet, please—"

"Please? Please?" It was obvious she wasn't going to let him speak. Six years of worry and pent-up frustration were erupting all over him. "How do you think I feel? How do think it felt to know that after six years you phone the DPA and ask to speak to Callum Ferguson? *Callum Ferguson?* You must have known I would be here. You must have known the news would spread like wildfire. I don't care that it's about a smallpox outbreak. I don't care that it's the scariest outbreak we've ever dealt with. I want you to stop for five minutes and think about what that felt like for me."

Wow.

One thing was for sure, she'd been waiting to say that for a long time.

If Violet could see him now she would see that for the first time in years he was hanging his head in shame. "Give me a break, sis."

"*Give you a break?* Right now, I'd like to break every bone in your body."

Ouch. Harsh. And definitely not Violet's normal response. During the biggest potential outbreak in years, she'd just found her lost brother. She must be stressed up to her eyeballs. The added fact that no one knew he was her brother couldn't be helping—and she wasn't finished yet.

"Why haven't you answered my texts? Why haven't you answered my phone calls?" He could hear it now. The tiny waver in her voice. Violet never liked anyone to know when she was upset. He could almost picture the glimmer of tears in her eyes.

He sighed. "I've been busy, sis. I've got some really sick kids here." He leaned back against the wall, "Plus I've got an invasion of DPA faces that I'd hoped never to see again."

He stopped talking. He didn't need to say any more. Violet knew exactly how he felt about all this. He'd never actually said the words to her, but his sister knew him better than anyone.

"You can do this, Sawyer." Her voice was almost a whisper. A cheerleading call for him. After all this time she was still trying to instill confidence and strength into him.

She was the one person in the world who could chew him out one minute, then fight to the death for him a second later.

Family. He'd almost forgotten what it felt like.

"I'm just in the wrong place at the wrong time again, Violet. Story of my life."

Silence again. She realized the enormity of his words. The price he'd paid the last time had almost destroyed him.

"Are you safe? Did you put yourself at risk before you realized what it was?"

It was natural question—a sisterly question—but it still grated. Especially when he'd been part of the DPA. "I was in the same room as the kids, breathing the same air. I took precautions as soon as I had reason for concern, but they didn't have the appropriate masks. I had to send the other member of staff away—she's pregnant."

He heard Violet's sharp intake of breath. She knew exactly the impact that must have had on him.

"So, for a couple of hours it was just me treating the kids. You know how it is, Violet. That's the way it's got to be. I've had my smallpox vaccination. Now I just need to wait."

"I don't like this. I don't like any of this. I've waited months to hear from you again—eight measly texts in six years—and now this? All I've ever wanted to know is that you were safe, Sawyer, but when I finally hear from you, you're in the most dangerous place of all. It just doesn't seem real."

Sawyer felt himself bristle. He didn't want to get into this with Violet. He didn't want to answer a million questions about where he'd been or what he'd been doing. That was a conversation for another day—and maybe not even then.

And even though he could hear the note of desperation in her voice, he just couldn't go there.

"How's Callum? Have you heard if he's okay? I tried to call the hospital earlier, but they wouldn't tell me anything."

There was hesitation at the other end. She was obviously

trying to decide what to tell him. "He's had a massive MI. They took him for angioplasty hours ago and apparently it went well."

There it was again. That tightening feeling around his chest. The way it always came when things were outside his control.

He hated the fact that even though he was a doctor he couldn't always help the people he loved.

He changed the subject.

"What do you know about Callie Turner? She seems a little out of her depth."

"You think?" Violet's answer was snappy, verging on indignant. She was obviously suffering from the same lack of sleep that he was. He was forgetting what time it was. "Callie's one of the best doctors I've worked with. She does everything to the letter. She's very focused, very ordered. Don't get in her way, Sawyer, she won't like it."

"Tell me something I don't know." In a way he was surprised. Violet was always honest with him. She would tell him if she had any doubts about Callie. The fact that she hadn't mentioned even one was interesting. He decided to take a new tack. "What about her scars?"

"What scars? Callie has scars?"

She sounded genuinely surprised. Didn't the women in the DPA locker room look at each other? Maybe he should call them all on their observation skills.

"Yeah. A big one, snaking right down her leg. She didn't get it at work, then?"

"How come you've seen Callie's scars? Ah...the protective clothing. I get it. No, I had no idea Callie had a scar. She definitely didn't get it at work. She's never had any accidents here. It must be from years ago."

He leaned against the wall just outside the children's room again. All of a sudden he was embarrassed. He hadn't had a proper conversation with his sister in the last few years and he was asking her about other people? He should be ashamed of himself. He took a deep breath, "How are you, Violet? Are you okay?"

"How do you think I am? The biggest potential outbreak in who knows how long and, oh, yeah, my brother's in the middle of it. The DPA's in an uproar. Some rooms are deathly silent and in others you can't even hear yourself think. We've got another couple of outbreaks in other places but none like this." She lowered her voice, as if she was hiding her conversation from someone near her. "What do you think? Do you really think it's smallpox?"

He blew a stream of air out through his lips. "That's the million-dollar question. I'm sure it's a pox—and it definitely isn't chicken pox. But am I sure it's smallpox?" He shook his head. "I just don't know, sis. That's for the lab rats to tell us."

He heard her laugh at his affectionate name for his friends who worked down in the labs. "By the way, Frank says hello. He also cursed a little. He was just about to start his vacation when your lab samples arrived. He says you owe him and his wife a trip to Hawaii."

Memories started to come flooding back into Sawyer's mind. Memories he'd blocked out for a long time. He'd worked with Frank Palmer for six years. They were the same age and had got married around the same time. When Helen had died, he just hadn't been able to stay in touch. Everything was a permanent reminder.

Frank's wife Lucy was a petite, gorgeous blonde who had probably had her suitcase packed with a different bikini for every day of their vacation. She would have been *mad*.

Helen and Lucy had been good friends. They'd made

plans together and enjoyed each other's company. Lucy had been heartbroken when Helen had died.

His heart gave a little squeeze. It wasn't just his sister he hadn't considered.

He hadn't considered other people. Other people who had been devastated by Helen's death. He'd been too busy focusing on his own grief to allow anyone else's to touch him.

"Tell Frank I'm sorry—no, tell Lucy I'm sorry." He hesitated for a second then asked, "Frank and Lucy—do they have any kids?"

It had been another of Helen and Lucy's grand plans, that they would all have kids at the same time. They'd always joked that their imaginary offspring could be prom king and queen together.

He heard Violet take a deep breath and her voice had a new edge to it, a harsher edge. "You've been away too long, Sawyer. Frank and Lucy lost their daughter last year to stillbirth. It was an extremely traumatic time—Lucy nearly died and had to have a hysterectomy. They can't have any more children."

He felt as if someone had just twisted a knife in his guts. For a few fleeting seconds he'd been jealous. Jealous that Frank still had Lucy. That he still had a future with his wife.

Violet's words sent chills across his body. It just showed you—you never knew. You never knew the minute when things could come crashing down all around you.

And now he was feeling something else. Disgust with himself. He hadn't been there to support his friends in their time of need. People who had reached out to him when he'd been at his lowest ebb.

It didn't matter that he'd walked away and ignored everyone. He could still remember every card, every phone call, every email, every handshake.

Helen would have been livid with him. He could almost hear her reading him the Riot Act.

Touching reality again was making him realize that her death hadn't affected only him. It had affected everyone around them.

Some of the contact tracers in the team could barely look at him today.

And it wasn't a reflection on them. It was a reflection on *him*.

They had no idea how he would react to them. How he would react if they brought up the past and expressed their sympathies about Helen—even after all this time

Violet cleared her throat at the end of the line and he snapped back to attention. "I take it you're still flying under the radar in there? They haven't made the connection between us?" he asked.

"No. No one knows." He heard her breathe a sigh of relief. "Or if anybody knows, they're not saying anything. Evan Hunter's walking around here like a bear with a sore head. I've spent the last few hours trying to avoid him. He didn't take it well that you're involved in this."

Sawyer couldn't help the smile that automatically spread across his face. "He'll get over it," he murmured. He looked at his watch. "Hate to say it, sis, but I need to go. I might have a chance to get my head down for a couple of hours. One of the pediatricians has just arrived to share the responsibility of the kids. We've just had to intubate one of them. This might be the only chance I get to sleep in a while."

"Okay, Sawyer. Stay safe and keep an eye on Callie. She has lots of good qualities. And keep your phone switched on. If I call and you don't answer…"

"I get it, sis. Keep your head down and stay out of Evan Hunter's way. He'll find something else to gripe about soon."

He stared at the phone as he heard her hang up, puzzled by her parting shot about Callie. It was almost like a little beacon, glowing orange in the dark sea. She knew exactly how to play him. Some things never changed.

CHAPTER SIX

Violet had only just replaced the receiver when Evan Hunter came stomping across the room, shouting orders as he went. They might be an hour ahead of Chicago but hadn't anyone told him it was six o'clock in the morning and most of the staff had been up all night?

"Somebody get that man a coffee," she grumbled as she slid her chair under the desk and pulled up the screen she'd been reviewing. It was a distribution model of the potential spread of the smallpox virus. They'd started working on this while they had still been trying to determine if the passengers on the plane had been exposed or not.

"Violet! *Violet!*"

Rats. It was almost as if he had an internal radar and could hear her thoughts.

"What?" She turned to face him as he hovered above her, obviously irritated by her lack of instant response. "What's happened?"

"Where have you been? I've been looking for you?"

Darn it. She'd only ducked out for five minutes to speak to Matt. How on earth could he have known that?

There was only way to shut him up. "Ladies' room." She gave him a sarcastic smile. That was all the information he would need.

He scowled at her. "I need you to get some background

on Matt Sawyer for me. Find out where he's been for the last six years. Find out how he managed to end up in an E.R. in Chicago."

She was stunned. It was the last thing she had been expecting. A few hours ago it had been a whole hullaballoo about a graph of the potential spread of smallpox. And, well, yes, she could almost understand it. That was just the kind of thing he wanted to appear instantly before his eyes. Stuff the grunt work. He practically expected people to work at the speed of light. It wouldn't be the first time she'd told him in no uncertain terms that data needed to be checked and rechecked, assimilated and analyzed beyond any shadow of a doubt.

But this? Asking her to investigate her own brother?

It was totally out of left field. A complete bolt from the blue.

Anyone else might have been intimidated by his stance, leaning over her. But Violet wasn't. She'd been this close to Evan before. About six months ago after a work night out.

The medic and her boss. Never a good idea.

Too bad she couldn't shift the inappropriate memories out of her head, which came up at the most inopportune moments.

"Violet? Did you hear me?"

She snapped back to attention. Back to reality. Sawyer and Evan Hunter had never got on. She'd no idea why and she didn't really care. Just as well she'd never told her boss that Sawyer was her brother.

She stared at him, unfazed by his annoyed face. Violet didn't do well on lack of sleep. It was the standing family joke that everyone should stay out of her way if she'd had a bad night on call as a resident. Her patience had just flown out of the window.

"Why on earth do you want me to check up on Sawyer?

Shouldn't we be focusing on the real issue—the potential smallpox outbreak? I thought you wanted a complete rundown on the potential spread? That's what I've been working on for the last few hours and I'm not finished yet."

Evan leaned closer. "Don't you dare tell me what to do right now. I'm the team leader around here. I decide what happens. Sawyer is irresponsible and reckless. He's the last person we can trust. And a few hours ago he phoned in the biggest threat to this country's health in years. Am I suspicious? Absolutely I am! Now..." he pointed at the computer "...find out where he's been and what he's been doing. I want to know now!"

He swept into the office next to her, slamming the door behind him as if he could knock it from its hinges.

Violet sagged back down into her seat. She didn't need to do what he asked. She'd been doing it for the last six years and had found nothing. *Nada.*

Apart from a few cursory texts since his wife's funeral and his departure from the DPA, she knew nothing.

His texts had only ever told her that he was safe. Nothing else. Not where he was or what he was doing.

The hard fact was that if she wanted to know where Sawyer had been she would have to ask him. And right now she had a distribution model to finish.

She stared at the slammed door. Violet was used to prioritizing her own workload.

She set her jaw.

Evan Hunter could wait.

He watched the walls shake around the door he had just slammed. What on earth was wrong with him?

Evan felt sick. He had potentially one of the most well-publicized outbreaks in the DPA's history to handle and at the heart of it all was a man he hated. A man he didn't trust.

And he was taking it out on the people around him—he was taking it out on Violet.

The last thing he should be doing.

The press was all over this. The media room at the DPA was currently packed out, with the phones ringing constantly. He could handle stress. It wasn't the first time he'd handled a major outbreak.

What he couldn't handle were his reactions to Violet.

Those were the things he couldn't control.

He was going to have to do something about it—and fast.

"Callie, phone."

Callie looked up from where she was standing, talking to Sawyer. The plans for the containment facility were almost complete. The nurse dangled the phone from her hand. "It's the lab."

Callie and Sawyer moved in unison, diving for the phone at the same time.

Their hands clashed and Callie shot him a dirty look and shoved him out of her way. "Callie Turner."

"It's Evan."

She really couldn't face any niceties. Her brain could only fix on one thing—and from the expression on Sawyer's face he felt the same way.

"What is it? What has Frank found?" Sawyer flinched next to her at the sound of Frank's name. What was that all about? Frank had worked at the DPA forever. They must know each other.

She could hear the deep intake of breath at the end of the phone. "Electron microscopy revealed a brick-shaped virus. It's definitely an orthopox."

Callie felt her insides twist. She knew better than to

say the next words. But she couldn't help it—it was automatic. "He's sure?"

Beside her she saw Sawyer drop his head into his hands. He knew exactly what was being said.

"He's sure."

She touched his arm and met his pale green eyes, giving him a silent nod. Sawyer let loose a string of expletives. The lab was only confirming what they'd all suspected. It was the first step in trying to classify the disease. It just made it all seem a little too real.

It was time to get down to business. "How long before he can be more specific?"

"He's still running the PCR. You know how this is— we could have something for you in twenty-four hours or it could take up to seven days. Direct fluorescent antigen testing has ruled out varicella. Tell Sawyer he was right—it's definitely not chicken pox." She heard Evan sigh. Those words must have been painful for him. "Your next stage is the move to the containment type C facility. Are you ready for that?"

Callie looked at the whiteboard on the wall next to her. Every detail was clearly displayed. Her team was good. "The power company's just been in touch to let us know the power has been reconnected. We're just waiting to hear back from the chief of police about closing the highway and getting the police escort. Once that's in order we'll be ready to move."

"Keep me posted. I'll be in touch if we have any more news."

Callie stood in a daze for a few seconds, the phone dangling from her hand. She was trying to assimilate the information she'd just been given. A warm hand closed over hers and replaced the receiver.

They didn't speak. For once it seemed that their minds were working in unison.

Callie looked around at her bustling colleagues. Someone was going to have to tell them. Someone was going to have to confirm that this was a real and credible threat. It wasn't just a suspicion any more. They'd moved a stage beyond that now.

And it was her job.

Her job to ensure the safety of her team under these confirmed conditions.

Her job to keep the staff informed.

Her job to be responsible for the patients who were—most likely—infected with smallpox.

Her job to help prevent the spread of the disease.

It was almost overwhelming. Could she really do all this?

Sawyer was watching her. He could see the tiny flare of panic in her eyes. And as much as this was the worst possible news, he knew it was time to step up.

They were close together, low enough for their voices not to be heard.

"What exactly did Evan say?"

"It's definitely an orthopox." The anxiety in her voice was palpable. But a little smile appeared on her face. "And Evan said to tell you that you were right—it's definitely not chicken pox. They've ruled it out."

He pulled back a little. "Evan Hunter said that?"

She nodded. "I think he was more or less pushed into a corner on that one." Her eyes swept the room, trepidation returning to them. "I need to tell the team. We have to move to the containment facility."

If only she could see what he did. At times she had a little-girl look about her, as if she was about to be swept away by a tidal wave. As if the situation and events were totally out of her control. But these were tiny, fleeting glimmers that disappeared in an instant.

Then she would tilt her chin and act exactly the way she should. Just like she was doing now.

She was pushing aside her own fears and focusing on the details of the job. Just like a good doctor should.

They were close together again. Hiding away from the rest of the world. Her eyes were much bluer this close up. Last time they'd been like this had been in a darkened room and he hadn't really had a chance to appreciate her finer features.

She was lucky. No lines marring her complexion, only some dark circles under her eyes. Her gaze met his and her brow wrinkled. "Can I do this, Matt?"

MATT. HARDLY ANYONE called him that. Just the way she said the word took him by surprise. He was so used to being called by his surname that it actually made him stop for a moment. He reached out and took her hand. She didn't flinch, didn't pull away. She just inched a little closer.

He saw the glimmer of fear register in her eyes. Her tongue peeked out and ran along her dry lips, moistening them and leaving them glistening.

He was fixated. He couldn't look away.

He bent down, his lips brushing the side of her cheek. "Of course you can do this, Callie. This is what you trained for."

If he turned his head just slightly his lips would be on hers. It was the most inappropriate, most inopportune moment. But Sawyer didn't care.

For the first time in a long time he was finally starting to feel again.

And everything else just paled in comparison.

He was getting another waft of that raspberry shampoo.

But then she moved, lowering her face beneath his and resting her hands on his shoulders. There was something else in her expression. It was almost as if she was taking a minute—as if she wanted to tell him something. And it was clear she had no idea about the thoughts currently circulating in his head.

He tried to focus. To take his gaze off her pink lips. She was close enough that he could smell the mints she'd been eating.

They couldn't stay like this. Any minute now someone in the E.R. would notice they were closer than normal.

He had to get some perspective before he did something he might regret.

He jerked back. "How long until we find out the diagnosis?"

If she noticed him pulling away she didn't react. "Evan wasn't sure. Anything from between another twenty-four hours up to seven days. But at the moment we still need to tell everyone the quarantine will last for seventeen days."

"Seven days is a long time to wait for a diagnosis."

She nodded and turned away from him. Focusing on work, getting back to the job. Staring up at the whiteboard. "I guess we'd better start vaccinating again. Everyone going to the type C unit needs to be vaccinated beforehand."

She was right. She was being professional. Her mind was focused on the job. Just where his should be.

He nodded and said the words he was supposed to. "Let's get to work."

How on earth was he going to manage in an enclosed space with her for the next seventeen days?

CHAPTER SEVEN

"Wow! How did they manage this in such a short space of time?"

Callie peered out of the transport-vehicle window as they approached the containment facility. It was more than impressive. A bright white building sitting in the middle of an industrial site.

It was almost the regulations personified.

A single building located at least one hundred yards from any other occupied facility. Non-shared air-conditioning, heating and adequate ventilation systems. Single rooms with negative air pressure. Advanced medical and laboratory systems. Dependable communication systems and controllable access.

Then, more than the obligatory one hundred yards away, another type R facility to host everyone who'd been exposed, vaccinated and hadn't developed any symptoms. All the patients who'd been exposed in the E.R. could now be safely housed and monitored for the next two weeks.

Sawyer pressed his face up against the window next to her. The slow-moving convoy had taken nearly forty minutes to get here. It had been a surreal experience. But, then again, it had been years since anything like this had happened. The fact that the ambulance transport crews were kitted out in masks, gloves, gowns and shoe covers probably hadn't helped. Particularly with the amount of news crews that surrounded the hospital.

Callie found that incredible. Who, in their right mind, news crews or not, would want to be that close to a possible smallpox outbreak? If she'd been any other kind of doctor she would have headed to the city limits as quickly as she could.

Callie shuddered at the thought of the news headlines that evening. The pictures of the crew transporting the 'infected' patients could be terrifying to the general public. She could only hope that Evan Hunter would be in charge of damage control.

"I guess it must have been something else. A school? Some kind of lab? A warehouse?" Sawyer wrinkled his nose, as if he was aware that none of those things really fitted. "Did Callum leave you any notes?"

Callie rummaged through the pile of papers on her lap. "I've been so busy sorting out the problems—getting the electricity and water turned on, medical supplies delivered—that I didn't really think about it. He just told me he'd identified 'suitable premises.' Ah, here it is." She dragged a pale cream piece of paper from the bottom of the pile.

"What's wrong?"

Her eyes were still scanning the page and what she was reading was obviously translating straight to her face. "It's just a little odd." She lifted her head and stared at the building again, "It was a research facility."

"What's odd about that?"

"It's apparently been here for the last hundred years." A strange sensation swept over her. "Do you think they used it for the last smallpox outbreak?"

"Now, there's a creepy thought."

They pulled up outside the buildings and both heads

turned to look again. Sawyer opened the door and jumped down, holding out his hand to help Callie. She left her papers on her seat and jumped out with him.

They stood next to each other, hands on their hips, trying to work out what was going on. "It looks brand-new," Callie muttered.

"It certainly does. Maybe it's just had a coat of paint?"

He stepped forward and touched the exterior wall. "It's certainly had new windows and doors."

Callie nodded. "And a new ventilation system." She gave a nod to the system that was clearly venting all its air outside through the designated HEPA filters. "They couldn't possibly have had that last time round. It must have been used recently."

She turned around as the rest of the transport started to pull up behind them. "Let's take a look inside."

Sawyer matched her step for step as they strode through the building. Everything about it was perfect. A laboratory, newly refurbished patient rooms and clinical treatment rooms. Then a whole separate building that fitted with type R requirements, with single bedrooms and bathrooms where all the people under the containment could be housed, with extra facilities available for them all. Kitchens, sitting rooms, children's playrooms, even a cinema room, it was extraordinary.

All with the proper ventilation systems to prevent the spread of infection.

Callie ran her fingers along the wall in the one of the corridors. She didn't feel uneasy. This place didn't have a bad feeling attached to it, but there was a certain air of mystery. "If these walls could talk, what would they tell us?"

Sawyer turned to face her, "What do you mean?"

She pointed to the nearest room. "This almost seems

too good to be true. This place has obviously been in use recently—though we did have to get the water and electricity switched back on. They haven't managed to do all this in twenty-four hours. I wonder what kind of research they did here?"

Sawyer pushed open the nearest room—full of state-of-the-art monitoring and ventilation equipment. "Does it really matter? We've got good facilities here." He nodded as Dan, the pediatrician, appeared at his back, entering the room to make sure it had everything he needed for the children.

A smile appeared across Dan's face. "These are the latest ventilators. I've been trying to get Chicago General to buy some. They cost serious money. They'll be perfect for the kids. But here's hoping I only need one." He gave a nod to Callie. "I don't know how you managed it but this is perfect."

That strange feeling spread again. "I don't know how I managed it either," she said quietly. Everything seemed to have miraculously fallen into place. Maybe her rant at Evan Hunter had worked. Someone in the DPA had excelled themselves here.

Sawyer placed a hand on Dan's shoulder. "How do you want to set things up? Do you want to have Jack and Ben in separate rooms? We've got the negative air pressure facilities here, we can use them."

He was obviously just trying to give Dan his place. As the only pediatrician, the care and responsibility of the two boys fell to him. It didn't make sense to bring in any other doctors. And although he wasn't a pediatrician Sawyer had already volunteered to assist with the care of Jack and Ben. Since he'd done the initial diagnosis he seemed reluctant to let them go. But he was quite happy to take instructions from Dan.

Dan shook his head. "Actually, no, I want to keep them together. They've been equally exposed anyway. Separating them at this time isn't going to benefit either of them. Unless you can tell me something different?"

Callie shook her head.

Sawyer cut in. "I'm with you, Dan. In that case, for the sake of the two of them, it's better they stay together. This place would be terrifying for a six-or seven-year-old on their own. There is no viable clinical or psychological reason to keep them apart. They're brothers. They're meant to be together. Let's not add to the stress."

Callie could feel her heart flutter in her chest. He couldn't possibly know or understand what those words would mean to her. It was just the fact that somebody, somewhere had even the slightest inkling about the connection between siblings. The reassurance of being together, no matter how unscientific. And the possible benefits for the boys.

She'd heard miraculous stories before about premature twins being reunited in the same special-care cot and the baby that had been expected to die had made an unlikely recovery.

She herself had been badly injured in the car accident, almost unconscious. But when it had become apparent that Isabel was going to die, an experienced nurse had insisted her trolley be pulled in next to her sister's. Then she'd lifted Isabel's hand to let Callie hold it as her sister's life had slipped away.

It had been the worst moment in Callie's life. If she hadn't been going straight to Theatre, they would have had to sedate her.

But now, with the benefit of hindsight, it was one of her most precious and treasured memories. She'd been able to say things to Isabel that she might never otherwise have had the chance to say. Even though she realized Isabel had probably not heard her, it had still given her comfort. It had also meant the world to her parents, who hadn't been able to make it to the hospital in time to see their daughter before she'd died.

So Sawyer's words and understanding meant more to her than she could ever possibly reveal.

Dan and Sawyer were already striding down the corridor, organizing the transfers from the ambulances. Staff were streaming past, carrying boxes that were systematically being unpacked into cupboards.

Callie walked back out and watched the rest of the people being shown into the other building, carrying their belongings with them. One of the planners came up and handed her a large plan of the building, complete with names assigned to every room. "Thought you'd need this, Callie."

She nodded as she looked over the plan, a smile crossing her face when she assimilated the sleeping arrangements. "We don't seem to have adequate laundry facilities." She lifted her head to the planner, who consulted his list and shook his head. "We need to get right on that. In the case of smallpox, laundry can be a risk. It can carry contaminated fluids. We need to make arrangements for the laundry to be put in biohazard bags and autoclaved." The planner scribbled furiously then walked away.

She felt Sawyer's hand on her shoulder. "Our home for the next, what, seventeen days?"

"Sixteen," she said firmly. "We've already done the first day." She gave a little smile. "Think you can stand me for that long?"

"I might be forced to give you a haircut."

"Ditto."

He jerked back a little. "Isn't that some crazy quote from a romance movie?"

"I don't know. I don't watch romance movies. I'm more an action girl myself."

"Really?" There was distinct tone of disbelief in his voice.

"Yeah."

He shook his head. "Just when I think I know you, even a little, you say something to surprise me."

"That I like action movies? If that surprises you, you've led a pretty sheltered life." She realized the stupidity of her words as soon as they left her mouth. But it was too late. They were out there.

Sawyer didn't react. He just pulled out some equipment from the back of one of the ambulances and gave her a weak smile on the way past.

She was cringing inside. A man whose wife had died on a DPA mission had obviously never led a sheltered life. How could she possibly last another sixteen days around him without making an idiot of herself?

He turned back to face her, his expression unreadable. "What about Alison? Did everything work out okay?"

So it was back to business. A few seconds of personal chat that she'd just ruined. She'd only herself to blame. She forced a smile onto her face. "I think in a few hours we'll all wish we were Alison."

"How come?"

"We couldn't bring her here because we couldn't vaccinate her. The next option in the plan is to isolate the person at home. But Alison didn't want to take the risk of being isolated at home in case she put her family at risk."

Sawyer nodded. He would know that being isolated at home would be the logical answer but not entirely practical. "So you had to think outside the plan? Interesting."

He folded his arms across his chest. "I bet that gave you a spasm. So what's happened to her?" The grin that had vanished a few minutes ago had reappeared. Callie resisted the temptation of rising to the bait.

"It seems that somebody in the DPA budget office was in a nice mood. They've rented out an entire boutique hotel for the next fortnight until we're sure she's symptom-free. Alison will be living in the lap of luxury."

Sawyer's response was instant. He shook his head. "Maybe to you or me. But not to her. Alison dotes on her kids. It will drive her crazy not to be with them for two weeks."

Callie tried not to grimace. She'd been thinking of the gorgeous surroundings, fabulous food, luxurious bedding and unlimited TV channels. She really hadn't thought much past the idea of ordering room service every night.

"I guess not," she murmured, as she followed him down the corridor as he dumped some more supplies in the treatment room.

"Let's grab our stuff and dump it in our rooms." They walked back outside and Sawyer lifted her rucksack and suit carrier from one of the vans. "Did you really travel this light? Or do you have a giant suitcase hidden somewhere?"

She laughed. "I do have a suitcase, but it's a carry-on." She looked around her, "I've no idea where it is, though. What about you?"

Sawyer lifted a polythene bag. "My worldly goods."

"You're joking, right?"

He shook his head. "I came to work to do a twelve-hour shift. I didn't realize I should have packed for a fortnight."

"Wow. We're really going to have to get you some clothes, aren't we?" She started to laugh. "What about all your hair products? Won't they need a suitcase all of their own?"

"Cheeky!" She ducked as he flung his bag at her head. The contents spilled on the ground. Another pair of Converses, a T-shirt, a pair of ripped jeans, a pair of boxers and a bunched up pair of socks. She raised her eyebrows as she stuffed the contents back in the bag and lifted up one shoe. "Two pairs?"

He shrugged. "That's the good pair. The scruffy ones are work shoes." She smiled at the kicked-in shoes she held in her hands. She wouldn't even have worn them to paint a fence—and these were the good ones. "Nothing else?"

"What? I wear scrubs at work all day. What else do I need?"

"I hate to think. You got anything to sleep in?"

"What kind of a question is that?"

"The kind of question from a woman who's sharing an apartment space, kitchen and bathroom with you."

Ever since she'd looked at the plan she'd felt nervous. Excited nervous, not scared nervous. Wondering what his reaction would be to the sleeping arrangements.

"Why aren't I sharing with Dan? Wouldn't that have made more sense?"

She nodded as they headed over to the building. "It does—and he's sharing with us too, along with one of the other DPA doctors. Four people per apartment. But I guess they figured you'd be doing the opposite shifts from Dan. Doesn't make sense for you to be working at the same time."

"Callie, Sawyer!"

They turned their heads as one of the nurses shouted over to them.

"We need you in the treatment facility. There's a few patients with symptoms that need checking out."

They looked at each other and swiftly dumped their bags at the entrance.

"Guess we can do this later," Callie said flatly.

His gaze met hers. "I guess we can."

There was something in the way he said it. The tone of his voice. The way his eyes held contact with hers. The way there was a hint of smile on his face. It sent a weird tingle down her spine.

All of a sudden that excited nervousness didn't seem so odd after all.

CALLIE LOOKED DOWN at her map as they walked along the corridor. "Next left," she said.

It was late and they were both tired. Checking over a few symptoms had taken a lot longer than expected.

Sawyer pushed open the plain white door with the number seven on the front. It opened into a large sitting room with white walls and red carpet and a sofa. It was much bigger than she'd expected. An open-plan kitchen stood at one end of the room with a door to another corridor at the bottom.

Callie was a little shocked. It was much better than she had expected. "I thought it would be like student accommodation." She gave a little shrug, "You know, kind of drab and definitely tiny." She pressed her hand down on the comfortable sofa with matching cushions. "I guess not. Who do you think stayed here?"

"Who cares?" Sawyer had made his way to the pristine white kitchen and started to rummage through a cardboard box sitting on one of the worktops. "Wonder where this came from? Gotta love those planners. I'm starving." He emptied the contents onto the surface—milk, bread, butter, cereal. Callie automatically opened the door to the fridge and started depositing the perishable items inside.

"Yes!" He punched his hand in the air as if he'd just won an award.

"What is it?"

"My favorites." He pulled out a packet of chocolate cookies and ripped it open. "I didn't realize how hungry I was." He tilted his head at her as the cookie disappeared in two bites. "Who sorted all this stuff out? Was it Alison?" He looked back in the box. "Because I swear, if I find a tuna pizza in here I'll—"

"You'll what?" She swatted his arm. She almost felt relieved. He was back to his relaxed self again. The way she preferred him. The way he was when he didn't feel as if he had the weight of the world on his shoulders. Along with two very sick kids.

He squinted. "It's a bit bright in here, isn't it?"

Her eyes swept around the unexplored apartment again. It was clear neither of their other colleagues had found their way here yet. She nodded and flicked the overhead light back off, plunging them back into darkness. She walked over and pulled the curtain at the window, which looked onto the rest of the industrial site. Dim light flooded through the kitchen. The moon was high in the dark sky outside and the external lights surrounding the buildings let a little more light into the room.

It was nice. Kind of private.

Sawyer flicked the switch on the kettle. "A coffee pot and some decent beans obviously weren't on the inventory."

"And that'll be my fault, will it?" In the dim light Sawyer didn't seem anywhere as near as intimidating as before.

Maybe that was what he needed. To be out of the hospital environment and the things he was obviously struggling with. Maybe this—an environment like someone's home—made him feel more chilled. More easy to be around.

Or maybe she was remembering the last time they'd

been in a darkened room together. Because she was feeling herself drawn towards him, her feet on autopilot.

She was up close, just under his chin. He turned back round and gave a little start at her close proximity. Was she reading this all wrong?

But from the lazy smile that came across his face she obviously wasn't.

He leaned one elbow on the counter top. "Did I say it was your fault?" He was so close that his breath warmed her cheeks.

"You didn't have to, but it always seems that way."

He lifted his hand and rested it gently on her hip. "Maybe you're just a little too uptight. Maybe you need to stop following the rule book all the time." He moved forward in the darkness, his lips brushing against her ear. "Maybe—just maybe—you need to learn to relax a little."

It was the way he said it. His tone of voice. She hadn't read anything wrong.

She was reading everything perfectly. He thought she couldn't throw the rule book away? Even for a second?

Under normal circumstances she would have been horrified. But nothing about this was normal. And nothing about how she felt drawn to this man was normal.

Maybe for just five minutes she could follow her own rules. Not the ones that felt safe.

She looked at him steadily in the dim light. "Maybe. I was just thinking the same thing about you. Maybe you need to learn to relax too," she whispered.

For a second nothing happened. Her breath felt caught in her chest. Her skin prickled. What would he do?

It was almost as if she could see him thinking, weighing up things in his mind. Had she just made a huge mistake? The wait was killing her.

Then she felt it—a warm hand slipping into hers. It

electrified her skin. He pulled her over towards the sofa and sat. He tugged her down next to him, the moonlight spilling over them both.

Maybe she should feel a little intimidated by how close they were. If she leaned forward right now she could brush her nose against his. But she didn't feel intimidated at all. She didn't feel they were close enough.

In the dim moonlight and up this close she had her best-ever view of his pale green eyes. She'd seen a previous stone that color once in a tiny boutique jeweler. It was called paraiba tourmaline and she'd never seen one again. Which was a pity because it was the exact color of his eyes. And she could see the little lines all around the corners of his eyes. Were they laughter lines? Or were they from the permanent frown that he usually saved for her?

His shaggy brown hair didn't annoy her nearly so much when she had a close-up view. She kind of liked it. In fact, for a split second she could see her fingers running through it in the midst of...

She shook that thought from her mind, squeezing her eyes shut for a second. *Wow. Where had that come from?*

But she didn't feel embarrassed. She didn't feel awkward. The heat emanating from his body was warming hers. And she was enjoying it. No matter how crazy that was.

When had been the last time she'd been in this position? This close to a man? It must have been over a year ago.

Harry. Like all the others, he hadn't worked out either. It wasn't that there had been anything wrong with him. He had been kind, handsome, considerate. Just what any girl would want. But she just hadn't connected with him. Hadn't been able to let herself go enough to plan ahead for a future with him in it. Because that would have meant letting him in. Telling him everything he'd needed to know. And she hadn't been there yet.

She hadn't been ready to share.

So what was so different about Sawyer?

Was it that he challenged her to let the rule book go? Was it that he pushed her to do better?

Or was it that he'd lived through the pain of loss himself? Maybe he would understand in a way that no one else could? Maybe that was the truth of why she was drawn to him—a fellow lost soul.

He moved. The shadows had gone from his eyes and there was no barrier between them—no shutters.

Callie's stomach was in a little knot. Was he finally letting down his guard? Would he actually talk to her about what had happened?

His hand came down on her the side of her leg. His warm hand instantly connected, shooting warmth through her thin scrub trousers.

"So, Callie, are you going to tell me?"

She turned to face him. His hand was still on her leg but now she'd angled her body around to face his so they were almost nose to nose.

"About what happened. To your leg."

This was it the moment she should pull away. The time for her to retreat into herself and hide away from the rest of the world.

She'd done it before. It was automatic. It was so easy.

Her hands moved, up around his neck.

She was about to take the biggest step she'd ever taken.

"Not now. Maybe later."

Four words. That was all.

But it felt like a giant leap forward.

It was the first time she'd ever even considered telling someone about what had happened.

He could never know the strength that had taken.

She was sure she started to hold her breath. She believe how distracted she was right now. She was sure he must think her a little crazy.

But she didn't have time to think of any of these things.

Because she was kissing Sawyer.

CHAPTER EIGHT

Callie wasn't quite sure who made the first move. She didn't think it was her, but then again she didn't think it was him. It was almost as if they read each other's minds and moved simultaneously.

There was no light-hearted kissing. No nibbling. Nothing gentle. Nothing delicate.

From the second their lips locked there were no holds barred. His lips devoured hers, fully, passionately without a moment's hesitation. And she liked it.

She could feel the scrape of his emerging bristles on his chin against her skin, abrading it as they kissed. Their teeth clashed and they both ignored it, his hand pressing firmly on her back to bring her even closer.

She wanted to run her hands over his body, across his chest and down his back. Everything about her was acting on instinct. The one thing she wasn't used to.

His kisses moved. Down her neck, along her throat. Then he groaned and shifted position, pushing her onto her back on the sofa and slowly moving on top of her. He pressed her arms above her head, straddling her body, and starting work on her neck again.

She was gasping now, willing him to go lower. Itching to let her hands feel his skin under her palms.

She wrenched one of her hands free and grabbed hold

of his hair, pulling his head back up towards her and capturing his lips again. She loved the feel of them. She loved the way he kissed her.

If this was what kissing a bad boy was like, she should have done it years ago.

She moved her head, kissing down his neck and releasing her other hand to slide it around his back. She was pulling him closer, working her hands under his scrub top, dancing her fingers up and down his spine.

She heard him groan and felt his muscles flex beneath her fingers. Somehow knowing she had some control made her feel bolder. She wanted to feel his skin against hers, she wanted to *see* his skin. She pulled at his scrub top, tugging it upwards until he'd no choice but to stop kissing her for a second and pull it over his head.

There. Just what she wanted. Sawyer, bare-chested.

She ran her fingers across the scattered dark hairs on his chest, wishing they were tickling her bare skin. But he hadn't moved quite as quickly as she had. His fingers were just edging beneath her top. Her back arched automatically towards him, willing him on.

He gave her that lazy smile. *Did this man know just how sexy he was?* Then he bent and whispered in her ear. "Have a little patience, Callie."

Patience. The last thing on her mind right now.

His voice was rugged, husky. A perfect voice for the middle of the night in a darkened room in a place that belonged to neither of them. It seemed all the more wicked. All the more illicit.

He started tugging her top over her head. His eyes widened at the pink satin push-up bra he revealed. Callie was a girl who loved her fancy matching underwear, no matter what clothes she was wearing on top. *Thank heavens for small mercies.* Just wait until he reached the thong.

He didn't hesitate for a second. His gaze was fixed on her breasts enclosed in the pink satin. "So you have a thing for pale colors and matching sets? Last time I saw you half-dressed it was in lilac."

His voice was lower. Growling. And it turned her on a lot. "I have lots of matching sets." She raised her eyebrows and gave him a calculating smile. "What's your favorite color?"

"Red," he groaned, as his palms skirted the outside of the bra cups. Her breasts seemed to be swelling at his touch. But the appreciation of her underwear was momentary. Sawyer cut to the chase—his patience obviously as limited as hers. He reached behind her back and released the clasp, her bra flung aside a moment later, releasing her breasts into his clutches. As his teeth brushed against her peaked nipple she could begin to feel the throb between her legs.

"Or maybe emerald green." He tweaked, licked and blew his hot breath across her as she moaned beneath him. Her hands kept trying to move, to make further contact with his skin, to get between them and reach down below. But he kept moving, changing position and diverting her attention.

This man had talent in the diverting attention stakes.

Her legs automatically widened and he moved from straddling her to bringing his legs between her thighs. Again she acted on instinct, raising her hips and tilting her pelvis towards him. Thin scrub trousers couldn't disguise what lay beneath and she gave a little gasp.

His hand slid beneath her scrub trousers, sliding first across her pelvis then down along her thigh, his fingers tracing the line of her scar. But she didn't flinch, she didn't jerk the way she had when some other lover had touched it. This felt easy, this felt natural. His hand ran back up the inside of her leg, sending a rush of blood to her groin, working his way around her buttocks and smiling as he played with her thong. He gave a little tug and there was an instant ping, along with a loosening sensation. Thirty dollars gone in one tug. She could almost visualize the thin gossamer straps breaking. It only excited her more.

His fingers crept back around to the front, coming into contact with her pubic curls. She moaned and opened her legs, willing his fingers closer, and her frustration built.

The scrub trousers were annoying her now. She didn't want any barrier between them. She didn't want anything between them at all. She moved his arms out of the way to give her a clear path to where she wanted to go.

She pushed her hand down the front of his scrub trousers, ignoring his boxers and sliding right inside. She could feel his back arch and she wrapped her hand around him. Finally. Just what she wanted.

His mouth was moving lower now, his fingers still dancing a fine tune as she moaned in response. This bad boy certainly knew how to play her.

"Anyone home?" The door of the apartment slammed loudly.

They froze. For a few seconds neither of them moved.

Dan. It was Dan. The bright light flicked on, sending illumination over their bare skin. Sending them both into instant panic.

Sawyer pushed himself up, pulling his hand out of Callie's scrub trousers and starting to stand. Callie's head jerked from side to side, trying to find where Sawyer had flung her bra.

That was as far as they got.

Dan had obviously walked the few steps into the apartment and his jaw dropped.

Callie could have died.

She didn't even have time to cover her breasts—her scrub top had been flung far behind her in the midst of passion. Sawyer let out an expletive and stepped in front of her. "Give us a second, will you, Dan?"

Dan gulped. "Sure." The color spread rapidly up his cheeks as he walked back outside in stunned silence.

Sawyer closed the apartment door and leaned against it.

Callie felt the tears rapidly building in her eyes. She wanted to die of embarrassment. She felt like some teenager caught in a compromising position.

The silence in the room was deafening. She moved quickly, threading her arms back through her bra, fastening it and pulling the crumpled scrub top over her head.

Dan's face was haunting her. He'd seen her almost naked. A guy she hardly knew.

Sawyer was still standing with his back against the door, his eyes not meeting hers. The obvious bulge was still apparent in his thin scrub trousers. And the irony of it hit her. *Another guy she hardly knew.*

This wasn't her. She didn't act like this. She sometimes didn't even kiss on the first date.

But Sawyer had literally been by her side since she'd arrived in Chicago and the attraction had been instant. Instant but ignored.

This was the worse possible time for her. She needed to be a leader—someone that people could respect and respond to. What if Dan told the others what he'd just seen? That the doctor in charge of the potential smallpox outbreak had been lying half-naked on the sofa with a guy she'd just met?

What if he told them that her mind certainly wasn't on the job? That she was focusing on something else entirely?

She squeezed her eyes shut and tried to push the horrible thoughts from her mind. Could this be any worse?

Yes, it could.

Sawyer still couldn't look her in the eye. He hadn't even moved to pull his scrub top back on. He was just leaning against the door, his eyes fixed on the window straight ahead.

What was worse than getting caught in a compromising position with the bad boy?

Getting ignored by the man who'd just kissed you as if his life depended on it.

"Are you ready?" His voice startled her. It was almost a growl. Almost as if he thought this was all her fault.

It made her bristle. It made her defensive. It hurt.

She had to work with this man. She had to *live* with this man for the next two weeks. It would be so easy to hide her scarlet cheeks, put her head down and walk out of this room. But she couldn't. Not like this.

"I'll be ready to go when you can look me in the eye, Matt."

His head shot up. He flinched. It was so unfair that he was still standing there, bare-chested, right before her eyes. Men had it easy. He looked startled by the use of his first name—she'd only ever called him that a few times.

Or was he just surprised she'd immediately called him on his reaction?

"Let's not get into this now." He turned his back on her, picked up his scrub top, clenching it in his fingers, and put his hand on the door.

"Why not?" She couldn't think straight. Not after what had just happened.

"What?" He was beginning to look annoyed.

"Why not get into it now?" She gestured towards the door. "I'm really not looking forward to going out there and facing Dan. I don't even want to think about how I'm going to have to appeal to his better nature not to tell everyone about this." She shook her head. "My guess is that the last thing he'll want to do is share an apartment with us. Who would? We've just behaved like a pair of hormone-crazed teenagers."

She stepped forward and put her hand on his chest and he visibly flinched again. *Actions spoke louder than words.* It told her everything she needed to know.

"We have to work together, Matt. We've been stuck together in close proximity, under pressure, for the last two days. I guess we're just going to have to chalk this up to experience."

Her heart was thudding against her chest. She had no idea if she'd just played him right. She was trying to remain detached. She was trying to be rational. But she didn't feel that way.

In truth, she was mortified.

Hot and heavy after a first kiss, after only a couple of days.

She didn't need to justify herself. She didn't need to explain herself. But she just couldn't let him think that was her normal behavior.

"I guess there's a first time for everything." She kept her voice as steady as she could. He'd finally raised his eyes to meet hers but the shutters were well and truly down again. "It's probably best for both our sakes, and for the people we're responsible for, that there isn't a repeat performance."

His face remained blank. As if he was listening to her words but not really hearing them.

"If you will let me pass, I'll go and face the music with Dan."

He stepped out of her way, remaining silent.

She opened the door and stepped out into the corridor.

His silence was angering her now. First he wouldn't look at her. Now he wasn't talking to her.

She turned her head to the side, praying he wouldn't see the tears glistening in her eyes. "Maybe you'd better try and sort out other sleeping arrangements. This situation is untenable."

ON THE OUTSIDE Sawyer was frozen to the spot, but on the inside he was a bubbling cauldron, full of sulfur and about to explode.

Dan had appeared at the worst possible time—that much was obvious.

And Callie was right. They both had to pray that he would keep things to himself; otherwise Callie's authority could disappear in the blink of an eye. And in a situation like this that could be disastrous.

He knew that she'd been hurt by his lack of response but the truth was that she was right, he couldn't look her in the eye. And after what they'd just shared Callie would have wanted some kind of sign. A sign as to whether this had been just a one-off mistake or if it could lead somewhere.

And the truth was he just didn't know.

Every nerve ending in his body was on fire. Every place that she'd touched his skin seemed to burn. She'd been so willing, so responsive. If Dan hadn't appeared, chances were nothing would have stopped them.

And how would he have felt then?

Feel.

That was the problem.

Sawyer had been down this road before. Meet a woman in a bar, exchange small talk, have meaningless sex, sneak out before morning.

But all of a sudden the road had changed direction.

No, scrap that, this was an entirely new road.

In the space of a couple of days this woman had started to get under his skin. To invade his senses. To make him feel things that he hadn't felt since he'd first met Helen.

And it felt like a betrayal. It didn't matter that Helen had been dead for six years. It didn't matter that she would have never have wanted him to lead this closed-off life. His impersonation of the walking dead was growing stale, even for him.

But on any of his chance encounters before, he'd never *felt* anything. Apart from the obvious. He'd just been going through the motions. Making sure everything still worked.

This was different. This was nothing like that.

From the moment Callie Turner had appeared on his radar everything had turned upside down.

At first he'd thought he was annoyed because Callum was sick, then he'd thought it was because she was inexperienced. Or struggling. Or getting things wrong. Or all of the above.

But the truth was he was looking for a reason—any reason—not to like Callie Turner.

He was fighting the way he was drawn to her—was curious about her and wanted to know more.

The sight of her getting changed into her scrubs. The scar on her leg. The almost kiss in the treatment room.

The way he'd felt as soon as his lips had touched hers. The way she'd reacted to his touch. The feel of her skin next to his. The arch of her back. The tilt of her pelvis. The small groan she'd made at the back of her throat.

All of it driving him crazy. All of it making him act on instinct. Something he hadn't allowed to happen in a long time.

How could he have gotten into this? How could he have ended up in a specialist containment unit for a seemingly extinct disease? All of this was so unreal. This had bad movie written all over it.

Wrong place, wrong time.

The words danced around his brain again. He'd first thought them when he'd raised the alarm about the apparent smallpox cases. The words had been so in tune with how he had been feeling. He couldn't wait to get out of Chicago General. He couldn't wait to get away from the whole situation.

But now the words made him feel uncomfortable. He still didn't want to do any of the infectious disease stuff. But his Hippocratic oath had him firmly by the short and curlies. He had to stay here and help look after these people. He had to work with the team from the DPA. He had a responsibility. To them. To the patients. To the staff. To Callie...

Everything came back to her. No matter where his head drifted off to, she was always the thing he came back to. Like an anchor point.

He could almost see the picture of Helen that still sat on his desk at home. Her smiling face, dark hair and dark eyes. Home? When was the last time he'd gone home? When was the last time it had felt like home?

He sagged against the wall again. Everything was bubbling to the surface, thanks to the way he was feeling towards Callie, and he just couldn't deal with this—not on top of the DPA issue all over again.

Did she even realize how hard this was for him? To be amongst these people again? To be amongst the people that reminded him at every glance of how much he'd failed his wife?

What kind of a husband couldn't save his wife? Maybe for a regular guy that could be acceptable. But he was a doctor. And his wife had died from a medical complaint.

One that, under normal circumstances, could have been treated and her life saved.

For a few hours with Helen he'd felt as if they had been trapped on a runaway train.

They hadn't got to experience the joy of a positive pregnancy test. They hadn't got to celebrate their child's arrival, planned or not. He felt cheated out of so many experiences—all because they'd been in the wrong place at the wrong time.

Worst of all, he didn't know who to be angry at most. Himself? The DPA? Evan Hunter? Helen?

It had been Evan who had sent Helen into the field, not him. Even though she hadn't been feeling one hundred percent. None of them had had any suspicion she might be pregnant—not even Helen. But their baby had decided to defy the odds of their contraceptive of choice. And by the time they'd known, it had been too late.

A ruptured ectopic pregnancy in the middle of nowhere. There had only been one possible outcome.

He had to get past this. He had to move on. Everything about this situation was wrong.

He couldn't begin to work out his feelings towards his past and the guilt he felt, in this new situation and his pull towards Callie. He felt pressured. Callie was pressured. It wasn't the right time or the right place. He had to step back. He had to step away.

And from the hurt look in Callie's eyes, he'd already done that. Whether he'd planned to or not.

He could hear mumbled voices through the door. They sent a cool breeze dancing over his skin, covering his chest and arms in goose-bumps. He grabbed his scrub top and pulled it over his head.

He had to go out there. He had to act as if nothing had

happened. He had to try and help Callie save face, because if word of this ever got back to Evan Hunter…

He had no intention of being around to face the fallout.

He glanced at his watch. Forty-eight hours. That was how long he'd lasted when a beautiful woman had been dangled under his nose.

The pull was just too strong.

But everything about this was wrong. They would be together for the next fourteen days. Fourteen days and nights with Callie Turner.

And he'd just made it all worse.

His hand hesitated on the door handle.

Because now he knew how her skin felt. Now he knew how she reacted to his touch. Before he could only have imagined. And that could have kept him safe. That could have kept him on a reasonably even keel.

But now…

He closed his eyes. And it was Helen's face he saw. Helen's eyes. Helen's smile. The instant image made him jump.

The sear in his chest was instant. Like his heart was being twisted inside his ribcage. He couldn't do this. He couldn't do any of this.

Callie was a career girl. He used to be the same.

But now he was a getting-by kind of guy. In two weeks' time, for the second time in his career, he would walk away from the constraints of the DPA. And nothing would give him greater pleasure.

No. He could do this. He could keep his head down. He could stay out of her way. He could work the opposite shift from her. He could make sure they were never alone together. He could make sure that opportunity didn't knock again.

Because that would keep him safe.

Because he wasn't entirely sure how he would react.

He straightened his shoulders and walked out into the corridor.

It was empty. Callie and Dan were gone.

CHAPTER NINE

Evan was impatient. The computer graphics filled the wide screen on the wall, mapping the potential spread across the world, along with the corresponding timescale. It was hours and hours of hard work and dedication. Every eye in the place was fixed on the simulation. The color-coded icons were blinking at him, the red ones demanding his full attention.

He turned round and folded his arms across his chest. Violet was wearing red today too. Almost as if she was marking a claim on the piece of work she'd just created. A fitted, knee-length red dress with a black belt capturing her waist. It was an unusual color for her to wear and he was surprised by how much it suited her. Her blonde hair sat on her shoulders and she peered through matching red-rimmed glasses. It was almost as if she was trying to divert his attention…

Then it struck him—she was.

His mind drifted back to a few months ago and a blurry night with drinks after work. She'd been wearing red then too. And he'd definitely been distracted. He felt the fire burn in his belly that she might have been thinking about that while getting dressed that morning and had deliberately chosen her outfit accordingly. His own thoughts made him feel distinctly uncomfortable and, consequently, irritable.

"Where's the stuff on Sawyer?" he snapped.

"What?" Delicate lines creased her forehead. She looked at him as if he was talking a foreign language.

"You know what," he accused. This was all becoming more and more obvious. "I asked you to do a background check on Sawyer. Find out where he's been and what he's been doing. I asked you more than two days ago. Where is it?"

She waved her hand in at him irritation. "Earth to Evan. I've been kind of busy on the save-the-planet-from-smallpox stuff."

He pulled his shoulders back in shock. Cheeky. Insolent. Not the way that Violet Connelly ever spoke to anyone—least of all him, her boss. She was really pushing him. And it didn't help that every time she came into his field of vision his eyes fixed on her lips.

Lips of which he'd already had experience.

He could see some ears pricking up around them, People craning their necks above their partitions to see how he was going to react.

Did anyone here know what had happened between them?

He had to make sure there were no suspicions. He couldn't let anyone think he would give Violet preferential treatment.

He placed a hand on her desk and leaned forward, drawing his head level with hers. Up close and personal she was a tiny little thing. His hands could probably span her waist. He could see her nibbling her bottom lip as if she was nervous. And she probably was with his big frame towering over her.

He pulled back a little and kept his voice calm. It wasn't

his job to entertain the crowds—they had enough work to be getting on with. "Dr. Connelly, I gave you a specific task to do a number of days ago. I expect you to have completed it." He caught the glimmer in her eye. It definitely wasn't fear. It was much more like rebellion!

"I've been busy." The words were firm, even if he could see the slight tremble in her hand as she picked up a pen.

"You're telling me that in the last two days you've found out nothing about Matt Sawyer? Nothing?" His voice was steadily rising now, despite his best intentions.

Was he imagining it or had she just pouted her lips at him? This woman was going to drive him crazy.

She shrugged her shoulders. "Oh, I've looked. But there's nothing to find. I've no idea what Matt Sawyer's been doing or where he's been." She raised one eyebrow at him and tilted her chin. "Why don't you ask him?"

She was baiting him. In front of a room full of colleagues. The hairs were standing on end at the back of his neck. It was all he could do not to growl at her.

"You've got two hours, Violet. Two hours to find out exactly what I requested on Matt Sawyer. If you don't deliver, I'm taking it to the director."

He turned on his heel and walked out of the room. The pen still dangling from Violet's fingers.

"Still nothing?"

The DPA guy shook his head as Sawyer leaned against the wall. It had been three days and they still had no word on the classification of the disease. They were still stuck in the no-man's land of a "brick-shaped orthopox", which told them something but pretty much told them nothing at the same time.

Sawyer had been doing his best impression of the invisible man. And it made him feel lousy.

When Callie worked days, he worked nights. When Callie was in the apartment, he was out, finding any excuse to be somewhere else. There had been a few awkward moments, a few "almost" bumps in the corridor, resulting in both of them jumping and staring at walls and floors instead of the person right before their eyes. A huge amount of avoidance tactics on his part.

He was beginning to find it almost comedic. The number of times he'd heard her voice behind a door he had been about to open, only to swerve and end up in a place he really didn't want to be, having conversations with people he barely knew.

On the other hand, yesterday he'd found himself in the children's playroom, leading the Portuguese soccer team on a quest for worldwide domination against the children in the US soccer team. It had been game controllers at dawn. But he'd had to let them win, even though he'd suspected they were playing dirty.

There were five kids, aside from Ben and Jack, in the containment facility, of varying ages and nationalities. None seem to have had any side-effects from the vaccine. And the minor ailments that had brought them into the E.R. in the first place had all been resolved. It was amazing what the threat of an infectious disease could do.

But spending time with the children had been fun. They were treating everything like a vacation. They could watch want they wanted on cable, play a mountain of console games and pretty much eat whatever they liked. He'd made a mental note that the children's playroom was now going to be his number-one place to go to avoid Callie.

Today had been torture. The trouble with a containment facility was that no matter how hard you tried to find somewhere else to sleep there really wasn't anywhere else to go so he had to stick to the apartment he'd been allocated.

The aroma of coffee had drifted under his door around lunchtime. He was supposed to be sleeping, but he'd only dozed on and off for a few hours. The temptation to get out of bed with his nose leading him directly to the coffee pot had been huge, but then he'd heard her voice. Callie was obviously in the kitchen, grabbing a bite to eat. And the last thing he wanted to do in his sleep-deprived state was run into her.

She was already destroying the few hours' sleep he was actually getting by invading his dreams. Sometimes happy, sometimes angry, but always in state of undress. Funny, that. It was taking him back to his teenage years.

And that probably wasn't a place he wanted to go. Violet had enough blackmail material on his misspent youth to last a lifetime.

The trouble with avoiding Callie was being out of the loop of information. She was the focal point around here—all paths led to Callie and if he wasn't communicating with her, he didn't always know exactly what was going on.

He had been sure that the DPA would have had a more definitive diagnosis by now. Frank Palmer would be working flat out. It didn't matter that he knew it could take up to seven days. He wanted to know *now*.

One of the nurses came and touched his shoulder. "Can you take a look at Mrs. Keating, Ben and Jack's mum? She's not feeling too good."

His stomach plummeted. It was the one thing they had all been waiting for—someone else to show signs of infection. He picked up Jill Keating's notes and started walking across the corridor. The thick bundle was packed full of assessments and observation notes. For a woman with no significant disease history it was surprising how quickly notes filled up in an isolation facility.

"What's she complaining of?" he asked the nurse.

There was another person that was having trouble looking at him.

But for an entirely different reason. The nurse's eyes would be full of unspoken worries and unanswered questions. Things that nobody wanted to say out loud right now.

Everyone was dreading someone showing signs of infection. It would give them all the confirmation of the infectious disease without the laboratory diagnosis.

"She has a low-grade temperature and a headache. Her pulse is fine and her blood pressure only slightly raised. But she's vomited twice."

Mrs. Keating was lying in bed in the darkened room. It had taken her more than forty-eight hours to finally leave the room that her children were in and have some rest. The woman was probably exhausted and that could explain the headache and the slight rise in blood pressure. But the temperature and vomiting?

He pulled on the protective clothing, regulation mask and gloves and pushed open the door. "Hi, Jill. It's Dr. Sawyer. Want to tell me how you're doing?"

She averted her eyes straight away as the light from the corridor spilled into the room. It sent an instant chill down his spine. "Wake Callie," he whispered over his shoulder to the nurse.

He spent the next twenty minutes examining Jill. She was definitely exhausted. And despite being surrounded by food and drink she was showing clinical signs of dehydration. The black circles under her eyes were huge and she vomited into a sick bowl again during his examination.

Callie was standing at the window in the corridor, looking anxiously through the glass. He'd signaled to her to wait outside.

She moved to the door as he came back outside and waited impatiently while he discarded his protective clothing.

"Well? What do you think?"

He started scribbling some notes on Jill's prescription chart. "I'm sorry that I woke you, Callie."

"Why? Is she okay?"

He nodded. "I can't say for certain but I suspect she is in the throes of her first-ever migraine. The only thing that doesn't really fit is the low-grade pyrexia. But everything else makes me think it's a migraine. And after the stress she's been under I wouldn't be surprised. I'm going to give her an injection then sit here and wait until her symptoms subside."

"And will they?"

He shrugged his shoulders. "I certainly hope so. This is a wait-and-see option. We need to give it a little time. An hour or so."

"Call me if there's any change."

He nodded. Disappointed. He'd half expected her to wait with him. This could be crucial in determining the nature of this disease. But it obviously wasn't to be. She couldn't get away from him fast enough.

And he couldn't really blame her.

Or maybe she was just showing faith in his competence as a doctor?

Whatever it was, he was just going to have to get over it. But his stomach was gnawing at the memory of how much he'd missed those eyes in the last few days.

His nose picked up the smell of toasted bagels. It was time to follow his stomach. This could be a long wait.

AN HOUR LATER Jill was in a deep sleep. The migraine relief seemed to have worked well and Sawyer was breathing a sigh of relief. He'd checked on the boys—both Jack and Ben were stable and showing no obvious signs of improvement or deterioration. It was four a.m. That horrible point of the night when nausea abounded and sleep seemed so far away.

He looked around. One of the nurses touched his shoulder. "Go and have some coffee, Sawyer, you look like crap."

"Thanks for that."

She smiled at him. "Oh, you're welcome. I'll page you if I need you—but I doubt it."

He headed down the darkened corridor. There was definitely a pot of coffee on the go somewhere. The smell seemed to be drifting towards him and making him follow it like the children had followed the pied piper. And he could hear some background noise.

He reached one of larger communal kitchens. The coffee pot was just on the boil. Just the way he liked it. Straight, black and hot.

He poured a cup and headed towards the noise. The kids must have left the TV on in the cinema room. It was something sappy. He slumped into one of the seats. If he just sat down for five minutes and drank this coffee, he would be fine. The caffeine would hit his system and keep him awake for the last few hours.

Five minutes.

"What are you doing here?"

He jumped. The voice cut through the darkness and he spilled hot coffee all down the front of his scrub trousers. "Hey!" He rubbed frantically at the stain, lifting the wet trousers from his groin area—some things just shouldn't get burned.

Callie appeared at his side and peered at the spreading stain. "You klutz." She started to snigger. That crazy middle-of-the-night kind of laugh that night shift staff got and couldn't stop.

Sawyer sighed and set down his half-filled coffee cup.

"I came down here for a coffee to help me stay awake and wondered what the noise was. What are you doing here?"

"I couldn't get back to sleep."

"So you came down here, rather than sit up with me next to the patients?" It sounded almost accusing and he didn't mean it to come out that way but in the middle of the night social niceties disappeared.

"I guess I didn't want to sit next to you, Sawyer."

Yip. It worked both ways. Night shift certainly did away with the social niceties.

He didn't want to get into this. Not here. Not now. He glanced at the big screen. "You told me you were an action girl, not a chick-flick girl. What happened?"

Their eyes turned in unison at the screen as the hero's eyes followed the heroine, staring at her unashamedly.

Even in the dark Callie's cheeks looked a little flushed. Maybe it was the intimacy of the scene. Not intimate in that sense. But intimate in the fact it was the first time the audience could see how smitten the hero was with the girl of his dreams.

And he could relate.

Here, in the middle of a darkened room, in the midst of an outbreak, Sawyer could totally relate.

He could see Callie's long eyelashes, the blue of her eyes dimmed by the light. But the flickering screen highlighted her cheekbones, showing the beautiful structure and lines of her face. He couldn't take his eyes off her.

Her eyes met his. "I am an action girl. But I was too late this time. It seems the kids are action fans too—and they all have DVD players in their rooms." Her voice was quiet, almost whispered. It made him naturally lean towards her to hear what she was saying above the background noise of the movie.

"I'm an action girl" were the words playing around in his mind.

She held up another DVD and tilted her head to the side, revealing the long line of her neck.

His hand went automatically to her waist and she didn't flinch, didn't move. Her arm stayed half in the air, still holding up the DVD, almost as if she was frozen.

Sawyer stepped forward, the full length of his body next to hers. He forgot about the damp coffee stain on his scrubs. This was where he should apologize. This was where he should tell her he was having trouble getting his head around all this.

This was where he should tell her about Helen. About the fight with Evan and the consequences. This was where he should clear the air.

Because if he didn't, he'd never move on.

But he didn't do any of those things.

He just kissed her.

His hands captured her head, winding his fingers through her hair and anchoring her in position.

But he didn't kiss her like he had before.

This time he was gentle. This time he was slow. This time he wanted her to know that he meant it. It wasn't just a reaction. It wasn't just a physical thing.

This was him, Matt Sawyer, wanting to make a connection with her, Callie Turner.

So he started on her lips. Brushing his against hers then moving along her jaw and down her neck.

He was just working his way back up the other side of her neck when Callie's hands connected with his shoulders, pushing him back firmly.

"No, Sawyer. Stop it."

He was stunned and immediately stepped away.

Even in the dark he could see tears on her cheeks. "I

can't do this. This isn't me. And I know you don't mean it. I can't do what we did a few days ago and then just walk away. You need to leave me alone." She started walking towards the door. Away from him. "Just leave me, Sawyer. Leave me alone."

"Callie, wait—" But his words were lost because she'd almost bolted out the door. He stared down at his hands. The hands that had just touched her. That hands that still wanted to be touching her.

He didn't blame her. His earlier actions had been pretty much unforgiveable. But the pull towards her was real. And it wasn't going to go away any time soon.

He sagged back down into one of the chairs. There was no point in going after her right now.

He needed the proper time and space to talk to her.

His eyes went back to the screen flickering in the darkness. They'd reached the point in the movie where the heroine was telling the hero she was marrying someone else.

Kind of ironic really.

CALLIE FLEW ALONG the corridor as if she were being chased by swarm of angry bees. He'd kissed her again. And she'd been so close to responding to him. So close.

But she couldn't let that happen again. She couldn't be caught in a compromising position with Sawyer. She had to keep her mind on the job.

That was the rational part of her brain talking.

Her heart was saying something else entirely.

She couldn't let him touch her again. She couldn't let him evoke those feelings in her again, only to walk away without a single glance.

She wasn't built that way. She couldn't deal with things like that.

Isabel had been entirely different. *Isabel* would have

been the one kissing Sawyer and walking away without a second thought. She had always been in control.

Not like *her*.

History had taught her that she hated things she couldn't control. And there were lots of elements of this spinning out of her control, without adding her feelings for Sawyer into the mix.

When were these feelings ever going to go away? She'd thought working at the DPA where she and Isabel had planned to be would have given her some comfort. But in the end it hadn't.

The guilt she felt about her sister still gnawed away at her. She constantly compared herself to Isabel, without ever really meaning to.

Even with the men she'd dated she'd kept her sister at the forefront of her mind. Would Isabel have approved? Would she have liked this one? Would she have thought that one good enough?

But with Sawyer it was different. She didn't even want to give them space together in the same thought. Why was that?

If Sawyer had met Isabel, would he have been attracted to her instead of Callie?

That thought made her feel physically sick. She felt a horrible creeping sensation over her skin, along with a realization of her continued exasperation with herself.

When would this go away? When would she feel as if she was living her own life and not doing penance for the loss of her sister's?

Everything in her work and personal life was so mixed up right now. And being stuck in an enclosed space with Sawyer wasn't helping.

Yesterday she'd spent time fretting over the plan. While all her instincts had told her that keeping the brothers together was ultimately the right decision, the truth was that the plan told her otherwise.

She'd spent a few hours weighing up the pros and cons of insisting the plan be followed before finally deciding to let it go. The only thing was, unease still gripped her. Gnawed away at her stomach and kept her awake at night.

Plans were evidence based. Plans had been researched within an inch of their lives. How would she defend her decision if challenged from above?

Sawyer had whispered to her to relax and stop following the plans a few nights ago and the truth was it hadn't been nearly as scary as she'd thought.

Just like making the decision about the brothers.

Her phone buzzed in her pocket and she pressed the answer button straight away. It was five in the morning so it had to be the DPA.

"Callie? How are you? How are you holding up?" Her footsteps froze.

"Callum?"

"Who else would call you at this time in the morning?"

Relief flooded through her and the tears that had just vanished came spilling down her cheeks again.

Callum. Her port in a storm. The one person she actually *did* want to talk to.

"You don't know how happy I am to hear your voice. How are you, Callum?"

She heard the hearty laugh she was so used to. The familiar sound made her miss him all the more.

"I'm fine. You were right—it was an MI. They whipped me down to the angio lab and inserted a stent. Missed most of the last few days because of the drugs. But I'm feeling great today."

She leaned against the wall, sliding down onto her

haunches. "If you're feeling great, why are you phoning me at five in the morning? Shouldn't you be resting?"

"Resting's for amateurs. Couldn't sleep and no one at the DPA will tell me anything useful. I blackmailed one of the nurses into letting me use her phone. It's been five days and I should have been officially discharged by now. Funny thing is, my doc won't discharge me to the containment unit."

She shook her head at his tenacity. She wouldn't put it above Callum to try and discharge himself straight to the containment unit. "You phoned the DPA?"

"Of course I did. I wanted to know how my favorite doctor was getting on."

She felt warmth spread across her chest. "I bet you say that to all the girls." It was so good to hear his voice. She'd heard about the stent but no one would actually say if they'd spoken to him. This made all the difference. She smiled. "And anyway who is your favorite doctor—me or Sawyer?"

He paused. Obviously deciding what to say next. "Yeah, Sawyer. Well, he used to be my favorite but you've taken over from him now. How are you getting on with him, Callie?"

His voice sounded a little strained. And the realization hit her. That's why he was phoning. That's why he was trying to get to the containment unit. He was worried.

"Ask me something else."

"Oh, I see. It's like that."

That was Callum. He knew her too well. She couldn't lie to him and try and dress this up but she didn't want to add to his stress. "Yes, it is. Ask me about the smallpox."

She heard the sigh at the end of the phone. "I'm assuming you don't have a definitive diagnosis yet."

"You're assuming right. We know it's an orthopox and

we know it's definitely not chicken pox. We've vaccinated all those exposed and moved to the containment facility. What was this place, by the way? I'm assuming you know."

He cleared his throat. "It's just a little place that was on the back burner."

"What does that mean? The building is old, but the facilities are state-of-the-art." Her curiosity was piqued now—no matter what the time.

"How are the patients?"

She gave half a smile. An obvious deflection. He knew it. And she knew it. Whatever this building had been, he'd no intention of telling her. "We've got two sick little boys—one ventilated. And we're monitoring symptoms in everyone else. Had a bit of a scare with the boy's mother but it turned out to be nothing. Oh, that reminds me. We had someone we couldn't vaccinate. A nurse who is eighteen weeks pregnant. She's currently holed up for a fortnight in an exclusive Chicago hotel."

"Oh, no." Callum's silence was ominous. She'd expected him to say something else or to ask more questions.

"Callum?"

"How's Sawyer? Was he okay about that? How did he deal with the pregnant nurse?"

She shifted her weight from one leg to the other. What could she say? That initially he had freaked out? But he'd managed to contain how he'd been feeling and had done the job? It was truthful, but was probably too near to the bone. "He was fine. I know that his pregnant wife died on a DPA mission but no one really knows the details. Want to fill me in?"

His answer was brusque. "Not really. Is he following protocol?"

"Ours or his?"

"So it's like that. I might have guessed. Sawyer's never

going to change." Even though he sounded a little exasperated, Callie could almost see the smile on his face as he said the words.

"If you tell me about him, Callum, maybe I'll understand him a little better. Maybe it will help us work together."

She could almost hear his brain ticking over at the end of the phone. "Are you having major problems with him? Professional problems?"

How did she answer that question? Because, like it or not, the professional problems were minor. It was the personal problems that were the real issue.

Callum had never been slow off the mark. He was a man who could always read between the lines.

"It sounds as if it's not up to me to tell you, Callie. It would be better coming from him." Words of wisdom from a man who was obviously seeing things much more clearly than she was. "Maybe I should give Sawyer a ring. Have you got his number? Did he ever change it?"

"Maybe you should relax. Maybe you should follow the post-MI protocol like a good patient."

"Give me his number."

"No."

"Dr. Turner, I asked for his number." His voice was rising now and he was obviously getting agitated. He only ever called her Dr. Turner when he was trying to tell her off. It made her smile.

"I'm hanging up now, Callum."

"Don't you dare!"

"Take care now."

She was smiling but still close to the floor on her haunches. Her legs were beginning to cramp.

She stood up and arched her back, trying to release the tension. Her head was beginning to thump, probably from lack of sleep and all the stress she was under. Nothing to do with Sawyer.

Nothing at all…

SAWYER WAS LYING on his bed, trying to get some sleep. He glanced at his watch for the tenth time. The sun was streaming through the windows. Seemed like no one had thought of blackout blinds for this place.

He picked up his phone and pressed in Violet's number. His guilt was starting to kick in now. He should have phoned her earlier. His excuses were weak—even he knew that.

She picked up straight away and let out a big sigh. "Perfect timing, bruv."

He sat up in bed. The chance of sleep was long gone. "What's up?"

He heard her slow intake of breath. "I've got Evan Hunter breathing down my neck. He wanted me to check up on you—find out what you've been doing these last few years."

"Well, I'll make it easy for you. I don't want you to be next on Evan Hunter's hit list. Check out Borneo, Alaska and Connecticut."

"What?" He could almost hear the wheels spinning in her brain at the eclectic mix of places he'd been in the last six years.

"There's nothing sinister to find, Violet. You know that."

Her answer was instant. "I know that, Matt."

"What's Evan's problem? No—scratch that. I know what his problem is—me. But what exactly does he think he's going to find?"

Violet sounded annoyed. "I have no idea. He threatened

to report me to the director if I didn't get back to him with a report in two hours."

"What? He asked you do to a report in the middle of the night?"

"Well, not exactly. He first asked me to do it five days ago. Then he gave me the two-hour time limit three days ago."

"And you still haven't done it?"

He could hear the casualness in her voice. "Yeah, well, I didn't really think he'd complain about me to the director. He was just growling at me. Trying to show me who's boss. Now you've given me the heads up I'll at least go and give him that to chew over. It should be enough to finally satisfy him you're not involved in this." He could hear the hesitation in her voice. "How are you, Sawyer? Is everything okay? Any other symptoms?"

"Not yet. We had a little scare earlier but it's fine. I'm fine." He paused. "Well, actually, I'm not fine."

There was a long significant pause at the end of the phone and he knew why. He'd never discussed anything with his sister before. He avoided personal issues at all costs.

"What's wrong?" Her voice was quiet, almost afraid to ask the question.

"It's Callie."

"Is something wrong with Callie? Does she have symptoms?" It was only natural for her to jump to the most obvious conclusion.

"No. It's not that. I kissed her."

"You did what?"

Well, that had got her attention. Other than their last conversation, he couldn't remember the last time Violet had ever shouted at him. But, then again, she was also defying Evan Hunter left, right and center, which was also unheard of. It seemed his sister had turned into a whole new person over the last six years. All while he'd been hiding in the outer parts of the planet.

"I kissed her." He flopped back down on the bed. The words seemed so much worse now he'd finally said them.

But they felt so much better. It was nice to finally offload.

"Why on earth did you kiss Callie Turner?" her voice hissed down the phone. She was obviously trying to keep anyone from hearing.

Sawyer felt like a teenager. Why did any guy kiss a pretty girl? "Because I wanted to. And I think she wanted me to."

"You mean she didn't slap your face?"

"Not quite."

Violet was obviously a bit stunned. "So, what's the problem?" She hesitated a second. "I mean, this isn't the first time you've kissed someone since Helen, is it?"

He let out a snort of laughter. "I think I can safely say no to that. But this is different."

"Different how?"

She'd put him on the spot now and he didn't quite know how to answer. "Different because I don't want to hurt her. But there's a definite attraction between us. And I know she feels it too."

"Has an alien inhabited your body?"

"What do you mean?"

"I mean that for the first time in years you're talking to me about your feelings. Since when have you done that?"

He couldn't answer.

"Okay, brother, I'm only going to say one thing. I like Callie. I mean, I *really* like her."

"Well, I think I like her too." There. He'd admitted it. To someone other than himself.

"Then don't mess this up. Don't hurt her." The words were blunt and straight to the point. Violet had never been one to mess around with how she felt.

"Can't you give me something else? Can't you tell me to handle this? You know her better than I do." He was beginning to sound desperate, but right now he didn't care.

"Really? Well, here's the clincher—I haven't been in a lip-lock with her, Matt. And I'm sorry but you don't reach the grand old age of thirty-six and ask your sister for dating advice. That ship sailed a long time ago, buddy. Probably around the time you told everyone about my high-school crush."

He cringed but it brought a smile to his face. He'd made a poster and stuck it up outside the school. Violet had locked herself in her room and hadn't spoken to him for days. She still hadn't got over it.

"So, no advice, then?"

"Absolutely not. Not on your love life anyway. Just stay safe, brother. And phone me if there's any problem. Any *work*-related problem."

"What about Evan?"

Her voice had a hard edge to it now. "Leave me to worry about him. I'm hoping I'll be out of his hair soon enough." She hung up before Sawyer had a chance to ask her what she meant.

He stared at the ceiling. Potential smallpox day five. Great.

CHAPTER TEN

"Wake up, Sawyer."

One of the nurses stood above him. Liz? Julie? He really couldn't remember. He sat bolt upright in the bed, not even thinking about hiding himself.

She turned sideways. "Cover yourself up, boy. And get dressed. Some guy from the DPA wants to talk to either you or Callie, and I can't find her."

Sawyer pulled the sheet half across his body, lifting a crumpled pair of scrubs from the floor and tugging them on. He smirked as the nurse rolled her eyes and handed him the matching top.

He let out a laugh as she walked to the door then stopped and threw him a can of deodorant. Then something registered with him. "What do you mean, you can't find Callie? Where can she be?"

The nurse shrugged. "I just know the guy said he had to speak to either one of you. He's been holding for a few minutes because I tried to find Callie first. When I couldn't, he said to wake you."

"Where's the phone?"

"At the nurses' station."

He jogged along the corridor. His brain was in overdrive. It was day seven. This had to be a diagnosis. But where on earth was Callie?

He picked up the phone. "Frank?"

"Finally. Sleeping beauty wakes up."

"Have you got something?"

"Is this Frank? Is this the man who is supposed to be in Hawaii with his devoted and gorgeous wife, who'd bought eight different bikinis for our long-awaited vacation?"

Seven days. He'd waited seven days for this. "Frank?" He couldn't hide the impatient tone in his voice.

"It's monkeypox."

"What?" Sawyer was stunned. He'd never seen monkeypox before. It had never really been on his radar.

Frank seemed to know exactly what to say. "You'll need to examine the boys again for bites, scratches and abrasions. Monkeypox usually only occurs in Western or Central Africa but strangely enough the last known case was in the U.S. in 2003, caused by prairie dogs."

"What?" Nothing about this made sense. His brain couldn't process what he was hearing.

"Monkeypox can be spread by squirrels, dogs, rats, mice and rabbits. That's why your boy had swollen glands. It's one of main differences in symptoms between smallpox and monkeypox."

Sawyer ran his hand through his hair. Where was Callie? He had to talk to her about this straight away. Things were starting to register in his brain. Should he have guessed this? He hadn't given too much thought to the swollen lymph glands—even though they were unusual in smallpox. He'd just assumed it was a viral response.

"What are our options?"

Frank cleared his throat. "None, really. No known treatment. It's less severe than smallpox and the smallpox vaccine can lessen the symptoms. But it can still be fatal—monkeypox can have a one to ten percent mortality rate. All the smallpox infection controls should remain in place."

They spoke for a few more minutes then Sawyer replaced the receiver. "Wow." He leaned against the wall.

His head was spinning. His eyes swept across the room. Everyone was going about their business quietly and efficiently. What effect would this news have on the people here?

In a way it was a relief to finally have a diagnosis but with no known treatment it still made things difficult. He racked his brain, trying to remember what he could about monkeypox. It wasn't much.

He only hoped there was a plan.

Had he just thought that? Him, Sawyer, wondering if there was a plan?

Callie was obviously rubbing off on him.

Callie—where was she?

He started walking along the corridor, stopping people on the way past. "Have you seen Callie? Do you know where Callie is?" Time after time his colleagues just shook their heads.

Finally, one of the contact tracers furrowed his brow. "I saw her go down there a little while ago." He pointed down one of the long corridors.

Sawyer strode along. He couldn't remember this part of the building on the plan. It was well away from the small labs and isolation ward. He reached a double door at the end of the corridor and pushed it open.

It took his breath away.

The tiny little room was extraordinary. A small stained-glass window was set into the facing wall, with the sun streaming through causing a kaleidoscope of colors across the white walls. It was like a magical light show.

Callie hadn't even heard him enter. She was sitting on

one of the wooden pews near the altar at the front. There was no particular religion celebrated here. It was one of those non-denominational rooms that could be used by anyone.

A quiet place. For contemplation.

He walked along the carpeted aisle and sat down next to her. She jerked, conscious of no longer being alone, and opened her eyes. He slid along a little. She was sitting directly in the stream of coloured light. Her face and skin were lit up like a rainbow. It was dazzling. He'd never wanted to reach out and touch anyone more than he did right now.

Papers were scattered all around the floor at her feet.

"What do you want, Sawyer?" She sounded weary, exhausted. The relief that had instantly flooded him when he'd heard the diagnosis disappeared. All of a sudden he could hear the countdown in his head. Now they had a definitive diagnosis, it was another step closer to getting out of there.

It was a step closer to getting away from the dreaded DPA. It was also a step closer to getting away from Callie.

And he wasn't prepared for the way that made him feel.

"Sawyer?"

He was still looking at her pale skin bathed in myriad colors. It was taking his breath away. As were the feelings sweeping over him.

He took a breath. "We have a diagnosis. It's monkeypox."

"Monkeypox?" Her voice rose automatically then she looked around her, as if conscious she shouldn't shout in a place of worship. She fell to her knees on the paper-strewn floor where papers had been tossed in all directions.

He joined her. "Do you think there's something about monkeypox in here?"

She nodded. "There is. It isn't much, just some basic information and guidelines." Her head shot back up, "Who did you speak to?"

"Frank. And before you ask, he was positive. He said you could call him back. He'll stay at the lab until he gets a chance to speak to you."

"Here it is!" She pulled a few crumpled pieces of paper from the floor. Her eyes started racing across the text. She was mumbling under her breath, "Same transmission precautions, slightly shorter incubation period." Her eyes lit up. "I'm not entirely sure—I'll need to check—but I think this is good news for Alison. It seems to be a larger droplet infection. There's a good chance she won't have been infected."

He nodded. "Actually, it still has a seventeen-day incubation period. She'll need to wait a little longer before she can go home."

Callie nodded but the smile reached all the way up to her eyes. "It's something. I was dreading a smallpox diagnosis."

"Me too." He looked around him. "How did you find this place?"

She let out a little laugh. "Curiosity got the better of me. It wasn't marked on the plans and I wanted to find out what was down here." She put her hands out. "Once I'd found this place I wanted to keep this little piece of paradise to myself."

"I don't blame you." His eyes met hers. He didn't want to fight. He didn't want a confrontation. Both of them knew they needed to talk. But this just wasn't the right time or place.

She looked down at the mess she'd made on the floor. A bright red folder had been pushed under one of the pews. "I came here to escape. To get out of the rat race." She edged the folder with her foot. "I had a bit of a disagreement with the plan. It sort of ended up all over the place."

He folded his arms and gave her a lopsided grin. "Shock, horror. Callie Turner threw the plan away?"

"I guess I did." She was biting her lip as she stared at the scattered papers. Didn't she know how much that distracted him?

He rested back against the wooden pew. Not exactly designed for comfort. Any minute now Callie would be off, her brain kicking into gear and taking off at full speed. He could picture her talking nineteen to the dozen and shouting instructions to everyone.

That's why he kind of liked this place.

"How long have you had this hidden gem?"

She arched her eyebrow at him and had the good grace to look embarrassed. "A few days. Right after we bumped into each other in the kids' cinema room. I needed somewhere I could have a little space."

"From me?" He didn't want her to say yes. He *really* didn't want her to say yes. But somehow it was more important that she was honest with him than that his feelings were hurt.

She sighed. "From you, from me, from everything." She threw up her hands but her voice was remarkably steady. "I had to sort a few things out in my head." She gave him a sad sort of smile. "I spoke to Callum. He wanted to call you—to interfere—but I wouldn't let him."

It was probably the first time in his life that he didn't automatically jump to his own defense. He didn't need to. He knew exactly what she would have said to Callum and exactly what he would have said in response.

"So, is he going to kick my ass?"

She let out a little snigger.

"Just as well I changed my number, then." He turned to face her. "Seriously, is he well enough to call?"

She nodded.

"Do you mind if I call him and tell him about the monkeypox? It might be the only thing that distracts him from tearing me off a strip or two."

"I think that would be fine." She stood up, her feet brushing against her paperwork. She looked a little lost. "I'll come back for this later. I still haven't really figured out if this is the place for me. I need to do a little more thinking."

"The place for you?" He looked around him in confusion. "A chapel?"

She shook her head slowly and took a deep breath. "No. The DPA."

There it was, he thought. The thing that was bothering her most. Him kissing her had only been a distraction.

And it was obviously the first time she'd said it out loud.

The underlying issue was still there. She was uncomfortable. She wasn't truly happy in her work—he knew it and she knew it. He'd known it right from the beginning. So he wasn't the main cause of her problems, only an antagonist.

"You're doing a good job, Callie." It seemed important to tell her. It seemed important to rally her confidence.

"You think so?" She'd reached the door now and turned back to face him.

He nodded. "I do. And don't think about things too long, Callie. Take it from someone who knows. Sometimes while you're doing all that thinking, life passes you by."

She pulled her shoulders back as if she was a little startled by his words. Her hand wavered on the doorhandle and then she came back and sat down beside him again.

It didn't matter that she had other things to do. Other

news to spread. Other plans to follow. Sometimes you just had to act on instinct. To take the moment before it passed.

"Is that what happened to you, Sawyer? Life has just passed you by?"

He froze, lowering his eyes and taking a few breaths. Her hand crept over and held his, interlocking their fingers.

He nodded, still looking at the floor. "I've lost six years," he whispered "being angry at everyone and everything."

His gaze rose again and fixed on the wall in front of him, staring at the beautiful light streaming through the stained-glass window. She squeezed his hand. Sometimes it was better to say nothing. Sometimes it was better just to give someone the time to say what they needed. Sometimes the best gift to give to someone was just to listen.

It struck her like gold. This was part of what she wanted to do. Not just for Sawyer but for her patients too.

"I was angry with Evan for sending her into the field. I was angry with myself for not knowing my wife was pregnant. I was angry with Helen for not realizing she was pregnant."

He turned to face her. His eyes were wet with tears and he wrinkled his brow. "I was angry that the plan didn't have any contingencies for things like this—a member of staff needing surgical intervention in the middle of nowhere."

He took a deep breath. "But most of all I was angry at myself for not being able to save her. I was her husband. I should have been able to save her..."

She let his voice tail off. She wanted to put her arms around him. She wanted to hug him as tightly as she could.

But there was a balance here that could so easily be tipped. He'd shared something with her that she doubted he'd shared before. What did that mean?

It seemed almost like a step towards her. But she couldn't be sure. And was she ready to take a step like that while she still had demons of her own?

Something twisted inside her. Could she talk about Isabel? Was she ready to share? She was still faltering. She still had to step out of Isabel's shadow before she could do anything else. Too much was happening all at once, so where did Sawyer fit into this equation?

She rubbed her hand over the top of his. Words seemed so futile now but she had to say something so she kept it simple. "Thank you for sharing, Sawyer. I know it was hard. And I'm glad you did." Her words were whispered and he gave her a little smile.

"I think it's time you went outside and faced the masses. Better share the good news and tell them what they need to know."

She nodded and slowly stood up. He needed some time. He needed some space. She could appreciate that.

And if she really cared about him, she had to give it.

"Come out when you're ready." She gave him a little nod and walked out.

Sawyer leaned back against the pew. In a matter of minutes it would be chaos out there again. Everyone would have questions and be looking for answers. The people currently quarantined would need up-to-date information. They would need to know what would happen next. Everything would have to be reassessed, re-evaluated, reconfigured.

As soon as the door closed behind her, Sawyer felt the air in the room become still. He didn't feel any urge to hurry after her. It would all still be out there in a few minutes—or a few hours. It was truly peaceful in here. No outside noises and far enough away from the clinical areas and staff to shield it from any external influences. Not even the noise of the birds tweeting outside.

He sat there for the longest time watching the colorful reflections from the stained-glass window dance on the wall to his right.

He looked at the scattered pieces of the plan around his feet.

Plans. He'd spent so long hating plans and everything about them. Blaming them and the DPA for the part they'd played in Helen's death.

It didn't matter that he was supposedly an intelligent, rational man. Nothing about his wife's death had seemed rational to him.

It had all seemed so random.

The DPA planned for every eventuality—or so he'd thought. But it hadn't planned for that. It hadn't planned for his wife to collapse with an ectopic pregnancy in the middle of nowhere and too far away for any emergency treatment.

And it had made him mad.

It had made him behave in a way that would have embarrassed Helen. He had questioned everything. He had torn up plans and set them on fire. He'd refused to follow any of the protocols that the DPA had set. And then he'd walked away from it all.

He'd walked away because he hadn't wanted to deal with anything.

He couldn't possibly believe that they'd just been unlucky. That Helen's death had simply come down to dumb, rotten luck.

He'd tried to forget everything and push everyone away.

But now it was time to stop all that. It was time to open his eyes.

It was time to remember—both the good and the bad.

And he remembered. He remembered everything about his wife that he'd loved.

And for the first time in a long time he took joy in remembering.

The dark shade of her hair, the chocolate color of her eyes. The fact that every item in her wardrobe had been a variation of a shade of blue. Her collection of bells that had sat on the window ledge in their bedroom. The smell of her favorite perfume, which she'd worn every single day. The candles she'd lit around her bath at night. The grey and blue felt hat she'd worn in winter that he'd always said made her look one hundred and five.

All the things that he'd been terrified to forget. Once—just once—he'd forgotten who her favorite author had been. It had sent an irrational, horrible fear through his entire body. How could he forget something about his darling Helen? Those books were still sitting on her bedside cabinet.

So he'd made lists and chanted things over and over in his bed at night. He hadn't been able to stand the thought of her fading from his memory. That the love that he'd felt for her would ever die.

He remembered their first date at the movies, their first kiss, their first fight and their first home. Their wedding day. Their wedding night.

And the way he'd held her on that last, horrible day when they'd both known she was going to die.

That nothing could save her. Even though he kept telling her she'd be fine.

The way she'd felt in his arms as he'd felt the life slowly drain from her body.

The way she'd told him she'd love him forever. And to live a good life.

Here, in this special place, it felt right. It felt right to remember her. It felt like a celebration.

Of life.
Of love.
Of forgiveness.

A single tear rolled down his cheek. He'd cried an ocean's worth of tears but now it was time for the last one.

Now it was time to let go.

Now it was time to live his life.

CHAPTER ELEVEN

The alarm started sounding sharply. Sawyer and Dan were on their feet almost simultaneously. Even though the ventilator was breathing for Jack, his blood results had shown that his organs were starting to fail.

"Cardiac arrest. He's in V-fib."

Sawyer was almost through the door before one of the nurses blocked his path. "Gown!" she shouted.

Dan hadn't been so forgetful and already had a gown half on and his mask in place. Sawyer hated this. What was the point? How effective were the masks really? How much protection did the gown really offer? Wouldn't it make more sense just to get in and defibrillate him?

He hauled the gown and mask on and entered the room just as Dan placed the paddles on the boy's chest. "Clear!"

Jack's little body arched and all eyes fixed on the monitor.

Still VF.

Callie ran into the room, her gown barely covering her shoulders. "No!" she gasped, and ran to the other side of the room.

It was then Sawyer heard the high-pitched squeal. The squeal of a little boy watching people attempt to resuscitate his brother and not having a clue what was going on.

He cursed and pulled the curtain between the beds. Why hadn't he realized? Why hadn't he even thought of that?

But Callie had. She had her arm around Ben's shoulders and was whispering to him through her mask. Her face was mainly hidden but he could still see her eyes. And there were tears in them.

Dan was moving quickly, seamlessly, shouting instructions to the surrounding staff. Jack's mother and father appeared at the window, horrified at what was happening to their son.

Jill Keating promptly dissolved into a fit of tears, her legs giving way beneath her.

They started CPR, a nurse with a knee on the bed using one hand on Jack's small chest. Regular, rhythmic beats. It was painful to watch.

The ventilator had been unhooked. Another doctor was bagging Jack down the tube already in place.

Drugs were pushed through Jack's IV. Anything to try and restart his heart.

"Everyone stop a second!" Dan shouted.

Callie's head shot up, a look of horror on her face. She moved from Ben's bed over to where Sawyer was standing. "You can't stop!" she shouted. "Don't you dare stop!"

A HAND TAPPED Violet on the shoulder. "You've to go the boardroom."

Her head shot up. "What for? I'm in the middle of something right now. Can't it wait?"

Maisey shook her head. "I seriously doubt it."

Violet spun around in her chair. Maisey's voice didn't sound too good. "What do you mean?" She had a horrible feeling in the pit of her stomach.

"I'm sorry, Violet."

Violet reached out and grabbed her sleeve as she tried to

walk away. "What do you mean, you're sorry? Why have I to go the boardroom?"

Maisey couldn't look her in the eye. "It's the director. Along with Evan Hunter. I think Evan's complained about the deadline you didn't meet—the report he's been waiting four days for."

Violet's heart started to thud in her chest. "But that's what I'm working on." She held up the crumpled piece of paper.

Maisey shook her head. "I'm sorry, Violet. The director said he wanted to see you straight away."

Violet stood up, trying to ignore the tremor in her legs.

Rats. She'd known she was treading on thin ice when she hadn't had the report ready for Evan on time.

The truth was she had been hoping he would forget all about it now they had a final diagnosis of monkeypox. Sawyer should be the last thing on his mind right now.

She scrabbled around her desk for the report she'd been writing. Not only was it very late, she'd also left the details scarce. It would hardly placate the director.

Was he about to fire her?

Was she about to get fired because she'd tried to cover for her brother?

Her heart pounded as she crossed the department on her way to the boardroom. At this rate she would be sick all over the director's shoes.

The boardroom—where all official business was carried out.

One thing was sure—if she was going down, she was taking Evan Hunter with her. Let Evan see what the director thought about the boss cavorting with his staff.

ALL HEADS TURNED towards her. Callie's heart was racing, sweat lashing off her brow and running down her back.

Sawyer stepped into her line of vision, blocking the view of Jack and the rest of the staff. It took her a second to focus.

"Callie. Calm down."

Her skin was prickling. The scar on her leg itching like crazy. Her head flicking back between Ben's fearful face on the bed behind her and Sawyer's wide frame standing in front of her.

Everything seemed to be spiraling out of her control. She didn't feel in charge any more. "We can't stop. We can't. It's not been long enough." She was shaking her head. This wasn't even her area of expertise. What did she know about resuscitating a child? The last time she'd been involved in a pediatric resuscitation she'd been a first-year resident. It had made her realize that pediatrics wasn't for her.

"Callie." His hands were firmly on her shoulders now. "Step away from this. It's under control."

That's when she lost it even more. "You think this is under control? Under control? How? How is this under control? Is this part of the plan?"

She moved closer to Sawyer and hissed in his ear, "If Jack's about to die, you need to tell his family. You need to give them a chance to say goodbye." Her eyes drifted back to the bed behind her. "You need to give Ben a chance to say goodbye. He should get to hold his brother's hand."

She was feeling frantic. She couldn't let this happen. It didn't matter that she wasn't a pediatrician. She was the doctor in charge of this outbreak so, at the end of the day, everyone should be doing what she told them.

Sawyer reached up and stroked her cheek. The action took her by surprise. It brought her instantly back to the here and now. "Callie, Dan's not stopping. He's only waiting for a few seconds to recheck the cardiac monitor—to see if Jack's heart rhythm has changed. Think, Callie. We always do this at arrests. Don't we?"

His voice was quiet, only loud enough for her to hear. Not that the rest of the staff were bothering. Most were still round Jack's bed, assisting with the arrest. Another nurse had appeared at Ben's side and was sitting with her arm around him, talking in his ear.

Ben.

He was terrified. He was crying. He was asking the nurse questions. Callie felt herself start to shake.

"We've got a rhythm!"

Both their heads turned towards the shout. Dan had just defibrillated Jack's little chest again and the monitor had given a little blip. Dan started shouting more instructions for different drugs. The room was a hive of activity. IV's were being hung and Mr. and Mrs. Keating had been gowned up and were being shown into the room.

Callie was trembling. She couldn't stop herself.

Then a warm hand slipped into hers and pulled her out of the room, walking her along the corridor and sitting her down in an easy chair. A cold drink was pressed into her hands and Sawyer sat in the chair opposite her.

He didn't say a word. He just sat.

The cold juice slid down her throat. The intense itch in her leg increased. She was clawing at her leg and couldn't stop. He bent over, his hand capturing hers and stopping her scratching. His head was underneath hers and he looked up at her. "Want to tell me what just happened in there?"

She felt her throat constrict. "I don't think I can."

He sat back in his chair. She could tell he was contemplating what to do next. What on earth must he be thinking of her?

His gaze was steady. It felt as if he was looking deep inside her. Somewhere she didn't want him to go. "It's time, Callie. Tell me about your scar."

She took a sharp breath. How did he know? *How did he know there was a connection?*

She laid her palm flat on her thigh. The desire to scratch was overwhelming. but she knew it was all psychological. No matter how hard she scratched, it wouldn't stop the itch. She'd just end up breaking her skin and drawing blood.

"I was in a car accident." She didn't know where the words had come from. It almost felt as if someone else had said them. But it was definitely her voice.

"How long ago?" It was a measured question. A prompt. It was almost as if he knew she just couldn't come out and tell him everything at once—it would be too painful.

"I was twenty-three."

"Were you badly injured?"

She took a deep breath. Although the scar was a permanent reminder, for the most part Callie had pushed all memories of her injuries aside.

Physical injuries could heal. Psychological injuries not so much.

"I had a fractured femur and tib and fib. Fractured ribs too."

"Wow. You must have had to take some time out of medical school."

"Only a few weeks. I became their first official online student. They recorded lectures for me and sent me notes. I did my assignments online for a couple of months."

It almost gave the game away and she could see the calculating expression on his face. Her professors had gone above and beyond their responsibilities and he had to be wondering why. Most medical schools would have told a seriously injured student to take time off, recuperate and come back the following year.

His gaze remained steady. It was obvious that he'd figured things out. "Who else was in the car, Callie?"

She was instantly on the defensive. "What makes you think someone else was in the car?"

"Who else was in the car, Callie?"

He'd just repeated the question. There was no fooling Sawyer.

Her throat was instantly dry again and her voice cracked. "My sister, Isabel."

He moved forward and took her hands again. "Isabel. What a beautiful name. Tell me about your sister, Callie." Again he was surprising her. He wasn't hitting her with a barrage of questions, he was just giving her an open invitation to talk.

"I can't," she whispered, as a single tear slid down her cheek. This was just too hard.

He reached up and caught it in his fingertips. "Yes, you can."

EVERYTHING HAD JUST changed color for Sawyer. He already knew her sister must be dead. The look on her face had said it all and the hairs currently standing on end at the back of his neck agreed.

He could see how much she was struggling. He could tell she wanted to run from the room like a frightened rabbit. She'd barely been able to get the words out.

A sister. Callie had a sister. Or she'd *had* a sister.

Now he understood her reaction when she'd heard about Violet. Now he understood why she'd been so angry with him. If she'd lost a sister and felt as if he'd abandoned his... well, her reaction was entirely normal.

"Isabel was a year older than me. She was at medical school too. She wanted to work at the DPA."

"Did you?" Things were starting to fall into place for

him. This was behind the reaction in the chapel earlier. This was why she wasn't sure of herself.

She hesitated. "I... I didn't know what I wanted to do."

"Was Isabel injured in the car accident?"

Callie couldn't speak now. She just nodded. The tears were spilling down her face. Her hands were icy, almost as if she was in shock. He rubbed them gently, trying to encourage the blood flow and get some heat into them again.

It was obvious that Callie didn't talk about this to people. Violet hadn't heard a single thing about this—he suspected that no one at the DPA knew. Hadn't anyone ever asked her about her scar?

It was one of the first things he'd noticed about her.

It was time to ask the ultimate question. He had to give her a chance to let go. "Did she die?"

And that's when the sobs were let loose. Big, loud gasping sobs. The kind where you couldn't catch your breath before the next one took over your body.

He knew how that felt. He'd been there too.

He moved, sitting on the arm of the easy chair, wrapping his arm around her shoulders and letting her rest her head on his shoulder as she cried. It was the most natural thing to do.

Grief was all-consuming.

"There was a nurse and she knew Isabel was going to die. My parents hadn't got there yet. They were about to take me to Theatre but she wouldn't let them. She pulled me over to Isabel and put her hand in mine. It was the best and worst moment of my life. She knew how important it was. And I never even got to thank her. Everything just turned into a blur after that. My parents arrived and..."

"That's why you wanted the boys to hold hands. Now I get it," he murmured. It all made sense now. The look of terror on her face, her reactions. They were all the actions of someone who had walked in those shoes. Only someone who'd had that experience could truly know what it all meant and how important the smallest thing could be.

Her voice tailed off. She couldn't talk any more. He lifted a damp lock of her hair and dropped a kiss on her forehead. "I understand, Callie. I understand better than you could ever know."

"How can you?" she whispered. Her whole body was shaking. "We were fighting. I've never told anyone this but Isabel and I were fighting. A car came round the corner on the wrong side of the road and I didn't have time to react. I didn't have time to react because I was distracted. I was trying to stop Isabel from getting her own way yet again."

He could see the pain written across her face. And more than anything he wanted to take it away.

The feelings almost overwhelmed him. It had been so long since he'd felt like this that he almost didn't recognize it. That intensity. That urge to protect.

The feelings of love.

Sawyer sucked in his breath. The pain spread across his chest. His heart thudded, his muscles tensed.

Every one of his senses was hyper-aware. He could hear her panting breaths, feel the dampness of her tears between his fingertips. He could smell the aroma of her raspberry shampoo and remember the taste of her on his lips.

And he could see her. All of her. Her bedraggled hair, damp around her forehead. The little lines etched around her clear blue eyes. The pink tinge of her cheeks. The dark red of her lips.

Her pink scrub top clung to her, outlining her firm breasts and the curve of her waist. The matching trousers hugged her hips and thighs. Her bright pink casual shoes cushioned her feet, with one dangling from her silver-starred toes.

All of this made up the picture of the woman that he loved.

The realization made him want to run. Made him want to escape for a few minutes to sort his head out and re-align his senses.

But he couldn't leave. He could never leave her like this. His hand rubbed her back and he tried to keep his eyes off her silver-starred toes and the pictures they were conjuring up in his mind.

"All siblings fight, Callie. That's normal. That's what being a brother or sister is all about. You were just unlucky."

She shook her head. "But it didn't feel like that." She pressed a hand to her chest. "Isabel had always been really competitive. Medical school was just making her worse." Her eyes turned to meet his. "Of course, her fellow students would never have said that. They all embraced that kind of lifestyle. As if everything was a race, every mark a victory. But she carried it home with her. And it made being her sister tough." Her voice cracked and sobs racked her shoulders once again.

Sawyer pulled her close. She was consumed with guilt. That much was obvious. Not just because she'd been driving the car but because of how she'd been feeling towards her sister.

"Callie, I know. I understand. Violet was the good girl in the family. The one who always looked perfect in pictures. Sometimes I even hated her."

"You did?" Her eyes widened, her expression was one of surprise.

"Of course I did—she's my sister. Family's like that. You can't love or hate anyone more than your immediate family. No one else generates the same emotional energy. The same tug. Even in love." He gave her a smile.

"I walked away a few years ago. If I'd stayed near my family they would never have allowed me to live the way I have. The first thing Violet did when I phoned her was chew me out. Just wait till I see her. There won't be anything left for you."

"For me?" The tone in her voice changed. Her gaze fixed on his.

He bent his face to hers, taking in her trembling lips. Right now he didn't care about the monkeypox. He didn't care about the quarantine and vaccinations. And he certainly didn't care about the plans.

All he cared about was the woman in front of him.

It didn't matter how long he'd known her. It didn't matter how much they'd have to work through. All that mattered now was that he wanted a chance with her.

A chance to see where life could take them.

"Callie, what would it take to make you happy?"

She shook her head. "What do you mean?"

He knelt down in front of her. "I want you to stop thinking about anyone else. Stop thinking about the situation we're in with work. Stop thinking about responsibilities. Stop thinking about what anyone else thinks about you." He clasped both her hands in his. "I've spent the last six years in a fog, Callie, and being around you has finally woken me up."

He looked around the plain white room they were in. "I can see the color in things again. I can see light again. And it's all because of you."

She took a deep breath and drew back a little. She looked scared. Not of him—but of what he was saying.

"But we're not a good match, Sawyer. We're nothing alike. Even Callum said we're like oil and water."

Sawyer smiled. Trust Callum to see things long before anyone else could.

"And opposites attract, Callie." He drew her closer and whispered in her ear, "And in case you haven't noticed, I'm really attracted to you."

"Ditto," she whispered.

Their eyes met. They were reliving the conversation in the kids' cinema room.

"Callie, do you really want to be part of the DPA?"

"What?" She looked shocked.

He held his hands out. "This, Callie, all this. Is this really what you want? Because I can see you're a good doctor but I have to keep convincing you of that." He laid his palm on her chest above her heart, "And if you don't feel it in here, I wonder if you're doing the job of your heart or if you're just doing your duty to your sister."

All of a sudden she couldn't meet his all-too-perceptive gaze.

He put a finger under her chin and gently made her look at him. "Sometimes you need someone else to put things into perspective for you. Callie, I see a beautiful woman who is a great doctor but who is clearly in the wrong job. Was it in your heart to come to the DPA? Or did you come because that was the path that Isabel had mapped out for you both?"

"We wanted to work together. It was our dream."

"Both your dreams? Or only hers?"

"Don't say that. I don't like the way you make that sound. It was our plan." Her eyes drifted away from his and became fixed on the blank wall. "When you don't follow the plan, things go wrong. That's what happened that night. I took a different road—I was just so sick of Isabel being in charge all the time. Planning what we were doing every second of every day. Even down to what we ate."

Her shoulders started to shake again, her widened eyes turning back to meet his. "Don't you see what happened? When you stick to the plan, things go fine. But when you don't...that's when things go wrong. We would never have been on that road if I hadn't fought with Isabel. If I'd just gone along with what she'd wanted, everything would have been fine."

"You don't know that. You *can't* know that." He touched her cheek. "And would you have liked this job any more if Isabel was working next to you? Or would you still hate it just as much but do a better job at hiding it—all to keep her happy? To stick to the plan?"

She opened her mouth to speak but Sawyer wasn't finished. "Sticking to the plan doesn't always work. Helen and I stuck to the plan. The plan didn't cover what to do in a surgical emergency with no equipment in the middle of nowhere. Because that's all it was—a plan. Nothing more, nothing less. Just another tool to have in your box. Life has a funny way of making its own plan, no matter what's down in black and white."

"And if you don't like it?"

"That's the beauty of having a plan, Callie. Knowing when to use it and knowing when to drop it." He crouched down in front of her, "Thinking of Isabel, does it still hurt?"

She hesitated. "Yes." Her voice was barely audible.

"Callie, if Isabel were here right now, what would she say to you?"

Callie shifted in her seat. "She'd tell me to get my act together." She looked Sawyer in the eye, "She'd tell me not to get distracted by other people. She'd tell me not to waste the last nine years of my career by throwing away my role in the DPA now." Was she trying to convince him or her?

"And if she could see you now—if she could feel how

you felt every day at work? Do you honestly think that's what she'd say?"

Callie sighed and he could see light dawn across her face. She was finally going to stop giving the answers she was expected to give. "No. She'd give me a boot up the ass and ask me why I hadn't said something sooner."

He smiled at her. "I think I would have liked Isabel."

She buried her head in her hands. "What will my parents think if I tell them I don't want to do this any more? They'll be so disappointed." Her voice drifted off and he could see pain flit across her eyes again.

"Callie, they've lost one daughter. They've gone through the worst pain imaginable. All they could want for you is to be happy."

He put his hand back on her heart. "Think of me as your own Aladdin's genie. I'm going to grant you a wish. And I'll do everything in my power to make it happen. What is it that you want, Callie?"

She was looking into his eyes, searching his face. He could tell she was terrified of revealing what she really wanted. He prayed he wasn't making her take a step too far.

But this felt right. It wasn't just him who needed to move on—it was her too. And they could do it together. Because nothing else could feel as good a fit as they did.

She sat for a few minutes. He could hear her deep breaths. He didn't want to push her any more. He knew how he would have reacted if someone had tried to push him too hard a few years ago.

She needed to be ready. She needed to be sure.

She lifted her eyes and they took on a determined edge. This was the Callie Turner who'd swept into his E.R. and told him she was in charge. This was the Callie Turner who'd made the decision to start vaccinating. This was the Callie Turner who hadn't blinked an eye at him watching her change her clothing. "I want more than one wish."

He felt relief wash over him. "Cheat. I'll give you two." His heart was thudding in his chest. He could only hope where this might go. "The first for work, the second for life." He felt his lips turning upwards, praying he wasn't reading her wrong.

She sucked in a breath and held it for a few seconds.

"The first for work," she repeated.

He nodded.

"I want to leave the DPA." As she said the words her shoulders immediately relaxed. It was almost as if someone had released the pressure in her and it had escaped. "I want to leave the DPA." She repeated the words again, this time more determinedly, with a smile starting to form on her lips.

The smile progressed, reaching across her face until her eyes started to light up. "I want to retrain. I want to work in family practice."

"You do?" He couldn't have picked that lottery ball if he'd tried.

She nodded. "I do." Those words sounded ominous. She met his eyes again and laughed.

"And your second wish?"

She stood up and pulled him up next to her. "This could be a difficult one."

Sawyer felt his heart plummet. "How so?"

She wrapped one arm around his waist. "I'm going to need some help while I retrain. I'm going to need some support."

He could see where this was going. "And where do you think you could get that support?"

"I'm kind of hoping I can rely on a friend."

"A friend?" His voice rose.

She stood on tiptoe and murmured in his ear. "It would have to be a special kind of friend. One who doesn't mind helping me study." She dropped a little kiss on his ear. "One who could make dinner and tidy up after himself because I'm going to be really busy."

He nodded. "Really busy. And where do you think you could find someone to meet all these demands?"

She ran her fingers down his chest. "I'm kind of hoping my genie can arrange it."

"Oh, you are?" He pulled her closer. She molded her body to his and wrapped her arms around his neck.

He got a waft of her raspberry shampoo. This was going to drive him crazy. Hopefully for the next fifty years.

She pulled back a little. "Come to think of it, most genies grant three wishes. I guess mine kind of short-changed me."

"Why, what would be your third wish?"

She stood on tiptoe again and whispered in his ear, with a sparkle in her eyes and a pink tinge to her cheeks.

"Now, that I *can* make happen straight away."

And he took her by the hand and led her down the corridor.

EPILOGUE

It was a perfect day.

The deep blue water was lapping up onto Osterman beach. Callie wiggled her feet and felt the sand shift under her toes. The ocean breeze blew her hair around her face, one side catching more of the breeze than the other. She grabbed a few strands and tucked them behind her ear.

The white canopy above her swayed in the wind, shading the guests from the early morning sun. She sighed and relaxed back into her white canvas chair and closed her eyes.

There hadn't been time for much sleep last night. Sawyer had just arrived back from his latest conference for the DPA and had been anxious to show her how much he had missed her. His new role as a DPA lecturer had been a surprise for them both. But he'd embraced it with more enthusiasm and vigor than he'd apparently possessed in years.

She could hear the ripple of voices around her. The ceremony was due to start in few minutes. There was a thud as Sawyer flopped into the chair next to her.

"How are you doing, beautiful?" He leaned over and dropped a kiss on her lips. She caught a whiff of his aftershave and touched his newly bare jaw.

"You've shaved. I was kind of liking the jungle warrior look." His hair was still slightly damp from his shower and she pushed it back from his eyes. "Next thing, you'll be having a haircut. Then I *really* won't recognize you."

He gave her a cheeky smile. "Never gonna happen."

She kept her hand on his face as she ran her eyes up and down his body. He was wearing a pale blue shirt with the sleeves rolled up and white cotton chinos. She stared down at his feet, at his toes pushing the sand around like her own.

"What happened to the shoes I bought you?"

He let out a laugh. "I decided to go native." He held out his hands at the beautiful scenery, "Somehow I don't think anyone will notice."

His phone buzzed and he pulled it from his pocket, a smile instantly appearing on his face. He handed the phone over. It was a text message with a photo of Jack and Ben, complete with Stetsons, on vacation in Texas. Jill had added the words *"With thanks to you both. xx."* Jack still looked a little frail and both boys still had pockmarks on their arms.

Callie sighed. "They look so much happier. I'm so glad they're doing well."

The music started and they both stood, turning to watch Alison, her husband and three kids walk down the sandy aisle between the chairs. Jonas, her eight-month-old, was held in her arms. He was wearing a white and blue sailor suit and hat and was chewing on his thumb.

He was older than the average baby who was christened, but Alison had wanted to wait until she could arrange something special. This was truly a baby to celebrate.

Callie felt a surge of warmth in her chest. He was the picture of health. It had been great relief to everyone that Alison had never shown any symptoms of monkeypox.

"Can we have the godparents, please?"

She felt a sharp nudge as Sawyer stood and held out his hand towards her. "Shall we?"

She slid her hand into his. It still gave her the same little tingle along her spine that it had all those months ago when they'd met.

Time had flown past. She'd handed in her resignation to the DPA and had started to retrain for family practice. From the first day and hour that she'd started, she'd known she'd made the right decision.

Family practice was so much broader than any other specialty. She got to see a little of everything and she loved it—from young people to old, from runny noses to lumps and bumps. More than anything she got to spend more time with her patients and follow through on their care. It was a better fit than she could ever have imagined.

She smiled and straightened her flowery summer dress before joining the family at the front.

The ceremony was over quickly. The family gave thanks and Jonas was officially named, with Callie and Sawyer the proud godparents.

Just when she thought it was time to head for the buffet lunch, Alison turned to face her friends and colleagues. "If you'll just give me a few more minutes." She waited for people to settle back into their seats.

She smiled at Sawyer and Callie. "Most of you will know how I met Jonas's godparents. And I'm delighted that they agreed to take the role today and join us in this beautiful location."

She paused, before giving Callie a knowing smile. "And it seems such a waste to let this be over so quickly." Then, in the blink of an eye, she sat back down.

Callie was stunned. Had she missed something? What had just happened? Was that it? Were they supposed to head off to the beautifully decorated buffet tables for lunch?

A glass was pressed into her hand, the cold condensation quickly capturing her attention. Sawyer was grinning at her. She took a quick sip. Champagne with a strawberry at the bottom. Delicious.

She watched as waiters appeared and passed glasses to all the guests. How nice. Had Sawyer arranged this to drink a toast to the baby?

He straightened up and cleared his throat. "I'm sorry for stealing Alison's thunder, but she gave me a severe talking to a few weeks ago." He gave her a little nod. "About not wasting time."

Callie felt her heart start to flutter in her chest. *No*. He couldn't be.

But he was. He'd dropped to one knee.

"Callie Turner, I've only known you for twelve months. And it's official—you drive me crazy."

The guests started to laugh.

"I've never met anyone who can burn mac n' cheese like you can. Or who can take up an entire closet with shoes."

She felt herself blush. Maybe she had gone a little overboard in making him build her a special shoes closet, particularly when she wasn't wearing any right now.

"But what I've realized in this life is that when you find someone who makes your heart sing like you do, who makes you think about everything that you do, and who you don't want to spend a day without, then you should never let them go." His pale green eyes met hers and she could see his sincerity.

"Callie, when I met you I thought I was in the wrong place at the wrong time. I couldn't believe I was so unlucky to come across an infectious disease and be stuck in the middle of it all again." He shook his head. "I didn't know how wrong I was."

"I'd been stuck in the wrong place and the wrong time for the last six years. This time—for once in my life—I was in the right place at the right time. Because it's where I met you."

The crowd gave a little sigh.

"Callie, the whole world knows that I love you. I want you to be the first thing I see every morning and the last thing I see every night. Would you do me the honour of becoming my wife?"

He'd opened a small box and a beautiful solitaire diamond glistened in the sun.

She couldn't speak. She couldn't say anything. She was too stunned.

Sawyer, the man who couldn't plan anything, had completely and utterly sideswiped her.

"I can read your mind, I know this isn't in the plan, honey, but do you think you can say something? I'm getting a cramp down here." Beads of sweat were breaking out on his forehead.

He was nervous.

For the first time since she'd known him Sawyer was nervous. It was kind of cute. But she didn't want to prolong his agony. She didn't want to panic the man she loved.

And she didn't want to give him a chance to change his mind.

She bent down and didn't hesitate. "How about a yes," she whispered.

"Yes!"

He swept his arms around her waist and swung her round.

She was laughing and he was squeezing the breath out of her with his enthusiastic grip. "Wait a minute, there's one condition."

He settled her feet back on the sand and slid the diamond ring onto her finger. "Anything, honey, you name it. Your wish is my command." He gave her a low bow.

She smiled. Plans could work both ways. "Well…" she ran her finger down his cheek "…since you made such good plans for today, I'm thinking that maybe you should be in charge of the wedding plans too."

His face dropped instantly then he tried to recover with a nervous smile. "If that's what you want, honey."

She reached up for him again and planted her lips on his. "Perfect."

* * * * *

Tamed By Her Brooding Boss
Joanna Neil

When **Joanna Neil** discovered Mills & Boon®, her lifelong addiction to reading crystallised into an exciting new career writing Mills & Boon® Medical Romance™. Her characters are probably the outcome of her varied lifestyle, which includes working as a clerk, typist, nurse and infant teacher. She enjoys dressmaking and cooking at her Leicestershire home. Her family includes a husband, son and daughter, an exuberant yellow Labrador and two slightly crazed cockatiels. She currently works with a team of tutors at her local education centre to provide creative writing workshops for people interested in exploring their own writing ambitions.

Dear Reader

Once bitten, twice shy... So the old saying goes. It's one that intrigues me... How, I wondered, would a young girl respond if the man she yearned for turned her away? Wouldn't she do her utmost to steer clear of him in the future?

That's exactly how it was for Sarah, after James Benson rejected her as a vulnerable teenager. Meeting him again, years later, she's alarmed to discover that she still has feelings for him—but she can't possibly act on them.

Besides, she has way too much going on in her life, with her young half-brother and half-sister to look after, as well as the responsibility of working as a doctor in a busy emergency department.

Add to the mix the tranquil setting of a picturesque Cornish fishing village—a favourite with me—and I think you'll agree we have the perfect prescription for romance!

Love

Joanna

Recent titles by Joanna Neil:

DR RIGHT ALL ALONG
DR LANGLEY: PROTECTOR OR PLAYBOY?
A COTSWOLD CHRISTMAS BRIDE
THE TAMING OF DR ALEX DRAYCOTT
BECOMING DR BELLINI'S BRIDE
PLAYBOY UNDER THE MISTLETOE

**These books are also available in eBook format
from www.millsandboon.com.au.**

CHAPTER ONE

'So, are you both okay…? Do you have everything you need?' Sarah's glance trailed over her young half-brother and half-sister, while she tried to work out if there was anything she had forgotten. It was a cool spring morning, with the wind blowing in off the sea, but the children were well wrapped up in warm jackets and trousers.

'Do you still have your money for the lunch break, Sam?' she asked, pausing to tuck a flyaway strand of chestnut-coloured hair behind her ear. He was such a whirlwind, she wouldn't have been surprised to learn that he'd lost it somewhere between the front door of the house and the school gates.

Ten-year-old Sam was clearly feeling awkward in his brand-new school uniform, but he stopped wriggling long enough to dig his hand deep into his trouser pocket.

'Yeah, it's still there.'

'Good. I'll organise some sort of account for you both with the school as soon as I can, but for now make sure you get a decent meal with what you have.' She gave Sam a wry smile. 'I don't want you to go spending it on crisps and junk food.'

His shoulders moved in brief acknowledgement and she turned her attention to Rosie. The little girl wasn't saying very much—in fact, both children had been unusually quiet this morning. Perhaps she should have expected that, since it was their first day at a new school. They didn't know this neighbourhood very well as yet, and they'd had to adjust to so many changes of late that it was understandable if they were struggling to take everything on board.

'How about you, Rosie? Are you all right?'

Rosie nodded, her expression solemn, her grey eyes downcast. 'I'm okay.' She was two years younger than her brother, but in some ways she seemed a little more mature than him. It looked as though she was coping, but you could never tell.

'I'm sure you'll be fine, both of you.' Sarah tried to sound encouraging. 'I know it's not easy, starting at a new school mid-term, but I expect your teachers will introduce you to everybody and you'll soon make friends.' She hesitated for a moment, but when neither child said anything in response she put an arm around each of them and started down the path towards the classrooms. 'Let's get you settled in—remember, if I'm still at work by the time school finishes, Murray from next door will come and pick you up.'

A few minutes later, she kissed them goodbye and left them in their cloakrooms, anxiety weighing heavily on her, but there was relief, too, when she saw that the other children were curious about the newcomers and had begun to talk to them.

Sarah pulled in a deep breath as she walked back to her car, trying to gather sustenance from an inner well of strength. It was difficult to know who felt worse, she or the children, but somehow she had to push those concerns to one side for the moment and get on with the rest of what looked to be a difficult day ahead.

It wasn't just the children who were suffering from first-day nerves—she would be starting out on a new job, riding along in the air ambulance with the immediate care doctor for the area. That would carry with it its own difficulties...but that wasn't what was troubling her. As a doctor herself, she hoped she was well prepared to cope with any medical emergency.

She set the car in motion, driving away from the small Cornish fishing village and heading along the coast road towards the air ambulance base where she was to meet up with James Benson.

Her hands tightened on the steering-wheel. Now, there was the crux of the problem. Even recalling his name caused a flurry of sensation to well up inside her abdomen and every now and again her stomach was doing strange, uncomfortable kinds of flip-overs.

How long had it been since she'd last seen him? A good many years, for sure... She'd been a teenager back then, naïve, innocent and desperate to have his attention. Her whole body flushed with heat at the memory, and she shook her head, as though that would push it away.

She'd do anything rather than have to meet up with him once again, but the chances of avoiding him had been scuppered from the outset. Maybe if she'd known from the start that he was a consultant in the emergency department where she'd wanted to work, she would never have applied for the post as a member of the team.

And how could she have known that he was also on call with the air ambulance? It was a job she'd trained for, coveted, and once she'd been drawn in, hook, line and sinker, there was no way she could have backed out of the deal.

She drove swiftly, carefully, barely noticing that she had left the coast behind, with its spectacular cliffs and rugged inlets, and now she was passing through deeply wooded valleys with clusters of whitewashed stone cottages clinging to the hillsides here and there. The bluebells were in flower, presenting her with occasional glimpses of a soft carpet of blue amidst the undergrowth. Small, white pockets of wood sorrel peeped out from the hedges, vying for space with yellow vetch. It was beautiful, but she couldn't appreciate any of it while her heart ached from leaving the children behind and her nerves were stretched to breaking point from anticipating the meeting ahead.

At the base, she drove into a slot in the staff car park and then made her way into the building, to where the air ambulance personnel had their office. Bracing herself, she knocked briskly on the door and then went inside.

The room was empty and she frowned. She couldn't have missed a callout because the helicopter was standing outside on the helipad.

She took a moment to look around. There were various types of medical equipment on charge in here, a computer monitor displaying a log of the air ambulance's last few missions, and a red phone rested in a prominent position on the polished wooden desk. To one side of the room there was a worktop, where a kettle was making a gentle hissing sound as the water inside heated up.

'Ah, there you are.' She turned as James Benson's voice alerted her to his presence. Her heart began to race, pounding as those familiar, deep tones smoothed over her like melting, dark chocolate. 'I'm sorry I wasn't here to greet you,' he added. 'We've all been changing into our flight suits and generally getting ready for the off.'

She nodded, not trusting herself to speak just then. He was every bit as striking as she remembered, with that compelling presence that made you feel as though he dominated the room. Or perhaps it was just that she was unusually on edge today. He was tall, with a strong, muscular build, and he still had those dark good looks which, to her everlasting shame, had been her undoing all those years ago, the chiselled, angular bone structure and jet-black hair, and those penetrating grey eyes that homed in on you and missed nothing.

He was looking at her now, his thoughtful gaze moving over her, lighting on the long, burnished chestnut of her hair and coming to rest on the pale oval of her face.

'I wasn't sure if it really would be you,' he said. 'When I saw your name on the acceptance letter I wondered for a minute or two whether it might be some other Sarah Franklyn, but the chances of there being two doctors in the neighbourhood with the same name was pretty remote. I know you went to medical school and worked in Devon.' His glance meshed with hers, and she steeled herself not to look away. He'd obviously heard, from time to time, about what she was doing. She straightened her shoulders. She would get through this. Of course she would. How bad could it be?

'I expect my taking up a medical career seems a strange choice to you, knowing me from back then.' Her voice was husky, and she cleared her throat and tried again, aiming to sound more confident this time. 'You weren't in on the interviews, so it didn't occur to me that we would be working together.'

He inclined his head briefly. 'I was away, attending a conference—it was important and couldn't be avoided or delegated, so the head of Emergency made the final decision.' His mouth twisted in a way that suggested he wasn't too pleased about that, and Sarah felt a sudden surge of panic rise up to constrict her throat. So he didn't want her here. That was something she hadn't reckoned on.

His glance shifted slowly over her taut features and she lifted her chin in a brash attempt at keeping her poise.

His grey eyes darkened, but his voice remained steady and even toned. 'Perhaps you'd like to go and change into your flight suit, and then I'll show you around and introduce you to the rest of the crew. We'll have coffee. The kettle should have boiled by the time you're ready.'

'Yes. That sounds good.'

At least he was accepting her presence here as a done thing. That was a small mercy. And it looked as though he wasn't going to comment on what had happened all those years ago. Just the thought of him doing that was enough to twist her stomach into knots, but for now perhaps she was safe. After all, she'd been a vulnerable seventeen-year-old back then, and now, some nine years later, she was a grown woman who ought to be in full control of herself. Why, then, did she feel so ill at ease, so uncertain about everything?

But she knew the answer, didn't she? It was because, sooner or later, the past was bound to come up and haunt her.

He showed her to a room where she could change into her high-visibility, orange flight suit, and she took those few minutes of privacy to try and get herself together. She'd keep things on a professional level between them, nothing more, no private stuff to mess things up. That way, she could keep a tight grip on her emotions and show him that she was a totally different person now, calm and up to the mark, and nothing like she'd been as a teenager.

She cringed as she thought back to some of the things she had done in her early teen years. Had she really driven Ben Huxley's tractor around the village on that late summer evening? He'd forever regretted leaving the keys in the ignition, and his shock at discovering his beloved tractor stranded at a precarious angle in a ditch an hour later had been nothing to the concern he'd felt at finding a thirteen-year-old girl slumped over the wheel.

And what had been James's reaction when she'd broken into the stables on his father's estate one evening and saddled up one of the horses? It had been her fourteenth birthday and she hadn't cared a jot about what might happen or considered that what she had been doing was wrong. She had loved the horses, had been used to being around them, and on that day she'd felt an overwhelming need to ride through the meadows and somehow leave her troubles behind. She had been wild, reckless, completely out of control, and James had recognised that.

'None of this will bring your mother back,' he'd said to her, and she'd stared at him, her green eyes wide with defiance, her jaw lifted in challenge.

'What would you know about it?' she'd responded in a dismissive, careless tone.

She'd been extremely lucky. No one had reported her to the police. She'd got away with things, and yet the more she'd avoided paying for her misdemeanours, the more she'd played up. 'Mayhem in such a small package,' was the way James had put it. No wonder he didn't want her around now.

He made coffee for her when she went back into the main room a short time later. 'Is it still cream with one sugar?' he asked, and she gave him a bemused look, her mouth dropping open a little in surprise. He remembered that?

'Yes...please,' she said, and he waved her to a seat by the table.

'Tom is our pilot,' he said, nodding towards the man who sat beside her. Tom was in his forties, she guessed, black haired, with a smattering of grey streaks starting at his temples.

'Pleased to meet you, Sarah,' Tom said, smiling and pushing forward a platter filled with a selection of toasted sandwiches, which she guessed had been heated up in the mini-grill that stood on the worktop next to the coffee-maker. 'Help yourself. You never know if you're going to get a lunch break in this line of work, so you may as well eat while you get the chance.'

'Thanks.' She chose a bacon and cheese baguette and thought back to breakfast-time when she'd grabbed a slice of toast for herself while the children had tucked into their morning cereal. It seemed a long while ago now.

'And this is Alex, the co-pilot,' James said, turning to introduce the man opposite. He was somewhere in his mid-thirties, with wavy brown hair and friendly hazel eyes.

'Have you been up in a helicopter before?' Alex asked, and Sarah nodded.

'I worked with the air ambulance in Devon for a short time,' she answered. 'This is something I've wanted to do for quite a while, so when this job came up it looked like the ideal thing for me.'

He nodded. 'James told us you'll be working part time— is that by choice? It suits us, because our paramedic is employed on a part-time basis, too.'

'Yes. I'll just be doing one day a week here, and the rest of the time I'll be working at the hospital in the A and E department.'

'Sounds good. You'll get the best of both worlds, so to speak. It's unusual to do that, though, in A and E, I imagine?'

'Not so much these days,' Sarah murmured. 'And it suits me to do things this way.' She bit into her baguette and savoured the taste of melted cheese.

'Sarah supplements her income by doing internet work,' James put in. 'She writes a medical advice column for a website, and one for a newspaper, too.'

How had he known that? She looked up at him in surprise, and his mouth made a wry shape. 'I came across your advice column when I was browsing one day, and there was mention there of your work for the newspaper.' He frowned. 'I'm not sure it's wise to make diagnoses without seeing the patient.'

'That isn't what I do, as I'm sure you're aware if you've read my columns.' Perhaps he was testing her, playing devil's advocate, to see what kind of a doctor she really was, but she wasn't going to let him get away with implying she might not be up to the job. Neither was she going to tell him about her personal circumstances and give him further reason for doubting her suitability for the post. She needed to work part time so that she could be there for Sam and Rosie whenever possible, and the writing had provided an excellent solution in that respect. Working from home was a good compromise.

'I mostly work with a team of doctors,' she said, 'and we pick out letters from people who have conditions that would be of interest to a lot of others. We give the best advice we can in the circumstances, and point out other possible diagnoses and remedies.'

'Hmm. You don't think the best advice would be for your correspondents to go and see their own GP, or ask to see a specialist?'

'I think a good many people have already done that and are still confused. Besides, patients are much better informed these days. They like to visit the doctor with some inkling of what his responses might be, or what treatment options might be available to them,' she responded calmly.

He nodded. 'I guess you could be right.' He might have said more, but the red phone started to ring and he lifted the receiver without hesitation. He listened for a while and then said, 'What's the location? And his condition? Okay. We're on our way.'

Food and coffee were abandoned as they hurried out to

the helicopter. 'A young man has been injured in a multiple-collision road-traffic accident,' James told them. 'He has a broken leg, but he's some thirty miles away from here, and the paramedics on scene feel they need a doctor present. He needs to go to hospital as soon as possible.'

They were airborne within a minute or two, and soon Sarah was gazing down at lush green fields bordering a sparse network of ribbon-like roads. James sat next to her, commenting briefly on the landmarks they flew over.

'There's the hospital,' he said, pointing out the helipad on top of the building. 'We'll be landing there when we have our patient secured.'

A little further on, they passed over a sprawling country estate, which had at its centre a large house built from grey, Cornish stone. It was an imposing, rectangular building, with lots of narrow, Georgian windows.

'Your family's place,' Sarah mused. 'Do you still live there?' It was large enough for him to have the whole of the north wing to himself. That's how things had been when she'd lived in the area, though he'd been away at medical school a good deal of the time, or working away at the hospital in Penzance. His younger brother had taken over the east wing, leaving the rest of the house to their parents.

He shook his head. 'I have my own place now. It seemed for the best once I settled for working permanently in Truro. It's closer to the hospital. Jonathan still lives on the estate, though he has a family of his own now. He has a boy and a girl.'

'I wondered if he might stay on. He was always happy to live and work on the family farm, wasn't he?'

James nodded. 'So you decided to come back to your roots. What persuaded you to leave Devon? I have friends who worked there from time to time and, from what I heard on the grapevine, you were pretty much settled there. Rumour had it your mind was set on staying with the trauma unit.'

'That's pretty much the way it was to begin with... I was hoping I might get a permanent staff job but then I was passed over for promotion—a young male doctor pipped me at the post, and after that I started to look around for something else.'

He winced. 'That must have hurt.' He studied her briefly. 'Knowing you, I guess his appointment must have made you restless. You wouldn't have let the grass grow under your feet after that.'

'No, I wouldn't, that's true.' She wasn't going to tell him about her situation—although it hadn't been voiced at the time, she was fairly certain that she'd lost the promotion because of her family ties, and now she had to do everything she could to find secure, permanent work. This job promised all of that, but she was on three months' probation to see how things worked out on both sides, and she didn't need him to go looking for excuses to be rid of her before she signed a final contract.

By now they had reached their destination, and as the pilot came in to land, she could see the wreckage below. It looked as though a couple of motorcyclists had been involved in a collision with a saloon and a four-wheel-drive vehicle, and there were a number of casualties. A fire crew was in attendance, and from the blackened appearance of the saloon, it seemed that a blaze had erupted at some point. She could only hope the occupants of the car had escaped before the fire had taken hold.

'You'll be shadowing me,' James said, unclipping his seat belt as the helicopter came to a standstill, 'so don't worry about getting involved with the other patients. We'll take them in strict order of triage.'

Sarah bit her lip. She had no objection to following his

lead and learning the ins and outs of this particular job, but surely she'd be of more use helping with the other victims of the crash?

'Okay, whatever you say. Though I do feel I could be of help with the rest of the injured.'

He was already on his way to the door of the helicopter, his medical kit strapped to his back in readiness. 'Let's see how it goes, shall we? According to the paramedics, our primary patient is in a bad way. He needs to be our main concern right now.'

Sarah followed him to the side of the road where a paramedic was tending an injured youth. There were police vehicles nearby and a young officer was directing traffic while another was setting up a road block.

She knelt down beside the casualty. He couldn't be much more than eighteen years old. He lay on the grass verge, well away from the traffic, and his face was white, blanched by shock and loss of blood. The paramedic was giving him oxygen through a mask.

'There are two people suffering from whiplash and sprains,' the paramedic told them. 'They're being looked after by my colleague, along with another man who has chest injuries—broken ribs and collarbone, from what we can tell so far. This lad is Daniel Henderson, motorcyclist. He and his friend were on their way to the coast when they ran into trouble. The two motor vehicles crashed at a road junction and the lads had no way of avoiding them.'

James was already assessing the extent of the boy's injuries. 'His lower leg's grossly deformed,' he said in a quiet voice. 'It looks like a fracture of both the tibia and fibula. That degree of distortion has to be affecting the blood supply.'

The paramedic nodded. 'He's in severe pain, he's very

cold and his circulation is shutting down. We can't give him pain relief because we can't find a vein.'

It was a bad situation, because if there was an inadequate supply of blood to Daniel's foot there was the possibility that gangrene would set in and he might lose his leg.

'Thanks, Colin. I'll do an intraosseous injection,' James said, reaching into his medical bag for a bone injection gun. He spoke directly to the boy. 'I'm going to give you something to take away the pain, Daniel. It's a strong anaesthetic, so after a minute or two you'll be feeling much better. There'll be a sharp sting and soon after that you'll start to feel drowsy. Are you okay with that?'

Daniel nodded and closed his eyes. It was a case of the sooner the better, as far as he was concerned.

'Shall I clean the injection site and prepare the ketamine for you?' Sarah asked, and James nodded.

'Yes, thanks.'

As soon as she had cleaned and draped an area on Daniel's upper arm, James located the injection site and pressed the device on the gun that would insert a trocar through the bone and into the soft marrow that was filled with blood vessels. Once he'd done that, he removed the trocar and taped the cannula, the small-bore tube, in place.

Sarah connected an intravenous tube to the cannula and then James was able to give the boy the medication he needed. 'How are you doing, Daniel?' he asked softly after a while. 'Are you okay?'

'I'm all right.' Daniel's voice became slurred as the drug began to take effect.

'Can you feel this?' James pressed a wooden tongue depressor against his leg.

Daniel shook his head.

'That's good, it means the anaesthetic's working,' James said. He glanced at Sarah. 'I think we can safely try to re-align the bones enough to restore his circulation. If you and Colin hold him still—Colin at his chest, and you, Sarah, take hold of his upper leg—I'll manoeuvre his ankle and start to pull. We'll need to take great care—we don't know how much damage has already been done to the blood vessels. Let's hope we can do this without too much of a struggle.'

He spoke softly so as not to alarm his patient, but Daniel was by now well anaesthetised and wasn't much concerned about what was happening. Sarah guessed he was simply glad to be free of pain at last.

James worked carefully to straighten out the broken bones as best he could, and as soon as he had achieved that to his satisfaction, he began to splint the leg to prevent any further movement.

'That should do the trick,' he said. 'His circulation should be restored now.'

Sarah kept an eye on Daniel the whole time. She was worried about him. He wasn't saying anything, and had appeared to be drifting in and out of consciousness throughout the procedure.

'We should put in a fluid line,' she said in an undertone. 'He's lost a lot of blood.'

'Yes,' James answered. 'Do you want to see to that, and then we'll transfer him to a spinal board?'

She didn't waste any time, and as soon as she had set up the line they worked together to make sure the young lad was comfortable and covered with a space blanket. Then they secured him with straps to the board so that he could be transferred to the helicopter.

James left them briefly while he went to check on the other patients, but he returned quickly and took his place beside Sarah in the helicopter.

'The others will be okay to travel by road,' he said. 'It'll take around an hour for them to get to the hospital, but they're in no immediate danger.'

He glanced at his patient. 'I've asked Tom to radio ahead and alert A and E to have an orthopaedic surgeon standing by,' he told Sarah. 'How's the lad doing?'

'His blood pressure's low and his heart rate is rapid, with a weak pulse,' she answered. The signs of shock were all there, but they'd done everything they could for now, and all they could do was wait.

Tom was already setting the helicopter in motion, lifting them up off the ground. Within minutes he had turned them around and they were heading out across the Cornish peninsula towards the hospital, some thirty miles away.

James checked on the injured youth, lifting the blanket to look at his feet. 'His toes are beginning to pink up,' he pointed out, glancing at Sarah.

'Oh, thank heaven,' she said. She smiled at him, her mouth curving, her green eyes bright with relief. With his circulation restored, the imminent danger of Daniel losing his leg had been averted. 'I'm so glad for him.'

James nodded. He gently tucked the blanket in place, but he didn't once take his gaze from Sarah. He was watching her closely, as though he was mesmerised, taking in the warmth of her response, the soft flush of heat that flared in her cheeks.

The breath caught in her throat, and a familiar hunger surged inside her as she returned his gaze. There was a sudden, dull ache in her chest, an ache that came from knowing her unbidden yearning could never be assuaged. He still had the power to melt her bones and fill her with that humiliating need that would forever be her downfall.

She closed her eyes briefly. How on earth would she be able to work with him over the weeks, months that lay ahead?

'We'll be coming in to land in about two minutes.' The pilot's voice came over the speaker.

'Okay, Tom. We'll be ready.' James turned his attention back to the boy on the stretcher. He was self-contained, in control, as always.

Sarah looked out of the window. She had to keep things between them on a professional footing. That was the only way she could survive. From now on it would become her mantra.

CHAPTER TWO

'You look as though you could do with a break. Has it been a tough week?' Murray laid a manila folder down on a corner of the pine kitchen table, avoiding the clutter of pastry boards and rolling pins. 'I brought the colour charts I promised you,' he added, tapping the folder. He stared at her, looking her up and down. 'You're not your usual jaunty self today. What's up?'

'Nothing's up.' Sarah smiled at her spiky-haired neighbour and waved him towards a chair. Perhaps she was a bit pale from being cooped up in the house, and since she was cooking with the children today there were probably traces of flour in her hair where she'd pushed it off her face with the back of her hand. 'If I look less than on top of the world, I guess it's because I was up till all hours last night, painting the walls in the living room. Sit down and I'll pour you some tea. We were just about to have a cup.'

'Sarah's going to paint our bedrooms next,' Sam put in eagerly. He was using a cutter to make gingerbread shapes, and he paused now to assess his handiwork. 'She said we can choose the colours—'cept for black. She won't let me have that.' His bottom lip jutted and he frowned as he thought about that for a second or two. Then his eyes lit up. 'Purple would be good, though—or bright red.'

'We helped Sarah with the living room,' Rosie put in.

'Well, I did. Sam kept going off and playing on his game machine.' She looked at her older brother and shook her head.

'You were both a great help, all the same,' Sarah said, her eyes crinkling at the corners. 'It's going to be a long job, though,' she admitted, glancing at Murray as she went over to the worktop at the side of the room. She lifted up the sunshine-yellow teapot. 'I knew there would be a lot of work when we moved in here a fortnight ago. This place was in a pretty wretched state when I bought it.'

Murray pulled a face. 'I guessed it was bad—the old man who used to live here wasn't able to do much in the way of maintenance—but I knew he was looking for a quick sale once he'd decided to go and live with his son and his family in Somerset. I did what I could to help him out with things, but there was a limit to what I could do, with company business getting in the way. There were orders for goods coming in thick and fast and supplies from the warehouses were delayed and so on. There's been a lot to sort out over the last few months.' He frowned. 'Perhaps I shouldn't have pointed the house out to you,' he finished on a thoughtful note.

She poured his tea and came towards him once more, placing the mug in front of him. 'You did the right thing,' she told him, laying a hand on his shoulder and squeezing gently. 'I'm really glad you told me about this place. I don't know what I'd have done otherwise. It was exactly what I needed.'

'Hmm... Well, I suppose a lick of paint here and there will work wonders.' He glanced at the children, busy laying out gingerbread men on a baking tray. Rosie's were perfectly symmetrical, with raisins placed in exactly the right place to represent eyes. Sam, on the other hand, was far more slapdash in his approach, and his men looked like cross-eyed vagabonds, with bits missing here and there. Sarah suspected he'd been surreptitiously tasting the uncooked mixture every now and again—the greasy smears around his mouth were a dead give-away.

Murray looked at Sarah once more as she placed the first batch of gingerbread men in the hot oven. 'How's the job going? Is it working out for you?'

She sat in a chair opposite him, leaving it to the children to finish rolling out the remains of the gingerbread mix on a pastry board.

'I think so. It's early days yet. My boss is watching my every move.' She gave a wry smile. 'I think he's worried I might slip up and inadvertently kill off one of our patients.'

James had not made it obvious that he was concerned about her ability to make the grade, but for the last week he'd checked everything she did, going over her charts and medication logs with a keen eye. Every now and again she would be aware of him assessing her actions, scrutinising the way she handled various procedures. She'd no idea why he was concerned about her abilities as a doctor, but in the past she'd always been headstrong and haphazard in her actions, and maybe he thought she'd breezed her way through medical school on a wing and a prayer.

Murray laughed. 'As if!' Then he sobered, glancing at the children, and added in an undertone, 'Seriously, though, are you finding it all a bit much? You have a whole lot on your plate these days.'

'It's okay. I'm beginning to get used to the new routine. It's just that...' She broke off, her expression rueful. 'I don't know,' she said, after a moment or two. 'I don't seem to have time to sit and think at the moment. Everything seems to be going at a breakneck pace—moving in here, the new job, finding a school for the children, taking on the internet work. It's all come about in a short space of time.' She straightened up and sipped at her tea. 'I'm sure things will sort themselves out, though. Like I said, these are early days.'

'Maybe it would help if I took the kids out for a while. That would give you some time to yourself—unless you'd like to come with us?' He gave her a thoughtful look. 'I need to head into town to pick up some hardware for my computer and I thought about dropping into the pizza place while I'm in the area.'

Sam's ears pricked up at the mention of pizza. 'When are you going? Can I go with you?'

'Sure.' Murray laughed. 'If Sarah thinks it's okay, that is.' He glanced at her and she nodded. She'd known Murray for years, ever since they'd both taken part in a rock-climbing course at an outdoor pursuits centre. He ran his own internet company, working from home most of the time, selling sports equipment and accessories, advising people on how to keep fit, and setting up weekend sporting activities. She'd always found him to be reliable and trustworthy. The children would be safe with him, that was for sure.

'That's fine with me. I think I'll give it a miss, though, if you don't mind. I think I need some time to get myself together.' It had been a stressful week, one way and another, and being with James every day had been harder to handle than she'd expected. She'd always known she should keep her distance from him, but now that she'd taken the job that was never going to happen. Every instinct warned her that whatever way she became involved with him, she might end up being hurt. He alone had the power to affect her that way. Emotionally he could leave her bereft.

She dragged her mind back to Murray's offer. 'I have to go and buy some groceries from the village store, and I could do with a walk along the clifftop and maybe even along the beach.' She smiled. 'Rosie and Sam never seem quite as keen on doing that as I am.'

Murray nodded and turned to look at Rosie. 'How does pizza sound to you, Rosie? Are you in?'

'Yes, please.' She looked at Sarah and said hesitantly, 'I don't mind going for walks…not really… It's just that…' She broke off, her shoulders wriggling. 'Mum used to take us along the seafront in Devon. Now… I get… I get all sad now when we go to the beach.' Her eyes were downcast, and her lower lip was beginning to tremble.

'Oh, Rosie…' Sarah's heart swelled with compassion, and she quickly stood up and went over to her. 'I know how you must be feeling, pumpkin.' She put her arms around the little girl and held her close. 'I do understand. It's hard…but you'll see, it'll get easier with time.'

'We used to play football on the beach with Dad sometimes,' Sam said, a wistful, far-away look in his blue-grey eyes. 'He used to dive for the ball and then he'd fall over and we'd wrestle him for it.'

Sarah reached out and gently stroked his hair. She didn't remember her father ever playing rough-and-tumble games like that with her when she'd been younger, but obviously he had changed, grasping a second chance of happiness after he had found her stepmother and started his new family. She felt for Rosie and Sam. They were going through something that no child should ever have to bear, but she was doing whatever she could to make life easier for them. It was difficult, though, because memories would come flooding in at unexpected moments, like this, putting her on the spot.

'Sounds as though you could all do with a bit of cheering up,' Murray said, coming to her rescue. 'I think pizza with all the toppings will probably do the trick—and we could take some of your game DVDs into the store and swap them for those you were telling me about, Sam, if you like?'

'Oh, yeah…that'd be great.' Sam's mood changed in mercurial fashion.

'Rosie, you might like to check out some of the dance games,' Sarah suggested, following Murray's lead. 'You have some pocket money saved up, don't you?'

Rosie brightened and nodded, causing her soft brown curls to flutter and gleam in the sunlight that poured in through the kitchen window.

'That's settled, then,' Murray said. 'As soon as you're ready, we'll be off.'

After they had gone, Sarah cleared away and set out the cooked gingerbread men on racks to cool. A few were missing already, since Murray and the children had decided they smelled too good to leave until later. Sam's pockets had been bulging as he'd left the house.

She looked around, suddenly feeling the need to go out and get away from all the jobs that were crying out for attention. Sam and Rosie would be gone for much of the afternoon, according to Murray, so maybe she would make the most of things and go and get some fresh air. The walk into the centre of the village would do her good and she could pick up some fresh supplies from the grocery store while she was there.

It was a beautiful spring day, with a blue sky overhead and patchy white clouds moving in from the coast. As she walked down the hill towards the seafront, past colour-washed cottages and narrow, cobbled side streets, she could feel the light breeze lifting her hair and billowing gently round the hem of her skirt. In the distance, boats were moored in the harbour, and closer to home fishermen tended their nets, laying them out on the smooth sand as they looked them over and prepared for the next trip out to sea.

Instead of going directly down to the beach, she took a path that led to a raised terrace overlooking the cove, and from there she gazed out across the bay towards the craggy promontory she had once explored as a teenager. It was some distance away, but she could see the waves dashing against the rocks, sending up fountains of spray to splash into the crevices. She'd gone there once with friends, and James had joined them. He had been on one of his brief visits home from medical school. He'd walked with her along the shore as she'd looked for shells buried in the warm sand. It had been a magical day, with the sun high in the sky and James by her side, a day that had almost made her dreams come true.

There was a movement beside her and it was almost as though by thinking of him she'd conjured him up. 'It must seem a long time ago since you spent your days searching for crabs in those rock pools,' James said, coming out of the blue to stand alongside her. He followed her gaze to the boulder-strewn beach some half a mile away.

She gave a startled jump, taking a step backwards as he went to place a hand on the metal railing in front of them. He quickly put his arm out to steady her, and then when she'd recovered her balance he let his hand rest on the curve of her hip.

'Are you all right? I'm sorry if I surprised you.' He sounded concerned and his glance moved over her to gauge her reaction. 'I didn't mean to creep up on you like that. I thought you'd be aware of me, but you must have been miles away in your head.'

'Yes... I'm okay.' She rested her fingers against her chest, on the soft cotton of her top, as though that might somehow calm the staccato beat of her heart. Where had he come from? She couldn't think straight while he was so close, with his hand spreading fire along her skin, sending heated ripples of sensation to spread through her hips and along the length of her spine. 'What…what are you doing here? Where did you come from?'

'I was on my way home from the hospital and I decided to stop and pick up something to snack on from the village shop. Then I saw you standing here.'

'Oh, I see.' She frowned. 'I thought this was your weekend off.'

He removed his hand and stepped closer to the rail, turning so that he could look at her properly. That ought to have made things easier for her, but instead her mind went blank for a moment or two as she unexpectedly felt the loss of his warm, intimate touch. Perversely, she wanted him to go on holding her.

'Yes, it is, but one of the junior doctors was anxious about a patient and phoned me to ask what he should do. Apparently the consultant in charge was busy dealing with another emergency.'

'Were you all right with that?' She'd watched him work hard all week, putting in long hours, staying on to make sure his patients pulled through and were definitely stabilised or on the road to recovery before he would leave. He seemed reluctant to hand over responsibility until he had done everything humanly possible to make sure they were safe. It must have taken a toll on him, but it didn't show. Despite all that supreme effort, he still managed to look fit and energetic, on top form.

Weekends were precious for everyone, but some senior medical staff guarded them as sacrosanct, a time to recuperate and recharge their batteries, something they'd earned after years of study and acquiring specialist qualifications. From what she'd heard, one or two consultants took a very dim view of things if juniors called them in to work out of hours. Of course, things tended to operate differently in the emergency department.

'I was fine with it,' James said. 'I'd sooner I was there to see a patient if there are any worries about his or her condition. Junior doctors do their best, but they need support, and I try to give it as much as possible. Sometimes you can do it over the phone, but other times there's nothing for it but to go in.'

'Yes, of course.' She had finished her foundation years, but she wasn't much more than a junior doctor herself—James was far more experienced than she was. He'd started his training while she'd been about to begin her worrisome teens, and he'd always put his heart and soul into medicine. 'What was the problem with the patient?' She might be in the same boat herself one day, in a quandary as to whether she should call him out, and it would be helpful to know what kind of things she ought to bring to his attention.

'A woman collapsed while she was being treated for an abdominal injury. The doctor followed all the protocols but she wasn't responding, so in the end he called me to ask for advice. The senior staff were all too busy with other emergencies. There was obviously something more going on than the problems with her injury, but her medical records weren't available. Her liver was damaged, nothing too major—at least, not enough to cause her total collapse. I've ordered a batch of tests, so we'll know better what's going on as soon as they come back from the lab. She's being given supportive treatment in the meantime.'

His glance wandered over her, taking in the pale-coloured cotton top that faithfully followed her curves, and the gently flowing skirt that skimmed her hips, drifting and settling around her calves as she moved. His grey eyes seemed to glimmer as he studied her, though of course it might simply have been a trick of the light. 'You're looking very summery…just right for this warm sunshine,' he said.

A wave of heat surged through her. She hadn't expected him to comment or even notice how she looked, but perhaps it was the contrast between how she looked now and the way she dressed at work that had sparked his interest. One day a week when she went out with the air ambulance, when she wore a flight suit, and the rest of the time at work she dressed in scrubs, the basic A and E outfit.

She gave a wry smile. 'It beats wearing scrubs, anyway, or even jeans. Just lately, when I'm at home I've been trying to get on with some decorating any chance I get, so it makes a change to be out of jeans for a while.'

'Ah…of course, you only moved back here a couple of weeks ago, didn't you? I imagine there's a lot to do, settling into a new place.'

'Yes, you're right there. My back certainly knows all about it.' She laughed, rubbing a hand over muscles that had only recently made themselves known to her.

'Perhaps it's just as well you're having the afternoon off, then. Are you taking some time off from the decorating to explore the village? I expect you want to get to know the place all over again.' He leaned back against the rail, at ease, his long body thoroughly relaxed as he watched her.

'Yes, I thought I'd wander around for a while. Though, like you, I need to get some supplies from the store. I did a big shop when we arrived but now I'm running out of a few things.'

She glanced at him. He was smartly dressed, in dark, clean-cut trousers and a deep blue shirt, the kind of thing he usually wore for work in the emergency unit when he wasn't in scrubs. Perhaps he'd left his jacket in his car, along with his tie. His shirt was open at the neck, exposing an area of smooth, suntanned throat. She looked away. 'Did you park up somewhere around here?' she asked.

He nodded. 'By the quayside. I don't live too far away from here, but it's more than a short walk and it's uphill all the way.' He pointed to the steps that were built into the hillside, with a protective rail to help along the way.

Sarah glanced at the steep, green slopes, covered with a rich array of grasses and shrubs. At intervals there were houses dotted about, overlooking the sea. 'Do you live in one of those?' she asked.

'No. You can't see my house from here. It's further back, about a mile inland. I walk to the village sometimes to stretch my legs and take in the scenery.'

'It must be a big change for you after all those years of living on your parents' country estate.'

'Yes, it is. But I like having my own space.' He looked out to sea for a while, and they both watched a sailing vessel move across the horizon. 'I wondered if you'd ever come back to Cornwall,' he said. 'You were in Devon for several years, weren't you? Did you stay with your father there? He'd remarried before you left here, hadn't he?'

'Yes, he had…and Sam was already a year old by then. I did stay with my father in Devon for a short time.' She moved restlessly, uncomfortable with memories that crowded her brain, and he followed as she began to walk along the cliff path.

'But then…?'

'I began to wonder if I might be in the way. What newly married couple wants a teenager around?' She pulled a face. 'Anyway, it wasn't long before I went away to medical school, and I was glad to be independent. And it was easier to rent my own place, once I found friends to share with me.'

'How did your father feel about that? After all, you and

he had quite a few years here in Cornwall when it was just the two of you together.'

She shrugged awkwardly. 'It was never all that comfortable for either of us once we were left on our own. He was withdrawn a lot of the time, and he preferred to be by himself. He'd have cut himself off from everyone and everything if it had been possible, but instead he had to go out to work to keep a roof over our heads. Then he met Tracy and everything changed.'

He frowned, looking at her with an intent expression. 'That must have been hard on you after all that time of being out in the cold, so to speak.'

She pressed her lips together briefly. 'She obviously sparked something in him that gave him a renewed zest for life. I guess I was glad he'd found some reason to join the human race once more.' The path led down from where they were to the centre of the village, where the grocery store and the post office stood side by side. 'I need to buy some fresh vegetables and a loaf of bread,' she announced. 'Are you heading in the same direction as me?'

'I am. I thought I might get some sticky buns and one of Martha's hot coffees to take away.' He sent her a quick glance. 'Perhaps you'd like to help me eat them—I didn't have breakfast and I missed out on lunch with being called out so early this morning. It's lazy of me, I know, but I can't be bothered to go back home and cook.'

Her green eyes widened a fraction. 'It's the middle of the afternoon,' she said in astonishment. 'You ought to know better than to go without food in our line of work.'

He nodded, his mouth making a crooked line. His whole countenance changed when he smiled, and her heart gave a small lurch. 'Consider me told off,' he said. 'How about the buns? Do you want to share?'

'Okay.' She pushed open the door of the shop and a bell

jangled to alert Martha, the proprietor, to her customers. 'But I'll go one better than that. Why don't you come over to my place and I'll heat up some soup and warm some bread rolls in the oven? Then you can have the buns for afters. I only live about five minutes' walk from here.' The suggestion was out before she had time to consider whether she was wise to get in closer contact with this man who had haunted her, metaphorically speaking, ever since her change from teenage brat to emerging womanhood.

'Well, that's too good an offer to miss…if you're sure?' His brow creased. 'I don't want to put you to any trouble.'

'It's no bother. But if you were to collapse through malnutrition, I wouldn't want to have it on my conscience.' She gave him an admonishing glance and he laughed.

'Thanks, Sarah. Besides, I'm curious to see where you're living now. I heard you'd bought a place, rather than renting. That sounds enterprising, coming from a girl who wanted to be free as a bird and explore new pastures.'

'Hmm.' Her cheeks flushed with warm colour. 'I was very young and naïve when I came out with that statement.' She'd been brash, full of youthful defiance, keen to let him know that she wouldn't be staying around for much longer. In truth, in her mind, she'd been running away. Her mouth made an odd twist. 'It's actually not up to much, and I think you might be quite disappointed when you see it. I know I was, but I was already contracted to buy it.'

He gave her a perplexed glance. 'You mean you bought it without seeing it?'

'That's right. It came up for auction and I didn't have time to suss it out before putting in an offer. It was just about as much as I could afford.' She lifted her arms in a futile gesture. 'And I was in a bit of a hurry.'

'It sounds like it.'

'Can I help you?' Martha bustled forward, ready to

serve them, her face creasing in a smile. 'Have you managed to sort yourself out, my dear?' she queried gently, looking at Sarah. 'You did quite a bit of stocking up last time you were in here, didn't you? I must say, you don't look quite as harassed as you did then.'

'I think it's all beginning to work out,' Sarah answered cheerfully. 'You had pretty well everything I needed to get me started with the cleaning and so on...but I just want a few bits this time around.'

Martha collected together everything off Sarah's list, and she and James left the shop a few minutes later, loaded with packages. James was munching on one of the buns he'd bought.

'Here, let me carry those for you,' he said, relieving her of a couple of bags. He peered inside them. 'There are a lot of vegetables in here for just one young woman.'

'Ah...perhaps you didn't know...' She sent him a quick, sideways look. 'I'm not on my own these days.'

'You're not?' His step halted momentarily and he frowned, glancing at her ring finger and then, seeing that it was bare, said, 'Have I missed something? Are you involved with someone?'

'No, it's nothing like that.' She walked determinedly up the hill towards her cottage.

He sent her a puzzled look, but they'd reached her house by now and she stood still, looking up at the blotchy, white-painted building with its peeling woodwork. 'This is it. This is where I'm living now.'

He stared, his gaze moving up to the roof where a few slates were cracked or missing altogether. To his credit, he managed to keep a straight face as he said slowly, 'I think you might have your work cut out here.'

She laughed. 'You said it...but that's nothing. Wait till you see the inside.' She'd already reinforced his view that she was as reckless as ever, buying on impulse, so what did it matter if he looked around and saw the pitiful state it was in?

They walked along the drab hallway to the kitchen, where he set the bags and packages down on the pine table. He glanced thoughtfully around the room for a moment or two, taking in the flaking ceiling and the windows that hadn't seen a lick of paint for quite some time.

'The cupboards and worktops look as though they're made of solid wood,' he commented after a while. 'I suppose they could be stripped back and restored to their original condition—or painted, depending on how you feel about it.'

'Hmm. Yes, you're right. I haven't quite decided what I'm going to do yet.' She smiled at him. He was being positive, and that made her feel much better. 'I'll put the soup on a low heat, and the rolls in the oven, and I could show you around the place while they're warming up, if you like?'

He nodded. 'Sounds good to me. Can I do anything to help? Shall I put the kettle on?'

'Okay, thanks. Mugs are over there, cutlery in the drawer.'

They worked together for a while, and then she took him on a whistle-stop tour of the three-bedroomed cottage, pointing out the best features, where she was able to find any.

'I knew the structure of the house was reasonably sound when I bid for it,' she told him, 'because Murray, my neighbour, is a good friend, and he knew about the property—from a layman's point of view, of course.'

'Ah... I see... I think.' He hesitated. 'Have you known him long?'

She nodded. 'For years, though of course we've been

out of touch until recently. He's been a great help to me.' They were in one of the bedrooms, and she waved a hand towards the small fireplace. 'I'm not sure quite what to do about that. As you've seen, there's a fireplace in each of the three bedrooms.' She frowned. 'They say you should keep any character features like that if at all possible when you're renovating, but they don't look too good at the moment, and anyway I'm wondering if the rooms might be a bit chilly with the open chimney.'

He shook his head. 'The chimney shouldn't make any difference, and from the looks of things you have central heating, which should keep everything cosy. I think it would be a good idea to keep them. The house is Victorian and pretty solid in most respects, and it would be a pity to lose its character. It should be a fairly straightforward job to renovate them—you have to get rid of any rust, of course, apply a coat of red oxide and then when that's dry rub in some black grate polish. It doesn't come off once it's done, and the fireplace will look as good as new.'

'You're probably right.' She was thoughtful. 'I'll put it on my list of things to do—it's getting to be quite a long list.'

'I could do it for you, if you like.'

She blinked in astonishment. 'You'd do that?' She was completely bowled over by his unexpected offer. Why would he want to spend time doing anything at all in this old, neglected house? And why would he do it for her?

'I think it's something I would enjoy.' He went over to the fireplace and ran his fingers lightly over the partially engraved cast iron. 'I often did restoration work in the family home, don't you remember? There was that time I was up a stepladder, trying to decide what colours to use on the ornate ceiling in the dining room, when you walked in.' He sent her an oblique glance, a glimmer sparking in his dark eyes.

'Oh.' The breath left her lungs in a small gasp. How could he have brought that up? Did he recall everything, every tiny instance of when she'd brought havoc into his life? 'How was I to know you were balanced on a ladder?' she said. 'I didn't mean to take you by surprise. All I knew was I was supposed to go to the house and find someone who would get me started on the apple picking. I should have gone to the study, but I went into the dining room by mistake.'

'And I narrowly avoided taking a nose dive.'

'Because I managed to steady the ladder just in time—'

'Only after I grabbed hold of the mahogany cabinet and regained my balance.'

'Yes, well...' Sarah clamped her mouth shut. Perhaps it was for the best if she didn't say any more. It was an experience that had alarmed her greatly at the time. For a number of years she had worked on the estate in the summer holidays and this particular season she had been scheduled to spend time in the orchards. She hadn't meant to catch her employer's son off guard, and the consequences could have been disastrous. 'You made a good job of the ceiling anyway,' she said, breaking her vow of silence.

He grinned. 'I guess I did, in the end. It took a while, though. A couple of weeks at least.' He moved away from the fireplace. 'I'll make a start with the fires as soon as I get hold of the red oxide and the polish...that'll be sometime next week, I expect.'

'Um, okay. Thanks. That would be really good. I'm really stunned that you should offer.' She looked around for a moment at the fading wallpaper and gave a soft sigh. It would all get done eventually.

'As you say, the house is sound in most respects,' James

commented, interpreting her rueful expression. 'It doesn't look much now, but with care and attention it could be something quite special.'

She smiled at him. 'Yes, you're right, of course.' She turned towards the door and said, 'I think you've seen everything now—shall we go and see if the soup's ready?'

The kitchen was warm from the old AGA, and Sarah soon had the table set for the meal. She put out butter, ham and cheese, along with a bowl of fresh salad, and invited James to sit and eat. Then she remembered the gingerbread men and laid some out on a plate, sliding it alongside the sticky buns James had bought.

'Help yourself,' she said, taking a seat across the table from him.

He smiled as he looked at the food, and sniffed the air appreciatively. 'Mmm,' he murmured, ladling soup from the tureen into his bowl. 'This smells appetising— like home-cooked vegetables in a rich, meaty broth.' He dipped his spoon in the soup and tasted the mixture, his eyes widening in surprise. 'Ah...this is wonderful. I don't think I've ever tasted anything quite like it.'

'Well, I'm glad to hear it—though if you're that hungry, I expect anything would taste good right now.' She grinned. 'Although I did spend a good deal of yesterday evening getting it ready.'

His dark brows rose, and he looked at her dubiously, as though he expected to see her nose grow like Pinocchio's had whenever he'd told a lie. 'You're kidding me,' he said in astonishment. 'You, spending time in a kitchen? I can scarcely believe it. As I recall, you'd sooner grab a burger or a baguette or stick something in the microwave so that you could be on your way. Wherever did you learn to cook?'

'Oh, here and there. It turned out to be a bit of a necessity once I was on my own.' She laughed. 'To be honest, I soon got very tired of convenience food and decided I needed to buy a cook book.' She helped herself to salad, adding grated cheese to her plate alongside the ham.

'You certainly look good on whatever it is you've been eating these last few years.' His glance trailed over her. 'You've filled out—as I recall, you were a skinny little thing with flyaway hair that was forever coming loose from the pins, or whatever it was you used to keep it in place.'

Her mouth made a brief, crooked slant. 'Not much change with the hair, then.' She'd brushed it before leaving the house, securing it in a topknot as best she could, and even now she could feel silky strands parting company with the clips.

She bent her head and pretended to be absorbed with her meal. He'd called her skinny. No wonder he'd not even looked at her the way she'd hoped for back then when she'd been seventeen. Warm colour filled her cheeks. Skinny. He'd made a twosome with Chloe, the daughter of the local innkeeper—she'd had curves aplenty, along with golden hair and dreamy blue eyes. She'd seen them having lunch together at a pub, and his defection had been the final straw to a love-starved teenager. She'd vowed then she would get away from the village and leave James far behind.

And yet now she was sharing a meal with him in her fading, love-starved cottage. She must be mad.

She gathered her composure and forced herself to look at him once more. 'I made another pot of tea—would you like a cup?' She was already reaching for the teapot.

He nodded. 'Thanks. That would be great.' He was staring absentmindedly at the plate of gingerbread men. Some had bits of leg missing, or half an arm, and that made him smile. 'They smell good—more wounded soldier than fighting men, I'd guess,' he said.

'Oh, yes. They're Sam's addition to the feast. He's always in too much of a hurry to bother with perfection.'

He frowned. 'Sam—so there's someone else, as well as Murray? Your life must be getting quite complicated.'

'Yes.' She glanced at him and said quietly, 'Perhaps you haven't heard what happened to my father and Tracy?' It had been a terrible shock, and she had never felt more alone in her life when she'd heard the news of their accident.

'Something happened to them?' His expression was suddenly serious, and Sarah nodded unhappily.

'They were caught up in a road-traffic accident.' She pressed her lips together briefly. 'Unfortunately their injuries were serious and they died almost instantly.'

He drew in a sharp breath, his features taut. 'I didn't know. I'm so sorry, Sarah. That must have been awful for you.'

'It was. It was a difficult time.' She closed her eyes fleetingly, resting a hand on the table, unable to concentrate on anything for that moment, while her mind was lost in the memory of those dreadful weeks when the world as she'd known it had come to a standstill.

His fingers closed over hers, in a comforting gesture that brought her back to the present and made her look up into his dark eyes.

'Did you have friends to support you?'

'Thankfully, yes.'

'I'm glad. I wish I could have been there for you.'

'Thank you.' She sent him a gentle smile. 'But I coped. The biggest problem for me back then was what to do about Sam and Rosie, of course...my half-brother and half-sister. Sam's ten years old, and Rosie's eight.' She frowned. 'I think you might have seen Sam when he was a baby...

at the wedding reception of a mutual friend. Anyway, they both live with me now.'

'But…surely there was some other relative who could have taken them in? An uncle and aunt, perhaps?' He looked shocked. 'How can it be that you're looking after them?'

Her shoulders lifted. 'There's no one else, so they're my responsibility now. That's why we moved back here, so that I could take up this new job and hopefully keep a roof over our heads.'

He shook his head, a perplexed expression on his face. 'I'd no idea, none at all.'

'Why would you?' she said quietly.

They finished their meal and James helped her to clear away. It was plain to see he was stunned by what she had told him, and later, when he was getting ready to leave, he said, 'You've taken on something that others would baulk at, you know.' His features relaxed. 'But somehow I might have expected it of you. You were always up for a challenge, weren't you?' His mouth twisted. 'Let's hope this one doesn't turn and bite back.'

CHAPTER THREE

'How are you feeling today, Nicola?' James picked up his patient's chart and then moved to the bedside where he gave the woman an engaging smile.

'So-so.' She tried to smile in return, but Sarah could see that she was extremely fatigued and clearly very unwell. Nicola Carter was in her mid-forties, with anxious grey eyes and brown hair that formed soft waves around her pale face. There was an intravenous drip connected to a cannula in her arm giving her lifesaving fluids. 'I feel a bit dizzy, and I keep being sick.'

'Mmm.' James nodded, showing his understanding and concern. 'It probably doesn't help that your blood pressure is very low. Your liver was bruised in the car crash and there was some bleeding inside your abdomen, which is why it is so important that you have complete bed-rest for a few days. You were in a bad way when you came into A and E on Saturday, and we still need to find out exactly what happened. It wasn't just the accident that caused you to collapse.' He glanced briefly at her notes. 'You haven't been eating much these last few months, have you? You've lost quite a bit of weight recently.'

'I just don't seem to have much of an appetite.'

'Well, we'll have to do something about that, and make sure we get you feeling better as soon as possible.' He laid a hand on hers. 'With any luck we should have the results of the latest tests by tomorrow. In the meantime, get as much rest as you can.'

'Okay.'

James moved away from the bedside, and Sarah followed. She'd gone with him each day on these rounds of the observation ward, and she was used by now to his gentle manner and matter-of-fact way of dealing with his patients. Somehow he managed to put them at ease so that they could feel reassured they were in good hands.

'I want you to follow up on Nicola's case,' he said now, replacing the chart in the slot at the end of the bed. 'With any luck, the internal bleeding will stop completely and she'll start to heal.'

'I'll see to it.'

'Good.' They walked together towards the A and E department, and he sent her an oblique glance, his grey eyes thoughtful. 'Thanks for giving me lunch the other day. I appreciated you taking the time and trouble to do that.' His mouth curved. 'And it was great to have the chance to look around your house.'

'Do you know—I enjoyed showing you? You actually helped me to see the place through fresh eyes.' She smiled. 'I wasn't sure what I was going to do about the children's bedrooms, how I was going to make them cosy and child-friendly, but you had some great ideas about using the old furniture in there. I'm going to spruce up the Victorian dressing screen and put it in Rosie's room—she'll find all sorts of ways to use it for imaginative games, I expect. And Sam will love to have the desk from the front room. He's really into drawing and writing these days.'

They left the observation ward and headed along the corridor, and James held open the fire door to let her pass through into the A and E department. 'I hadn't realised you'd taken on quite so much, with the children, especially. It must be difficult for you. I mean, you're so young, and you have your whole life ahead of you. Were there really no other options?'

Sarah shook her head. He wouldn't understand her reasoning because he was a bachelor, used to the freedom of his bachelor lifestyle. 'Even if there were, I wouldn't have taken them. I know what it's like to be left, to lose a parent, and they lost both of theirs. I wanted to smooth things for them, to show them that they still had family, someone who cared about them and who would be there for them.'

His mouth made a crooked slant. 'Given your background, I suppose I shouldn't have expected you to do anything else.'

'I guess so. Their situation is different from mine, of course, but they've had to put up with a lot, leaving their home behind, moving from Devon to Cornwall, settling into a new house and a new school. It's all happened quite fast, but I think they're beginning to make friends, so it should be a little easier for them from now on. I'm trying to involve them in the renovations as well, asking them for ideas and so on and giving them small jobs to do so that they feel they're part of it.' At least she could give them love and tenderness, things that had been sadly missing in her own early years.

'With your help, I'm sure they'll do all right. And doing up the house is a project that's going to keep all of you busy for the next few months.' He sent her a questioning glance. 'Speaking of which, I could come round this evening to make a start on the fireplaces, if you like…if that suits you?'

'That would be great, thanks.' It was good to know that he'd meant what he'd said about helping.

'I'm sure Sam will be happy with his new bedroom.'

James chuckled. 'Didn't you say you're going to paint one of the walls red? Better that than the all-round black he was talking about.'

'I think he must be going through a Goth phase.' She laughed with him. 'I thought of compromising and doing a midnight blue ceiling with stars. I haven't made up my mind yet, though.'

'Who knows,' he said in an amused tone, 'if you encourage an interest in the stars and planets, he might grow up to be an astronomer.'

'Yeah, maybe. I wonder if they do astronaut suits in black?'

'Ah...there you are, James.' The triage nurse looked pleased to see him, and hurried towards them as they made their way to the central desk. 'I was just about to page you.' She paused to catch her breath. 'We've a young girl, Rachel, about seventeen years old, coming in by ambulance. She's been partying all weekend from the sound of things. It's a regular thing with her, apparently. She collapsed at a friend's house—they say she'd been drinking and experimenting with Ecstasy.'

James winced. 'We've been getting far too many of these cases lately. And they seem to be getting younger.' He glanced briefly at the white board that detailed patients being treated in the emergency unit. 'Thanks, Gemma. We'll take her into the resuscitation room.'

'Okay. Do you want me to stand by?'

He shook his head. 'Sarah is shadowing me for these first few weeks, so she'll assist me on this one. I can see from the board that you have enough on your hands already.'

'Too right. It's been frantic here this morning from the outset.' Gemma walked swiftly away, leaving them to go and meet their young patient at the ambulance bay.

A paramedic was giving Rachel oxygen through a mask. 'She was talking at one stage—very upset and not making any sense, something about her family—but now she's unresponsive,' he told them. 'Her temperature's raised and her heart rhythm is chaotic. Blood pressure's high, too.'

By the time they had wheeled her into Resus, the girl had begun to have seizures, her whole body jerking in an uncoordinated fashion. James gave the teenager an injection of a benzodiazepine to control the convulsions while Sarah did a swift blood glucose test.

'She's hypoglycaemic,' she said, and James nodded.

'Give her dextrose, and thiamine to help with the alcohol problem. As soon as the seizure stops, we need to get in a fluid line.'

'Will do.' Sarah worked quickly to gain intravenous access. They both knew that the biggest danger to their patient right now was dehydration. Alcohol consumption caused loss of fluid volume due to increased urine output, and that could bring about problems with the heart and blood pressure and lead to collapse.

'I think it will be safer if we intubate her,' James said, gently introducing a short, flexible tube into the girl's windpipe and connecting it to a respirator. 'This way we can be sure she won't choke on her own vomit. And we need to get her temperature down.'

'I'll get the cool-air fan.' Sarah set that up and then paused for a moment to look down at the girl lying on the hospital bed. Her waif-like face was damp with perspiration so that her long brown hair clung to her cheeks and temples. She was dressed in party clothes, a skinny rib top and short skirt, with dark-coloured leggings that only emphasised her painfully thin frame.

'Apparently she talked about family,' she said quietly. 'From the notes, it looks as though Gemma hasn't been able to contact the parents yet. Perhaps I should talk to her friends and see what I can find out.'

'That's a good idea.' By now, James had set up the ECG machine to monitor the teenager's heart rhythm, and he had begun to write out the medication chart. 'I'm worried about the effect the alcohol and the Ecstasy are having on her heart,' he said, his mouth making a flat line. 'She's so young, and all this is such a waste.'

'They call it the love drug, don't they? It's supposed to make you feel warm and fuzzy and you want to hug everyone around you. Perhaps that was what she was looking for.'

'Maybe so, but she's ended up with a whole lot more that she didn't bargain for. If she comes out of this all right, she'll be a very lucky young woman.'

'I guess you're right. But perhaps we all do things we regret sometimes.'

He frowned, looking intently at her, his dark gaze searching her face.

She looked away, a rush of heat filling her cheeks. She didn't want to recall the things she'd done...especially that one time she'd had too much to drink...and she fervently hoped he'd forgotten it, that it hadn't made an impression on him. It had been as though she'd been determined to throw herself headlong into disaster. She shuddered, trying not to think about it. She wasn't the same person now.

She ran a hand through her long, silky, chestnut hair. 'I went a little crazy after my mother left. But I've had a lot of time to go over it in my mind.' She frowned. 'I think, all the time I was acting up, I was looking for something— something that would help me to make sense of my life and give me a reason to go on. After my mother walked out, I was hurt, desperately hurt, and bewildered more than anything else. I was sure I'd done something wrong, that I'd made her hate me so that she left me behind. I kept asking myself why else would she have done that. Didn't she know that I needed her? For a long, long time I went through a kind of grieving process.'

Her eyes clouded as she thought about those months, years of despair, and for a while she was silent, turning over the events of the past in her mind. Even now, she felt the bitter sting of that moment, watching her mother walk away, not knowing that was the last time she would ever see her—the revelation that she had gone from her life came later on, and it hit her as keenly now as if it had happened only yesterday.

'I'm sorry.' James placed the medicine chart on the bed and reached for her, his hand lightly circling her arm. 'You were only twelve years old when she left. It's no wonder that you were devastated after she'd gone.'

He drew her away from the bedside. 'Let's go and get a cup of coffee, take a break for a while. We can go outside in the fresh air if you like.'

'I... I don't know. Are you okay with leaving Rachel?' They'd been on the go for the last two or three hours and she could do with a short break, but even so she glanced doubtfully at the monitors. They were flashing up numbers and bleeping occasionally, signalling trouble, and for an instant she was uncertain what to do.

'The duty nurse will keep an eye on her. We've done all we can for her for the moment.' He signalled to a nurse who was writing up names and treatments on the white board and she nodded and came over to them.

She was young, conscientious and good at her job, but she coloured prettily as James handed her the medication chart. 'I've given her the first dose of cardiac medication,' he said, 'so her heart rhythm should begin to settle before too long. Let me know if there are any adverse changes, will you?'

'I will.' The nurse smiled at him, and Sarah wondered at the softening of her features, the molten glow of her eyes and the pink curve of her mouth. It was odd how he had that kind of effect on the women all around him. She'd seen it before, with the female foundation-year doctors, as well as with the ancillary staff. They all fell for him.

Perhaps it was understandable. She was far from immune herself, but of necessity she'd learned to steel herself against his inherent charm. Like she'd said, self-preservation was a powerful instinct. She'd heard on the grapevine that he'd dated a couple of young women doctors, but rumour had it he didn't want to commit and he'd let the relationships slide when it looked as though they were getting too heavily involved.

They bought coffees from the cafeteria and took them outside to the landscaped grounds beyond the building. Here the earth was gently undulating, grassed over, with trees and shrubs providing a pleasing backdrop, and here and there were bench tables and seats where the hospital staff could sit and eat while enjoying the sunshine.

James led the way to a table that sat in the shade of a rowan tree. The tree's pinnate leaves were dark green, rustling softly in the light breeze, a pleasing contrast to the clusters of creamy white flowers that adorned its branches.

'I'm sorry you were upset just now,' he said. His eyes darkened. 'I could see that it was difficult for you, going back over what happened.'

She gave a brief, awkward smile. 'It's all right,' she said, in a voice that was suddenly husky with emotion. 'I was young and troubled, but I found a way of getting through it eventually...with Murray's help. He helped me to see things in a different light.'

'Murray. Your neighbour.' He said it in a measured tone, a muscle flicking in his jaw. 'He seems to have been a strong influence on your life...both then and now.'

'Yes. He persuaded me to take up medicine.' Truth to tell, James had actually been the biggest influence in her life, but she wasn't about to admit that to him. He'd been patient, talking to her, making an effort to understand her, and she'd thrown it all back at him, too impulsive and reckless to care that he'd been trying to help her.

Her shoulders lifted in a negligent shrug. 'We kept in touch. Murray was always a good friend. He never judged me. Somehow he was just always there for me.'

'I suppose your father wasn't much help.'

'No, not much.' She pulled a face. 'I didn't get it at the time, why he didn't talk to me about my mother. He just clammed up, withdrew into himself. So, after I'd finished blaming myself for her leaving, I started to think it must have been his fault. He was the reason she'd walked away from us. He didn't talk about it. He kept his emotions locked up inside himself and I couldn't reach him so I started to kick out at anything and everything. I didn't care much about anything. And after the hurt there was just anger, a blinding, seething anger that seemed to grow and grow. The adults in my life had let me down and why should I worry any more about what anyone thought?'

'Do you ever hear from her or find out where she went?'

She shook her head and then sipped slowly at her coffee. 'Occasionally there would be cards. I think my dad tried to find her once, but by the time he tracked her down, she'd moved on. I know he wrote to her at the address he'd found, and a couple of months later there was a birthday card for me in the post. I was sixteen. It broke my heart.'

She rested her palm on the table, and he gently stroked

the back of her hand as though he would comfort her in some small way. 'Did you ever try to get in touch with her?'

'Yes, I did, from time to time…when I got over my anger and frustration. I just wanted to know why she did it, why she went away without a word of warning. I wanted to understand how she could have been so heartless. So I wrote to the address my father had found and hoped that my letter would be forwarded on to her. I thought, if she could send cards, there must be a tiny bit of remorse for what she did, somewhere deep down. But she never replied.'

She pressed her lips together, making her mouth into a flat line. 'I still want answers, even now, but I haven't been able to find her. The Salvation Army made some enquiries for me, but nothing came of it. It's very frustrating.'

'Perhaps it would be better if you gave up on searching for her. It isn't getting you anywhere, is it?'

'I don't think I can do that. It eats away at me, the not knowing. I need answers, and somehow, without them, I don't feel as though I can move on.'

He shook his head. 'After all this time you have to find a way of putting it behind you. Going on the way you are, you might simply be raking up more heartache for yourself.'

Her chin lifted. 'Then that's the way it will have to be. I can't give up.'

They finished their coffee and went back to A and E. Sarah sought out the friends who had come along with Rachel to the emergency department and spent some time with them, trying to find out more about the demons that had driven this troubled young girl to drink herself into a coma. It seemed to her that it was a very thin thread that separated her from this teenager. By all accounts, both of them had to face up to insurmountable problems...or maybe the difficulty was that they weren't facing up to them.

At the end of her shift she was glad to go home and leave the worries of A and E behind her for a while. More patients had been admitted to the observation ward, and when she left the hospital Rachel was still unresponsive for the most part. It would be several hours before her blood alcohol level reached a safe point, and likewise the problems that the Ecstasy had caused with high blood pressure and overheating would take some time to resolve.

Murray had collected the children from school for her, and she spent half an hour chatting to him before going back to her own house with Sam and Rosie.

'My boss is coming to help out with getting the house shipshape,' she told the children as they had dinner together later in the warm kitchen. 'I'll be painting the walls in your room, Sam, so maybe you can play in the living room this evening. I don't want you and Rosie arguing while we're busy.'

Sam didn't answer, but his upper lip jutted out in a scowl, and it seemed to Sarah that might be a bad sign. He was obviously keeping his options open as far as keeping the peace was concerned.

'He had a fight with a boy called Ricky at school,' Rosie confided. 'Ricky ended up with a bruise on his leg and he told the teacher Sam did it.'

'You didn't have to tell,' Sam complained, his expression dark and his eyes giving out flint-like sparks.

'Yes, but Murray has the letter from the teacher,' Rosie said with a holier-than-thou attitude. She looked at Sarah. 'He must have forgotten to give it to you.'

There was a tap on the kitchen door at that moment,

and Murray poked his head into the room. 'Is it all right if I come in?' he asked, and Sarah nodded.

'We were just talking about you,' she told him. 'Apparently you have a letter for me?'

He nodded, and held out an envelope. 'Sorry, it went out of my head when we were talking about your internet article. I came to give it to you as soon as I remembered.' He saw Sam's belligerent expression and added, 'Cheer up, old son. It could have been worse, and neither of you came out of it unscathed. Have you shown Sarah your war wounds?'

Sarah's jaw dropped. 'War wounds? What on earth happened?'

Sam began to fidget, hunching his shoulders as if he'd rather be elsewhere.

'Show me,' Sarah demanded, and he reluctantly held out his arm and rolled back the sleeve of his shirt. There were several red scratches along his forearm.

'I think you'd better explain,' she said, keeping a level tone.

'It wasn't nothin',' he muttered. 'Ricky said I couldn't play football 'cos I didn't have no football boots and I said I didn't need any, and I could play better football than him any day. Then we got into a fight.'

His grammar had gone to pieces, a sure sign that he was uptight. Sarah scanned the letter from the teacher. 'They're not taking any action because it happened outside the school grounds,' she said, and then added, 'Heavens, this all took place yesterday morning, after I dropped you off at school.' She looked at Murray, her eyes widening.

'The other parent complained to the head,' he explained. 'I didn't hear anything about it until the teacher handed me the letter today. Both boys have been reprimanded.'

'Hmm.' She glanced at Sam. 'Next time anything like

this happens, you tell me straight away so that I know what I'm dealing with.' She sighed. 'And I suppose we'll have to get you some football boots. They weren't on the list, so how was I to know? We'd better go into town after I finish work tomorrow.'

Sam allowed himself an exultant grin. 'Yay!'

'Never mind "Yay",' she said. 'No more fighting.' The doorbell rang, and she stood up. 'That'll be James,' she murmured. 'Excuse me. I'll go and let him in.'

James was waiting patiently outside the front door. He looked incredibly sexy. He was dressed in casual clothes, black chinos teamed with a dark shirt that skimmed his flat stomach and draped smoothly over broad shoulders. He was long and lean and as she looked at him her heart missed a beat. Heat began to pool in her abdomen and an unbidden yearning clutched at her, causing the breath to catch in her lungs.

He studied her, those grey eyes all-seeing, assessing her in return, and a faint smile hovered on his lips. 'Aren't you going to invite me in?'

'Oh. Yes, of course. Come in.' She opened the door wider, stepping back a pace and waving him into the hallway. 'We're in the kitchen. We were just having a bit of a discussion about problems at school.'

He looked at her curiously. 'What sort of problems?'

'Boys. Fighting,' she muttered, as though that said it all.

'Uh-huh.'

They went into the kitchen, and she introduced him to Murray first of all. 'We met years ago at the rock-climbing club at the coast,' she said. 'Murray showed me all the things I needed to know, like how to use a belay device and hammer pitons into rock crevices for anchor points.' She frowned, seeing that the men were looking at one another with oddly quizzical expressions. 'Do you two actually know each other?'

'I think we may have met before,' James said, eyeing up Murray's lanky, relaxed figure. 'Didn't your company supply the equipment for one of the activity weekends on my father's estate? We held a gymkhana and a dog trial course, if I remember correctly. You came to help set everything up for the event.'

'That's right.' Murray was impressed. 'You've a good memory—that was some years ago.'

'Mmm.' James studied Murray, his grey eyes taking in everything about him, from his jeans and supple leather jacket to the square cut of his jaw and the protective, intent expression that came into his blue eyes when he glanced at Sarah.

Sarah thought back to those summer days she'd spent on the Benson estate. She remembered being invited to the events that were held there from time to time, and the gymkhana stood out particularly in her mind. She'd ridden one of the horses that day. Over the previous months James's father had had his stable manager teach her how to ride—maybe he'd taken pity on the girl whose mother had abandoned her. Whatever, she had been performing that day, and when she'd come to the end of a faultless round, she'd slid down from her horse into James's waiting arms. He'd laughed as he'd caught her, and in that moment, as his arms had closed about her, she had fallen hopelessly, instantly in love.

What girl wouldn't have lost her heart to a man as sexy and charismatic as James Benson? To a naïve sixteen-year-old, he was everything she'd ever dreamed about, and when he'd wrapped his strong arms around her she'd been in heaven, a state of bliss that she'd wanted to go on for ever and ever. She'd felt the warmth of him, his long, firmly muscled body next to hers, and as he'd steadied her and led her away to the refreshments tent, she'd felt that at last the world had granted her deepest heartfelt wish. He'd noticed her, he'd held her, and life couldn't get much better.

Except of course, it hadn't really been like that, had it? For James's part, he had simply been acting the host for his father's community endeavour, and it had been his role to make the contestants feel comfortable and at their ease. His natural charm had taken care of the rest.

She drew in a deep breath and tried to unscramble her brain. 'James is going to help with the renovation work,' she said now, breaking into the silence that had fallen between the two men.

'Ah, that's good. I'm glad you're getting some help.' Murray straightened, and perhaps he felt uncomfortable under James's dark scrutiny because he started towards the door. 'I'll leave you to it, then.' He glanced at the letter lying on the kitchen table. 'I wouldn't worry too much about that, if I were you.'

'No. Well, Sam is going to have to stop fighting and find some other way to solve his disputes.' She glanced at Sam, who responded with a look of benign innocence on his face.

Murray left and Sarah offered James coffee. 'We'll take it upstairs with us,' she suggested. 'I thought I'd make a start with the red paint in Sam's room.' She turned to the children. 'It means you'll have to share Rosie's room tonight,' she told Sam. 'Murray helped me to shift your bed in there earlier today,' she added.

Rosie's mouth opened in protest. 'Share with him? No way!' She placed her hands on her hips, taking a mutinous pose, and Sarah's mouth made a downward quirk.

'It's only for a couple of nights, so that the smell of paint can evaporate,' she said. 'Why don't you both go and call for the children next door? See if they want to play in the garden for a while, and after that you can go into the living room.'

Sam headed for the back door, quickly followed by Rosie, who was marshalling more arguments against sharing with her brother. 'You'd better keep your hands off my game pad,' she warned him, 'or you'll be sleeping on the landing.'

'See if I care.' The door swung shut behind them.

'They love each other really,' Sarah said. She frowned. 'At least, I think they do.'

James laughed. 'I guess we should get started on the room while we have the chance.'

'True. Who knows when things might erupt?'

All was peaceful, though, for the next hour or so, and Sarah found that she was beginning to relax in James's company. He worked on all three fireplaces, scrubbing hard to remove any rust and debris that had accumulated over the years, and then he cleaned everything down with a sponge and cloth.

'There shouldn't be any dust in the air to affect your paintwork,' he said as he worked with her in Sam's room. 'You're doing the far wall, so that's well away from here.'

They worked together in harmony, with music playing on the radio in the background, and every now and again they stopped to comment on a favourite tune or a particular melody.

'I danced to that music at Sam's christening,' Sarah commented some time later.

'It's a popular number even now.' He headed for the door. 'I'll go and wash my hands.'

She'd finished painting the wall by now, had tidied away brushes and roller, and was standing back to look at the result. It didn't look bad at all, and she'd actually managed to keep the paint off her hands and clothes. She rubbed moisturiser into her hands and turned around to study the fireplace.

James had applied a coat of red oxide to the heavy iron. At the weekend, he'd said, he would finish it off with the grate polish.

He came back from washing his hands in the bathroom to find her with a dreamy expression on her face. 'Sounds as though this tune has some special meaning for you,' he said, listening to the gentle rhythm of the music.

'I remember floating around the room feeling as though I was on a cloud.' She laughed. 'That was probably down to the wine that I had with the celebratory meal after the church service. And little Sam was so sweet, with his mop of black hair and his lovely blue-grey eyes that seemed to look deep into your soul. He was nine months old then, looking around and taking notice of everything, and I thought he was adorable…my half-brother, my family. I felt this huge surge of love for him.'

She closed her eyes, thinking about that moment, letting the music flow through her, over her and around her. 'The music stopped, and I looked at my stepmother. She was holding Sam in her arms and he was almost asleep. He had that soft, sleepy look that babies have, he was trying to stay awake and enjoy the fun, but his eyelids kept slowly closing, and Tracy was looking down at him with such love, such overwhelming happiness. And I…' She broke off, the words catching in her throat. 'I thought, Why couldn't my mother love me like that?'

James slid his arms around her. 'Don't do this to yourself, Sarah. You don't know why she left, what went through her mind. You have to find a way to move on.'

'I know…but I don't know how…'

He held her close, his hand gently stroking the length of her spine, drawing her near to him so that their bodies meshed and her soft, feminine curves melted against the hard contours of his strong, masculine frame.

'You said it yourself, everything has happened so quickly of late. You lost your father and Tracy and you found yourself responsible for two young children. Then there was the move here, the new job. It's no wonder that you're feeling this way—your emotions are all over the place because now that you finally have time to breathe and take it all in, it's all coming home to you. You haven't had time to grieve properly.'

'I suppose you're right. It hadn't occurred to me.' She leaned against him, accepting the comfort he offered, drinking in the warmth of his body, taking refuge in the arms that circled her, keeping her close.

He kissed her lightly on the forehead, a kiss as soft as gossamer. She could barely feel it, and yet his touch seared her, its aftermath racing through her body like flame. 'I'm right,' he murmured, his voice deep and soothing, smoothing a path along her fractured nerves. 'All this will pass, and you'll get your life back together, you'll see. You've done so well to come this far.'

She wanted him to kiss her again, to hold her and kiss her on the lips, her throat, along the creamy expanse of her shoulders. He could make everything all right again. He was the only one who could do it. She laid her palm lightly against his chest. Her whole body trembled with longing, even as she knew it couldn't happen.

She'd been here before, yearning for his kisses, wanting him, only the memory of that time still haunted her dreams. She'd been seventeen, and she'd learned that the family was to move to Devon to start a new life. A new life away from James. That was how she'd thought of it, and she'd dreaded going away and leaving him behind. He had been all she'd had in the world. Her father and Tracy had been wrapped up in one another and she had simply been an outsider, looking in. How was she going to let him know how much she wanted him?

Just a few drinks, that's all it had taken, an opened bottle of wine in the fridge...no one would notice that she'd helped herself. Her father would think Tracy had drunk it, and Tracy would imagine her husband had finished it off.

It was pure Dutch courage. It was what she'd needed to give her the confidence to go and find James and show him that he needed her as much as she needed him.

And the clothes, of course...they were important, they had to be just right, extra-special. She had to look her best. And that was where her bridesmaid's dress came in, the one she'd worn to her father's wedding. It was the perfect creation for her, an off-the-shoulder cream dress in a filmy, soft material that clung to her curves and draped itself gently around her ankles. How could he resist her? Surely he would want her, and he would show her once and for all that she was the only woman in the world for him?

All she had to do was go to him, find him in his apartment in the big country house. It was late autumn and he was home for Christmas, celebrating the beginning of his second year as a foundation doctor. She set off along the quiet, country lane to walk the half-mile to the estate.

James always left the side door unlocked until late at night, so it was easy to gain entrance to the north wing of the house. He was so startled, his eyes widening as she walked—no, sashayed—into his sitting room. Heady from the wine she'd drunk, she'd put her arms around him, letting her fingers trail through the silken hair at his nape, and she pressed her body close to his, her breasts softening against his chest. She lifted her face for his kiss. He had to want her. She wanted him, needed him desperately...

But there it all went wrong. His hands went around her

in an involuntary motion, smoothing along the length of her spine, his palm coming to rest lightly on the curve of her hip. Then he sucked in his breath and his fingers gently circled her wrists, drawing her arms down from his neck, away from him.

She was stunned. This wasn't what she expected. This shouldn't be happening.

'I'm sorry, Sarah,' he said. 'I can't do this. You should go home. Come on, let me see you back to the house.' And he took off his jacket and wrapped it around her, taking her out of the room, out into the darkness of the night. The moon silvered the path, lighting their way, and she felt sick at heart. He didn't want her. He had rejected her, and she had made an almighty fool of herself. How could she face him ever again?

'Are you all right, Sarah?' The softly spoken words took her by surprise, and it was a moment before she realised that she was back in the present day, and they were standing in Sam's room, with the smell of paint filling the air and the music on the radio winding down to a soft murmur.

'I... Yes, I'm fine.' She eased herself away from him, her fingertips trailing across his shirtfront as she stepped back, putting distance between them. 'You're right,' she said huskily, 'these last few months have been an emotional roller-coaster. I'm probably overwrought and not thinking as clearly as I might.'

'Maybe you need to spend some time relaxing, instead of working on the house,' he suggested. 'A day on the beach, perhaps, or a visit to the village spring fayre. The change might do you a world of good.'

She nodded. 'I'm sure you're right. I'll have to sort something out.'

He smiled, looking at her a little oddly, as though he was trying to fathom what was going on in her head.

But she was safe enough, wasn't she? He couldn't possibly know what she'd been thinking, how close those memories had encroached on the here and now. Could he?

CHAPTER FOUR

'Will you be coming along to the village's spring fayre?' James was writing up his patient's notes on the computer, but he looked up as Sarah came over to the desk.

'Um, when is it?'

He laughed. 'You're telling me you haven't seen all the notices posted up around the village?'

'I'm afraid I haven't.' She had the grace to look shame-faced. 'When I'm home I tend to dash about here and there, and the only things that tend to filter through to me are what to make for dinner, how did the laundry bin get full so quickly, and if Sam's managing to stay out of trouble.'

His mouth made a crooked line. 'Like I said, you need a break.'

'Yeah. Don't we all?' She bent her head so that he wouldn't see her reaction to his comment. That's what he'd told her last night, that she needed a break, and a wave of heat ran through her as she thought about it. She didn't want to recall those tender moments when she had been wrapped in his arms, but despite her misgivings the memory of that embrace had haunted her ever since. It had brought with it so many searing emotions, recollections of that earlier time when he had held her close. It was difficult enough seeing him every day, working with him, without being reminded of the foolish crush she'd had on him for all those long years.

To hide her discomfort, she began searching through the lab reports in the wire tray. 'So tell me about the fayre. I suppose I ought to support it if it's to do with the village.'

'It's tomorrow, from ten in the morning. Any money that's collected will go towards the fund for the new swimming pool—we want to build it in the grounds of the village school, so that all the local children will get the chance to learn how to swim from an early age. Being surrounded by the sea, as we are, it's really important that we keep them safe, but at the moment they have to go into the nearest town if they want to learn, and that's quite a drive for most villagers.'

She nodded. 'I see your point. It sounds like a really good cause. How's the fund doing?'

He smiled. 'Pretty well. I'm pleased with how things are going. We're almost there, and if the spring fayre brings in a goodly amount we should soon be able to start work on the pool.' He sat back in his chair, watching her, completely relaxed, his long legs stretched out in front of him. How could he be so laid back when she was distracted simply from being near him?

He was waiting for her answer and when she stayed silent he said, 'So, what do you say? Are you up for it?'

'Uh...yes, okay. I expect Rosie and Sam will enjoy a day out.'

'Good.' His mouth curved with satisfaction. 'I'll come and collect you, if you like, at—what time? Would around midday suit you?'

'Um, thanks, that will be absolutely fine.' He was only offering to do that so that he could show her the way, wasn't he? He didn't have any deep-seated interest in her, other than as a colleague, so there was nothing for her to read into his suggestion, was there? He was good with everyone at work, helping them out whenever they had problems. Why would she be any different? A peculiar frisson of dismay crept through her at the thought, but she hastily pushed it away.

Anyway, wasn't one rejection enough for her? Why would she even entertain the idea of getting involved with him outside work? It didn't count that he was helping her with the house—he'd probably taken one look at it and made up his mind that she needed all the help she could get.

'Ought I to contribute something to the stalls?' She pursed her lips, trying to decide what she might take along. 'Some groceries, perhaps, or a cake? I could make a fruit cake and ice it. Rosie's really keen on baking these days and Sam's always up for joining in.'

He seemed to be quite taken with that suggestion. 'A cake sounds like a good idea,' he said cheerfully. 'We could have a guess the weight of the cake competition.'

She nodded, giving it some thought. 'That would certainly bring in some more money. It means I'll have to make a cake that looks fairly scrumptious if it's going to end up as a prize.' A niggling doubt crept in and she added in a rueful tone, 'Perhaps I should have had a bit more practice at cake decoration.' Then a thought struck her and her eyes narrowed on him. 'You're giving this whole thing the big sell—are you on the organising committee or something?'

'Uh…you could say that. The fayre's being held in the grounds of my house, and I've had quite a say in what's being included. And of course we have to make provision for all kinds of weather, so part of the house will be opened up as well.'

'Oh, I see.' She frowned. How would he come by the

land that would be needed for such an enterprise? 'Going on past experience, an event like that could take up a big area…but you told me you weren't living on the family estate any more, didn't you? So how is it possible for you to do it?'

'You're right. I moved out some time ago. But I inherited a property from my great-grandparents—well, strictly speaking, my brother and I both shared the inheritance, but I bought out his half. He was happy for me to do that.'

'Even though he has a wife and children? Wouldn't he have welcomed the chance to have a property of his own instead of sharing with your parents?'

'Jonathan's comfortable staying on the family estate. There's plenty of room for them all there, and they have a separate wing to themselves. He acts as manager of the estate for my parents, so it's really convenient for him to be living on site.'

'I imagine it would be.' She hadn't reckoned on this, and it took some getting used to, discovering that James had not moved to an ordinary detached property, as she'd imagined, but instead he'd inherited another grand house. It just went to show that there was still this huge divide between them and perhaps she ought to have realised that his wealthy background would always be a part of him.

Giving herself a moment to absorb all this, she glanced at the paper in her hand and then frowned as she read through Nicola Carter's test results.

'Is something wrong?'

'Not wrong…a bit worrying, perhaps. I have the results here for Mrs Carter, the patient who collapsed after the road accident with bruising to the liver. From the looks of these lab-test results, she has a secondary adrenal insufficiency. Both the ACTH and the cortisol levels are low.'

His expression was thoughtful. 'We'd better do an MRI

scan to see if anything's going on with the pituitary gland. In the meantime, we'll go ahead with steroid treatment and see how she responds to that.'

'I'll see to it. I'm going to look in on Rachel, too, to see how she's doing. Hopefully, she's over the worst as far as the drug abuse goes, and the alcohol should be out of her system by now, so I might be able to talk to her, and maybe find out if she needs counselling of some sort.'

'They all need counselling when they get into that state,' he said in a dry tone. 'It wasn't an unusual situation for her, by all accounts. Her blood-alcohol level was sky high, and drug-taking has been a common thing for her.'

'Well, I'll do what I can for her in the meantime. Are we going to move her on to a medical ward?'

'Yes, and Mrs Carter, too, as soon as we have the results of the scan.'

Sarah nodded, and hurried away to set things in motion. She was relieved to be able to put some distance between James and herself. It was more difficult for her than she had expected, working with him. It had shocked her to the core to relive all those old humiliating feelings last night, when she'd been in his arms. What must he think of her? And yet he'd said nothing, either then or now... and he'd certainly never commented on her immature, futile attempt at seduction when she was in her teens. It was hard to know whether that made things better or worse.

The rest of the day passed quickly, with a flurry of emergencies being brought into A and E after a traffic accident and a near-drowning off the coast at Land's End. They brought their patient, an eleven-year-old boy, back from the brink of death, and Sarah couldn't help thinking that James was right about the need for swimming lessons. The sea could be a dangerous place for the unwary.

Rachel was able to sit up in bed by now, and the endotracheal tube had been removed so that she was breathing unaided, but she looked pale and unhappy when Sarah went to see her. Her long brown hair was lank and her hazel eyes were dull and lacking in any kind of interest in her surroundings.

'Hello, Rachel,' Sarah greeted her. 'How are you feeling today?'

'Tired. My chest hurts... I'm a bit breathless.'

Sarah nodded, and checked the heart and respirations monitor. 'It's an after-effect of the Ecstasy you took,' she explained. 'You've had some problems with your heart rhythm, but things are beginning to settle down. That would have been worrying enough on its own, but the alcohol added even more complications. It does seem as though you've set yourself on a bit of a downward spiral. I'd like to think we could help you to get your life back on course. Maybe we could talk about anything that's bothering you.'

'There's no point.' The girl turned her head away.

'There's a lot of point, surely? Your friends have been to see you, I hear. They're obviously very worried about you.'

Rachel didn't react, apart from a slight movement of her shoulders, as though she could scarcely find the energy to respond. Sarah said softly, 'Is there anyone we can contact for you—your parents, for instance? I saw from your notes that you're living in a flat, so I presume you left the family home a while ago.'

Rachel shook her head. 'There's no one.'

'I'm sorry.' Sarah frowned. 'Do you want to tell me about it? Did something happen to your parents?'

'No. Not really. We were always arguing, it was a bad atmosphere, and I decided it would be better if I moved out. My brother left a couple of years ago, and I thought I'd do the same.'

'Do you keep in touch with your brother?'

'Not lately. I used to see Harry every now and again, but since I left home last year I haven't heard from him. He was sharing a house with a friend, but he's not there any more.'

'But you used to get on well together?'

Rachel nodded. She closed her eyes, and Sarah could see that even this short conversation had been too much for her. If they could find this brother, perhaps he could do something to lift his sister out of this self-destructive pattern of behaviour. 'I'll leave you to get some rest,' she said quietly. 'Try to drink plenty of fluids—I see your friends have left you some orange squash. The nurses will keep your water jug topped up. Just ask them if you need any help while you're not able to get out of bed.'

After work, Sarah picked up the children from Murray's house and took them into town to buy football boots for Sam and new shoes for Rosie. 'I think we'll pick up some ingredients for sugar paste and some food colouring, while we're about it,' she told them.

'Why? Are we making cakes?' Rosie asked. 'We did sugar paste at school and made all these little flowers. They were lovely. And you can eat them, too.'

'Well, just one cake,' Sarah explained, 'for the village fayre. We'll make it after we've had our evening meal. And then tomorrow, when it's completely cool, we'll have a go at icing it.' It meant she would be spending what was left of the evening searching the internet for tips on how to decorate cakes but, then, it was all in a good cause.

'There we are... I think that's turned out pretty well, don't you?' she said later that evening, as she took the rich fruit cake from the oven and slid it onto a rack.

'It looks yummy,' Rosie commented, admiring the luscious, deep golden brown cake.

'And it smells good,' Sam agreed. He pulled a face. 'But I think we ought to be able to keep it after the fayre and eat it.'

'Mmm. Sorry about that.' Sarah smiled. 'But whoever guesses the weight gets to win it and take it home.'

His expression brightened. 'We'll just weigh it, then,' he said, licking his lips in anticipation.

'Away with you! That would be cheating.' She laughed. 'Anyway, I'm sure there'll be lots more goodies for you to try when we go to the fayre tomorrow.'

The next day, Sarah was up early, anxious to ice the cake before James arrived to take them over to his house. She was a little bit apprehensive, thinking about the day ahead, being with James away from work, and the only way she could counter those feelings was to keep busy. She covered the cake with a layer of marzipan and then spread the white icing over the top and sides.

It had been a long, long while since she had spent a day out with James, and it was one thing to do that on neutral territory, but somehow the prospect of being with him on his home ground was a different thing altogether. It was far too intimate a setting, and not at all what she had envisaged when she'd made up her mind to keep things on a professional basis between them. She gave a rueful smile. Her plans in that regard had probably been scuppered from the outset, what with having lunch with him and with him helping her to renovate the house. Hadn't it always been that way in her dealings with James? Whatever she decided, life had a way of turning everything upside down.

'What are we going to do?' Rosie asked, yawning as she came into the kitchen some time later. She blinked, trying to accustom her eyes to the sunshine that filtered into the kitchen through the slats in the blinds at the window. 'Are we going to cover it with icing sugar flowers, or ribbons and bows? Or both?' She looked at the collection of decorative materials that Sarah had set out on the pine table.

'I'm not sure yet,' Sarah said. 'We'll have to think about it while we have breakfast.'

'I think we should do a water picture, if it's to get money for the pool,' Sam announced, coming to join them at the table. He was still dressed in his pyjamas, and his shoulders slumped as though he would much rather be snuggled up in bed but hadn't wanted to miss out on anything.

'That's actually quite a good idea,' Rosie said in a surprised tone. She looked at her brother as though she didn't quite know him. 'It'll be good to have a swimming pool at the school. Everyone will be able to have lessons, or practise, won't they?' Then she frowned. 'Mum taught us how to swim when we were small. It was fun, and we used to go to the pool every week. She said we were her little water nymphs.' Her grey eyes clouded momentarily and Sam's expression dissolved into sudden anguish.

Sarah sucked in a silent breath. 'Maybe we should make this a special cake, then,' she suggested, thinking quickly. 'We could do a design to show we're thinking of your mother, with a garden pond, perhaps, and two water nymphs sitting on flower petals nearby. What do you think?'

'Oh, yes, that'd be brilliant.' Sam was smiling now, and Rosie had a thoughtful look about her.

'We should have a blue colour for the pond,' she said, 'and there should be some water lilies on it. You'll need green sugar paste for those, and white and yellow for the flowers.' She inspected the bottles of food colouring that were set out on the table. 'And then some bigger flowers for the water nymphs to sit on.'

'Or they could be in trees, with little houses in them.' Sam was looking pleased with himself, excited about the project. 'And there could be a frog on the pond and a boy fishing.'

'That sounds lovely, but let's not get too carried away,' Sarah laughed. 'The simpler the better, I think. After all, we only have a few hours before James comes to pick us up, and I'm not exactly used to doing this sort of thing.'

BY THE TIME James arrived at midday, they were just about ready, with the children dressed and raring to go and Sarah putting the finishing touches to her make-up. She was wearing dark blue jeans and a smooth-fitting cotton top, and she'd pinned her hair up into a loose topknot.

'Hi. Are you all set?' James asked. He gave her an admiring glance and then relieved her of the holdall she was carrying and tested the weight with his hand. 'Heavens, what have you packed in here? We're going for an afternoon out, not a week's trekking expedition.' He grinned.

'It's just a few extras—an emergency first-aid kit and clothes in case the weather turns to rain, or one or other of the children manages to fall into a mud pile or some such.'

He laughed. 'That's hardly likely to happen, is it?'

She sent Sam a surreptitious look. 'Don't you believe it,' she whispered. 'I still haven't recovered from taking them to the zoo last month.'

'That wasn't my fault,' Sam put in with a frown. There was obviously nothing wrong with his hearing. 'I didn't start it. I was looking at the monkeys and Rosie got fed up waiting and pushed me out of the way.'

'Did not!' Rosie let out a shriek of indignation. 'I was trying to get by him.'

'Did too. And so I pushed her back and then we got into a fight and we both ended up rolling down the slope.

Wasn't my fault it had been raining and the ground was all messy.'

Sarah groaned. 'Oh, please...don't remind me.'

James looked puzzled. 'I take it things got a bit out of hand?'

She nodded. 'As they do quite often.' She studied him briefly. 'You seem surprised. But you must know how these things are...you're used to children, aren't you? You said your brother had a boy and a girl.'

'Yes, but they're only one and two years old.' He gave her a doubtful look. 'There are never any problems with them...not that I can see, anyway.'

'Oh, dear.' She gave him a sympathetic look. 'I can see this is all new to you. For myself, I've watched Rosie and Sam growing up, and I have friends whose offspring are always up to something or other, so nothing much surprises me any more where children are concerned. You've been well and truly sheltered, haven't you, living the bachelor lifestyle these last few years?'

'I suppose I have.' He smiled as they walked out to his car, a sporty, silver streak of mouth-watering beauty. It had a soft top, and the hood was down to leave the occupants free to enjoy the sunshine and fresh breeze. 'Hop in the back, you two,' he said to the children, tossing the holdall into the boot. He glanced at Sarah. 'Is that the cake you're carrying? Do you want me to put it in here along with the holdall?'

'I think I'd rather keep it with me,' she said, guarding the cake tin as though it was something precious, not to be let out of her sight. 'After all the work we've put into it, I want to be sure we get it there in one piece.'

'I can't wait to see it. Do I get to have a peek now?'

'Okay.' She carefully prised the lid off the tin. 'You won't be able to see the sides this way. Rosie and Sam decided we needed pale green fronds all the way round, to represent reeds.'

He looked into the tin and gave a low whistle of appreciation.

'So, you like it?' she asked.

'I certainly do. That's a real work of art. If I won it, I wouldn't be able to bring myself to cut into it.' He glanced at her, his gaze full of admiration. 'What a brilliant idea, to have a water theme. I love those little water nymphs.'

She nodded. 'That came from Sam. He's quite a deep thinker, underneath it all. And both of the children helped, especially with the flowers and leaves.' She'd made the wings for the water nymphs herself, lovely gossamer creations made from golden spun sugar strands.

'I can see why you want to keep it safe,' he said, waiting as she carefully replaced the lid on the tin. He held open the car door for her as she slid into the passenger seat. 'You're amazing…definitely a woman of hidden talents.'

She mumbled something incoherent in return and he gave her a quizzical look as he slid behind the wheel of the car. As if he'd ever wanted to explore those talents. The thought came to her unbidden, and she swiftly pushed it away. She had to keep her mind off that track. The past was done with, finished, and it was high time she acknowledged that, if only for her own peace of mind.

He followed the coast road for a while, and then turned off down a winding country lane. At first there were houses clustered together but these gradually became more and more isolated until finally they came to what must have been a large farmhouse at one time. James took them along a wide driveway, bordered on either side by manicured lawns, where stalls were set out. Some displayed goods for sale, while others offered games to be played and prizes to be won.

'Here we are,' he said, pulling up in front of the house and cutting the engine. 'This is my place.'

'Wow.' Sam was impressed. He jumped out of the car and stared up at the wide frontage of the two-storey building. 'Do you live here all by yourself?'

'I do. But a lady comes from the village to clean up for me a couple of days a week. She does a bit of cooking, too, because she's afraid I might starve to death, left to my own devices.'

Rosie frowned. 'Would you really? Starve, I mean?' She was obviously worried by that. 'You could always put stuff in the microwave, you know. It's easy to do that. That's what my mum used to do when we all wanted different things.'

'That's what I do, too, sometimes.' He smiled at her. 'You should come and see my kitchen. I've just had it remodelled, and there's a microwave and a tabletop slow-cooker in there, as well as a built-in oven—all kinds of equipment that I still have to learn to use.'

'You should ask Sarah to help you out,' Rosie suggested helpfully. 'She's had to learn how to do all sorts of cooking 'cos she says we're not allowed to eat rubbish. We have to grow and be strong and healthy.'

Sam flexed his muscles. 'I've been eating lots,' he said. 'I'm going to get big so's I can beat Ricky Morton.' He began to jab at the air with his fists, like a boxer.

Sarah raised her eyes heavenwards. 'What did I say about no fighting?' she reminded him.

'Yeah, well...if he comes at me, I'll be ready for him.' He made another lunge with his arm.

Sarah looked once more at the house as they started to walk towards the stalls. It was built of mellow, sand-coloured stone, and there were lots of Georgian-style windows, with an entrance porch at the mid-point. Jasmine rambled around and over the porch canopy, its waxy, star-shaped white flowers adding a purity and delicate beauty to the archway. The walls were covered in part with dark green ivy, lending the house an old-world charm. 'It's lovely,' she said, smiling appreciatively.

'I'm glad you like it.' James looked fondly at his home, set against a backdrop of mature trees and colourful shrubs. 'It's always had a special place in my heart— not just because of the house, though it is beautiful, but because my grandparents lived here before they bought the house where my parents live now. There are so many memories locked up in this place that I couldn't bear to see the house go onto the open market. It belongs within the family.'

There was a far-away look in his eyes. 'My brother and I used to come here on visits, and we had our own rooms when we stayed over.' He winced. 'After my grandparents left, it was let out as apartments for holidaymakers for a number of years. It's taken a while but it's good to have it restored to a family home once more.'

She nodded, understanding how he must feel. 'And to think I worry about my small renovations,' she said with a laugh. 'I couldn't even begin to tackle something like this.'

'Can we go on the bouncy castle?' Rosie asked, looking eagerly towards where children were jumping and squealing with delight. 'I can see Frances from school, and her brother, Tom. He's in Sam's class.'

'Yes, that's okay. We'll be looking at the stalls over here when you've finished.'

The children hurried away. 'We could put your cake on the table next to where the raffle is being drawn,' James suggested. 'One of the helpers made up a "Guess the weight" chart, so there's nothing else that needs to be done.'

'All right.' They put the cake in pride of place on the table, and straight away a small crowd formed, oohing and aahing over it.

'It's already looking as though that will be a money-spinner,' James said. 'Perhaps Rosie was right…you could give me a few tips on how to cook.' He slid an arm around her waist as they walked away, drawing her close to him and setting up a tingling response in her that rippled through her from head to toe.

'I'd be happy to do that, though I can't see you spending much time in the kitchen, state-of-the-art equipment or not,' she answered, trying to ignore the heat that was spreading through her. 'You're far more likely to drop by Martha's shop for doughnuts and sticky buns.' She looked him over, lean and muscled in chinos and T-shirt, with not an ounce of fat to spare. 'Heaven knows how you manage to stay so fit looking.'

He grinned. 'It must be all that hands-on exercise I get in A and E that does it. It certainly seems to work for you, anyway.' His glance shimmered over her, and Sarah felt a small glow start up inside her. At least he wasn't calling her skinny any more.

'I don't think that's just down to the work at the hospital. There are two energetic youngsters who have a big hand in keeping me on my toes.'

'True.' They wandered around the stalls for a while, trying their hands at spinning the wheel to win a soft toy, and knocking down skittles for a bag of sweets. Rosie and Sam came to join them after a while, playing hoopla and firing water pistols at toy ducks to see if they could knock them off the stand. Then the children sat for a few minutes while their faces were painted and they were transformed into a glittery princess and a fiery tiger.

'You look fantastic,' Sarah told them, and James nodded in agreement.

'But we came here with Rosie and Sam,' he said with a puzzled frown. 'Any idea where they've gone?'

Rosie giggled.

They spent some time at the barbecue, munching on succulent chicken and rice, kebabs and salad. Then Rosie and Sam wandered over to one of the toy stalls, keen to spend some of their pocket money on new treasures. They came back a few minutes later, eager to grab Sarah's attention.

'Can we go round with Frances and Tom for a bit?'

'There are pony rides round the back of the house,' Sam added, 'and we want to have a go. Their mum says it's all right. She said we could meet up with you in the refreshments tent at four o'clock, if that's all right with you.' He pointed towards Frances's mother in the distance, who mouthed carefully and gesticulated that she would look after them.

Sarah nodded and mouthed 'Thank you' in return. She'd met and talked with Kate Johnson on several occasions and knew she would carefully watch over them. 'Okay. That's fine with me. If you need us before then, we'll be out here somewhere, looking at the stalls.'

'Or maybe we'll be in the house,' James put in. 'I thought I might show Sarah around.'

'Okay.' The children ran off to join their friends, and James took Sarah's arm, guiding her towards the tombola table. 'Let me buy you some tickets,' he said. 'I'm sure you'd love to win a basket of fruit, wouldn't you?'

'I certainly would,' she said, eyeing the basket that had pride of place amongst the beans, sauces and pickles. Instead, she ended up with a jar of strawberry jam. 'That's an excellent jam,' she said, looking closely at the jar. 'I love it, but Sam will pick out all the strawberries and put them to one side.'

'Tut-tut...' James smiled, his mouth crooking attractively. 'That's sacrilege.' They reached the coconut shy, and he took careful aim with a wooden ball, hitting the target full on.

A minute or so later he weighed the coconut in his hand and said in a droll tone, 'I don't even like coconut...and have you ever tried to open up one of these things?'

She chuckled. 'I dare say a hammer and chisel would come in pretty handy.' She walked with him to the plant stall, picking out a selection of plants for her small garden. 'I don't have a lot of room out back,' she told him, 'but I thought I could brighten the borders with begonias and marigolds. And I love antirrhinums, so I have to find a spot for those.' She gazed into the distance, looking at his beautifully landscaped gardens, where flowering shrubs added swathes of colour to the front of the house. There were low-spreading berberis with an abundance of orangey-yellow flowers, magnificent cotoneasters and attractive yellow cytisus.

'I'll carry these for you,' James said, helping to place her purchases in a plastic plant tray. He wedged the coconut in one corner. 'Perhaps we should drop these off at the house, and I'll give you the grand tour?'

'That sounds good to me.' She smiled at him, and realised that she had enjoyed these last few hours. Away from work, relieved of responsibilities for an hour or two, she'd been able to relax, and she discovered that being with him was fun. They talked, shared anecdotes, and took pleasure in the simple things of life. Perhaps she was living dangerously, being this close to him, watching him smile as he looked around and saw how everyone was making the most of their day out, but for the moment she was glad to cast her anxieties to one side.

'I've had quite some time to make the changes here,' he said as he led the way into the house. Some of the rooms had been opened up to the visitors to the fayre, and French doors were open to allow easy access. There were cake stalls in here, and a table set up with a tea urn and cups and saucers. A few tables and chairs had been laid out so that people could take a few minutes to sit and chat over a cup of tea, with cake or scones, or even appetising sandwiches cut into small squares.

'Let's go through to the rooms that aren't being used for the fayre,' James suggested, taking her through an archway into a spacious hall. He'd taken the precaution of labelling the doors in here with signs saying 'Private'. They went into a large room, filled with light from a number of tall windows along one side. 'I use this as a study,' he said. 'If I need to keep up with the latest medical research, I come in here to sit at the desk and use the computer. Or if I want to read or listen to music, I have everything I need in here.'

'You certainly have a lot of books,' Sarah remarked, looking around. Bookshelves lined one wall, filled with an assortment of reading material, from medical and scientific volumes to travel books and a collection of the latest bestsellers. There was an armchair by the open fireplace, cosy and inviting, with well-stuffed cushions and a footstool close by. 'I could curl up in here for a week, just reading the murder mysteries you have on this shelf alone.' She trailed a finger over the spine of one novel, her eyes shining. 'I love anything by this writer,' she said. 'I've read everything he's ever published.'

'You're welcome to drop by any time and make yourself at home,' he offered, his grey glance moving over her like the lick of flame. 'I'd be more than happy to have you spend time here.'

Heat filled her cheeks. Was this how he managed to charm all the women at work? She was more than tempted to take him up on his offer, but a cautious inner voice warned her that it could only lead to trouble.

'Seriously, if you want to borrow any of the books, that's fine, just help yourself.' He smiled at her. 'I might have known you'd have a taste for the more exciting, edge-of-the-seat kind of writing. That daredevil, always-up-for-a-challenge girl has never really gone away, has she?'

'Oh, I wouldn't say that. I've learned that there are other kinds of challenge, like medicine, for example, that can be just as stimulating.'

'Yes, you're right.' He nodded, becoming serious once more. 'I think I've always wanted to be a doctor deep down, especially since I realised that you can make a difference by stepping in when someone's seriously ill or suffering from life-threatening trauma. I wanted to be first on the scene, with the ability to save lives—but you need to have a good team working with you. That's why I try to get the best of both worlds, by working in the hospital and outside with the air ambulance. It makes for a good balance, and stops the work from becoming mundane.'

'Yes, I'm with you there.'

They wandered from room to room, and it became clear that he had an eye for what was elegant and uncluttered. Everywhere was tastefully furnished, with colours that reflected nature, soft greens, pale gold and shades of russet. There were period pieces here and there—a couple of Hepplewhite chairs and a Georgian inlaid card table in the study, and a grandfather clock and oak settle in the sitting room.

The floorboards here were covered with luxurious oriental rugs and there was a wood-burning stove to provide warmth on chilly evenings.

The kitchen was just as he had said, completely fitted out with modern equipment, all discreetly blended with natural oak cupboards and marble worktops, and an island bar where you could sit and enjoy a cup of coffee while watching TV on a pull-down screen. At one end of the room there was a table and chairs next to the window that overlooked the landscaped garden. On another wall there was an antique oak dresser displaying beautiful hand-painted crockery.

'Mmm…you have everything you could possibly want in here,' she said. 'It's a dream kitchen. It would be a crime not to whip up some delicious meals in here.'

'I suppose so…though I've learned I can get by quite happily on take-away food, especially since the Chinese restaurant set up in the village a few months ago. They do a fantastic chop suey and egg fried rice.'

'Oh, don't!' she said on a soft sigh. 'I've eaten lunch, but I could still work my way through chop suey, chow mein and sweet and sour chicken. They're my absolute favourites.'

He chuckled. 'Perhaps we'd better move on from the kitchen. I'll show you upstairs.'

He led the way, showing her onto a wide landing, where several doors led off in various directions. 'There are four bedrooms, all with their own en suites,' he told her. They walked from one to the other, and Sarah was impressed by each one in turn.

'What do you think?' he asked. 'I've done them out in pale, restful colours, and carpeted them so that they're quiet and comfortable. I know some people don't like carpets, but I tend to wander about in bare feet first thing in the morning, and having wool underfoot seems to make life so much more relaxing.'

'I think they're just perfect. Especially this master bedroom.' She could imagine him padding about in here, bare-chested, yawning and stretching as he looked out of his window onto the garden below. This room was filled with his presence...everything in here reflected his calm, understated vitality. It was something she'd always admired in him, that effortless way he had of moving, all that latent energy waiting to be unleashed. And now...now she began to feel hot and bothered, overwhelmed by a sudden rush of hormonal feverishness. A pulse started to throb at the base of her throat and her chest felt tight.

'Are you all right?' He moved closer to her, searching her face, a small frown indenting his brow, and for once she couldn't hide the flush of heat that swept along her cheekbones. Small beads of perspiration broke out on her forehead.

'I'm fine. A bit hot, that's all,' she said huskily. 'Perhaps we should go.'

He shook his head. 'Sit down for a while. You look as though you're going to faint or something.' He waved a hand towards the bed. 'I'll open a window.'

'No, I'll be fine, really. There's no need for you to do that. Perhaps the salad dressing I had earlier was a little salty. I should have had something to drink.'

'I'll get you some water. But you need to sit down,' he insisted, taking her gently by the arm and leading her over to the bed. 'In fact, maybe you should lie down for a while.' He felt her forehead with the back of his hand. 'You're really very hot.'

'I'm... It's nothing, really...' Her voice faded, and suddenly as James moved away from the bed it seemed like a good idea if she were to lie back for a while. Perhaps he was right after all. Maybe it wasn't hormones that were troubling her. She'd rushed about yesterday evening, seeing to the children, preparing the cake and studying cake decoration late into the night. And then from early this morning she'd been on the go, sorting the laundry, doing the chores and icing the masterpiece. And there'd been the notes she'd had to finish for her internet article. She'd been working to a deadline...

Her eyelids were heavy. It wouldn't hurt to close them for a second or two, would it? She heard him moving about in the bathroom, that gloriously cool room with the bathroom suite that gleamed palely and the ceramic tiled walls that reflected exquisite good taste. Her mouth was dry, and she could feel heat rising along the column of her throat. It felt damp to the touch.

There was something attached to her arm. She looked at it in vague disbelief. A blood-pressure monitor? James was taking her blood pressure?

'What are you doing?' she said, frowning, a headache starting at her temples.

'Your blood pressure's way too high,' James murmured, releasing the cuff from around her arm. 'No wonder you felt strange. Here, drink this.' He slid a hand behind her shoulders and gently raised her to a sitting position. With his other hand, he held a glass to her lips and she felt the cold drops of water trickle into her mouth.

She drank thirstily, and when she had finished he carefully laid her down again.

'You should get some rest,' he said, giving her a concerned look. 'I think you've probably been overdoing things lately. With that, and the move from Devon to Cornwall, and taking on the care of the children, you've had a lot to take on board. Your body's telling you to slow down, take time to breathe.'

She tried to sit up. 'The children,' she said. 'I should go and take over from Kate.'

'No. I'll see to it. You stay here. Try to get some sleep. There's nothing to bother you here, no one to worry about. I'll see to everything.'

'I'm so sorry,' she muttered. 'I can't believe this is happening. It has been such a lovely afternoon.'

'It still is,' he said, his mouth tilting at the corners. He laid a hand lightly on her shoulder, and she thought for a moment that he was going to brush her cheek with his hand, but then he brought his fingers down to her cotton top and he slowly began to undo the buttons at her throat.

'I... You...' She tried to protest, but the words wouldn't come out, and she simply stared at him, wide eyed, her lips parting a fraction.

'There's no need for you to panic,' he said. 'I'm not trying to take advantage of you. I'm only undoing the first few buttons to cool you down. There's nothing for you to worry about.'

'No?'

It was a query, and he answered with a smile. 'Any other time, maybe it might have been different...but right now I want to look after you,' he said. 'You'll be safe here, I promise. Close your eyes and get some sleep.'

Any other time... Her mind did a strange kind of flip as she absorbed that, but then caution overtook her once more. 'The children...' she said, her voice slurring as weariness overcame her. 'You don't know how to...'

'They'll be fine. I'll let them loose on my DVD collection. And when they're tired of that, we'll make supper.'

'All right.' She closed her eyes and let herself sink into the soft, cushioning duvet. 'Thanks.'

She didn't know what was happening to her but it was

sheer bliss to simply lie here and do nothing, to let the healing power of sleep overtake her.

Her mind drifted, oblivion taking over. She thought she felt him move closer, lean down and brush her forehead with a kiss that was as soft as a cotton-wool cloud.

But he wouldn't do that, of course. She must be dreaming.

CHAPTER FIVE

Sarah slowly opened her eyes. She wasn't sure what had woken her, but the room was dark, and for a while she lay there, trying to recall where she was and what had happened. The last thing she remembered as she'd drifted away had been the heavenly feel of the mattress beneath her, as though she was being enveloped in softness. Later, she'd stirred, feeling a chill in the air, but soon afterwards there had been the sensation of something floaty being draped over her, and she'd sunk back into a blissful, deep sleep.

Now she tried to sit up, her eyes becoming accustomed to the shadows and the faint glow of moonlight that seeped into the room through the curtains.

'I didn't mean to disturb you,' James said softly, his voice deep and reassuringly calm. He switched on the bedside lamp, and a pool of golden light shimmered around her. 'I saw that you were a bit restless, so I made some hot chocolate.'

'Oh, thank you, that was thoughtful of you,' she murmured, still drowsy. She frowned. 'What time is it? How can it be dark? Surely I haven't slept for all that long?'

He placed a tray on the bedside table and sat down on the edge of the wide bed. 'It's around ten o'clock. Once you settled down, you were well away.'

'Oh, no... I can hardly believe it. How could I have done that?' It suddenly struck her that she was supposed to be looking after the children, and she sat up straight in a panic. 'The children...'

'They're fine. They're fast asleep in the guest rooms. I told them they could sleep in their underwear for tonight.'

'But... Oh, this is awful. I let them down. I should go to them...'

He laid a hand on her shoulder and gently pressed her back against the pillows. 'You don't have to go anywhere. I explained to them that you were very, very tired and that you needed to rest. Of course, they wouldn't take my word for it and they insisted on coming up here to see you. Once they knew you hadn't been kidnapped or whisked away anywhere, they were fine. They watched a DVD and then we made sandwiches and popcorn.'

'You had popcorn in your kitchen?' She sent him a doubtful look and he grinned, handing her a mug of hot chocolate.

'Drink that. It'll help you settle for the night. The popcorn was Sam's. He bought a bag from the food stall and Rosie showed us how to heat it up in the microwave. I had no idea you could do that with corn.'

Her mouth curved. 'Well, I guess we learn something new every day.' She sipped the creamy chocolate and sighed with contentment. 'This is delicious.' Then she frowned. 'I really should get them home.'

'No, you don't have to do that.' He shook his head. 'It would be a shame to wake them.'

She chewed at her lower lip. 'We've been a lot of trouble to you, disturbing your peace. You probably had plans for this evening.'

'I didn't, beyond finishing off the fireplaces at your house.' He laughed. 'How sad is that?'

'Oh, enormously sad, for a man in his prime.' She laughed with him. 'Seriously, though, thanks for taking care of Sam and Rosie. It can't have been easy for you if you're not used to children.'

'It was okay.' A small line etched its way into his brow. 'They never stop, do they, kids? You think you have them settled, that everything's sorted, and they come up with something you never thought of...like "Can we sleep in a tent in the garden?" That was Sam. And "Why don't we make a spaghetti Bolognese?" That was Rosie. "You only need mince and tomato puree and herbs," she said, "and spaghetti, of course." Which would have been fine, seeing that I had some herbs in the kitchen.'

'And the rest of the ingredients?'

'Unfortunately, no.' He shook his head, his mouth making a wry shape. 'She doesn't have a very high opinion of my culinary efforts, I'm afraid.'

She smiled, swallowing more of the chocolate, before looking at him curiously. 'Did you ever think about having a family of your own? I mean, seeing your brother settled with his wife and children, did you think you might want to do that some time?'

'Some time, maybe, with the right woman.' His gaze rested on her intently for a moment or two, his gaze dark and unreadable, then he shrugged awkwardly and appeared to give the matter some thought. 'I've been too busy, up to now, with one thing and another, working my way up the career ladder. There have been a lot of specialist exams, different hospital jobs along the way. A wife and family probably wouldn't have fitted in too well with all that.'

'I suppose not.' Was that the reason he hadn't wanted to get more deeply involved with any of the women he had dated? From what she'd heard back at the hospital, there were more than a couple of women who mourned the fact that he hadn't wanted more than a light-hearted romance. She put down the mug.

His glance trailed over her, lingering on the burnished chestnut of her hair that framed the pale oval of her face, before he let it glide over the silken smoothness of her arms. 'What about you? I'd have expected someone to have snatched you up by now.'

She shifted a little under his dark-eyed scrutiny. She was still dressed in jeans and cotton top, but her buttons were undone, exposing the creamy swell of her breasts, and the light from the lamp added a soft sheen to her bare arms. She was covered with a light duvet, and now she pulled this up around her. 'I don't think I'm settling-down material, I'm afraid. I have this problem believing in happy ever after.'

'Ah…yes.' There was a regretful note in his voice. 'I can see how you might feel that way. When your mother went away, she left you with a scar that refuses to heal, didn't she?'

She glanced at him briefly from under her lashes. Her mother hadn't been the only one to do that to her, although the pain he'd caused her had been done unknowingly. 'Something like that.'

'But you've had boyfriends?' He was looking at her intently, a faint glitter in his eyes.

She nodded. 'Some.' She wasn't going to enlarge on that. Either they'd become too keen and she had ended the relationships, or they just hadn't gelled with her. Anyway, there was only one man she'd ever really wanted and he'd made it pretty clear years ago that he didn't want her.

James laid his hand over hers. 'You should get some sleep,' he said. 'It'll do you the world of good to rest and rid yourself of your cares for a while. I'll look in on the children, but I don't think you need have any worries on that score.'

'But this is your room... I'm in your bed.' She tried to sit upright once more but the duvet hindered her, wrapping itself around her.

'Mmm...' His mouth quirked wickedly and there was a gleam in his eyes as his gaze shimmered over her. 'I'd be more than happy to join you...breathtakingly happy, in fact...but I've a feeling that would be a big mistake. You're vulnerable right now, and you'd probably hate me in the morning.'

She drew in a sharp breath, her eyes widening. Was he really, actually saying that he wanted her? She made a second attempt to sit up.

He gently urged her back down, laying his hands on her shoulders in such a way that stirred up a fever inside her. 'Relax,' he said. 'I'll be in the room next door. If there's anything you need, just call out.'

The mere thought of doing that made her heart begin to throb heavily in her chest, banging against her ribcage. Should she wind her arms around him and tell him just how much she wanted to keep him close? What if she were to call out for him in the night and wait for him to come to her? Would he reject her this time, as he had done once before? Undoubtedly not, from the looks of things...but dared she risk everything in doing that?

But then he stood up, looking down at her for a moment or two before heading towards the door. She gave a soft sigh of relief mingled with regret. She wasn't thinking straight. How could she even imagine how it would be to lose herself in him...this man who couldn't commit?

After he'd gone, she switched off the lamp and lay down, snuggling under the warmth of the duvet. Her body ached with longing for what might have been.

In the morning, after a deep sleep, she woke feeling renewed, refreshed and full of energy. When she drew back the curtains, it was to a bright day with the sun making the colours of nature even more vivid than usual. She opened the bedroom window, breathing in the crisp, fresh air, and if she listened carefully, she was sure she could hear the sea in the distance, dashing against the rocks. James had a truly wonderful home, in a perfect setting.

She showered quickly, washing her hair, and then wrapped herself in a clean, white towelling robe that she found in the airing cupboard. She'd washed her underwear and cotton top, and left them on the heated towel rail to dry. They wouldn't need ironing, and within an hour or two they should be ready for her to put back on. There was a hairdryer in a drawer in the bedroom, and she sat for a few minutes at the dressing table, blow-drying her long hair.

James was in the room next door, he'd said, so she sought out the other two guest rooms and looked in on the children. They were both fast asleep, Rosie, pink cheeked, her arms flung out on the duvet, Sam curled up under his covers, with only his nose peeping out.

She smiled, and quietly left them, making her way downstairs. To her surprise, James was in the kitchen.

'I didn't realise you were up,' she said. 'I thought it was early.'

'It is.' His gaze seemed transfixed on her for a moment, and she wondered belatedly if it had been a mistake to come downstairs wearing just a towelling robe. It fitted to just below her knees, but there was still a good expanse of her legs showing. She pulled the robe a little more closely around her.

'I hope you don't mind. I showered and washed my clothes through.'

His gaze wandered over her hair, the rich chestnut

tresses spilling over her shoulders in a silken swathe. 'No… uh…um…' He seemed to be having trouble with his voice, and he cleared his throat. 'Not at all. I…uh… I'm an early riser. And I thought I'd make a start on breakfast. I'm sure you must be hungry, after you missed out on supper.'

'I'm starving,' she admitted.

'Good. You'll be able to tuck in, then.' He seemed to have recovered from whatever was bothering him and waved her to a chair. 'Sit down. There's some fresh tea in the pot. And while you're relaxed, I'll take your blood pressure again.'

'Oh, there's really no need for you to do that,' she protested. 'I'm absolutely fine. Having those few hours of sleep did me a world of good.'

'Even so, I just want to be sure.' He fetched a blood-pressure monitor from a cupboard and began to wrap the cuff around her arm.

'How many of these things do you have secreted about the place?' she teased.

'Just one.' A smile hovered on his lips. 'You were pretty much in a state of collapse yesterday, so I dashed down here to grab this machine.' The monitor beeped and he checked the reading. 'That's great,' he said. 'Back to normal. Like I said, it must have happened because you'd been overdoing things.'

'I knew it would be all right.' She gave a rueful smile. 'Anyway, it wouldn't go down too well if a doctor couldn't stand up to a little pressure, would it?'

'There are different kinds of stress,' he pointed out, putting the monitor back in the cupboard. 'As I said before, you haven't really had time to come to terms with your father's death, as well as the worry of having to sell his house and find somewhere for you and the children to live. You can't manage on an adrenaline rush for ever. Sooner or later something has to give, and perhaps being able to relax for once led to meltdown.'

'I suppose you could be right.' She poured tea for both of them. 'I'll help you with breakfast. What were you planning on having?'

'I hadn't worked that out yet.' He looked in the fridge. 'I've plenty of eggs, fresh tomatoes, mushrooms, and there's some bacon and gammon, too.'

'How about I whip up an omelette while you make toast?'

He nodded. 'Sounds perfect to me. We'll make a great team.'

He fished pans out of the cupboard and laid slices of bread on the grill pan. 'Is there anything else you need?'

'A whisk? A simple hand-held one will do.'

He frowned, searching through the cutlery drawer until with a flourish he triumphantly produced one. 'One whisk.'

'And a bowl to mix the eggs in.'

'I can do bowls.' He produced a selection and she chose one of them.

'Thanks. I'm all set now. Do you want to put plates to warm?'

They worked in harmony for the next few minutes, and the kitchen soon became filled with the appetising smell of cooked bacon and golden fried mushrooms.

Rosie and Sam appeared as James was buttering toast and setting it out on plates at the table. 'You're just in time,' he said. 'Grub's up.'

'I'm not eating grubs.' Sam pulled a face, and James looked nonplussed for a moment or two.

'Are you sure?' he teased. 'I heard they were really good for you.'

Rosie laughed. 'There are no grubs,' she told Sam. 'It's

your favourite—bacon and mushrooms and omelette.' She sniffed the air appreciatively.

'So that's one more dish I've learned to cook,' James said, and Rosie nodded.

'That makes two, then, if you add popcorn to the list.' Rosie gave him a serene smile as she dipped her fork into the fluffy egg, leaving the others to dissolve into laughter.

After breakfast the children went to play in the garden, where they discovered an old swing and a rope ladder tied to a tree. There was a tyre, too, suspended from the sturdy branch of an apple tree, and Sam took to it with relish.

'They seem to be having a good time,' Sarah said happily, watching them through the kitchen window. 'Were those things put up when your grandparents lived here?'

James nodded, coming to stand beside her. His long body brushed against hers, and the warmth coming from him permeated through her towelling robe, bringing a flush of heat to her cheeks. 'My brother and I used to spend hours out there. We had a great time. My grandfather knew how boys needed to burn off energy with lots of outdoor activities, so he made sure we had our very own adventure playground. I renewed the ropes and kept everything as it was because I thought maybe Jonathan's children would enjoy them some day.'

'I'm sure they will. It was thoughtful of you to do that.' She smiled at him. He'd taken a lot of care in renovating this house and making it into a home, and it showed his love of family in the way he'd kept this playground for his niece and nephew. This house and its garden were made for family life, but would they ever be given over to that? Would there come a time when James decided he wanted a wife and children of his own? A small frisson of alarm rippled through her at the thought. How could she bear it if James were to set up home with another woman?

'What is it?' He gave her a quizzical look.

'Nothing…' She faltered. 'I wondered… I don't think I'll ever settle into a relationship. Too much can go wrong, and I'm just not up to coping with that. But it's a shame, because I was thinking that I'd like children of my own one day. I have Sam and Rosie to care for, of course, and they'll always be precious to me, but I would still have liked to have a baby, or babies, at some point.' She sighed. 'Anyway, it wouldn't work—Sam and Rosie wouldn't understand, would they? I'd hate them to feel that they were being pushed out.' She gazed at him, her green eyes troubled.

Perhaps there was something in her expression that tugged at him, because he quickly put his arms around her and drew her close. 'Is that how it felt for you, when your father married again and started a second family?' Her silky hair hung loose about her shoulders, and now he brushed away glossy tendrils that had fallen across her cheek, hiding her face.

'I don't know. I'm not sure quite how I felt about things at the time.' All she could think about just now was that it was really good to be in his arms. He made her feel warm and safe, as though he truly understood and cared about her. 'I loved them from the first…but somehow I began to feel that I was in the way, intruding on their family life. It wasn't anything that was said or done, but I felt a bit like an outsider, looking in. I don't ever want Rosie and Sam to feel like that.'

'I'm sure they won't.' His voice was gentle and reassuring. 'They think the world of you, and they know how much you love them. I can see it in the way they talk to you and the way they act around you. It says a lot that they're confident enough to make friends and go out there and enjoy being children. Things could have been very different if you hadn't taken on the responsibility of looking after them.'

'Maybe. I want them to be happy.'

He gazed down at her. 'And what do you want for yourself? Don't you deserve a shot at happiness, too? You've worked really hard to get this far—it's no wonder you collapsed yesterday. Perhaps it's time to start thinking about what you want out of life.'

'I have what I want.' It was true. Right now, she was blissfully content simply to be wrapped up in his embrace. She could kid herself that she was cosseted, cherished almost, as his fingers splayed out over her spine and his other hand rested warmly on the curve of her hip. It didn't matter that he was simply comforting her, offering to share her burden.

'Do you?'

She lifted her face to him, and was immediately lost in the intensity of his gaze. 'For now, anyway.'

He shook his head, frowning as though he was battling with himself over something. She couldn't tell what he was thinking. But after a moment or two it seemed to pass, and now flame shimmered in the depths of his eyes and a smile hovered on his lips—lips that were just a breath away from hers. He lowered his head, and heat surged in her as she realised what he was about to do. Her heart lurched inside her chest, and then his lips touched hers, soft and compelling, achingly sweet, leaving a trail of fire in their wake.

A pulse began to throb in her throat, and she wanted to lean into him, to let her soft curves mesh with his hard body, but most of all she wanted him to kiss her again, to want her, to need her and take all she had to offer. She hardly dared believe that he might truly want her. Shakily, she ran her hands up over his chest, curving them around his shoulders and gently kneading the muscular contours with the tips of her fingers.

He sucked in his breath, and then a ragged, shuddery sigh escaped him. His hands moved over her, shaping her, moulding her to him and tracing a path as though he would learn every dip and hollow and commit it to memory. His mouth came down on hers, crushing the softness of her lips, tasting, exploring, and growing ever more passionate as she hungrily returned his kisses. She clung to him, wanting this moment to go on and on.

Then, with shocking suddenness, the kitchen door clattered open and the electric tension in the air was shattered, lost in time as they broke apart and turned to see what had caused the interruption.

'Rosie won't let me go on the swing.' Sam's chin jutted with indignation. 'She's been on it for ages. You have to tell her that it's my turn.' Thankfully, he was so het up about his grievance that he didn't notice there was anything at all wrong with either of them.

Sarah was breathing deeply, trying hard to slow the heavy, thudding beat of her heart. She was in a state of shock, overcome by the realisation that for a while she'd forgotten completely where she was and how she should behave. What was she doing, getting herself involved with James? How many times had she told herself that she must steer clear of any entanglement with him? Was she determined to set herself up for more hurt?

'Tell her she has five more minutes,' she said, pulling in a deep breath and finding her voice, 'and then you must swap over. I'll let you know when the time's up.'

'Wha-a-t? That's not fair!' Clearly, he wasn't happy with the five-minutes rule, but Sarah was in no mood for a drawn-out discussion.

'You heard what I said.'

Sam went out again, muttering to himself, and a moment later they heard him shout triumphantly, 'Five minutes, then you've gotta give me a go or you're in big trouble. Sarah says so.'

James looked at her. He was frowning, and she guessed he was as troubled as she was. 'Sarah, I...'

'It's all right.' She shook her head. 'It's just as well he came in. We were both carried away there for a while. It's been a strange couple of days. I don't think either of us is thinking straight.'

His expression was sober. 'I don't want to hurt you, or cause you any more problems. The truth is I wasn't thinking at all.'

'No...well, it doesn't matter.' Perhaps he'd discovered that she wasn't a skinny teenager any more, and being a red-blooded male he'd been carried away with the heat of the moment. It hadn't meant anything to him...nothing of any importance, at any rate...and that was why he'd said he didn't want to hurt her. 'Let's forget it happened, shall we?' She was giving him a get-out clause.

'Okay. If you say so.' His voice was ragged.

HE TOOK THEM home a couple of hours later, and spent time finishing off the fireplaces with the black grate polish, while Sarah caught up on chores and Rosie and Sam went to play with the children next door.

'I'll have a go at sanding the floorboards downstairs another time, if you like,' he offered when she went to admire his handiwork a little later. The fireplaces looked magnificent, as good as new, and she really appreciated the work he had done.

'You've done a great job,' she said. 'I can't ask you to do any more. I've already asked too much of you. And I don't want you to feel obliged to help me out. I can manage, I'm sure. It takes time, that's all.'

'It's not a problem. Like I said, I'm interested in renovation...it's good to see a property fulfil its potential, and these floors are basically sound. They need a bit of care, that's all. And I have a machine that will do the job in no time at all.'

She smiled. 'Okay, then. Thanks. For everything.'

He nodded. 'I'd better go.' His grey gaze slanted over her. 'I'll see you at work tomorrow.'

'At the air ambulance station, yes.' She looked forward to those days that were spent out of the hospital, attending to on-the-spot emergencies. They weren't good for anyone unfortunate enough to be involved in an accident, or to be taken ill suddenly, of course, but from a professional point of view it was good to know that they could give immediate lifesaving help in that first all-important golden hour.

She went with him to the door and watched him slide into the driver's seat of his car. He hadn't made any attempt to touch her since Sam had burst into his kitchen, and while she was glad of that, she was sad about it, too. She was mixed up inside, emotionally vulnerable, and at a loss to know how to deal with her feelings.

James didn't appear to be having any problems on that score. Kissing her had been a momentary lapse and now he was back to his normal self, confident, energetic and ready to move on. It would take her a little longer to get there.

IN THE MORNING, she was at the air ambulance base when the first call came in. 'Okay, it looks as though we're on our own on this one,' Tom, the pilot, said. 'James is still attending an incident that came in an hour ago. It was only a couple of miles away, so he took the rapid-response car. The paramedics wanted a doctor on the scene.'

'Do you think you can handle this without him?' the co-pilot asked as they scrambled for the helicopter. 'An ambulance is on its way to the scene, but apparently it's been held up.' Alex frowned, running a hand through his wavy, brown hair. His hazel eyes were concerned.

'I'll be absolutely fine, Alex,' she said quickly. 'You don't have to worry. I won't let anyone down.'

'Sorry, Doc.' Tom looked embarrassed. 'Alex worries about all the new people who join the crew. It's not meant to be a personal criticism—but we were hoping James would be back before we took off.'

They were airborne within a couple of minutes, and Sarah concentrated on finding out all she could about the incident they were about to attend.

'It's a ten-year-old boy who has fallen down a mine shaft,' Alex told her. 'An old copper mine, apparently. They're dotted all around the area. Trouble was, they were closed down decades ago, and when they were abandoned the entrances to the shafts were covered with timber and soil. I think, over the years, the timbers have begun to rot, and every now and again they cave in.'

'That's awful,' Sarah said, her heart going out to the child who had unwittingly been swallowed up into a deep chasm in the ground. 'I can't believe that no one's taken responsibility for them.' She thought about the child lying at the bottom of the shaft, cold and most likely wet, too. He was the same age as Sam. 'Are his parents at the mine, do we know?'

Alex shook his head. 'He was with his older brother when it happened. The police have been trying to find his parents, but they're not at home.'

They flew over heath, covered with mauve heather and yellow gorse, and soon the helicopter landed in a safe area close by the mine. Police and fire crew were already there, and Sarah was beginning to see why Alex might have been worried about her working on this venture. Someone would have to go down into that mine shaft to rescue the child. It was more than likely he was badly injured after such a fall, and was probably suffering from broken limbs—if he was still alive. That new anxiety struck her forcibly.

'Has he been talking?' she asked one of the fire crew. 'Has anyone been able to speak to him?'

'He's said a few words...nothing much, nothing intelligible, anyway.'

That could mean he was semi-conscious, making it all the more important that he have medical attention as soon as possible. 'I can see you have the winch in place. I'll need to get into a harness to go down to him. Will you help me with that?'

'Are you sure you're up to it?' The man gave her a doubtful look. 'It can be dangerous going down into these shafts. There could be loose timbers, rock falls—perhaps it would be better if you gave instructions to one of our crew. He'll tell you how the boy is doing, and you could maybe tell him how to go on from there.'

She shook her head. 'I can't see that working. Your fireman might not be able to take precautions against spinal or pelvic injury, and I doubt he'll know how to give injections or set up a fluid line. You need a medic down there.' She started to walk towards the winch. 'Will you help me get set up?'

Reluctantly, he did as she asked. The harness was designed to fit snugly around the person, and there were lots of buckles to be fastened and checked. It was imperative that everything be fixed in place so as to be perfectly secure.

'What's going on here?'

Sarah had started to climb into the harness when

James's voice cracked through the air like a whip. She looked up at him, startled to see his face etched in taut lines, his mouth flat, compressed.

'I'm going down into the shaft to look after the boy,' she said. 'His name's Ross. He's fallen about twenty feet into a cavern and might be semi-conscious.' She gave him a brief smile. 'I'm glad you made it here after all.'

'So am I. Step out of the harness, please, Sarah. I'll go down in your place.'

She stared at him in disbelief. 'But I'm all ready to go.'

'Not any more. This is way too risky for you.'

Affronted, she tilted her chin, and said firmly, 'For you, too, I'd have thought. I've had a lot of rock-climbing experience. I'm quite prepared to go down there and see to the boy. I don't see it as a problem.'

'You may not, but I'm afraid I do. Rock climbing is not the same as caving or potholing, and I have experience in both of those, so I'll go in your place. Step out of the way, Sarah, please.'

Everything in her told her that she must stand her ground, but she was all too conscious of time passing while they argued, with danger to the boy increasing with every minute. Neither did she want to create a scene in front of the police and fire crew, so she said in a low, exasperated voice, 'What gives you the right to stop me?'

'Seniority.'

She gave him a furious glare and finally stood to one side, leaving him to get into the harness. How could he do this to her? What had possessed him to play the seniority card like that, when she was perfectly capable of going down that shaft?

He had his medical kit with him, and she handed him a torch. 'It'll be pitch black in there,' she said.

'I know. Thanks.'

All she could do now was watch and wait while James descended the shaft, followed by one of the fire crew. It was galling to have to stand there and do nothing.

After several minutes a stretcher was lowered down, and more time passed before James indicated that they were ready to come back up. The firemen began to winch up the stretcher, and slowly hauled the boy to safety.

'How's he doing?' Sarah asked as soon as James came to the surface. She was still smarting at his treatment of her, but her focus had to be on the child.

'He has rib and pelvis fractures,' he answered quietly. 'He's not doing too well at all, I'm afraid. I think there must be massive internal bleeding. His blood pressure is falling and his heart rate's rapid.' James hesitated briefly, and she could see that he was acutely disturbed by this young boy's condition. Now that the child had been brought to the surface, he set about finding intravenous access and began to put in a fluid line to help resuscitate him. 'I'm worried that he might go into shock, so we have to get him to hospital as soon as possible. I've given him painkillers and stabilised the fracture with a pelvic sling, so that should compress the area and stop some of the bleeding.'

Sarah knelt down beside the stretcher. 'He's struggling to breathe,' she said in an urgent, low voice, glancing at James. The boy was being given oxygen through a mask, but it obviously wasn't sufficient to help him. 'His condition's deteriorating rapidly.' She studied the rise and fall of his chest and said quickly, 'Something's not right. There's a segment of his ribcage that's not moving in tune with the rest.' She frowned. 'There must be several rib fractures—part of the ribcage has broken and become detached.'

He winced. He had the fluid line in place now. 'A flail chest,' he said in a low tone. 'I suspected as much, but it was too dark down there to see properly.'

Sarah quickly examined the boy, who was lying motionless but groaning in pain. 'I know this must be uncomfortable for you, Ross,' she said softly, 'but we'll look after you and help you to feel better. It won't be too long before we have you in hospital.'

She turned back to James. 'His windpipe has deviated to one side and his neck veins are distended. One of the ribs must have pierced his lung.' This was more bad news. It meant that air was collecting in the pleural cavity and had nowhere to escape. As it built up, it was disrupting other organs and tissues. 'We have to act quickly.' If they didn't act promptly to do something about it, the child could go into cardiac arrest and they might lose him.

He nodded. 'I'm on it.' He reached for equipment from his medical pack and then carefully injected anaesthetic between the boy's ribs. Then he made an incision in the chest wall and slid a catheter in place. There was a satisfying hiss as trapped air escaped, and Sarah sealed off the end of the tube in a water-filled bottle that acted as a one-way valve.

'Okay, I've taped the tube in place.' He glanced at her. 'I'll stabilise the flail segment with a gauze pad and then we can be on our way.'

'Good.' She didn't say any more. She was too annoyed with him to speak to him about anything other than work, and her only concern at that moment was that Ross needed to be transported to the hospital in a matter of minutes. By the time he was there, perhaps his parents would have been located and would be in time to visit him and reassure him before he went to Theatre for lifesaving surgery.

They loaded Ross into the bay of the helicopter and within a couple of minutes they were on their way. The ambulance still had not arrived, and Alex told her it had been held up by a road-traffic accident that had happened while they'd been on their way to the mine. She absorbed the news with a sombre expression. Without medical intervention, it was doubtful Ross would have been alive by the time the paramedics arrived. This way, he at least had a chance of survival.

Once they were at the hospital they handed Ross over to the trauma team, who whisked him away. His parents were there, waiting for him, and Sarah breathed a faint sigh of relief as his anxious mother hurried forward to hold his hand.

She walked back to the helicopter without looking at James. She held her head high, ready to deal with Tom's and Alex's comments. They were all too aware that James had set her to one side like a spare part.

Strangely, though, they were quiet on the subject. Were they on her side? Or did they think that, as a woman, she shouldn't be taking on such risks? It was such an old-fashioned viewpoint.

James had no such inhibitions. 'I was horrified when I saw you getting ready to go down into that mine,' he said as they took their seats on the helicopter. 'All I could think about was the danger you were putting yourself in.'

'You didn't seem to have any qualms about going down,' she answered in a terse voice. 'And from the looks of things, you didn't come out of it unscathed.' Now that she had the chance to look at him properly, she saw that he had a deep gash on his forehead, hidden for the most part by an unruly lock of dark hair. There was a graze on his hand, too, she noticed, when he pulled on the seat belt and fastened it in place. 'If I'd been allowed to do my job and go down, I would have accepted injuries as one of the hazards.'

'And that's okay, is it, to risk your life in the course of the job?'

Her eyes widened in astonishment. 'Why on earth should that be all right for you and not for me?' she demanded.

'I'm not the one with a family to care for,' he said bluntly. 'I shudder to think what might have happened to you. What do you imagine will happen to Sam and Rosie if you're injured or worse? How will they react if anything bad happens to you? Who will look after them? Haven't they suffered enough? Surely you can't think purely of yourself now, if you really mean to act as a permanent guardian to them?'

She was stunned by what he said. It was true she hadn't thought beyond helping the boy, but what would he have her do? This was her job, and if he weren't around, wouldn't she do the same again?

He was right about Rosie and Sam, though. If she was serious about taking care of them, she had to rethink her priorities. It troubled her deeply, thinking about that. Perhaps, on the face of it, he'd had good reason to step in and take over, but the intrusion still needled her. He'd pulled rank, and that annoyed her intensely.

CHAPTER SIX

'How is Ross doing?' Sarah asked the specialist nurse in charge of the paediatric intensive care unit. 'The poor child was in a really bad way yesterday. I couldn't bring myself to start work without coming here to check up on him first.'

'He's still in a critical condition, I'm afraid.' The nurse gave her a sympathetic smile. 'It was dreadful, what happened to him. His parents have been beside themselves with worry and I've had to send them down to the cafeteria to take a break. Otherwise, I don't think they would have eaten since yesterday.' She frowned. 'I doubt he would have survived if it hadn't been for you and Dr Benson. But the good news is he had surgery on his pelvis yesterday, almost immediately after you brought him into A and E. Mr Norris managed to stop the bleeding, but of course the lad had lost a lot of blood already.'

Sarah nodded and looked down at the white-faced child lying in the hospital bed. There were drips and tubes taped in place so that he could receive lifesaving fluids, oxygen and medication, and where his broken pelvis had been treated there were post-operative surgical drains.

His blood pressure was still low and his heart rate fluctuated as she watched the monitors.

'On top of everything else, he was dreadfully cold when

he arrived here,' the nurse told her. 'We were all very worried about him.'

'I know you're taking good care of him,' Sarah told her. 'We can't do anything more but wait now to see what happens.'

'Mmm. He doesn't look very strong to start with, does he?' The nurse gave Ross one last look before excusing herself to go and see to another patient.

Sarah stood by the bedside for a while longer. 'You have to get better, Ross,' she urged. 'Be strong. You can do it.'

There was a movement beside her, and she looked around to see that James had come to join her. She might have known that he would come to see how the boy was getting on. They were in tune when it came to how they felt about their patients. She checked him out surreptitiously and, as ever, when he was at work, he was immaculately dressed in a dark grey suit, with the jacket open, showing a pristine shirt and soft blue-grey tie.

'You're obviously worried about him,' he said, 'but from what I heard, the surgery went well, and they've done X-rays of his chest to show that the chest tube is in the right place. They're giving him strong painkilling medication at the moment, so hopefully his breathing will be more comfortable.'

'Yes, it looks as though they're doing everything they can for him.' Her expression was rueful. 'I can't help feeling particularly involved with this young lad. Looking at him, it feels as though time's going backwards.' She sighed, thinking of what had happened some time ago. 'It was a boy like Ross that caused me to take up medicine in the first place.'

'Really?' He studied her thoughtfully, his dark brows lifting a fraction in query. 'What happened?'

'I was on a rock-climbing weekend with Murray when

we heard a shout. A moment later we saw a boy come tumbling down the cliff face near where we were. I think he must have climbed over the safety fence then lost his footing and slipped over the edge. We called out the emergency services, and started to go back down the cliff to where he had landed on an outcrop.'

Even now, it was distressing to think back to that worrying time. 'He'd broken his arm, and his foot was at a weird angle to his leg. Murray used dressing pads from his emergency first-aid kit to stem the bleeding, and we splinted his limbs as best we could using tape from the pack. I was glad we were there for him because he would have been terrified if he'd been on his own. At least we were able to comfort and reassure him, otherwise I don't know how long he would have lain there before anyone found him.'

'It was a good thing you knew what to do.'

She winced. 'It was Murray who knew what to do. He'd done a first-aid course because as a climber he was worried about these sorts of situations cropping up. It made me think seriously about doing a course myself, but in the end I decided to go in for medicine instead.'

He smiled. 'There's a huge amount of difference between those two choices. For what it's worth, I think you made a good decision.'

'Yes.' She gave a wry smile. 'Contrary to popular opinion, I did manage to make one or two back then.' She said it in a droll tone, and he sent her a quick glance.

'I'll hazard a guess that you're still annoyed over what happened yesterday. Would I be right?'

'You could say that.' She flashed him a sparking glance. 'Annoyed is such a mild word, don't you think?' She moved away from the bedside. 'You undermined me in public and stopped me from doing my job. You were way out of line.'

'I did what I thought was right.'

'Of course you did.' Her mouth made a flat line. 'Anyway, I don't want to talk about that now. I'm a few minutes early and I want to go and look through the lab results before I start my shift on A and E.'

'I'll come with you.'

'Fine.' She didn't say any more, and responded to his conversation with brief one-word answers. The more she thought about it, the more she resented his actions.

Once they were in the A and E unit, she went over to the central desk and looked through the wire tray for lab and radiology reports. 'There's an update here on Nicola Carter,' she told him, glancing through the patient's file. 'It's no wonder she suffered an adrenal crisis. The radiologist's report says she has a tumour on the pituitary gland.'

His mouth made a downward turn. 'We'd better get the endocrinologist to take a look at her,' he said. 'Let's go and bring these scans up on the computer.'

They went into the annexe, and brought up the patient's notes on screen, but Gemma, the triage nurse, came looking for them a moment later. 'There's someone asking to see you, Sarah. He says he's Rachel Veasey's brother, Harry. I've shown him to the relatives' waiting room.'

'Oh, brilliant. Thanks, Gemma. I'm glad we managed to find him.'

'You're welcome.' Gemma walked away, in a hurry to see to incoming patients.

'How did that come about?' James asked with a frown. 'This is the girl who collapsed through drink and drugs, isn't it? I thought she didn't have any family.'

'She told me she had a brother, and her friends said they thought he was living in a village in Somerset, so I tried to track him down. I thought he might be on the electoral register, and when I looked I found there weren't that many

Veaseys listed, so I took a chance and contacted one of them. I wrote to him.' Her mouth curved with pleasure. 'It seems I might have been lucky and managed to find the right person.'

'You went to a lot of trouble to get in touch with him.' He studied her curiously. 'Is this because you feel the need to bring families together?'

'I suppose it must be. I think Rachel needs someone from her family to care about her. There was a void, and I wanted to fill it.'

'Because you can't fill the void in your own life?'

She pulled in a deep breath. His calm, penetrating assessment shocked her. 'Maybe.' She shrugged awkwardly. 'I know you don't think it's a good idea, but I've never given up on finding my mother. I want to know why she walked out, and the question keeps eating away at me. I feel as though I can't move on until I have an answer. I can't settle. I can't get my life in order.' She ran a hand through her hair. 'The card I had from her last Christmas was postmarked London, but I just don't seem to be able to track her down.'

'It would surely be easier for her to get in touch with you? She probably doesn't want to be found—I can't help thinking you're laying yourself open for trouble if you insist on looking for her.'

'That's as may be. I'm still determined to try.'

He smiled wryly. 'I guessed that might be the case.' He was pensive for a moment or two. 'It's possible she could have remarried, I suppose. Maybe you need to get in touch with the General Register Office and see if you can track down a marriage using her maiden name. Hopefully, that will give you her new name.'

She blinked, looking at him in stunned surprise. 'Oh,

wow! You're right, of course. Why on earth didn't I think of that?'

He smiled, his head tilting slightly to one side as he studied her. 'Perhaps because you're too close to the problem?'

'Yes, I see that.' Her green eyes were wide, shimmering with a sudden film of joyful tears. 'Thanks, James,' she said huskily. She was so overwhelmed by the significance of this new idea that she wrapped her arms around him and gave him a hug. 'I absolutely forgive you for everything. You're a genius.' She lifted her face to him, ready to plant a swift kiss on his cheek, but at that moment he turned his head and their lips met in a soft collision. She heard his sharp intake of breath, and tension sparked like a flash of wildfire between them.

There was an instant of complete stillness and then, with a muffled groan, he pulled her to him, covering her mouth with his. He kissed her hard, a deep, fervent kiss that caught her off balance so that she clung to him, revelling in this exhilarating, heat-filled moment.

Almost as soon as it had begun, though, it was over. James lifted his head and held her at arm's length as though he needed space but was reluctant to let her go completely. The air between them was thick with unbidden yearning. His breathing was ragged, coming in short bursts, and Sarah stared at him, her whole body feverish from that brief, close encounter.

His features were taut, and his eyes were dark and troubled. 'I shouldn't have done that,' he said in a roughened voice. 'I mustn't do that. I'm your boss. You're on a probationary three months and it isn't right. It isn't a professional way for me to behave. I'm sorry.'

Sarah's throat was suddenly dry and she swallowed carefully. 'It was my fault. You shouldn't blame yourself.

I was carried away by the heat of the moment, thinking I might be able to get in touch with my mother after all this time. I shouldn't have flung myself at you.' The ethics of the situation didn't seem relevant to her—after all, she was a qualified doctor, not a student in training, but it obviously bothered James, and she wasn't going to try to persuade him otherwise. Perhaps he was looking for an excuse to keep away from her. She had no real idea what made him tick as far as she was concerned. Maybe he was as confused as she was.

He released his hold on her and she moved away from him, not knowing what else to do or what to say. 'I'll... I'll go and talk to Harry, and then I'd better see who Gemma has lined up waiting for me.'

'Okay.'

She made a hurried escape. Her heart was still thudding from the intensity of that kiss, but the whole episode puzzled her. What did James really feel for her? He clearly wanted her, but was it just a whim, a passing fancy, a fleeting passion? The whole thing was bewildering.

She spoke to Harry for a few minutes and then took him to Rachel's ward. The young girl was still thin and pale looking, and she was very tired, probably as a result of the irregular heart rhythm she was suffering as a result of her use of Ecstasy. Sarah checked her notes, satisfying herself that everything was being done to help her to recover.

'Harry?' Rachel's face lit up with pleasure. 'You're here... I didn't think... Oh, I'm so glad to see you.'

'Me, too.' Harry pulled up a chair and sat down at his sister's bedside, and Sarah decided it was time to leave the two of them to talk to one another in private.

'I'll be in A and E if you need me,' she told Harry. She wrote her phone number down on a scrap of paper and handed it to him. 'Here's my number in case you want to talk to me or if there's anything I can do to help your sister.'

He thanked her, and she went back to the emergency department, feeling lighter at heart now that Rachel had someone dear to her close by.

'There's a girl waiting to be seen in the treatment room,' Gemma told her a minute or so later. 'She's twenty years old. A friend called the ambulance. Apparently she passed out a couple of times and was out of it for a while. The paramedics said her blood pressure and pulse were both low. She just had a break-up with her boyfriend, so the friend thinks it might be something to do with that…an emotional reaction.'

'I'll look at her and see if we can find out what's happening. Thanks, Gemma.' Sarah went to the treatment room and introduced herself to the young woman who was waiting for her there. She was a pretty girl, blonde with blue eyes and a slender, shapely figure. She told Sarah that her friend had gone to get them both a coffee from the machine.

'Okay, Ann-Marie, do you want to tell me what happened?'

'I collapsed,' the girl told her. She was pale, and her eyes were red rimmed as though she'd been crying. 'I felt really strange all at once, and it was as though I couldn't breathe. I was dizzy and light-headed.'

'Did you have breakfast this morning?'

'Yes, I had a bowl of cereal.'

Sarah smiled. 'That's good. You're not watching your weight, or anything like that?'

Ann-Marie shook her head. 'No, not at all.'

'So, did anything happen just before you started to feel this way—a bang on the head or has something out of the ordinary happened recently?'

This met with another shake of the head, but Ann-Marie added huskily, 'I had a text from my boyfriend. He wants us to break up…says things aren't working out.' Tears welled up in her eyes and she sniffed and dabbed at them with a tissue. 'It upset me, and after that I started to feel strange. It was as though everything drained out of me.' She hesitated. 'It's not the first time I've fainted, though… so I'm not really sure if it's the break-up that made me ill.'

'It must be distressing for you, but try not to upset yourself.' Sarah brought her stethoscope from her pocket. 'I'll examine you, if I may, and see if we can find out what's wrong.'

The examination didn't reveal anything untoward, but Sarah said quietly, 'That all seems to be okay, but I think we'll admit you to our observation ward so that we can run some tests and keep an eye on you for a while. I'll ask the nurse to set up an ECG to monitor your heart rate and exclude any problems there.'

She made the arrangements and went to see the rest of the patients on her list. Some time later, when she was treating a man suffering from an asthma attack, James came to find her and drew her to one side.

'Keep him on the nebulised salbutamol for the time being,' she told the nurse, 'and let me know if there's any change in his condition.' She left the room with James.

'Is something wrong?' she asked. She saw he had Ann-Marie's file in his hand.

'Gemma tells me you've admitted this woman to the observation ward,' he said. 'We've quite a high number of admissions already and I'm wondering if it's really necessary to keep her here. After all, her symptoms are probably something her GP could deal with…they could even have a purely emotional basis. Perhaps she's overwrought and not coping too well with her love life. That's not strictly something we should be dealing with here.'

'That's all possibly true, but something's bothering me. I have an instinct about her.' Sarah was on the defensive. 'She said it had happened before, and I want to get to the bottom of it. She was in a state of collapse when the paramedics picked her up, and I'd sooner we were on hand to deal with the situation if it happens again.'

'All right. But if she's stable in the morning, you should send her home with a letter for her GP.'

She nodded. 'I will.' At least he hadn't overridden her decision, and she was glad about that. She might be wrong about Ann-Marie, but it was a case of better safe than sorry as far as she was concerned.

James glanced at her as she started to walk back towards the treatment room. 'If it's all right with you, I could come round to your place to start on the floors after work today. I know you're always busy with one thing and another, but I won't get in your way. I've hunted through the mountains of stuff in the outbuildings and found the sanding machine, so it should make fairly light work of them.'

'You don't need to do that,' she said quickly. After what kept happening between them, perhaps it would be for the best if she avoided any more contact with him outside work. Going on as they were was surely like playing with fire? Sooner or later, she'd find her fingers were burned.

'I know that, but I'd like to get to work on them. It's very satisfying, seeing things restored to their former glory. Will you be at home?'

'Yes.' She frowned, searching for excuses. She didn't want to be blunt and tell him to stay away, but everything in her was telling her she needed to steer clear of him away from work. 'I'll be very busy, though, working on the internet article for next week's topic. And I promised Rosie and Sam I'd take them to the local library to choose some books. So, you see, you could be making a wasted journey and I don't want to put you out. You really don't need to worry. I'll get around to doing the floors myself some time. My priority right now is to get the roof repaired, and I've made an appointment for a roofing company to send someone round.'

'Yes, I can see that's important. It might not be too big a job, though. Let's hope so, anyway.' He didn't say any more, and she hoped he'd taken the hint. It was a relief. It would surely be far better if they kept their work and private lives separate from now on.

The rest of the day flew by as she dealt with a steady stream of patients and by the time she went home and picked up the children from Murray's house, she was more than ready for a break. Sam was unusually subdued, she noticed, but Murray didn't have any clue what that was all about.

'He hasn't said anything to me, except that he has to get some information together for a school project. He's supposed to present it to the class some time next week and he hasn't made a start yet, apparently.'

Sarah's expression was rueful. 'Perhaps it's just as well we're making a trip to the library, then. With any luck he might find something there to inspire him.'

They arrived back at the house some time later, armed with several colourful books, and Sarah began to prepare supper while the children disappeared into their rooms. Murray came round to collect a book she'd picked up for him, and she invited him to stay and eat with them.

'It's nothing much, just a casserole. I put all the ingredients together this morning and set the automatic timer, so it should be ready any time now.'

'It smells wonderful,' Murray said, sniffing the air, and

when she served up the meal a short time later, they all ate appreciatively.

Sam was still morose, not saying very much, and Sarah tried to wheedle out of him what was wrong, while she stacked crockery in the dishwasher, but it was no use. He wasn't talking.

Then the doorbell rang and Murray went to answer it. He came back a moment later, saying, 'You have a visitor.'

She looked up, and was startled to see James standing next to him. 'James? I hadn't expected— So you decided to come after all?'

'I did. After all, you didn't expressly tell me not to come.' He glanced at Murray and then looked back at Sarah. 'I hope I'm not intruding on anything. I can always leave.'

'No...no, not at all. You're welcome to stay.'

'I'd better be going, anyway,' Murray said. 'Thanks for the meal, Sarah. It was delicious. I'll return the favour some time.'

'I'm glad you enjoyed it.' She went with him to the kitchen door, waving him off.

'You and he must spend quite a bit of time together, with him living next door,' James said speculatively, his dark eyes narrowed. 'You seem to get along very well with one another.'

'We do.' She looked at him fleetingly, not wanting to dwell too long on his powerfully masculine frame, made all the more impressive by the clothes he was wearing. Dark jeans moulded themselves to his strong, muscular legs, and a T-shirt hugged the contours of his chest. 'I see you've brought the sanding machine with you,' she said. 'You must mean business.'

'If that's all right with you?'

'I... Yes, of course. I haven't cleared any of the furniture out, though. I was pretty sure you wouldn't be coming.'

'That's not a problem. I'll see to it.'

Rosie had stayed quiet so far, but now she looked carefully at the machine. 'What's that for?' she asked.

'It's for getting all the old dirt and sealant off the wooden floorboards so that they come up looking clean and new,' James told her. 'Then, when that's done, they can be sealed again with polyurethane to give them a fine sheen.'

'That'll be good,' she said approvingly. 'They look old and grotty now, don't they?' She smiled. 'I can help you move the furniture if you like. Do you think you might start with the dining room?'

'That sounds like a good idea, though I don't want you hurting yourself moving furniture.' He glanced at Sarah. 'Is it all right with you if I start in the dining room? What do you think?'

'Yes, that's okay.' She glanced at Sam, conscious of how quiet he was being. 'Perhaps you'd like to help us get the furniture out of the room, Sam?'

Sam lifted his shoulders but didn't make any attempt to answer, and James said in a sympathetic tone, 'Are you all right, Sam? You're not saying very much, and that's not like you at all. Is everything okay?'

Sam pressed his lips together and seemed to be thinking hard about something. Then he looked at Sarah and said, 'If you're doing the floors, does that mean we're staying here, or are you making the house look good so you can sell it?'

'Heavens, where did that thought come from?' She looked at him in surprise. 'What makes you think we would be leaving? Is that what's been troubling you these last few hours?'

'Ricky Morton says we're not a proper family—you're not our mum, he says, and we don't have a dad. And he says if you get fed up of looking after us we won't have anybody and we'll have to go into care. Then you can sell the house and get somewhere just for you.'

Sarah reeled back from that as though she'd been kicked in the stomach. It took her breath away momentarily and she struggled to get herself together again. 'That's an awful lot of guesswork from Ricky,' she said at last. She was still shocked and flummoxed by Sam's innocent outburst. 'Why on earth would I get fed up with looking after you?' Sarah hugged him close to her, shocked that he could even think such a thing. Rosie came and huddled next to her and she put a protective arm around each of them.

'It seems to me Ricky's saying an awful lot of things that he doesn't really understand,' she said carefully. 'He's wrong. Perhaps he has problems of his own that make him think that way, but it isn't going to happen. I'll always want to take care of you.'

Sam gazed up at her, his expression earnest and pleading at the same time. 'Do you promise?'

'I promise, Sam. I love both of you, and we can be a family, the three of us. There are lots of families where there's only one parent.' She looked at James and saw that he was frowning. 'Isn't that true, James?' she said, willing him to back her up in this.

'It is,' he responded, 'and things often work out very well for them.' He hesitated for a moment, and then went down on his haunches by the children and said carefully, 'I think you're very lucky to have Sarah taking care of you. She's changed her life so that the three of you can be together. And as to making the house look good, she's doing it because she can see it's a solid house with big rooms and she wants it to be perfect for you.'

Sam slowly nodded. 'I was scared. Mum and Dad went away, and I don't want Sarah to do the same.'

'I don't ever want to go away,' Sarah told him softly,

bending to kiss him lightly on the forehead. She hugged them both tight. 'Everything I'm doing, I'm doing for both of you.'

'And that means making a start on the dining-room floor,' James said, standing up. 'Do I have some helpers?'

'Sarah and I can move the chairs,' Rosie decided, already on her way out of the kitchen.

'Can I have a go with the sander?' Sam wanted to know.

Some half an hour later James was ready to make a start, and after Sam made a few forays with the machine alongside the wall where the cupboards used to stand, the children disappeared upstairs to play in their rooms. There was half an hour left before bedtime and Sarah advised them to make the most of it. Two minutes later an argument erupted between them as Sam tried to muscle in on Rosie's computer game, and Sarah had to go and sort things out.

She came downstairs a short time later and made coffee. 'It was difficult earlier,' she said, offering James a cup, 'finding the right thing to say to Sam. I know they worry, and I do what I can to reassure them, but I can't promise them that everything will go smoothly. You were right about me taking risks going down the mine shaft, but I didn't want to admit it. Sometimes, when it's called for, we have to do what we think is the right thing. And it seemed that way to me at the time. If I had to choose between taking a chance on saving that boy's life or doing nothing, I'd take a chance, without even thinking about it. It doesn't mean I don't care about Rosie and Sam.'

He swallowed some of the hot liquid and set his cup down on the mantelpiece. 'I know that. The truth is, when I saw you getting ready to be lowered down into that pit, I was shocked at the thought of what might happen to you. It overrode my better judgement, if you like. If it had been anyone else, I'd probably have suggested that I go down into the mine alongside him or her, but with you, somehow, it's different. Perhaps I was wrong, but I can't say that I wouldn't do exactly the same thing if those circumstances arose again.'

Her jaw dropped a fraction. He'd done it because he cared about her and hadn't wanted to see her heading into danger. Her heart made a tentative leap within her chest. He cared about her and wanted to keep her safe. That was more than she could ever have hoped for. Even so, for her own sake, she knew she mustn't read too much into it.

She gave a rueful smile. 'I have to make choices and face the consequences, and I have to do it on my own. You're a caring, thoughtful person, but it isn't right that you should have to worry about my wellbeing.'

His mouth twisted. 'I don't think it works quite that way.'

'No?' She sent him a quizzical glance. 'I accept I have responsibilities now. I have to look out for Rosie and Sam, and I'm doing it the best way I can. I'm really glad you backed me up earlier…it helped a lot. It made me feel better, and I could see the children were reassured, too.'

'I'm pleased about that, too.' He frowned. 'It's difficult looking after children, isn't it? They can be quite a handful. It's not just a question of sorting out fights at school, or stopping them from rolling about in mud at the zoo… there are all these undercurrents going on as well, not to mention the everyday problems of getting them to where they need to be and keeping them from laying into one another.' He brooded on that for a few seconds. 'It must have been difficult for you…but you seem to have the perfect temperament for it.'

'I don't know about that. I've not really had a choice.' She sipped her coffee, watching him over the rim of her cup. 'I've had to learn how to do things. I'm still learning.'

'Yeah.' He smiled and reached for the sanding machine. 'It's a hard lesson, but you seem to be handling it pretty well. I'm amazed by the way you've got to grips with everything and turned your life around. You should be proud of yourself.'

He started up the sander and set to work, and Sarah stood by, watching him for a while, enjoying the way he moved, at one with the machine, making calm, steady inroads into the years of accumulated grime that had discoloured the wooden floorboards. Then she wandered away, going back into the kitchen and switching on her computer so that she could start work on her internet article.

Her fingers hovered aimlessly over the keyboard. James obviously felt something for her, or why would he be looking out for her? And he wanted her…when she was in his arms his kisses left her in no doubt of that. Despite his misgivings, she was certain he wanted more, and this time she wasn't a naïve seventeen-year-old. She was a woman, and if she pushed things, she was pretty sure his resolve would melt like snow in the sunshine.

But that didn't mean he was ready for anything other than a heady affair, did it? And even if he was, how could they ever have a future together when she was so uncertain about the steadfastness of relationships? Hadn't her own mother abandoned her? Why should James be any different? She couldn't bear it if one day he chose to turn his back on her.

CHAPTER SEVEN

'Hey, look at you! You're doing really well, young Ross. It's great to see you out and about. Last time I saw you, you were flat on your back in Intensive Care.' James gave the boy a beaming smile, watching as his mother pushed him in a wheelchair into the emergency department. She came to a halt by the central desk, and James exchanged a few words with her before turning his attention back to her son. 'You're looking so much better than you did a few days ago,' he said, raising his hand, palm open. 'High five?'

Ross slapped hands with him, grinning from ear to ear. 'I wanted to say thank you for getting me out of the mine,' he said. 'I was really scared, and I didn't think anyone would come to get me.'

James nodded. 'I can imagine how you must have felt down there. It was pitch black and you were in a lot of pain. But luckily for you, your brother sounded the alarm…so we came and found you as soon as we heard.' James looked him over. 'How are you feeling?'

'I'm okay.' Ross made a small frown. 'They give me tablets for the pain, and someone comes to help me exercise my legs. I can walk a bit on crutches, but the nurse says it might take a few weeks before I'm back on my feet properly.'

'Yes, it can take a while, but you're out of bed and on

the mend, and that's very good. I'm really pleased to see you up and about. Well done.'

'Yeah. I can't wait to get back home and see my mates.'

Sarah watched the interchange from the other side of the desk, where she was looking through her patients' notes on the computer. For all James had implied he didn't understand children too well, he seemed to be learning fast. He was naturally compassionate and it came across in his dealings with them.

It was plain to see that the child was still troubled by his experience, and clearly he was still in some pain, but, as James had pointed out, he was on the mend, and that was great news to hear. Ross's mother was smiling, happy to see her child lively and animated once more. They left A and E a few minutes later, with James promising to go and visit Ross on his ward.

'It's wonderful to see things turn out so well,' she said, and he nodded.

'That's the thing with children…they pick up so quickly. Perhaps it's because they're eager to get on with their lives, and they have so many things going on to distract them from their troubles.'

He came around the desk to look at the computer screen. 'This is Nicola Carter's file…so you're still keeping track of her?'

Sarah nodded. 'Some patients come into the emergency unit, get treated and then they're on their way, but with others it's not quite so simple. I want to know what happens to them after they leave us…like Ross, for instance. Technically, he's no longer our concern, but neither of us can resist checking to see how he's doing, can we?'

He laughed. 'True. So what's happening with Nicola? She was waiting for an appointment with the endocrinologist, last I heard.'

'She's already seen him and he arranged for her to have surgery to remove the tumour. He told her it was stopping the pituitary gland from functioning properly and that was why she collapsed and needed to be given steroid treatment. She'll be going to Theatre later today.' She frowned. 'I hope she'll be all right. She has a husband and three children, and they're all very worried about her.'

'I'm not surprised. Any surgery can be worrying, but for most people brain surgery's a frightening thing to contemplate. Let's hope the neurosurgeon manages to leave the pituitary gland intact. That way, it can start to produce the right amount of hormones and she at least has a chance of getting her life back.'

'From what I heard, he's new to the team…a youngish man, not very communicative.'

'Surgeons can be like that.' He gave a wry smile. 'They don't need to have much of a bedside manner when their patients are unconscious on a slab in Theatre, do they?'

Sarah had opened her mouth to answer him when Gemma came hurrying towards her. 'There's a problem with the patient you admitted to the observation ward—Ann-Marie Yates. Her boyfriend has just been in to see her and she's very upset, and now she's unwell again.' She shook her head. 'It's such a shame. Things started off all right. She's been fine since she was admitted, and we disconnected all the monitoring equipment as soon as we knew she was to be discharged this morning. She was getting ready to go home with her friend—apparently they share a flat—and then he walked in and they started to argue. And soon after he left, she collapsed again.'

'Oh, dear. She's not having too great a time, is she? Get her back onto all the monitoring equipment straight away and I'll come along and see her.'

'Okay. Thanks.' Gemma swivelled around, her sleek, black hair swishing as she hurried away.

James frowned, and Sarah jumped in before he had a chance to speak. 'I know you want me to refer her to her GP, but I still think we should investigate each episode thoroughly just in case there's something else going on.'

'I agree with you.' He said it in a calm, even tone, and she looked at him in surprise.

'You do?'

'You're an excellent doctor, Sarah. You've proved to me over these last few weeks that you're extremely competent, and the least I can do is go with your instincts. I'll come along with you to see how she is.'

She hadn't expected anything like that, but she was extraordinarily pleased and a little glow started up inside her. 'Okay. Thanks.' She led the way to the observation ward and arrived at Ann-Marie's bedside in time to see her struggling for breath and lying back against her pillows in a state of exhaustion.

'Hello, Ann-Marie,' Sarah greeted her. 'I can see you're unwell again. What seems to be the problem?'

'My chest hurts,' the girl whispered on a breathless note. 'I can't...breathe... I...'

'That's all right. Try not to worry. We'll give you something to help you feel more comfortable,' Sarah said in a reassuring tone.

'I'm...dizzy... I...' Ann-Marie's voice trailed off, her words becoming a jumble of incoherent sound.

'Let's get her some oxygen,' James said to Gemma, who had just finished taking the girl's blood pressure.

Gemma nodded and quickly went to fit a face mask over Ann-Marie's nose and mouth. 'Relax, and try to take deep breaths,' she told her.

'Her blood pressure's very low, and her heart rate is

forty beats a minute and dropping,' Sarah said in a quiet voice. 'This isn't a straightforward emotional upset.'

'I think you're right.' James was studying the readout from the ECG machine. 'Her heart rate is way too low. We'd better put in an intravenous line and get ready to give her atropine. That should stimulate more output.'

Sarah was already seeing to that, but a short time later it was clear that the atropine wasn't working. Ann-Marie's heart rate had dropped even further and was at a dangerous level. 'We need the defibrillator on hand,' she told Gemma. 'I'm going to give her an epinephrine infusion, but if that doesn't work, we'll have no choice but to try transcutaneous pacing.'

It was a worrying situation. The electrical impulses in Ann-Marie's heart weren't stimulating the heart muscles to contract and pump blood around her body, and if her heart rate dropped any further she could soon go into cardiac arrest.

Sarah set up the infusion and they waited to see what would happen, but after some time James shook his head. 'There's no change and we can't waste time trying any other medication while she's in this state. There's only one thing for it...we'll have to go ahead with the transcutaneous pacing after all.' He started to prepare sedative and painkilling medication while Sarah did her best to explain to their patient what they were about to do.

She couldn't be sure Ann-Marie was fully aware of what was going on around her, but she persisted in her efforts, saying, 'You might find this procedure a bit unpleasant, but we'll give you medication to help you feel more comfortable.'

James was already applying pads to the girl's chest and back, and Sarah started to set the controls on the machine. 'Okay, here we go. I'm starting the electrical impulses, low to begin with and increasing in strength until we have the rhythm we're looking for.'

'What's happening to her?' A man's voice cut into the tense silence of the room a minute or so later. 'Ann-Marie...'

Sarah glanced at him. He was in his early twenties, she guessed, tall, with unruly dark hair and anguished grey eyes.

'You'll have to stand back, sir,' Gemma said firmly. 'She's very poorly, and we need to get her condition stabilised before you can talk to her.'

'M-Marcus...?' Ann-Marie's voice was weak, but it was clear that she was coming round from her dazed state. Her blood oxygen level was improving as her heart began to beat a little faster, and a short time later Sarah stopped the machine from emitting any more shocks.

'We have a normal rhythm,' she announced, relieved that the procedure had worked.

'Ann-Marie, I'm sorry,' the young man said. 'I'm here. I couldn't stay away. I was stupid... I thought... I thought you were seeing someone else.'

Gemma intervened once more. 'She needs to rest,' she told him. 'If you want to stay with her, you have to be quiet.'

He nodded, gulping back what he had been about to say. He hesitated. 'I'll just hold her hand...is that okay?' He looked around the room and Sarah nodded.

'If there's any sign that her treatment is being undermined, you'll be asked to leave,' she said. 'Am I making myself clear?'

Marcus nodded. 'As crystal. I won't do anything to upset her, I promise.'

Ann-Marie pulled the oxygen mask to one side and looked anxiously at James. 'Will I need to have that done again?' she asked in a breathless voice. 'What's happening to me?'

'It's possible,' he told her, 'but now we know what's happening we'll try to give you medication to regulate your heartbeat and avoid the necessity for such drastic treatment. From the looks of things, your heart's electrical system isn't working properly, so you might need to have a pacemaker fitted at some point in the near future.'

'Oh. I see.' She was struggling to take this in, but she glanced up at Marcus for reassurance. He gently squeezed her hand.

'In the meantime,' James said with a smile, 'we'll make arrangements for you to see a specialist. You don't need to worry about it. You'll be well looked after.'

'Thank you.'

Ann-Marie closed her eyes briefly, and Marcus pulled up a seat alongside the bed, continuing to hold her hand. 'How could you believe I'd go off with anyone else?' she muttered under her breath.

'I think we can leave her in Gemma's care for now,' Sarah said, her mouth curving as she sent James a quick glance. She finished writing up the medication chart and handed it to the nurse. 'Thanks for your help, Gemma.'

She walked back to A and E with James. 'Aren't you glad I didn't send her home yesterday?' she said with a crooked smile.

His mouth quirked. 'Rub it in, why don't you?' Then he sobered and said thoughtfully, 'I dare say I'd have come to the same conclusion as you if I'd examined her and taken a history. It goes to show you should trust your team.'

'Am I one of your team?' she asked softly. 'I'm still on probation, aren't I?'

'I think we both know what the outcome of that will be,

don't we?' He smiled. 'Your job's safe, so you can relax as far as your future here is concerned.'

'I'm glad.' She gave a soft, shuddery sigh. 'It's a relief to know that you have faith in me.'

His gaze burned into her. 'I do, Sarah.'

Her green eyes glimmered as she returned his gaze. 'I'm just thankful one of my biggest worries has been taken away. I want to be able to tell the children their future is secure.'

James nodded and keyed in the security code to unlock the door to the emergency department. 'I've been thinking about that…especially about young Sam's worries. A lot's happened to him and Rosie in these last few months and maybe they both need a little more reassurance. It might help if we all spent some time together this weekend. What do you think? We could go down to the beach— try to get Rosie and Sam used to going down there once more. I know they have trouble with that… Rosie told me. Between us, though, we should be able to cope with any problems that come up.'

'You're making it hard for me to refuse when you put it like that,' she said.

'Do you want to refuse?' He sent her an oblique glance, looking at her keenly as though her response was all-important.

'No…not at all. An afternoon on the beach sounds like a great idea.' The idea of spending an afternoon with him was suddenly enormously attractive, and her heart made an excited leap inside her chest. She had to remind herself that he was only doing this for the children.

'Good. I'll come to your place around lunchtime on Saturday. It'll be good to spend time together. We could perhaps start off by having something to eat at the local inn?'

'I think that would be lovely.' Inside, she was bubbling with anticipation. 'I'll look forward to it.'

By the time Saturday came around, Rosie and Sam were eager to be off. Sam swivelled around in his seat by the computer. 'Will we be going in James's sports car?' he wanted to know. 'I wish I could drive it. It's well good.' He started to turn an imaginary steering-wheel with his hands and made brumming sounds like an engine roaring off into the distance.

'I expect so. The inn is a couple of miles from here, so I doubt we'll be walking.' She frowned, glancing around the room. Rosie was rummaging through a holdall on the dining-room table, anxious to make sure that all the preparations were in hand, but Sam was being his usual self, oblivious to any need to do anything other than play his game.

'Are you two about ready?' she asked, fetching coats from the hall cloakroom. 'Come away from that computer, Sam. You need to find your beach shoes if you're going on the sand—I don't want you ruining your best trainers. Make sure you put them in your bag. And find your swimming stuff.'

'Aw...can't you do it for me?' Sam protested. 'I'm in the middle of this war game. We're holed up in a cave in the mountains and the rebels are coming after us.'

'No, I can't. James will be here in a few minutes and I still have to go and look in the shed for buckets and spades. You can put your swim trunks on under your clothes. Save the game and play it later, or I might have to switch you off at the wall socket.' She came over to the computer table and let her hand hover over the plug.

'Spoilsport,' Sam complained. 'I'm nearly up to level ten...another few minutes and I'll have cracked it.'

'Crack it some other time.' Sarah waited while he saved

the game and then she switched off the computer. 'Rosie, put a couple of bottles of pop into the backpack for me, will you, please? We're bound to need a drink down on the beach.'

'Okay.' Rosie went to do as she asked, and Sarah followed her into the kitchen, on her way to the back door.

'Are you all right about this afternoon's trip?' she asked. 'We don't need to stay for too long if it bothers you, but I thought it would be nice for you to have the chance to splash in the sea for a bit and maybe play ball with Sam on the beach.'

'I think so. I don't know.' Rosie looked up at her, a variety of expressions flitting across her face. 'I feel a bit peculiar inside.' She slid bottles and tumblers into the bag and glanced at Sarah. 'It'll be different, though, going with James. I like him. He showed me how to set up my new dance game when he came to do the fireplace in my room, and when I was cross with Sam for being a nuisance, he took him away and helped him with his war game.'

'Yes, I've noticed he's good at finding solutions to things.' James didn't make a big song or dance about anything, but somehow or other he managed to smooth the path whenever there was a problem.

She went out to the shed and rummaged around for a bit. It was full of stuff from the children's former family home in Devon, as well as bits and pieces that Sarah had brought with her.

A few minutes later she went back to the kitchen with her hands full of buckets, spades, plastic sieves and a large beach ball. She was startled to see James standing by the table, talking to Rosie. As she entered the room his glance skimmed over her.

'You look great,' he said, his eyes lighting up, and her cheeks flushed under his avid scrutiny. She was wearing jeans that clung where they touched and a simple, short-sleeved top that outlined her curves. He was equally casually dressed, in dark jeans and a T-shirt. 'Rosie let me in,' he said. 'She told me you were almost ready, but apparently we're waiting for Sam to find his shoes.'

'Except he's upstairs playing on his game pad,' Rosie commented drily. 'Shall I go and tell him to hurry up?'

'Better not, or there's bound to be a fight. You could find some tissues and put them in my handbag, if you like.' Sarah smiled. 'I'll go and see what Sam's up to in a minute when I've found a home for these buckets and spades.'

'I'll put them in the boot,' James murmured. He grinned, looking at the bags and accumulated paraphernalia. 'Are you sure you haven't forgotten anything...folding table, portable gas stove, water canisters?'

'Oh, very funny,' she retorted, flicking him a pert glance as they went out to his car. The top was down, reflecting the warmth of the summer's day. The sky was blue, with no clouds in sight, and the air was fresh and clean. 'Like I said before, you've no idea how much preparation goes into a trip where children are involved.'

'Obviously not. Though we are only going for the afternoon, you know.' There was a glint in his eye as he gave her a sidelong look. 'Unless, of course, you wanted to make a weekend of it. It's not beyond the realms of possibility that we could go for longer...there's a lovely Smugglers' Inn along the coast where they do rooms.'

There was a hint of devilishness in his voice, sparking her pulses into a throbbing beat. He wasn't being serious, of course, but even so, she had to take a moment or two to calm herself down before answering him.

She carefully arranged the buckets and spades to one side of the car's boot. Then she looked at him, raising finely shaped eyebrows. 'It isn't going to happen. I'm not seventeen years old any more, you know. I hope I've a little more sense than to go throwing myself at you as I did back then.'

'No? Are you absolutely sure about that?' He was teasing her now, with laughter in his eyes and a roguish smile playing around his mouth.

'Definitely not. That was a big mistake. I can't think what came over me…and it certainly won't happen again.' She went hot all over, thinking about how she'd pressed her soft curves up against him and wound her arms around his neck. Her green eyes narrowed on him. 'Besides, I seem to remember you saying something recently about keeping things on a professional footing between us.'

'Hmm.' His mouth made a downward turn. 'I guess I've been fooling myself about that all along. I must have had a change of heart somewhere along the way. Perhaps seeing you in total command of yourself in A and E over these last few weeks has made me realise I should never have insisted on the three-month trial period in the first place. I was being over-cautious.'

'I'm glad you think so.' She moved away from the car as Rosie came out with the bags. 'Sweetheart, you should have left those for me,' she said in consternation, seeing her struggle with the weight.

James took the bags from Rosie and loaded them into the car. 'You did well to manage these,' he said. 'I was just telling Sarah she's packed everything bar the kitchen sink.'

Rosie chuckled. 'She wants to make sure everything is just right. I think she would have packed a hamper, but you said we were going out for lunch, didn't you?'

'I certainly did.' He glanced at the expensive watch on his wrist. 'And I think we should be getting on our way. Is there any chance of dragging your brother out of game paradise, do you think?'

Rosie shook her head. 'I don't think so. He doesn't even listen after he's loaded it up.'

'Uh-huh…we'll see about that.' Sarah went to fetch him, and within a minute or two they were all installed inside the car and were on their way. The children were hungry and already debating what there might be to eat, and Sarah admitted that it had been a long time since breakfast for her, too.

'I had a slice of toast before the children were up, and ate it while I skimmed my emails and read through my letters. They were a bit disappointing really, just bills and a printed estimate for the roof repairs.'

'Were you looking for something more?' James drove along the coast road, and Sarah leaned back in her seat, enjoying the feel of the breeze riffling her hair. The children were absorbed in watching the gulls circle the bay and trying to count how many boats were moored in the harbour.

'I was hoping there might be something from my mother.' She winced. 'I checked the marriages for the postmarked area over the last few years, and there weren't all that many with my surname and my mother's first name. So I followed them up, and I think I've found her.'

James shot her a quick glance. 'That must have come as a bit of a shock after all this time. Did you find an address?'

She nodded. 'Yes. I wrote to her, and I've been waiting to hear ever since. I gave her my email address and my phone number.' She sighed. 'There's been nothing so far. I keep kidding myself that she might be on holiday, or that I have the wrong person, but I suppose I have to accept that the truth is she probably doesn't want to know.'

'I'm sorry.' He clasped her hand in his briefly, keeping one hand on the steering-wheel. 'I'm not convinced that getting to know her again is such a good idea, anyway. As time's gone by you've been gradually getting your life back together, and I can't help thinking that if she turns up you'll find yourself drawn into an emotional whirlpool all over again.'

'It was never going to be easy, was it? Anyway, from the looks of things, it probably won't come about.'

They drove on for a while, until they came to an attractive, seventeenth-century inn, set back from the road. James parked the car and Sarah took a moment to look around at the white-painted building. It had lots of sash windows and there were hanging baskets at the front, filled with red geraniums and bright petunias. Wooden tables and chairs were set out on the forecourt, each group with its own red umbrella, and there were stone tubs dotted about, laden with flamboyant, crimson begonias and trailing foliage.

'Have you been here before?' James asked, and she shook her head.

'No, I haven't, but if the outside is anything to go by, it's lovely.'

'I asked the landlord to reserve a table for us by a window,' he said, shepherding the children out of the car and along the path. 'We can eat and look out at the sea at the same time, and if Sam and Rosie are finished before us, they can go to the play area at the back of the pub. We'll be able to see them from where we're sitting.'

'That's great.' She sent him an approving glance. 'It sounds as though you've thought it all out.'

He nodded. 'I want you to have a good time and be able to relax for a while.'

'Thanks.'

They went inside, and Sarah admired the low, wooden beams and the huge fireplace filled with logs. There was wooden bench seating on two sides, made comfortable with luxurious padded upholstery, and tables and chairs were grouped in cosy, recessed areas brightened with the golden glow of wall lamps. There was some raised decking, and their table was on one of these sections, by a tall, wide window that allowed daylight to pour into the room and gave them a beautiful sea view.

'Seafood's the specialty here,' James explained, handing her a menu, 'but there are all sorts of other dishes for you to choose from.'

'I want the chicken nuggets,' Sam decided, with the speed of lightning.

'As if you ever eat anything else.' Rosie studied the menu for a little longer. 'Could I have gammon and fries, please?' she asked.

'Of course, whatever you like.' James looked at Sarah, his dark brow lifting in query. 'What would you like?'

'I'll have the sea bass,' she said with a smile. 'They say it's cooked with lemon, ginger and honey. Yum...it sounds delicious.'

'It is. I can recommend it.'

James chose the same, and they spent a pleasant hour enjoying the good food and looking out over the coastline, watching the waves roll gently into the bay. They talked about all sorts of things—the times when Sarah had been learning how to climb rocks, and her job in Devon when she'd gone out and about with the ambulance service. James told her about his efforts to do up the house he'd inherited, and of his visits home, when he helped his brother with the running of the farm estate.

'The orchards are massive, aren't they?' Sarah commented. 'I remember when I worked there in the summer holidays there were tons of apples to be picked. And you would come round with scrumpy cider for all the workers when we were on our lunch breaks.'

'Mmm... Technically, you weren't supposed to have it.

It was pretty lethal stuff. But I think I gave you just a taster and made up the difference with orange juice.'

She laughed. 'Yes, I remember that now. I was so cross at the time.'

'You were cross about a lot of things back then.'

'Why were you cross?' Rosie asked, and Sarah gave a small start. She had forgotten the children might be listening in.

'It was because my mother had gone away,' she said quietly. 'I thought she should have stayed.'

Rosie frowned. 'Why would that make you cross? Our mother went away, but we were sad about it, not cross.'

Sarah took a moment to think how she should answer that. 'Yes, of course, that's understandable. But your mother didn't have a choice. Mine did. She chose to go away. She didn't want to stay.'

Sam's gaze was troubled. He reached out and patted her hand. 'It's all right, Sarah. We're here for you now.'

Sarah's eyes misted over at his innocent, sweet gesture of compassion. She blinked hard and swallowed against the lump that had formed in her throat. 'That's good to know, Sam,' she said huskily. 'I'm glad I have you and Rosie.'

James sucked in a deep breath. 'What more could anyone ask?' He smiled at the children and then glanced at the debris of crockery that littered the table. 'Except maybe for lots of ice cream and strawberry sundaes…'

'Yay… I'll have one of those!' Sam exclaimed. 'Can I?'

James nodded. 'They do them with fresh strawberries.'

'Yummy, scrummy, scrumptious,' Rosie said happily. 'They're my favourites.'

'Mine, too.' James gave their order to the waitress, and then glanced at Sarah. 'Are you okay?' he asked in a low voice. He reached for her hand, and folded it within his own.

'I'm fine.' She nodded. Rosie and Sam were busy colouring in the pictures on the printed sheets of paper that the waitress had given them and weren't taking any notice of what she and James were doing. 'I'm glad they feel the three of us belong together. Little gestures like that make it all worthwhile somehow, don't they?'

'They do.'

The children finished their desserts and Sarah sent them out to play on the climbing apparatus for a while. She and James took a few more leisurely minutes to drink their coffee, and turned the conversation to good food and wine.

When Sam and Rosie tired of the small adventure playground outside, they gathered up the baggage from the boot and headed down a winding path towards the beach. Here there were smooth stretches of sand broken up by rocks and boulders scattered around the base of the cliffs, and the children headed over to the rock pools with whoops of delight.

'Did we bring the fishing nets?' Sam asked, and Sarah had to shake her head.

'Sorry, we didn't.'

'You can use the small buckets to scoop things up,' James said. 'Here, let me help.' James walked alongside Sam, looking in the pools left behind by the tide, searching for crabs and other small crustaceans, while Rosie stayed with Sarah, picking up shells and examining patches of seaweed that had been washed up by the sea.

Later, the children slipped off their outer clothes and ran into the sea in their swimming gear, splashing in the shallows as the waves broke on the shore, before venturing further out and jumping with the bigger waves that came along. 'That's far enough,' Sarah told them. 'Stay close by the shore.' She and James rolled up their jeans and went into the water with them, laughing as an unexpected wave drenched them from the knees down.

James slid an arm around her waist and helped her run back to the shore as another wave threatened to overtake them. Still laughing, they dropped on to the sand, looking out over the sea to where the children played.

James was still holding her, and Sarah was content to lean back against him, folded into the crook of his arm. It seemed so natural to be with him this way, and as the sun warmed her bare arms and dried out her jeans, she thought how good it would be if the afternoon could go on for ever.

It couldn't, of course. As time went by, a breeze blew up, and Rosie and Sam were getting cold and ready to scramble out of their wet things and into their dry clothes. Sarah covered them in beach towels and helped them to get dressed, and then they all trooped back to the car.

'That was terrific,' Rosie said, settling back in her seat and lifting her face to the gentle wind as James drove them home.

'Especially the rock pools and the ice creams,' Sam added. 'The crabs were well good. I saw ten. Wait till I tell Ricky. He'll want to come as well next time. Can we bring him with us one day?'

'I expect so.' Sarah lifted her brows as she turned in her seat to look at him. 'Does that mean you're best friends now?'

'Yeah.' Sam didn't volunteer any more than that. He drew his game pad out of his pocket and concentrated on the screen.

Sarah smiled. 'I guess I shouldn't have worried,' she murmured, and James chuckled.

'I guess not.'

They arrived home a few minutes later and the children disappeared into their bedrooms. Sarah flicked the switch on the coffee percolator and started to set out mugs for her and James.

'I had a great time this afternoon,' she said, smiling at him as he came to stand beside her.

'So did I.' He wrapped his arms around her, drawing her to him and lowering his head so that his forehead lightly touched hers. 'It was good to hold you, out there on the beach, but I wanted to do so much more than that.'

'You did?' She looked up at him, her green eyes questioning. She trailed her hand lightly up across his chest, her fingers coming to rest on his powerful biceps.

'Oh, yes,' he said, his voice becoming rough edged, his lips hovering close to hers. 'I've tried so hard to keep my distance from you...physically, at least...these last few weeks, to avoid touching you or getting too close to you, but I'm fighting a losing battle. I know how much you worry about getting involved, but whenever I'm near you I want to kiss you and hold you and show you just how much I want you.'

'I'm glad,' she whispered. 'I want you, too.'

His body reacted instantly, as though she'd delivered him an electric shock. His hands pressed her to him, tugging her even closer than before and she gloried in the feel of him, in the way their bodies fused, one into the other, her soft curves blending with his taut, muscular frame. Her fingertips slid upwards into the silky hair at the nape of his neck, and she clung to him, loving the way his arms encircled her. His thighs moved against hers and his hands began to make a slow detour over her body, worshipping each and every rounded contour.

A shuddery sigh escaped her as his hand tenderly cupped her breast, and he covered her mouth with his, cutting off the soft groan that formed in her throat.

Hunger surged in her, raging through her body like a

firestorm, and as he lovingly caressed her she realised, through the haze that filled her head, that he must feel the same way. His heart was pounding, so much so that she could feel the thunderous beat of it against her breasts, and the knowledge filled her with a heady, tingling exhilaration. He wanted her every bit as much as she wanted him.

'I need you, Sarah,' he said huskily. 'I'm glad you're not seventeen any more. I don't know how I can go on without you...' His heated gaze swept over her, burning in its intensity, and he kissed her again, his hands roaming over the swell of her hips and easing her against him until pleasure built up in her and threatened to spill over in wave after wave of heady, tantalising desire.

'I want...' She started to say something, to tell him how much she wanted him, too, but something disrupted the heightened tension in the atmosphere, piercing it as though it was a pocket of hot gas that had built up and was ready to explode.

'What was that?' James suddenly became still, frowning as he, too, sought to find out where the disturbance was coming from.

They heard hissing, popping and bubbling sounds that were coming from behind them, and Sarah said in a bemused voice, 'It's the percolator.' She looked at James. 'I'd forgotten all about it.'

'Me, too.' He reluctantly eased himself away from her so that he could turn it off, and would have reached for her once again if it hadn't been for Rosie coming into the kitchen at that moment.

'Can I use the laptop?' she asked Sarah. 'I want to see if my friends from Devon are on line, but Sam's on the other computer.'

Sarah pulled in a deep breath, trying to get back to something like normality. She sent James a quick, sorrowful look. The mood had been broken, and they couldn't get back to where they'd been. He inclined his head briefly, sadly. Perhaps he felt it, too.

With the change in atmosphere, along came a niggling doubt. James hadn't wanted her all those years ago. Why did he want her now? Were his feelings purely a physical response?

'Yes, that's okay.'

Rosie sat down by the table and ran her fingers over the keyboard. There was a tinkling sound, and she said, 'Oh, you have some emails. They've just come in.' She glanced up at Sarah, her grey eyes wide. 'I think there's one you've been waiting for. The heading says, "Getting in touch".'

'Uh... I...' Sarah felt winded all at once, and a little dizzy. Her head was still up in the clouds somewhere from being with James, and now this had come at her, out of the blue.

She couldn't think what to do, and it was James who said quietly, 'I think you'd better sit down and read it, don't you? I'll see to the coffee.'

She floundered for a moment or two and then managed to find her voice. 'Okay, thanks.'

Rosie smiled. 'I'll come back in a couple of minutes, shall I? I'll go and text my friend from school while I'm waiting.'

'Yes, that's a good idea. I won't be long.' Sarah sat down and opened up the email. It was short, just a few lines, and she read through it quickly. Then she frowned and stared at the screen, not knowing what to think.

'What's wrong?' James asked, his expression guarded as he slid a mug of coffee towards her.

'I... Nothing, really. I mean, she's got back to me...my mother...which is what I wanted after all.'

'But? There is a but.'

'I'm not sure.' She read the email once more.

'Doesn't she want to meet up with you, is that the problem?'

'No. I mean, yes...she wants to see me. She's suggesting that I go over to London and have lunch with her some time at a local restaurant. She doesn't have a lot of time to spare, she says.' She looked up at him. 'That's okay, I suppose, isn't it?'

It wasn't quite what she'd expected. Maybe she'd been hoping for something with a little more warmth, an expression of joy at being able to link up with her after all this time. Not this cool, brief invitation to lunch as though she was a mere acquaintance who'd happened to drop her a line. She was her daughter, but she might as well have been a stranger. Sadness clouded her eyes. It was like being abandoned all over again. Was she really so undeserving of love?

James looked at her with concern, and he put his mug of coffee down on to the worktop next to him. 'You're asking me if it's okay? I don't know, Sarah. My instincts tell me it isn't, and from the look on your face, you feel the same way. Is that all she says? After all this time it doesn't feel as though it's enough. Not by any means.'

Sarah pressed her lips together. 'Well, she wants us to get together, and that's what I wanted after all. Only... I think I'd expected something more.'

A muscle flicked in his jaw. 'Of course you did. She walked out on you, her only child. She's made no effort to find you through all these years, and now she can't even be bothered to go to the trouble of coming here to see you? I'm sorry to be blunt, but at the very least she might have suggested you stay over at her place for a couple of days.'

'Perhaps she's afraid we won't get on. Or maybe she has a family of her own now.'

'And you aren't her family? Who has the better claim?'

'Even so…'

Exasperated, he came over to her. 'May I read what she has to say?'

'Of course.' She nodded and turned the laptop around so that he could see the screen.

A second or two later he sucked in his breath. 'Sarah, please tell me you're not going to dignify that by agreeing to go and have lunch with her. That's the chilliest invitation I've read in a long time. There's not even an expression of regret for what she did. You deserve so much better than that.'

She ran the tip of her tongue lightly over her lips. 'It might not be such a bad idea to go and see her. At least it would be a start.' He made a stifled sound, and she added, 'I'm not sure what I'm going to do yet. I have to think about it.'

'What is there to think about?' His voice was terse, reflecting the anger in his expression. 'She has the nerve to say that she's busy and can't spare you much time. She has a business to run…an online business, for heaven's sake, selling handbags and fashion accessories. How difficult can that be? Doesn't she know you're a doctor, working weekends sometimes, out on call at other times too? Did you tell her that?'

'Yes, I did. I told her quite a bit about myself and about my father and the children. I was sort of hoping she'd tell me more about herself.'

'The woman is selfish, Sarah. Always has been, always will be. Perhaps you should face up to the fact that she isn't going to change. When are you going to realise that you can't let her ruin your life any longer?'

'Like I said, I have to think about this.'

He shook his head, as though he was trying to rid himself of the whole idea. 'I almost wish she had never answered your letter. This is going to stir everything up all over again, isn't it? You were doing so well, getting yourself back on track, and now she's going to drag you down into her cold, self-centred world once more. She'll destroy you, and make you feel worthless all over again. Hasn't she already started the process with that wretched little note? I can see how badly it has affected you.'

He moved restlessly. 'I'd hoped there might be a chance for us...for you and me to get together, for us to be a couple. But you'll never settle to that, will you? Oh, it might be all right for a while, but there will always be doubt at the back of your mind, won't there? The worry that you'll be abandoned all over again?' He looked into her eyes, his gaze searing her. 'You know I want you, Sarah. Do you think we have any kind of a future together?'

Her lips parted as she tried to answer him. She'd waited so long to hear him say that they were a couple, that they would be together... Of course she knew he wanted her. He'd made that clear over the last few weeks, the way he'd been there for her, cared for her. But he was right, there was always a niggling doubt in the back of her mind that things would not work out for them. How could he love her, and want to be with her for ever? Had he ever mentioned love? And what of the other women, from the hospital and other walks of life, who'd set their hearts on him and had had their hopes and dreams dashed? Was she to become another one of them?

'James, you have to understand, it's hard for me to trust, to put my faith in anyone. I've been badly hurt, and I don't know how to put that behind me. I try, but something always gets in the way. I don't know how to change. You said once that being abandoned was like a scar on my mind, and maybe you were right— perhaps it has damaged me for ever.'

He sighed heavily. 'Then I guess I have my answer, don't I?' He turned away from her, picking up his car keys from the worktop. 'There's no hope for us.'

'James...'

'I'm sorry. I have to go. I can't do this any more. I have feelings too, you know.' He was already striding towards the door. 'I need to get some air and maybe drive around for a bit. You must do what you think right where your mother is concerned.'

He walked out, and Sarah sat at the table for a while after he had gone. What had been a wonderful day had turned to ashes, and for the moment she didn't have any idea how to deal with the aftermath. She stared into space, wishing with all her heart that James had stayed, that she'd been able to give him the answer he wanted.

'James has gone. You were arguing with him, weren't you? I heard you.' Rosie was shocked, and there was disbelief in her voice. 'How could you let him go like that?'

'We weren't arguing, Rosie. We were just...'

'You were. I heard you. Your voices were loud and he was angry.' Her face crumpled. 'Now it's all gone wrong.'

Sarah stood up, seeing the distress in Rosie's face. 'Rosie,' she said gently, putting an arm around the small girl, 'it wasn't an argument, not really. We just don't agree on some things, that's all. Sometimes grown-ups have differences of opinion. It's all right to do that.'

'No, it isn't,' Rosie sobbed. 'I like James. I wanted him to stay. We could have been a family, and now it's all ruined.'

Sarah hugged her, shocked by all those expectations that had been slowly simmering beneath the surface. She glanced across the room and saw Sam standing in the doorway. 'Did you feel that way, too?' she asked quietly, and he nodded, white faced.

'I wanted him to stay as well.'

'I'm sorry.' She held out an arm to him and he came into her embrace. They were echoing her own thoughts, but right now there wasn't a thing she could do about it.

Her mother's leaving had always been at the heart of her problems, making her uncertain, insecure and feeling unloved...unlovable. James had been dealing with that for some time, and now he'd decided enough was enough. He'd gone, and things might never again be the same between them. She couldn't bear it.

CHAPTER EIGHT

Sarah's pager went off, alerting her to an incoming emergency, and she winced inwardly. She was looking after a man who had suffered an angina attack and she really didn't want to leave him right now. He was frightened, fearful of the pain and desperately worried about what was happening to him.

'The nitroglycerin spray will help relieve the pain,' she told him. 'It widens the blood vessels and helps the heart pump blood around your body more easily. Just try to breathe slowly and evenly, and it should soon start to pass.'

She glanced at the nurse who was assisting her, and said in a quiet voice, 'I have to go and attend to another emergency. Will you stay with him and make sure that he's comfortable?' She reached for the medication chart and made some notes. 'I've written up his medication, but if there are any problems, call the registrar. He's due to take over from me in half an hour.'

The nurse nodded. 'I'll take care of him.' She held the oxygen mask to the man's face. 'Take it nice and slowly. Deep breaths. That's right. That's fine. You're doing really well.'

Sarah glanced at the ECG printout and saw that the attack was receding. 'You're in good hands,' she told her patient. 'You should feel better very soon.'

She hurried away, heading for the resuscitation room, and found herself walking swiftly alongside James. Her heart seemed to clamp into a tight knot inside her. She'd hardly had a chance to speak to him all day, and it looked as though they were still going to be tied up with work now, when it was nearly the end of her shift. There was so much she needed to say to him but here at work their conversation was muted, constricted by their surroundings, by work and the constant bustle of colleagues all around them.

'It looks as though we've both been paged for the same case,' he said with a frown.

'Yes. Do you know what it's all about?'

He shook his head. 'I was dealing with an appendicitis case—it's been non-stop all day.'

'You're right. I didn't even get to stop for lunch.'

'It goes like that sometimes.'

'Yes.' She sent him a quick glance. 'I tried to phone you yesterday, but all I got was your messaging service telling me you'd been called out to the hospital. It looks as though the rush started yesterday for you.'

'I had to come in to do some emergency surgery.' He pushed open the door to the resuscitation room and Gemma hurried to update them on the situation.

'This is Lucy Myers. She gave birth to a baby girl about eight hours ago. She was sent home as normal, but she became unwell and started to bleed heavily so her husband turned the car around and brought her straight here to A and E.'

'And the husband is...where?' James glanced around as he went to introduce himself to the young woman.

'In the relatives' room with the baby.'

'Okay.'

Lucy was already connected up to the monitors via various pads and electrodes, and it was plain to see from the readings that she was in a bad way. She was being given oxygen through a face mask but appeared not to be aware of her surroundings.

'She complained of dizziness and feeling faint,' Gemma said, 'and she's suffering from palpitations. It's hard to estimate how much blood she's lost, but from her condition it's a fair amount, I'd say.'

James spoke quietly to their patient, trying to calm her down and let her know that she would be safe. It was difficult to know how much she was able to take in, because the loss of blood was having a system-wide effect on her. 'I'm going to take some blood from your arm so that we can see if there's anything to pinpoint what might be causing this,' he said. 'But you had a prolonged labour, from what the records tell me, and that can sometimes lead to problems like this.'

Sarah made a careful examination and gently palpated the woman's abdomen. 'It looks as though the uterus isn't contracting as it should,' she murmured. Usually, after the placenta came away, there would be some bleeding, which would gradually stop as the womb contracted and compressed the blood vessels.

James relayed that information to Lucy. 'I'm going to put in an intravenous line so that we can give you fluids to help make up for what you've lost, and at the same time give you medication to help make the uterus contract,' he said.

Lucy didn't say anything. She was conscious, but too exhausted and debilitated to take any notice of what was going on.

'She's not responding too well, is she?' Sarah remarked softly. 'I've been massaging the uterus, but it hasn't helped to stimulate the contractions.'

'No.' James checked the monitors. 'Her heart rate's far

too high. I'll give her oxytocin and see if that starts things off.' He turned to Gemma. 'Alert Obstetrics and Gynaecology, will you, please, Gemma? They need to be aware of what's going on.'

'Will do. Do you want me to have Theatre on standby, too?'

He nodded. 'That would be for the best. I'm hoping it won't come to that, but it's possible she'll need surgery to stop the bleeding.' He frowned. 'You'd better talk to the husband about the possibility—he might have to sign the necessary consents if his wife isn't up to it.'

'Okay.'

James gave Lucy the medication through the intravenous catheter, and then he and Sarah stood back away from the bed for a while, waiting to see if her vital signs improved.

Sarah stretched, easing her aching muscles. It had been a long day.

James glanced at her. 'Are you okay?'

'I'm fine.' He seemed calm and relaxed, and there was no sign of any tension in his manner towards her. She wanted to talk to him about what had happened between them on Saturday afternoon, but this was hardly the place to do that. Instead, she kept to safe ground, talking about their work. 'I checked on Nicola Carter this morning,' she told him. 'Apparently the tumour was benign.'

James smiled. 'Yes, I read her notes. That must be a great relief for her family.'

'I imagine so.'

'What's happening with the girl you were worried about? Rachel, the one who had a bad reaction with Ecstasy?'

'She's doing much better. Her heart rhythm has settled down, and it's possible she'll be discharged soon.'

'To go back to her old lifestyle?'

Sarah shook her head. 'I don't think so. Her brother put her in touch with her parents, and from what I heard they all had a heart to heart and managed to sort things out. I think she'll be going back home to live with them.'

'That's good.' His gaze swept over her. 'At least somebody's family has been put back together again.'

'It goes to show that it's possible sometimes.' She lifted her chin. 'It all comes down to both parties making an effort to meet each other halfway.'

'Yeah, maybe.' He checked the monitors once more and went to carefully examine Lucy. 'The uterus is still soft and relaxed, and there are no contractions,' he said, under his breath. 'We'll try one more medication and if that doesn't start things off, there's nothing else for it—she'll have to go up to Theatre for surgery to clamp the blood vessels.'

'What are you going to use? Methylergonovine?'

'Yes. It might mean she won't be able to breastfeed for a few days, because it could pass into the milk, but I don't see that we have a choice.' James was already preparing the intravenous injection.

Once the injection had been given, they waited once again for it to take effect. 'Perhaps her husband could come in now?' Sarah suggested in a low voice. 'If this works, it would be good for her to see him and the baby…it might help with the bonding process. She had a long, exhausting labour, and then she collapsed, so she's had very little time to hold her baby. The midwife said she wasn't able to hold her for more than a minute or two because she was so weak.'

James frowned. 'So why was she discharged after only a few hours?'

'They had no beds and a couple of emergencies came

in. I don't think they had much of a choice, once her temperature and blood pressure were okay.'

His expression was sombre. 'The days are gone when new mothers would at least stay in hospital overnight.'

He went over to the bed and examined Lucy once more. 'The uterus is contracting,' he told Sarah. 'It looks as though her condition's about to stabilise.'

Lucy gave a low moan and stirred briefly. Then her eyelids flickered open.

'Hey,' he said softly, 'you're back with us. That's terrific. Are you okay, Lucy? How are you feeling?' The monitors showed that her blood oxygen level was up and her heart rate was gradually coming down to a more normal level.

Lucy nodded, pushing the oxygen mask to one side. 'I'm okay,' she said in a thin, tired voice. 'What happened to me? I feel wiped out.' Then, anxiously, 'Where's my baby?'

Sarah smiled. It was great that she was asking after her newborn infant. 'She's on her way. Your husband is looking after her. The nurse has gone to fetch them.'

The husband arrived in Resus a few minutes later, armed with a fresh, warm bottle of milk formula for the baby. 'I think she's hungry,' he said, looking down at the squalling infant in his arms. 'She's been asleep all this time, and then she suddenly woke up and all hell was let loose. She has a good pair of lungs on her and that's no mistake.' He smiled at his wife, and went to stand beside her. 'The nurse went to fetch the milk for me.'

Lucy held out her arms for the baby, and he carefully lowered the crying infant down to her. She snuggled her close in the crook of her arm and tested the milk for heat against the back of her hand. Then she gently eased the teat into the infant's mouth and there was instant peace in the room, with only soft sucking and gurgling sounds coming from the contented baby.

Sarah watched them, a tender smile on her lips. There was a hint of sadness in her expression too, though, and James looked at her curiously and murmured, 'It's good to see them together like that, isn't it? We'll let her recover for a while and then admit her to the observation ward.'

She nodded, but didn't say anything. They started to walk out of the room. Their job here was finished, and she could go home now, secure in the knowledge that their patient was out of the woods.

He asked quietly, 'Is something bothering you?'

'Not really. But I can't help wondering how my mother felt when she held me for the first time. Perhaps she never experienced that glow of motherhood. For her, having a baby might have been a burden, something that she felt she had to do to please her husband.'

His brows shot up. 'What makes you think that? Have you spoken to her about it?'

'We've exchanged a few emails. She says she never wanted children. She wanted to have a career, but my father was keen for them to start a family, so she went along with it.'

'Good grief.' His expression was bemused. 'I'm surprised she would admit to something like that.'

She gave a faint smile. 'I had pretty much the same thought, but I'd asked her to be honest with me, so I suppose I can't complain. Anyway, I'm going home now, so I'll be able to see if she has anything else to say.' She glanced at him as she reached for her purse from a locked cupboard behind the central desk. 'Will you be going off duty soon?'

'In about half an hour.' He caught hold of her arm as she would have walked away, gently circling it with his fingers. 'Sarah, I was wrong the other day when I suggested you shouldn't go and see her. It's not up to me to say what you should or shouldn't do. You have to do what you think is best. I just don't want to see you hurt.'

'I know. I understood that.'

'I'm glad.'

He might have said more, but Gemma called him to go and look at a patient, and Sarah made her way out of the department and set off for home. She was sad because her mother had turned out to be not quite what she'd expected, but at least she was in touch with her now, and gradually they would begin to get to know one another.

Now that she was over the initial shock of making contact, she'd realised that what bothered her most of all was not how she and her mother would go on but the state of her relationship with James. When he'd walked out on Saturday, she'd been lost, as though she'd been cast adrift.

She collected the children from Murray's house, and took them home to give them tea and biscuits to stave off the hunger pangs while she prepared the evening meal.

'Don't go eating too many, Sam,' she warned as he went to dip his hand in the biscuit barrel for the third time. 'I know it's been quite a while since lunchtime, but it's important that you eat all your dinner.'

'What are we having?'

'Beef risotto.'

'No problem. I love it.'

'Even so...' She replaced the lid on the biscuit tin as his fingers began to stray once more. 'You've had enough for now.'

'Can I fry the onions?' Rosie asked. 'I know how to do them until they're golden brown.'

'Okay.' Sarah smiled. Inside, she was aching a little for all that might have been, but Rosie and Sam kept her from thinking too hard about that. Whenever she was in danger of sinking into thoughts of James and how things could ever work out the way she wanted, one or other of them demanded her attention. 'Let's see, we need onions, mince, a little garlic...'

'Tomatoes and peas,' Rosie added.

'Yes, you're right.' She checked the items off one by one as she placed them on the kitchen table. 'I think that's about everything, don't you?'

'It won't be any good without the rice,' Sam said, frowning. 'Whoever heard of risotto without the rice?'

Sarah laughed. 'It's a good job you're here to keep me on course, isn't it?'

He gave them both a smug smile, and then went off to his bedroom to play for a while.

Some twenty minutes later the appetising smell of risotto filled the kitchen. 'We'll give it another fifteen minutes or so,' Sarah said. 'That'll give you time to do some colouring or—' She broke off as the doorbell sounded. 'It can't be Murray,' she said with a frown. 'He said he was going out this evening to have dinner with his girlfriend.'

She went to the front door and found James waiting in the porch. 'Oh...hello,' she said, her heart giving a small leap inside her chest, a smile curving her mouth. 'I thought...well, it's good to see you.' She waved him into the hallway, but he stopped, standing still and sniffing the air approvingly.

'Something smells really good,' he said. He looked uncomfortable. 'I didn't mean to barge in on you when you were about to sit down to your meal.'

'That's okay. You can stay and eat with us. We made plenty.'

He followed her as she walked towards the kitchen, and Sarah glanced up as she saw Sam flit across the landing upstairs. 'Hi, James,' he said, and then disappeared into his room once more.

Rosie greeted him with a sweet smile. 'Hi,' she said. She stared at him for a while and then added, 'I was afraid you might not come here again.'

'Oh, why's that?' James frowned.

Rosie's shoulders did a strange little wiggle. 'Because you and Sarah had an argument last time.'

'No...no...' He glanced at Sarah, his expression sombre. 'That was just a bit of a difference of opinion, that's all.'

'That's what Sarah said.' Smiling happily, she went to join her brother upstairs.

Sarah listened for a moment or two, waiting for them to start arguing, but nothing happened, and she turned to James. 'I'm really glad you came,' she said. 'I was miserable when you went away. I wanted to see you again, to talk to you properly, without worrying about being at work with people all around.'

He came over to her and took her in his arms. 'I was thinking exactly the same thing. I thought I should stay away, but I can't. I need to be here with you.'

'You're not still cross about my mother getting in touch?'

His mouth flattened. 'That was the least of my worries. But I think I was afraid that you would always be living in your mother's shadow, worrying about why she didn't care enough to stay, and it seemed such a waste. All these years you've been scared that there was no future for you, that you wouldn't have a family of your own because in the back of your mind you felt you didn't deserve it. You have to know that you can enjoy these things the same as everyone else. Your mother didn't reject you—she rejected the idea of motherhood. It doesn't mean that you're unlovable.'

'I think I'm beginning to realise that.' She pressed her

lips together briefly. 'I don't know what I was hoping for… to find some reason that turned her against me and my father, I suppose. But it wasn't that after all. It was simply that she never wanted a family. She wanted a career and freedom to do as she pleased without being tied down. And one day it all became too much for her, so she left to go and live her life the way she'd always wanted to.'

He ran his hand lightly down her arm. 'I'm sorry. Have you decided what you're going to do? Will you go and see her?'

'Maybe, one day, but not for some time. I thought it would be better to take things slowly. We can exchange emails, photos, get to know one another that way, and then perhaps we can talk on the phone at some point. I'm still not sure quite how I feel, but somehow it's as though a weight's been lifted off me. I really thought there was something wrong with me, and that she'd walked away from me…but now I know that she's the one with the problem. It's made me look at things in a whole new light. It made me think that I was wrong in believing none of my relationships could ever work out.' She looked up at him. 'I mean, I was wrong in thinking things would never work between you and me.'

He exhaled slowly. 'I'm glad you've come to realise that. I was hoping you would see things that way, but I didn't think it was possible.' His arms circled her, wrapping her in his warm embrace. 'I care about you so much, Sarah. I want you to know how I feel about you, but I needed you to know that things can be good between us. Everything doesn't have to turn sour.'

She lifted her face to him, her eyes troubled. 'I know you want me, but I don't really understand what you feel for me. You didn't want me when I was a teenager…you turned me away then…so what's changed? Why is now any different? I'm still the same person—a little curvier perhaps, not so impulsive and reckless, but basically I'm still me.'

'Ah, Sarah...' He bent his head and dropped a kiss on her startled mouth. 'I always wanted you. It took every ounce of willpower I had to turn you away that night. But I had to do it. You were so young and vulnerable, so confused... After your mother left, you put on this tough exterior, but I knew it wasn't for real, you were a young girl crying out for attention, and I couldn't take advantage of you. I wanted you more than anything, but I knew you'd hate me the next day, perhaps for always.'

He frowned. 'Besides, I had to go away to work. It wasn't as though I could stay close by. You had your future ahead of you. I knew you had to get rid of the demons that were driving you before you could settle to any kind of relationship.' He gave a rueful smile. 'I just didn't think it would take this long.'

She stared at him in bewilderment. 'You're saying that you wanted me back then? That you've wanted me all along?'

'More than that. I love you, Sarah. I couldn't let you know. I didn't want you to fling yourself into a relationship with me then realise you'd made a mistake and blame me later. I wanted you to be sure of your feelings. I love you and I'll always be here for you. That's why I've never been able to settle into a relationship with anyone else. You're the only woman I've ever loved. I'll never leave you, you need to know that, but do you think you can conquer your doubts?'

Joy welled up inside her. She lifted her arms, wrapping them around him, and lifted her face for his kiss. 'I've always loved you,' she said. 'I never had any doubts about that. I was afraid you wouldn't be able to love me in return.'

She made a choking little laugh. 'I was such a pain back then. I think I wanted to do my worst to prove to myself that no one could possibly love me.'

'It didn't work,' he said. 'It just made me want to protect you all the more.' He kissed her tenderly, brushing his lips over hers, trailing kisses over her cheek and along the smooth column of her throat. 'I love you and I want to spend the rest of my life with you.'

Her eyes widened. 'Do you really mean it?'

'I do.' He gently stroked her cheek, gazing down at her. 'Will you marry me, Sarah?'

She smiled up at him. 'Yes, please. It's what I want more than anything.' But then her expression sobered as she thought of something else that might be a stumbling block to mar their happiness. 'You realise, don't you, that it means you'll be taking on not only me but Rosie and Sam as well?'

'Oh, I think I can cope with that,' he said confidently, swooping to kiss her once more. 'We'll be a family, you, me, Rosie and Sam. You won't need to worry about anything.'

She snuggled against him, wrapped securely, satisfyingly in his arms, and for the next few minutes they were lost in one another, oblivious to everything around them. Sarah sighed happily. It was exhilarating, being held this way, having him kiss her and show her just how much he loved her. She wanted this moment to go on for ever and ever.

EPILOGUE

'Are you ready? Do you have everything you need? Something old, something new...?' Sarah's mother fussed around her, adjusting the folds of Sarah's ivory silk wedding gown and carefully draping the lace edged veil over her bare shoulders. 'Oh, you look so beautiful. I just can't believe... I never imagined I would see this day.' She wiped away a tear with the edge of her white handkerchief.

'Something old...' Sarah fingered the silver necklace she was wearing. Her father had given it to her when she had been a bridesmaid at his wedding, and she had treasured it ever since. 'Something new...' She smiled. 'James bought me these earrings to wear.' She turned her head this way and that, to show them off.

'They're lovely, absolutely exquisite.' Her mother's eyes were misting over once more.

They were diamond droplets, with an emerald at their core. 'To match your beautiful eyes,' James had said, and Sarah's mouth curved at the memory. 'Something borrowed, something blue...that's how the saying goes, isn't it?' She glanced down at the white silk ribbon that tied her bouquet of pink roses and fragrant orchids. 'I'll give this back to you later. I understand how much it means to you.' She hadn't understood the significance at first, but when her mother had explained that it was the ribbon from Sarah's christening gown, tears had come to her eyes. After all that had happened, her mother hadn't been able to part with this one tender memento of her baby girl.

Her mother nodded. 'I'll have new memories to treasure after this, though, won't I?' A line creased her brow. 'Can you ever forgive me, Sarah? Getting to know you all over again, and seeing you with James and Rosie and Sam has made me realise how badly I've behaved and just how much I've been missing. I'm so proud of you.'

'I forgive you,' Sarah said softly. On this day, of all days, she was thinking only of the future…of the wonderful, love-filled life that she was going to share with James.

Her mother sighed heavily, the breath catching in her throat. 'Thank you. It's more than I dared expect.' She frowned as a car drew up outside and there was a knock at the door. 'Oh, the taxi's here… I have to go.' Her voice rose in agitation. 'Where are Sam and Rosie? They have to come with me.'

'It's all right, we're here, we're ready,' Rosie said, coming into the sitting room. 'Murray was showing us pictures of the seaside where he's taking us for the next two weeks—him and his girlfriend. I like her, she's fun…and there are caves and rock pools and lots and lots of sand.'

'It'll be well good,' Sam joined in. 'He says we can go on sail boats and try out body surfing and stuff.'

'I think you'll have a great time,' Sarah said. 'But you'd better phone me every day, or else,' she warned.

Rosie laughed. 'We will.' She gave a twirl, showing off her pink silk dress and letting the skirts billow out around her. 'Do I look all right?'

'You look stunning, as pretty as a picture.' Sarah turned to Sam. 'And you make a wonderful pageboy, Sam. You're so smart in your suit, and I love that silk waistcoat. Do you think you can keep it clean until after the ceremony?'

He gave her a nonchalant smile. 'Of course.'

Sarah saw them out to the waiting taxi and waved them off. In just a few short minutes she would be setting off herself in the wedding car, with Murray by her side to do the traditional 'giving away' of the bride.

She was suddenly overcome by nerves. Would James like the way she looked? What was he thinking right now? This was the biggest commitment either of them would ever make, and she wanted everything to be over with so that she could be with him, just the two of them for a short while, to start their new life together.

Some twenty minutes later she stood in the stone archway by the church door, calmly waiting while Murray, looking splendid in a morning suit, chivvied the children into their places behind her. Everything would be all right. She remembered the love token that James had given her to pin to the inside of her dress. It was a small silver hoop that held a trio of tiny charms—a carriage to represent their journey together through life, a silver horseshoe for luck, and the something blue—a sapphire heart, to show the love that he would always have for her.

The wedding march sounded out, cutting into her reverie, and she took Murray's arm, walking slowly down the aisle towards the man she was to marry.

James turned to look at her as she approached. His lips parted in stunned surprise, his eyes widening as he gazed at her, and then he smiled. At the same time the sun shone through the stained-glass windows of the church, lighting up the altar and the gleaming silver candlesticks and spreading its warm rays over the flowers that decorated the pedestals.

He came to stand beside her. 'You look sensational,' he whispered, clasping her hand in his, his grasp firm and assured. 'I love you.'

The vicar stepped forward. 'Dearly Beloved,' he said, 'we are gathered here today…' And the service began. Sarah glanced at James from time to time, and each time he responded, looking into her eyes, showing her all the love that was in his heart.

'With this ring, I thee wed.' James slid the gold ring onto the third finger of her left hand, and Sarah felt a lump rise in her throat. This ring bound them together for all time. It was what James had promised when he'd slipped the diamond engagement ring on her finger just a few short weeks ago, and now this simple act in the wedding service completed that promise.

He held her hand as he walked with her down the aisle a few minutes later, and they stepped out into the sunshine, to be greeted by cheering friends and family, who showered them with confetti and clamoured for him to kiss the bride.

He took her in his arms and obliged cheerfully, kissing her with a thoroughness that took her breath away and pleased the onlookers enormously. 'My lovely wife,' he said, some time later. 'I feel as though I've waited for this moment for an eternity. I can't believe how lucky I am.' His gaze travelled over her. 'From this day forward,' he murmured, quoting from the wedding service, 'I'll always be here for you, Sarah. Don't ever doubt it.'

'I won't,' she said softly. 'We'll be together, for ever.'

And then he kissed her again, to the great delight of the photographer and everyone around.

* * * * *

Keep reading for an excerpt of a new title
from the Western Romance series,
LAST CHANCE ON MOONLIGHT RIDGE
by Catherine Mann

CHAPTER ONE

HER WEDDING DRESS still fit.

The marriage, however?

It was exploding at the seams.

Hollie O'Brien smoothed her hands down the fitted lace gown, tiny seed pearls beading under her fingertips just as they'd done two decades ago. Even though she hadn't been able to do up the buttons in back just now, the satin-and-lace creation felt the same against her skin, molding to her figure without being too snug.

Thank goodness it wasn't too small, since she'd put off pulling it from the back of her closet until the very last minute. Avoiding memories?

Absolutely.

But now, time was up, and she had to face all this gown represented—all that she'd lost. She spun in front of the antique full-length mirror, her bedroom suite behind her in a rustic chic wash of blue velvet brocade and dark pine walls.

She'd put such care in choosing the dress back then, full of hope, confident that she and Jacob could withstand any storms life sent their way. She'd been naive—and so very wrong.

This definitely wasn't the way she'd expected to celebrate her twentieth—the china—anniversary. Maybe that porcelain was prophetic, in some way, about the fragile nature of happiness. She and Jacob had exhausted every option—every alteration, so to speak—in hopes of salvaging their fractured union.

How ironic that they had built a thriving business focused on mending broken hearts and damaged relationships. Their Top Dog Dude Ranch perched in the Great Smoky Mountains was a success—and yet none of that reputed healing magic had shimmered over onto them.

At least she didn't have to hang on much longer. She just had to make it through the next two weeks with her sanity intact. Their dude ranch was featuring a massive spring weddings event. Non-stop weddings for the next fourteen days.

What pure torture, especially now.

When they'd planned this event a year ago, it had seemed like a brilliant idea to combine their anniversary month with a spring weddings theme. As part of the promotion, she'd gotten roped into putting on her gown for a photo shoot to be featured alongside images from their original ceremony.

But the positive press from the event was crucial for drumming up business. They needed the extra cash now more than ever. The expansion to a second Tennessee locale would give them each a place to live and autonomy in running their own division of the business. Otherwise, they would have to sell off the whole enterprise and split the proceeds once their divorce was final.

Hitching up the hem, she bunched lace in her hands, her buff-colored cowgirl boots tapping on the hardwood floor as she turned. She'd dreamed of passing the gown on to a daughter one day.

Even thinking of children brought a hitch to her throat and an ache all the way to her soul over so many losses. Miscarriages. Infertility. Her body had failed her.

Dropping on the end of her four-poster canopy bed, she

sagged back, fingertips tracing the patterns in the creamy tapestry throw blanket like a talisman. Rumor had it the bed came from an old saloon. She prided herself on decorating the ranch with authenticity, the cabins with a Western vibe. She'd thrown herself into the business to fill empty hours.

To distract her thoughts from the grief that had hovered at the edges of her marriage for so long.

Her gray tabby leaped from the floor, to the navy paisley cushion, then settled onto her lap, purring. She threaded her fingers though the cat's fur, medium length and plush rather than the typical shorter tabby coat. Pippa purred louder, pressing closer. Most people didn't know a cat's purr matched a hertz level that supposedly increased bone density and healing. She'd told ranch attendees that this was just one of the beauties of nature they utilized to help ranch guests. It was a miracle and science all wrapped up together. How many times had she preached that people who trusted the animal-assisted pack-tivities would feel the Top Dog healing boost?

Right now, she doubted that even a litter of kittens could mend her broken heart. Pippa mewed, nestling further into her lap as if to comfort Hollie's unspoken pain. Petting under her cat's chin, she took a deep breath. Then another.

She faced such a lonely future without her husband, without even her child. They'd finally embraced hope through adoption, welcoming a precious baby boy into their lives, only to have the birth mother change her mind and take the child back.

That had been the true beginning of the end for them. The blow had been fierce when, as a couple, they had already given all they had left inside. She hugged Pippa closer, only to realize she'd gotten fur on her dress, kitty hair dark against the white satin and stubbornly wrapped around seed pearls.

Standing, she eased Pippa to the floor and searched for the lint roller. A bark outside the bedroom door gave her only a second to react before a border collie Lab mix puppy bolted inside.

"Bandit, settle," she called.

The pup ignored her, bounding and barking. Close on his heels, her Scottish terrier—Scottie—trotted, quietly, but radiating energy with each speedy wag of his stubby tail.

Pippa hissed, hair standing up along her spine.

Uh-oh.

The feline darted under the bed in a blur of mottled fur. Bandit took chase. Scottie shot beneath the puppy, taking the lead.

Squealing, Hollie stumbled out of the way. "Pippa, Bandit, Scottie, please…"

She searched for the best way to corral them without tripping or diving onto her knees after them. The photo shoot would be ruined if she showed up in a torn and muddy gown, her hair sticking out every which way.

Grabbing the bedpost with one hand, she clapped the other to her chest to anchor her dress in place. Her booted feet tangled in the hem. She heard a rip and cringed, struggling to loosen her hold to save the gown that had suddenly become more precious than she would have admitted an hour ago.

Satin slithered from her grip, the fabric pooling at her feet. A gasp behind her sent her gaze flying up to the mirror again.

Her gaze met the reflection of—her husband.

JACOB O'BRIEN BRACED a hand against the door frame, his world rocked by the sight of his gorgeous wife, a wife he hadn't held or seen naked in months. Although technically, she wasn't naked, but close enough to make his blood sizzle.

Hollie stood with her wedding gown around her ankles, her wide blue eyes appearing every bit as stunned as he felt. Her dark brown hair tumbled over her shoulders in waves. The white satin of her strapless bra cupped her breasts, making his hands itch to sweep it away and take her to the bed, to their bed.

His mind scrolled back to the first time he'd seen her in the gown and when he'd peeled it from her that night on their honeymoon cruise. Their marriage had seen struggles, but they'd always connected on a physical level—until their son had been taken back by his birth mother.

Just the thought sent a stab of pain clean through him, echoed by scrolling memories of JJ's cherub cheeks and baby laugh. His eyes shifted to the place by their bed where JJ's basinet had rested.

A movement just past that too empty space shifted his attention back to the present.

The cat shot from under the four-poster bed, reminding him that he didn't want to risk anyone else seeing Hollie half-clothed. He closed the door quickly, throwing the bolt. Even though their quarters were private, that didn't preclude someone from the ranch staff searching for them. The day had turned into utter chaos—in more ways than one.

Jacob strode deeper into the room, kneeling to scoop her dress upward. Rising, he met her halfway as she bent forward at the same time. Their eyes met, so close he could see her pupils widening with awareness.

He needed distance.

He wanted his wife.

And there wasn't a chance he would get either.

Hollie took her dress from his fists, the brush of her touch electric, the lilac scent of her heady. His mouth watered for a taste of her.

Hitching the dress back up, she inspected every inch for damage as she pulled it in place again. A tiny tear showed along the hem. "I should have locked the door."

"At least the photographer wasn't with me." A dry smile kicked across his mouth. "Although I wouldn't mind having a few boudoir photos of you, for old time's sake."

"Not funny." She waved him away. "Go tell the photographer I'll be there as soon as I can get dressed. At least the rip is small and only in the hem."

Watching her struggle to reach behind herself, he finally said, "Do you, uh, need help?"

"Actually, yes. With the buttons." She sighed in exasperation. "I didn't think this through, and I can't reach them. How much longer do I have?"

"The photographer's ready to roll. There's not time for me to do anything more than help you." He steeled his resolve, cupped her shoulders and turned her around.

She swept aside her flowing brown hair, sun through the part in the curtains shimmering on the barest hint of auburn. He barely succeeded in biting back a groan of appreciation at the thin strip of flesh leading from the nape of her neck to the top of her sweet bottom.

"Jacob?" She looked over her shoulder, her blue eyes wide.

Clearing his throat, he began fastening the tiny pearl buttons. Heaven help him, there were so very many of them, and as much as he wanted to take his time, that wasn't an option. So he just soaked up the feel of her velvety skin under his knuckles as he made fast work of closing the gap. "Who took care of this the first time?"

"My mother." Her voice washed over him, soft and musical. "She did my makeup and even arranged the flowers. She had such a gift."

"I'm sorry she can't be here to help you now—during this transition, I mean." He hated to think of her alone.

He also hated to think of her moving on with another man.

"It's not like our split is a surprise, Jacob. I've had time to adjust. It's the waiting that's the hardest part right now."

Time to adjust? How could she be so glib about their life being torn apart? Her calm rationale cut right through him—and pissed him off. He fastened the last button. "There. All set."

"Thank you." She let her hair slide back into place, the strands slithering over his hand.

"You look...gorgeous."

"That's kind of you to say, but not needed." She pivoted to face him again, her eyes full of so much awareness, pain...memories.

All that raw emotion, feelings echoing inside him, threatened to drive him to his knees. "Hollie, babe—"

Shaking her head, she flattened a hand on his chest. "I guess we should get moving if we want to finish up before the first of the wedding couples arrive. I'll just staple the hem. No one will notice."

"Oh, man." He thumped himself on the head. "I came here to tell you about the change in scheduling."

"What change?" She frowned as she hastily put on dangly pearl earrings.

"The vans for the kiddie camp are running ahead of time. They'll be here an hour early." Thank goodness his efficient wife would have seen that details were ready far ahead of time. He didn't know how he would manage without her—in so many ways.

"We need to get moving, then." She suddenly shifted

into high gear, gathering her leather workbag full with her tablet and notes. She fished out a stapler, and with two quick clicks, the rip disappeared. She hastily threw in a makeup bag and a brush. "That's going to cut it close with getting the photo shoot complete and checking in the wedding couples and then changing back into the Western gear, but we should be able to pull it off before the kids arrive."

"Um, the bus with the first two wedding parties is stuck on the road because a bear is blocking the way."

"A bear?" Her face flooded with pure panic. "Jacob, that means all those kids will be arriving at the same time as the wedding parties. It's going to be chaos."

Chaos? Yep. He'd thought the same thing at the idea of a bear in the road. It was like even the animals were conspiring against them.

He just needed to get through the next two weeks. Then he could hunker down and recover. Not for the first time, he wished he would be the one moving to the new locale. All the memories of Hollie—of their son—would be a specter he wasn't sure how he would navigate.

"HERE COMES THE BRIDE." From the pond's dock, the photographer pivoted, silk scarf on his shoulder billowing behind him into the breeze.

Hollie picked her way down the wooded trail, her lace dress bunched in her hands. Her assistant held the train off the ground in a pseudo bridesmaid style as they made their way to the promo shoot. Spring caressed the branches of the trees reaching over the water, a splash of light greens and flower buds swaying in the cool mountain air. Jacob would be joining her as soon as he changed into his "groom's" gear for the photography session.

At least they were out of the house, with the buffer of other people—and her dress wasn't down around her ankles.

Her heart still hammered double time in her chest, her skin clinging to the memory of his touch along her back as he buttoned her gown. She needed to get her head out of the past, ditch all the memories of their wedding, their marriage, and focus on nailing this photo shoot.

The dock provided a prime spot to showcase the ranch, the mountains and valleys, so lush right now after the saturation of hefty winter storms. A couple paddled a lazy canoe in the distance, adding to the idyllic tableau. The waters narrowed into a stream that trickled over the rocks, and it followed for a mile, it connected to the hot springs inside Sulis Cave.

A breeze blew through, the mountain air cool even with approaching summer. She rubbed her arms against the chill.

"Do you want my jacket?" her assistant offered as they closed in on the photographer and reporter.

Ashlynn had joined their team last fall to help during the transition. A dear friend and foster sister of the co-owner of the new branch outside of Nashville, Ashlynn was a perfect fit for their Top Dog family. She floated back and forth between the two Tennessee locations for now, and would settle with Hollie at the new branch once the transition was complete for her to leave Moonlight Ridge.

Home.

"I'm good for now," she said, swallowing down a lump and waving to the photographer in the distance as he walked around, checking lighting. "Thank you, Ashlynn."

"I came prepared. I have a Top Dog windbreaker in my bag." She held up a boho bag, opening it to reveal not only an extra jacket, but also a makeup bag, brush, and hair spray, for the photo shoot, no doubt. Ashlynn was a gem.

"If you're sure. I wouldn't mind draping one over my shoulders." She plucked out the windbreaker with the Top

Dog logo. "Hopefully we'll get started soon. It's going to be a zoo around here having two buses arrive at the same time."

If it had been another wedding party showing up ahead of schedule, that would have been more manageable, since the welcome packet and activities were the same. But the vans with the children required a whole different type of welcome.

On the plus side, maybe the photographer would feature the children, too. Two dozen kids in the foster care system had been gifted with scholarships for a vacation at the ranch. One of the wedding guests had come up with the idea to make that his gift to a bride and groom. A truly lovely sentiment from a philanthropist, and one Ashlynn had taken a special interest in overseeing, given her own experience in foster care. Photo releases had been obtained for each child, with the hope of encouraging people to foster.

The whinny from a horse had Hollie looking over her shoulder. Jacob strode down the path, surefooted, leading Nutmeg—a blood bay Thoroughbred they had helped rescue and rehab from a neglect situation. Delicate sprigs of jasmine were threaded throughout the horse's reddish-brown mane. Nutmeg's neck arched majestically, making him look like something from a fairy-tale book. Her husband, decked out in wedding finery for the photo shoot, took her breath away every bit as much now as he had when they first married. He wore a black tuxedo with a bolo tie, a Stetson and cowboy boots. He was her every fantasy wrapped up in muscles and determination, honor and charm.

Except fantasies often didn't hold up to the harsh light of reality. He'd been supportive during the fertility treatments and cancer battle, but she'd seen the strain on him. Not that he shared his worries and fears with her.

She pulled her attention back to the photographer. He was new to the paper, but she'd met him last week to determine the schedule and show him to the cabin they'd designated for his use to save time driving to the ranch every day. "Thank you for being a part of our spring weddings event, Mr. Clark. Where would you like us to stand?"

"Call me Milo. Please." The photographer tugged on his graying beard, eyeing the landscape, his camera dangling around his neck. "I was thinking we could start out there on the little bridge over the stream. Will it hold up with the horse?"

Jacob stroked a hand along Nutmeg's muzzle. "Absolutely. Everything here is built to code. We've even hosted an entire dinner party on that bridge."

Milo waved them on. "Lead the way. I can get photos as we walk as well. How about hitch up the train and clasp hands with your husband. Mr. O'Brien, you lead the horse and pretend I'm just a regular guest who's taking a tour. Forget about the camera."

Easier said than done.

Hollie shrugged off the jacket and passed it to Ashlynn before linking fingers with Jacob, his touch warm and familiar. His warm brown gaze held her as firmly as his hand. Authentic? Or for the camera?

There'd been a time when this was so easy and natural for them. Now it was all just staged for business. The sound of the camera clicking serenaded them from behind, capturing images she knew would break her heart when she viewed them later.

Ashlynn walked alongside them, hitching her cavernous boho bag onto her shoulder. She tugged free strands of black curls that snagged under the strap before flashing the photographer a curious smile. "Milo, how much do you know about the history of Moonlight Ridge? It's got quite a special legend."

"I'm new around here," the photographer answered, sweeping to the side for more photos. "Fill me in on the details so I can include it in our feature."

"Well," Hollie said, "there is a cave with hot springs. We have hours it's open for any patrons, like a pool. Our guests can also schedule time slots to indulge as a family, couple, or private party. One of the bridesmaids has reserved it for a bachelorette party."

"What a unique idea." The photographer jogged ahead, huffing, then knelt for another shot.

Hollie tried to ignore how she and her husband's steps had synched up, a habit of two decades together, instinctive. "We have another bridal party indulging in a spa day. Lonnie and Patsy—our massage therapists—have worked with us from the start and assist with many of our events. They're also renewing their vows."

"Mr. O'Brien, could you put your arm around your wife's waist? Is the spa day at the springs?"

Her thoughts scattered at the strength of his arm, the spicy scent of his aftershave.

"The spa day can be at the springs." Jacob picked up the conversational slack before the silence grew too noticeable. "But the massage therapists can travel to different locations at the ranch. The hot springs are called also called Sulis Springs. It's reputed that magic carried from the Old World still lives with nearby animals."

"Tell me some more about that." Milo gestured for her to rest her head on Jacob's shoulder as they neared the bridge over the creek.

Had Jacob kissed her on top of the head? Instinctively?

Or for show? Either way, she tingled all the way to the roots of her hair.

"Once upon a time," Jacob said, his deep breath rustling her hair, "when my ancestors were settling into this area from Scotland and Ireland, they followed a doe to the cave opening. It wasn't just any old doe, though."

Hollie slid into their routine easily, taking comfort in the familiarity of it. Had she used the rituals to avoid real connection before now? Very likely. "She was the Queen of the Forest, and she glowed like starlight."

"My ancestors knew the type of animal well." Jacob stopped at the foot of the bridge, bringing her hand to his chest as the camera snapped away. "They used to roam Scotland and lead wayward souls to safe places and healing waters that offered respite and a way to connect. My ancestors met all sorts of challenges in getting settled into this region. They wanted to give up on the land—even on each other. But legend has it, when they were at the end of their rope, they followed the Queen of the Forest to the cave mouth."

Milo eased down toward the creek, using the lower angle to aim the lens up at them. "Keep going. This is all good stuff."

"There was a lost pup in the cave whimpering." Her mind echoed with the memory of her child's cries, a sound that still tortured her dreams as she wondered if he wept for her, wondering why she wasn't there to comfort him. "They searched and searched. Just when they'd given up hope, they found the scruffy little creature shivering, its paw caught between some rocks. They worked it free—but the real miracle is that the puppy didn't even growl or bite during the process."

Jacob's brown eyes darkened, as if he sensed her thoughts. "So, while they waited for a pot of coffee to brew over the fire, they cleaned up the young pup. As they rinsed the puppy, their bond was renewed. Healed. They found a way to work with the land, with each other."

Silence stretched, a woodpecker's rhythm conspicuously loud, but she had nothing to offer up. Her mouth had gone dry. Jacob simply stared back, his eyes awash with pain he never acknowledged.

Ashlynn cleared her throat. "It's magic," she interjected. "Much like how our hot springs have healed and gathered people to Moonlight Ridge for over a hundred years. We have a reputation for bringing people together because of it."

Together?

She felt like a total fraud, peddling snake oil. No matter how many couples and families she saw healed after their time at the ranch, it felt hollow with her own life falling apart. Her hands went cold, a chill that iced all the way to her soul.

Just as she started to angle away, to call an end to this torture, the photographer's voice cut through.

"Mr. O'Brien," Milo announced, "you may kiss your bride."

MILLS & BOON
Book Club

Why not try a Mills & Boon subscription? Get your favourite series delivered to your door every month!

Use code ROMANCE2021 to get 50% off the first month of your chosen subscription PLUS free delivery.

Visit **millsandboon.com.au/pages/print-subscriptions**
or call Customer Service on
AUS **1300 659 500** or NZ **0800 265 546**

No Lock-in Contracts

Free Postage

Exclusive Offers

For full terms and conditions go to millsandboon.com.au
Offer expires 31st Feb 2022

3 STORIES IN EACH VOLUME

Island Escapes

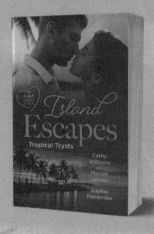

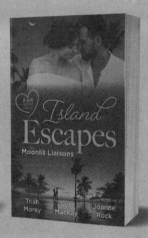

Book 1

February 2022

Book 2

On-sale April 2022

MILLS & BOON

millsandboon.com.au

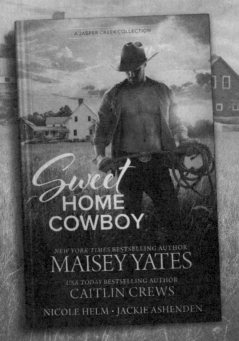

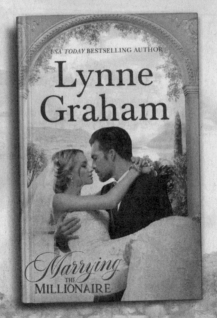

More LARGER PRINT books for you to enjoy!

Larger Print is now available in the following series lines:

MODERN

Forever

MEDICAL

INTRIGUE

DESIRE

MILLS & BOON

millsandboon.com.au